THE WHEEL OF
OSHEIM

THE WHEEL OF OSHEIM

THE RED QUEEN'S WAR
◆ BOOK THREE ◆

MARK LAWRENCE

ACE BOOKS, NEW YORK

ACE

An imprint of Penguin Random House LLC
375 Hudson Street, New York, New York 10014

Library of Congress Cataloging-in-Publication Data

Lawrence, Mark, 1966–
The wheel of Osheim / Mark Lawrence.
pages ; cm. — (The Red Queen's War ; Book three)
ISBN 978-0-425-26882-7 (hardcover)
I. Title.
PS3612.A9484W48 2015
813'.6—dc23
2015030737

FIRST EDITION: June 2016

PRINTED IN THE UNITED STATES OF AMERICA

10 9 8 7 6 5 4 3 2 1

Cover illustration by Jason Chan.
Interior text design by Laura K. Corless.
Map reprinted by permission of HarperCollins Publishers Ltd © 2014 Andrew Ashton.

Penguin
Random
House

Dedicated to my father, Patrick

ACKNOWLEDGMENTS

Many thanks to Diana Gill and the other good folk at Ace who have worked hard to put this book in your hands. Agnes Meszaros has also been of great help in bringing this book to fans of Jalan and Snorri. I'm indebted to her for kindnesses including beta reading, proofreading, wine, and chocolate. Thanks too for early reads from Mia Caringal and Nadine Kharabian. Finally, let's have another round of applause for my agent, Ian Drury, and the team at Sheil Land for all their sterling work.

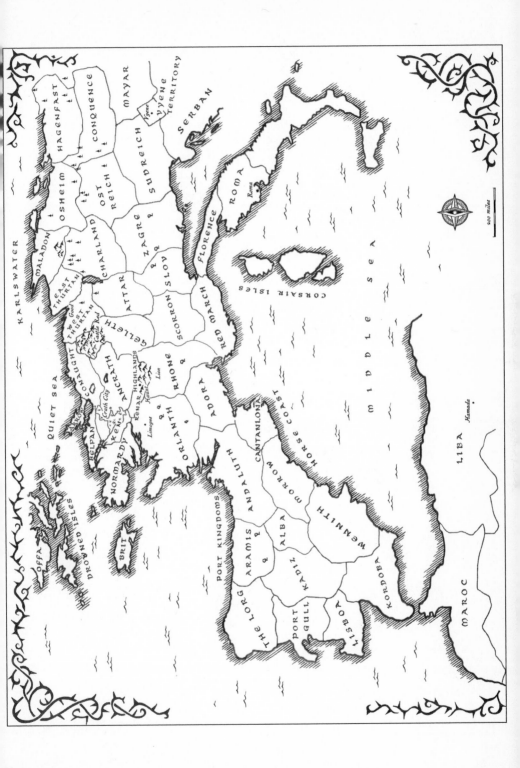

AUTHOR'S NOTE

For those of you who have had to wait a year for this book I provide brief catch-up notes to Book 3, so that your memories may be refreshed and I can avoid the awkwardness of having to have characters tell each other things they already know for your benefit.

Here I carry forward only what is of importance to the tale that follows.

1. Jalan Kendeth, grandson to the Red Queen, has few ambitions. He wants to be back in his grandmother's capital, rich, and out of danger. He'd also love to lord it over his older brothers Martus and Darin.

2. Life has become a little more complicated of late. Jalan still lusts after his former love, Lisa DeVeer, but she's now married to his best friend. Additionally he's still in massive debt to the murderous crime lord Maeres Allus, and wanted for fraud by the great banks of Florence. Plus, he's vowed revenge on Edris Dean, the man who killed his mother and his sister. His sister was still in his mother's womb and the necromantic sword Edris used (that Jalan now carries) trapped her in Hell, ready to return as an unborn to serve the Dead King. Jalan's sister had the potential to be a powerful sorceress and will make a very dangerous unborn— such potent unborn require the death of a close family member to return to the living world.

3. Jalan has travelled from the frozen north to the burning hills of Florence. He began his trip with Norsemen Snorri and Tuttugu of the Undoreth, picking up a Norse witch named Kara, and Hennan, a young boy from Osheim, on the way.

4. Jalan and Snorri were bound to spirits of darkness and light respectively: Aslaug and Baraqel. During their journey those bonds were broken.

5. Jalan has Loki's key, an artefact that can open any door. Many people want this—not least the Dead King who could use it to emerge from Hell.

6. In this book I use both Hell and Hel to describe the part of the afterlife into which our heroes venture. Hel is what the Norse call it. Hell is what it's called in Christendom.

7. Tuttugu died in an Umbertide jail, tortured and killed by Edris Dean.

8. We last saw Jalan, Snorri, Kara, and Hennan in the depths of the salt-mine where the door-mage, Kelem, dwelt.

9. Kelem was hauled off into the dark-world by Aslaug.

10. Snorri went through the door into Hel to save his family. Jalan said he would go with him, and gave Loki's key to Kara so it wouldn't fall into the Dead King's hands. Jalan's nerve failed him and he didn't follow Snorri. He pickpocketed the key back off Kara and a moment later someone pushed the door open from the Hel side and hauled him through.

11. More generally: Jalan's grandmother, Alica Kendeth, the Red Queen, has been fighting a hidden war with the Lady Blue and her allies for many years. The Lady Blue is the guiding hand behind the Dead King, and the necromancer Edris Dean is one of her agents.

12. Aiding the Red Queen are her twin older siblings, the Silent Sister—who sees the future but never speaks—and her disabled brother Garyus, who runs a commercial empire of his own.

13. The Red Queen's War is about the change the Builders made in reality a thousand years previously—the change that introduced magic into the world shortly before the previous society (us in about fifty years) was destroyed in a nuclear war.

14. The change the Builders made has been accelerating as people use magic more, in turn allowing more magic to be used—a vicious cycle that is breaking down reality and leading to the end of all things.

15. The Red Queen believes the disaster can be averted—or that she should at least try. The Lady Blue wants to accelerate to the end, believing that she and a select few can survive to become gods in whatever will follow.

16. Dr. Taproot appeared to be a circus master going about his business, but Jalan saw him in his grandmother's memories of sixty years ago, acting as head of her grandfather's security and much the same age as he is now . . .

17. The Wheel of Osheim is a region to the north where reality breaks down and every horror from a man's imagination is given form. Kara's studies indicate that at the heart of it was a great machine, a work of the Builders, mysterious engines hidden in a circular underground tunnel many miles across. Quite what role it plays in the disaster to come is unclear . . .

PROLOGUE

In the deepness of the desert, amid dunes taller than any prayer tower, men are made tiny, less than ants. The sun burns there, the wind whispers, all is in motion, too slow for the eye but more certain than sight. The prophet said sand is neither kind nor cruel, but in the oven of the Sahar it is hard to think that it does not hate you.

Tahnoon's back ached, his tongue scraped dry across the roof of his mouth. He rode, hunched, swaying with the gait of his camel, eyes squinting against the glare even behind the thin material of his shesh. He pushed the discomfort aside. His spine, his thirst, the soreness of the saddle, none of it mattered. The caravan behind him relied on Tahnoon's eyes, only that. If Allah, thrice-blessed his name, would grant that he saw clearly then his purpose was served.

So Tahnoon rode, and he watched, and he beheld the multitude of sand and the vast emptiness of it, mile upon baking mile. Behind him, the caravan, snaking amid the depths of the dunes where the first shadows would gather come evening. Around its length his fellow Ha'tari rode the slopes, their vigilance turned outward, guarding the soft al'Effem with their tarnished faith. Only the Ha'tari kept to the commandments in spirit as well as word. In the desert such rigid observance was all that kept a man alive. Others might pass through and survive, but only Tahnoon's people lived in the Sahar, never more than a dry well from death. Treading the fine line in all things. Pure. Allah's chosen.

Tahnoon angled his camel up the slope. The al'Effem sometimes named their beasts. Another weakness of the tribes not born in the desert. In addition, they scrimped on the second and fourth prayers of each day, denying Allah his full due.

The wind picked up, hot and dry, making the sand hiss as it stripped it from the sculpted crest of the dune. Reaching the top of the slope, Tahnoon gazed down into yet another empty sun-hammered valley. He shook his head, thoughts returning along his trail to the caravan. He glanced back toward the curving shoulder of the next dune, behind which his charges laboured along the path he had set them. These particular al'Effem had been in his care for twenty days now. Two more and he would deliver them to the city. Two more days to endure until the sheik and his family would grate upon him no longer with their decadent and godless ways. The daughters were the worst. Walking behind their father's camels, they wore not the twelve-yard thobe of the Ha'tari but a nine-yard abomination that wrapped so tight its folds barely concealed the woman beneath.

The curve of the dune drew his eye and for a second he imagined a female hip. He shook the vision from his head and would have spat were his mouth not so dry.

"God forgive me for my sin."

Two more days. Two long days.

The wind shifted from complaint to howl without warning, almost taking Tahnoon from his saddle. His camel moaned her disapproval, trying to turn her head from the sting of the sand. Tahnoon did not turn his head. Just twenty yards before him and six foot above the dune the air shimmered as if in mirage, but like none Tahnoon had seen in forty dry years. The empty space rippled as if it were liquid silver, then tore, offering glimpses of some place beyond, some stone temple lit by a dead orange light that woke every ache the Ha'tari had been ignoring and turned each into a throbbing misery. Tahnoon's lips drew back as if a sour taste had filled his mouth. He fought to control his steed, the animal sharing his fear.

"What?" A whisper to himself, lost beneath the camel's complaints.

Revealed in ragged strips through rents in the fabric of the world Tahnoon saw a naked woman, her body sculpted from every desire a man could own, each curve underwritten with shadow and caressed by that same dead light. The woman's fullness held Tahnoon's eye for ten long heartbeats before his gaze finally wandered up to her face and the shock tumbled him from his perch. Even as he hit the ground he had his saif in hand. The demon had fixed its eyes upon him, red as blood, mouth gaping, baring fangs like those of a dozen giant cobras.

Tahnoon scrambled back to the top of the dune. His terrified steed was gone, the thud of her feet diminishing behind him as she fled. He gained the crest in time to see the slashed veil between him and the temple ripped wide, as if a raider had cut their way through the side of a tent. The succubus stood fully displayed and before her, now tumbling out of that place through the torn air, a man, half-naked. The man hit the sand hard, leapt up in an instant, and reached overhead to where the succubus made to pursue him, feeling her way into the rip that he'd dived through headfirst. As she reached for him, needle-like claws springing from her fingertips, the man jabbed upward, something black clutched in his fist, and with an audible click it was all gone. The hole torn into another world— gone. The demon with her scarlet eyes and perfect breasts—gone. The ancient temple vanished, the dead light of that awful place sealed away again behind whatever thinness keeps us from nightmare.

"Fuck! Fuck! Fuck!" The man started to hop from one bare foot to the other. "Hot! Hot! Hot!" An infidel, tall, very white, with the golden hair of the distant north across the sea. "Fuck. Hot. Fuck. Hot." Pulling on a boot that must have spilled out with him, he fell, searing his bare back on the scalding sand and leaping to his feet again. "Fuck! Fuck! Fuck!" The man managed to drag on his other boot before toppling once more and vanishing head over heels down the far side of the dune screaming obscenities.

Tahnoon stood slowly, sliding his saif back into its curved scabbard. The man's curses diminished into the distance. Man? Or demon? It had escaped from Hell, so demon. But its words had been in the tongue of the old empire, thick with the coarse accent of northmen, putting uncomfortable angles on every syllable.

The Ha'tari blinked and there, written in green on red across the back of his eyelids, the succubus stretched toward him. Blinked again, once, twice, three times. Her image remained, enticing and deadly. With a sigh Tahnoon started to trudge down after the yelping infidel, vowing to himself never to worry about the scandalous nine-yard thobes of the al'Effem again.

ONE

All I had to do was walk the length of the temple and not be seduced from the path. It would have taken two hundred paces, no more, and I could have left Hell by the judges' gate and found myself wherever I damn well pleased. And it would have been the palace in Vermillion that I pleased to go to.

"Shit." I levered myself up from the burning sand. The stuff coated my lips, filled my eyes with a thousand gritty little grains, even seemed to trickle out of my ears when I tilted my head. I squatted, spitting, squinting into the brilliance of the day. The sun scorched down with such unreasonable fierceness that I could almost feel my skin withering beneath it. "Crap."

She *had* been gorgeous though. The part of my mind that had known it was a trap only now struggled out from under the more lustful nine tenths and began shouting "I told you so!"

"Bollocks." I stood up. An enormous sand dune curved steeply up before me, taller than seemed reasonable and blazing hot. "A fucking desert. Great, just great."

Actually, after the deadlands even a desert didn't feel too bad. Certainly it was far too hot, eager to burn any flesh that touched sand, and likely to kill me within an hour if I didn't find water, but all that aside, it was alive. Yes, there wasn't any hint of life here, but the very fabric of the place wasn't woven from malice and despair, the very ground didn't suck life and joy and hope from you as blotting paper takes up ink.

I looked up at the incredible blueness of the sky. In truth a faded blue that looked to have been left out in the sun too long but after the unchanging dead-sky with its flat orange light all colours looked good to my eye: alive, vibrant, intense. I stretched out my arms. "Damn, but it's good to be alive!"

"Demon." A voice behind me.

I made a slow turn, keeping my arms wide, hands empty and open, the key thrust into the undone belt struggling to keep my trews up.

A black-robed tribesman stood there, curved sword levelled at me, the record of his passage down the dune written across the slope behind him. I couldn't see his face behind those veils they wear but he didn't seem pleased to see me.

"*As-salamu alaykum*," I told him. That's about all the heathen I picked up during my year in the desert city of Hamada. It's the local version of "hello."

"You." He gestured sharply upward with his blade. "From sky!"

I turned my palms up and shrugged. What could I tell him? Besides any good lie would probably be wasted on the man if he understood the Empire tongue as poorly as he spoke it.

He eyed the length of me, his veil somehow not a barrier to the depth of his disapproval.

"Ha'tari?" I asked. In Hamada the locals relied on desert-born mercenaries to see them across the wastes. I was pretty sure they were called Ha'tari.

The man said nothing, only watched me, blade ready. Eventually he waved the sword up the slope he'd come down. "Go."

I nodded and started trudging back along his tracks, grateful that he'd decided not to stick me then and there and leave me to bleed. The truth was of course he didn't need his sword to kill me. Just leaving me behind would be a death sentence.

Sand dunes are far harder to climb than any hill twice the size. They suck your feet down, stealing the energy from each stride so you're panting before you've climbed your own height. After ten steps I was thirsty, by halfway parched and dizzy. I kept my head down and laboured up the slope, trying not to think about the havoc the sun must be wreaking on my back.

I'd escaped the succubus by luck rather than judgment. I'd had to bury my judgment pretty deep to allow myself to be led off by her in any event. True, she'd been the first thing I'd seen in all the deadlands that looked alive—more than that, she'd been a dream in flesh, shaped to promise all a man could desire. Lisa DeVeer. A dirty trick. Even so, I could hardly have claimed not to have been warned, and when she pulled me down into her embrace and her smile split into something wider than a hyena's grin and full of fangs I was only half-surprised.

Somehow I'd wriggled free, losing my shirt in the process, but she'd have been on me quick enough if I hadn't seen the walls ripple and known that the veils were thin there, very thin indeed. The key had torn them open for me and I'd leapt through. I hadn't known what would be waiting for me, nothing good to be sure, but likely it had fewer teeth than my new lady friend.

Snorri had told me the veils grew thinnest where the most people were dying. Wars, plagues, mass executions . . . anywhere that souls were being separated from flesh in great numbers and needed to pass into the deadlands. So finding myself in an empty desert where nobody was likely to die apart from me had been a bit of a surprise.

Each part of the world corresponds to some part of the deadlands— wherever disaster strikes, the barrier between the two places fades. They say that on the Day of a Thousand Suns so many died in so many places at the same time that the veil between life and death tore apart and has never properly repaired itself. Necromancers have exploited that weakness ever since.

"There!" The tribesman's voice brought me back to myself and I found we'd reached the top of the dune. Following the line of his blade I saw down in the valley, between our crest and the next, the first dozen camels of what I hoped would be a large caravan.

"Allah be praised!" I gave the heathen my widest smile. After all, when in Rome . . .

More Ha'tari converged on us before we reached the caravan, all black-robed, one leading a lost camel. My captor, or saviour, mounted the beast as one of his fellows tossed him the reins. I got to slip and slide down the dune on foot.

By the time we reached the caravan the whole of its length had come into view, a hundred camels at least, most laden with goods, bales wrapped in cloth stacked high around the animals' humps, large storage jars hanging two to each side, their conical bases reaching almost to the sand. A score or so of the camels bore riders, robed variously in white, pale blue, or dark checks, and a dozen more heathens followed on foot, swaddled beneath mounds of black cloth, and presumably sweltering. A handful of scrawny sheep trailed at the rear, an extravagance given what it must have cost to keep them watered.

I stood, scorching beneath the sun, while two of the Ha'tari intercepted the trio of riders coming from the caravan. Another of their number disarmed me, taking both knife and sword. After a minute or two of gesticulating and death threats, or possibly reasoned discourse—the two tend to sound the same in the desert tongue—all five returned, a white-robe in the middle, a checked robe to each side, the Ha'tari flanking.

The three newcomers were bare-faced, baked dark by the sun, hook-nosed, eyes like black stones, related I guessed, perhaps a father and his sons.

"Tahnoon tells me you're a demon and that we should kill you in the old way to avert disaster." The father spoke, lips thin and cruel within a short white beard.

"Prince Jalan Kendeth of Red March at your service!" I bowed from the waist. Courtesy costs nothing, which makes it the ideal gift when you're as cheap as I am. "And actually I'm an angel of salvation. You should take me with you." I tried my smile on him. It hadn't been working recently but it was pretty much all I had.

"A prince?" The man smiled back. "Marvellous." Somehow one twist of his lips transformed him. The black stones of his eyes twinkled and became almost kindly. Even the boys to either side of him stopped scowling. "Come, you will dine with us!" He clapped his hands and barked something at the elder son, his voice so vicious that I could believe he'd just ordered him to disembowel himself. The son rode off at speed. "I am Sheik Malik al'Hameed. My boys Jahmeen." He nodded to the son beside him. "And Mahood." He gestured after the departing man.

"Delighted." I bowed again. "My father is . . ."

"Tahnoon says you fell from the sky, pursued by a demon-whore!"

The sheik grinned at his son. "When a Ha'tari falls off his camel there's always a demon or djinn at the bottom of it—a proud people. Very proud."

I laughed with him, mostly in relief: I'd been about to declare myself the son of a cardinal. Perhaps I had sunstroke already.

Mahood returned with a camel for me. I can't say I'm fond of the beasts but riding is perhaps my only real talent and I'd spent enough time lurching about on camelback to have mastered the basics. I stepped up into the saddle easy enough and nudged the creature after Sheik Malik as he led off. I took the words he muttered to his boys to be approval.

"We'll make camp." The sheik lifted up his arm as we joined the head of the column. He drew breath to shout the order.

"Christ no!" Panic made the words come out louder than intended. I pressed on, hoping the "Christ" would slip past unnoticed. The key to changing a man's mind is to do it before he's announced his plan. "My lord al'Hameed, we need to ride hard. Something terrible is going to happen here, very soon!" If the veils hadn't thinned because of some ongoing slaughter it could only mean one thing. Something far worse was *going* to happen and the walls that divide life from death were coming down in anticipation . . .

The sheik swivelled toward me, eyes stone once more, his sons tensing as if I'd offered grave insult by interrupting.

"My lord, your man Tahnoon had his story half right. I'm no demon, but I did fall from the sky. Something terrible will happen here very soon and we need to get as far away as we can. I swear by my honour this is true. Perhaps I was sent here to save you and you were sent here to save me. Certainly without each other neither of us would have survived."

Sheik Malik narrowed his eyes at me, deep crows' feet appearing, the sun leaving no place for age to hide. "The Ha'tari are a simple people, Prince Jalan, superstitious. My kingdom lies north and reaches the coast. I have studied at the Mathema and owe allegiance to no one in all of Liba save the caliph. Do not take me for a fool."

The fear that had me by the balls tightened its grip. I'd seen death in all its horrific shades and escaped at great cost to get here. I didn't want to find myself back in the deadlands within the hour, this time just another soul detached from its flesh and defenceless against the terrors that dwelt there. "Look at me, Lord al'Hameed." I spread my hands and glanced down across my reddening stomach. "We're in the deep desert. I've spent less than a quarter of an hour here and my skin is burning. In another hour it will be blistered and peeling off. I have no robes, no camel, no water. How could I have got here? I swear to you, my lord, on the honour of my house, if we do not leave, right now, as fast as is possible, we will all die."

The sheik looked at me as if taking me in for the first time. A long minute of silence passed, broken only by the faint hiss of sand and the snorting of camels. The men around us watched on, tensed for action. "Get the prince some robes, Mahood." He raised his arm again and barked an order. "We ride!"

The promised fleeing proved far more leisurely than I would have liked. The sheik discussed matters with the Ha'tari headman and we ambled up the slope of a dune, apparently on a course at right angles to their original one. The highlight of the first hour was my drink of water. An indescribable pleasure. Water is life and in the drylands of the dead I had started to feel more than half dead myself. Pouring that wonderful, wet life into my mouth was a rebirth, probably as noisy and as much of a struggle as the first one given how many men it took to get the water-urn back off me.

Another hour passed. It took all the self-restraint I could muster not to dig my heels in and charge off into the distance. I had taken part in camel races during my time in Hamada. I wasn't the best rider but I got good odds, being a foreigner. Being on a galloping camel bears several resemblances to energetic sex with an enormously strong and very ugly woman. Right now it was pretty much all I wanted, but the desert is about the marathon not the sprint. The heavily laden camels would be exhausted in half a mile, less if they had to carry the walkers, and whilst the sheik had been prodded into action by my story he clearly thought the chance I was a madman outweighed any advantage to be gained by leaving his goods behind for the dunes to claim.

"Where are you heading, Lord al'Hameed?" I rode beside him near the front of the column, preceded by his elder two sons. Three more of his heirs rode further back.

"We were bound for Hamada and we will still get there, though this is not the direct path. I had intended to spend this evening at the Oasis of Palms and Angels. The tribes are gathering there, a meeting of sheiks before our delegations present themselves to the caliph. We reach agreement in the desert before entering the city. Ibn Fayed receives his vassals once a year and it is better to speak to the throne with one voice so that our requests may be heard more clearly."

"And are we still aiming for the oasis?"

The sheik snorted phlegm, a custom the locals seem to have learned from the camels. "Sometimes Allah sends us messages. Sometimes they're written in the sand and you have to be quick to read them. Sometimes it's in the flight of birds or the scatter of a lamb's blood and you have to be clever to understand them. Sometimes an infidel drops on you in the desert and you'd have to be a fool not to listen to them." He glanced my way, lips pressed into a bitter line. "The oasis lies three miles west of the spot we found you. Hamada lies two days south."

Many men would have chosen to take my warning to the oasis. I felt a moment of great relief that Malik al'Hameed was not one of them, or right now instead of riding directly away from whatever was coming I would be three miles from it, trying to convince a dozen sheiks to abandon their oasis.

"And if they all die?"

"Ibn Fayed will still hear a single voice." The sheik nudged his camel on. "Mine."

A mile further on it occurred to me that although Hamada lay two days south, we were in fact heading east. I pulled up alongside the sheik again, displacing a son.

"We're no longer going to Hamada?"

"Tahnoon tells me there is a river to the east that will carry us to safety." I turned in my saddle and gave the sheik a hard stare. "A river?"

He shrugged. "A place where time flows differently. The world is cracked, my friend." He held a hand up toward the sun. "Men fall from the sky. The dead are unquiet. And in the desert there are fractures where time runs away from you, or with you." A shrug. "The gap between us and whatever this danger of yours is will grow more quickly if we crawl this way than if we run in any other direction."

I had heard of such things before, though never seen them. On the Bremmer Slopes in the Ost Reich there are bubbles of slo-time that can trap a man, releasing him after a week, a year, or a century, to a world grown older while he merely blinked. Elsewhere there are places where a man might grow ancient and find that in the rest of Christendom just a day has passed.

We rode on and perhaps we found this so-called river of time, but there was little to show for it. Our feet did not race, our strides didn't devour seven yards at a time. All I can say is that evening arrived much more swiftly than expected and night fell like a stone.

I must have turned in my saddle a hundred times. If I had been Lot's wife the pillar of salt would have stood on Sodom's doorstep. I didn't know what I was looking for, demons boiling black across the dunes, a plague of flesh-scarabs . . . I remembered the Red Vikings chasing us into Osheim what seemed a lifetime ago and half-expected them to crest a dune, axes raised. But, whatever fear painted there, the horizon remained stubbornly empty of threat. All I saw was the Ha'tari rear-guard, strengthened at the sheik's request.

The sheik kept us moving deep into the night until at last the snorting of his beasts convinced him to call a halt. I sat back, sipping from a water skin, while the sheik's people set up camp with practised economy. Great tents were unfolded from camelback, lines tethered to flat stakes long enough to find purchase in the sand, fires built from camel dung gathered and hoarded along the journey. Lamps were lit and set beneath the awnings of the tents' porches, silver lamps for the sheik's tent, burning rock-oil. Cauldrons were unpacked, storage jars opened, even a small iron oven set above its own oil burners. Spice scents filled the air, somehow more foreign even than the dunes and the strange stars above us.

"They're slaughtering the sheep." Mahood had come up behind me, making me jump. "Father brought them all this way to impress Sheik Kahleed and the others at the meet. Send ahead, I told him, get them brought out from Hamada. But no, he wanted to feast Kahleed on Hameed mutton, said he would know any deception. Desert-seasoned mutton is stringy, tough stuff, but it does have a flavour all its own." He watched the Ha'tari as he spoke. They patrolled on foot now, out on the moon-washed sands, calling to each other once in a while with soft melodic cries. "Father will want to ask you questions about where you came from and who gave you this message of doom, but that is a conversation for after the meal, you understand?"

"I do." That at least gave me some time to concoct suitable lies. If I told the truth about where I had been and the things I had seen . . . well, it would turn their stomachs and they'd wish they hadn't eaten.

Mahood and another of the sons sat down beside me and started to smoke, sharing a single long pipe, beautifully wrought in meerschaum, in which they appeared to be burning garbage, judging by the reek. I waved the thing away when they offered it to me. After half an hour I relaxed and lay back, listening to the distant Ha'tari and looking up at the dazzle of the stars. It doesn't take long in Hell before your definition of "good company" reduces to "not dead." For the first time in an age I felt comfortable.

In time the crowd around the cooking pots thinned and a line of bearers carried the products of all that labour into the largest tent. A gong sounded and the brothers stood up around me. "Tomorrow we'll see Hamada. Tonight we feast." Mahood, lean and morose, tapped his pipe out on the sand. "I missed many old friends at the oasis meet tonight, Prince Jalan. My brother Jahmeen was to meet his betrothed this evening. Though I feel he is rather pleased to delay that encounter, at least for a day or two. Let us hope for you that your warning proves to have substance, or my father will have lost face. Let us hope for our brothers on the sand that you are mistaken." With that he walked off and I trailed him to the glowing tent.

I pushed the flaps back as they swished closed behind Mahood, and stood, still half-bowed and momentarily blinded by the light of a score of cowled lanterns. A broad and sumptuous carpet of woven silks, brilliantly patterned in reds and greens, covered the sand, set with smaller rugs where one might expect the table and chairs to stand. Sheik al'Hameed's family and retainers sat around a central rug crowded with silver platters, each heaped with food: aromatic rice in mounds of yellow, white, and green; dates and olives in bowls; marinated, dried, sweet strips of camel meat, dry roasted over open flame and dusted with the pollen of the desert rose; a dozen other dishes boasting culinary mysteries.

"Sit, prince, sit!" The sheik gestured to my spot.

I started as I registered for the first time that half of the company seated around the feast were women. Young beautiful women at that, clad in immodest amounts of silk. Impressive weights of gold crowded elegant wrists in glimmering bangles, and elaborate earrings descended in multipetalled cascades to drape bare shoulders or collect in the hollows behind collarbones.

"Sheik . . . I didn't know you had . . ." Daughters? Wives? I clamped my mouth shut on my ignorance and sat cross-legged where he indicated, trying not to rub elbows with the dark-haired visions to either side of me, each as tempting as the succubus and each potentially as lethal a trap.

"You didn't see my sisters walking behind us?" One of the younger brothers whose name hadn't stuck—clearly amused.

I opened my mouth. *Those were women?* They could have had four arms and horns under all that folded cloth and I'd have been no wiser. Sensibly I let no words escape my slack jaw.

"We cover ourselves and walk to keep the Ha'tari satisfied," said the girl to my left, tall, lean, elegant, and perhaps no more than eighteen. "They are easily shocked, these desert men. If they came to the coast they might go blind for not knowing where to rest their eyes . . . poor things. Even Hamada would be too much for them."

"Fearless fighters, though," said the woman to my left, perhaps my age. "Without them, crossing the barrens would be a great ordeal. Even in the desert there are dangers."

Across from us the other two sisters shared an observation, glancing my way. The older of the pair laughed, full-throated. I stared desperately at her kohl-darkened eyes, struggling to keep my gaze from dipping to the jiggle of full breasts beneath silk gauze strewn with sequins. I knew by reputation that Liban royalty, be it the ubiquitous princes, the rarer sheiks, or the singular caliph, all guarded their womenfolk with legendary zeal and would pursue vendettas across the centuries over as little as a covetous glance. What they might do over a despoiled maiden they left to the horrors of imagination.

I wondered if the sheik saw me as a marriage opportunity, having seated me amid his daughters. "I'm very grateful that the Ha'tari found me," I said, keeping my eyes firmly on the meal.

"My daughters Lila, Mina, Tarelle, and Danelle." The sheik smiled indulgently as he pointed to each in turn.

"Delightful." I imagined ways in which they might be delightful.

As if reading my mind the sheik raised his goblet. "We are not so strict in our faith as the Ha'tari but the laws we do keep are iron. You are a welcome guest, prince. But, unless you become betrothed to one of my daughters, lay no finger on them that you would rather keep."

I reddened and started to bluster. "Sir! A prince of Red March would never—"

"Lay more than a finger upon her and I will make her a gift of your testicles, gold-plated, to be worn as earrings." He smiled as if we'd been discussing the weather. "Time to eat!"

Food! At least there was the food. I would gorge to the point I was too full for even the smallest of lustful thoughts. And I'd enjoy it too. In the deadlands you starved. From the first moment you stepped into that deadlight until the moment you left it, you starved.

The sheik led us in their heathen prayers, spoken in the desert tongue. It took a damnable long time, my belly rumbling the while, mouth watering at the display set out before me. At last the lot of them joined in with a line or two and we were done. All heads turned to the tent flaps, expectant.

Two elderly male servants walked in with the main course on silver plates, square in the Araby style. Sitting on the floor I could just see a mound of food rising above the dishes, roast mutton no doubt, given the slaughtering earlier. God yes! My stomach growled like a lion, attracting nods of approval from Sheik Malik and his eldest son.

The server set my plate before me and moved on. A skinned sheep's head stared at me, steaming gently, boiled eyes regarding me with an amused expression, or perhaps that was just the grin on its lipless mouth. A dark tongue coiled beneath a row of surprisingly even teeth.

"Ah." I closed my own mouth with a click and looked to Tarelle on my left who had just received her own severed head.

She favoured me with a sweet smile. "Marvellous, is it not, Prince Jalan? A feast like this in the desert. A taste of home after so many hard miles."

I'd heard that the Libans could get almost as stabby if you didn't touch their food as they would if you *did* touch their women. I returned my gaze to the steaming head, its juices pooling around it, and considered how far I was from Hamada and how few yards I would get without water.

I reached for the nearest rice and started to heap my plate. Perhaps I could give the poor creature a decent burial and nobody would notice. Sadly I was the curiosity at this family feast and most eyes were turned my way. Even the dozen sheep seemed interested.

"You're hungry, my prince!" Danelle to my right, her knee brushing mine each time she reached forward to add a date or olive to her plate.

"Very," I said, grimly shovelling rice onto the monstrosity on my own. The thing had so little flesh that it was practically a grinning skull. The presence of a distinctly scooped spoon amid the flatware arranged by my plate suggested that a goodly amount of delving was expected. I wondered whether it was etiquette to use the same spoon for eyeballs as for brain . . .

"Father says the Ha'tari think you fell from the sky." Lila from across the feast.

"With a devil-woman giving chase!" Mina giggled. The youngest of them, silenced by a sharp look from elder brother Mahood.

"Well," I said. "I—"

Something moved beneath my rice heap.

"Yes?" Tarelle by my side, knee touching mine, naked beneath thin silks.

"I certainly—"

Goddamn! There it was again, something writhing like a serpent beneath mud. "I . . . the sheik said your man fell from his camel."

Mina was a slight thing, but unreasonably beautiful, perhaps not yet sixteen. "The Ha'tari are not ours. We are theirs now they have Father's coin. Theirs until we are discharged into Hamada."

"But it's true," Danelle, her voice seductively husky at my ear. "The Ha'tari would rather say the moon swung too low and knocked them from their steed than admit they fell."

General laughter. The sheep's purple tongue broke through my burial, coiling amid the fragrant yellow rice. I stabbed it with my fork, pinning it to the plate.

The sudden movement drew attention. "The tongue is my favourite," Mina said.

"The brain is divine," Sheik al'Hameed declared from the head of the feast. "My girls puree it with dates, parsley, and pepper then return it to the skull." He kissed his fingertips.

Whilst he held his children's attention I quickly severed the tongue and with some frantic sawing reduced it to six or more sections.

"Fine cooking skills are a great bonus in a wife, are they not, Prince Jalan? Even if she never has to cook it is well that she knows enough to instruct her staff." The sheik turned the focus back onto me.

"Yes." I stirred the tongue pieces into the rice and heaped more atop them. "Absolutely."

The sheik seemed pleased at that. "Let the poor man eat! The desert has given him an appetite."

For a few minutes we ate in near silence, each traveller dedicated to their meal after weeks of poor fare. I worked at the rice around the edge of my burial, unwilling to put tainted mutton anywhere near my mouth. Beside me the delicious Tarelle inverted her own sheep's head and started scooping out brains into her suddenly far less desirable mouth. The spoon made unpleasant scraping sounds along the inside of the skull.

I knew what had happened. Whilst in the deadlands Loki's key had been invisible to the Dead King. Perhaps a jest of Loki's, to have the thing become apparent only when out of reach. Whatever the reason, we had been able to travel the deadlands with less danger from the Dead King than we'd had during the previous year in the living world. Of course we had far more danger from every other damned thing, but that was a different matter. Now that the key was back among the living any dead thing could hunt it for the Dead King.

I was pretty sure Tarelle and Danelle's sheep had turned their puffy eyeballs my way and I didn't dare scrape away the rice from my own for fear of finding the thing staring back at me. I managed, by dint of continuously sampling from the dishes in the centre, to eat a vast amount of food whilst continuing to increase the mound on my own plate. After months in the deadlands it would take more than a severed head on my plate to kill my appetite. I drank at least a gallon from my goblet, constantly refilling it from a nearby ewer, only water sadly, but the deadlands had given me a thirst that required a small river to quench and the desert had only added to it.

"This danger that you claim to have come to warn us of." Mahood pushed back his plate. "What is it?" He rested both hands on his stomach. As lean as his father, he was taller, sharp featured, pockmarked, as quick to shift from friendly to sinister with just the slightest movement of his face.

"Bad." I took the opportunity to push back my own plate. To be unable to clear your plate is a compliment to a Liban host's largesse. Mine simply constituted a bigger compliment than usual, I hoped. "I don't know what form it will take. I only pray that we are far enough away to be safe."

"And God sent an infidel to deliver this warning?"

"A divine message is holy whatever it may be written upon." I had Bishop James to thank for that gem. He beat the words, if not the sentiment, into me after I decorated the privy wall with that bible passage about who was cleaving to whom. "And of course the messenger is never to be blamed! That one's older than civilization." I breathed a sigh of relief as my plate was removed without comment.

"And now dessert!" The sheik clapped his hands. "A true desert dessert!"

I looked up expectantly as the servers returned with smaller square platters stacked along their arms, half expecting to be presented with a plate of sand. I would have preferred a plate of sand.

"It's a scorpion," I said.

"A keen eye you have, Prince Jalan." Mahood favoured me with a dark stare over the top of his water goblet.

"Crystallized scorpion, Prince Jalan! Can you have spent time in Liba and not yet tried one?" The sheik looked confounded.

"It's a great delicacy." Tarelle's knee bumped mine.

"I'm sure I'll love it." I forced the words past gritted teeth. Teeth that had no intention of parting to admit the thing. I stared at the scorpion, a monster fully nine inches long from the curve of the tail arching over its back to the oversized twin claws. The arachnid had a slightly translucent hue to it, its carapace orange and glistening with some kind of sugary glaze. Any larger and it could be mistaken for a lobster.

"Eating the scorpion is a delicate art, Prince Jalan," the sheik said, demanding our attention. "First, do not be tempted to eat the sting. For the rest customs vary, but in my homeland we begin with the lower section of the pincer, like so." He took hold of the upper part and set his knife between the two halves. "A slight twist will crack—"

Out of the corner of my eye I saw the scorpion on my plate jitter toward me on stiff legs, six glazed feet scrabbling for purchase on the silver. I slammed my goblet down on the thing crushing its back, legs shattering, pieces flying in all directions, cloudy syrup leaking from its broken body.

All nine al'Hameeds stared at me in open-mouthed astonishment.

"Ah . . . that's . . ." I groped for some kind of explanation. "That's how we do it where I come from!"

A silence stretched, rapidly extending through awkward into uncomfortable, until with a deep belly-laugh Sheik Malik slammed his goblet down on his own scorpion. "Unsubtle, but effective. I like it!" Two of his daughters and one son followed suit. Mahood and Jahmeen watched me with narrowed eyes as they started to dismember their dessert piece by piece in strict accordance with tradition.

I looked down at the syrupy mess of fragments in my own plate. Only the claws and stinger had survived. I still didn't want to eat any of it. Opposite me, Mina popped a sticky chunk of broken scorpion into her pretty mouth, smiling all the while.

I picked up a piece, sharp-edged and dripping with ichor, hoping for some distraction so that I could palm the thing away. It was a pity the heathens took against dogs so. A hound at a feast is always handy for disposing of unwanted food. With a sigh I moved the fragment toward my lips . . .

When the distraction came I was almost too distracted to use the opportunity. One moment we sat illuminated by the fluttering light of a dozen oil lamps, the next the world outside lit up brighter than a desert noon, dazzling even through the tent walls. I could see the shadows of guy ropes stark against the material, the outline of a passing servant. The intensity of it grew from unbelievable to impossible, and outside the screaming started. A wave of heat reached me as if I had passed from shadow to sun. I barely had time to stand before the glow departed, as quickly as it came. The tent seemed suddenly dim. I stumbled over Tarelle, unable to make out my surroundings.

We exited in disordered confusion, to stare at the vast column of fire rising in the distance. A column of fire so huge it rose into the heavens before flattening against the roof of the sky and turning down upon itself in a roiling mushroom-shaped cloud of flame.

For the longest time we watched in silence, ignoring the screams of the servants clutching their faces, the panic of the animals, and the fried smell rising from the tents, which seemed to have been on the point of bursting into flame.

Even in the chaos I had time to reflect that things seemed to be turning out rather well. Not only had I escaped the deadlands and returned to life, I had now very clearly saved the life of a rich man and his beautiful daughters. Who knew how large my reward might be, or how pretty!

A distant rumbling underwrote the screams of men and animals.

"Allah!" Sheik Malik stood beside me, reaching only my shoulder. He had seemed taller on his camel.

That old Jalan luck was kicking in. Everything turning up roses.

"It's where we found him," Mahood said.

The rumbling became a roar. I had to raise my voice, nodding, and trying to look grim. "You were wise to listen to me, Sheik Mal—"

Jahmeen cut across me. "It can't be. That was twenty miles back. No fire could be seen at such—"

The dunes before us exploded, the most distant first, then the next, the next, the next, quick as a man can beat a drum. Then the world rose around us and everything was flying tents and sand and darkness.

TWO

I could have lost consciousness only for a moment for I gained my senses in time to see a dozen or more camels charging right at me, maddened by terror, eyes rolling. I lurched to my feet, spitting sand, and dived to one side. If I'd had a split second to think about my move I would have gone the other way. As it was, almost immediately I slammed into someone still staggering about while the rumbles of the explosion died away. Both of us followed my planned arc but fell short of the point I would have reached unimpeded. I did my level best to haul my screaming companion out from underneath me to use as a shield but just ended up with two handfuls of gauze and a camel's foot stamping on my arse as it thundered by.

Groaning and clutching my rear, I rolled to the side, discovering that I appeared to have stripped and possibly killed one of the sheik's daughters. The moonlight hid few details but with her hair in disarray I couldn't tell which of the four it was. Figures closed on me from both sides, the sand settling out of the night as they came. Somewhere someone kept shrieking but the sound came muffled as if the loudness of detonation had reduced all other noise to insignificance.

The sheik's elder sons pulled me to my feet, keeping an iron grip on my arms even after I'd stood up. A grey-haired retainer, bleeding from the nose and with the left side of his face blistered, covered the dead daughter with his tunic, leaving himself naked from the waist up, hollow-chested and wattled with the hanging skin old men wear. The sons were shouting questions or accusations at me but none of them quite penetrated the ringing in my ears.

The sand cleared from the air within a minute or so and the moon washed across the ruin of our camp. I stood, half-dazed, with Jahmeen's knife to my throat, while Mahood shouted accusations at me, mostly about his sister, as if the destruction of the camp were as nothing compared to the baring of two breasts. However fine. Oddly I didn't feel scared. The blast had left me somehow separated, as if I floated outside myself, an unconcerned observer, watching the surroundings as much as I watched Mahood's raging or Jahmeen's hand around the hilt of the blade at my neck.

It looked as if a hurricane had blown through leaving no tent standing. Those of us who had been inside when the night lit up were largely unharmed. Those who had been outside showed burns on any exposed flesh facing the direction of the explosion. The Ha'tari on patrol had fared better, though one looked to be blind. But the tribesmen who had been sitting around their prayer pole, unveiled in the darkness, had been burned as badly as the servants.

The camels had taken off but many of the caravaneers had gathered around the base of the nearest dune where the wounded were being treated, leaving me with the two brothers and three retainers out on more exposed sands. It was damnable cold in the desert night and I found myself shivering. The brothers might have thought it from fear, and Jahmeen grinned nastily at me, but some cataclysms are so terrifying that my habitual terror just up and runs, and right now my fear was still lost somewhere out there in the night.

It wasn't until Sheik Malik approached from the dunes with two Ha'tari, leading half a dozen camels, that I suddenly settled back into myself and started to panic, recalling his light-hearted talk of gold-plating the balls of any man who laid hands on his daughters.

"I never touched her! I swear it!"

"Touched who?" The sheik left the camels to the Ha'tari and strode into the middle of the small gathering around me.

Jahmeen lowered the knife and the two brothers hauled me around to face their father. Behind him the column of fire continued to boil up into the night, yellow, orange, mottled with darkness, spreading out across the sky, huge despite the fact it would take a whole day to walk back to where it stood.

"This was a Builders' Sun." The sheik waved at the fire behind him.

My mind hadn't even wandered into why or what yet but as the sheik said it I knew that he was right. The night had lit brighter than day. Had we been a few miles closer the tents would have burst into flame, the people outside turned into burning pillars. Who but the ancients had such power? I tried to imagine the Day of a Thousand Suns when the Builders scorched the world and broke death.

"The infidel has despoiled Tarelle!" Mahood shouted pointing at the figure sprawled beneath the robes.

"And killed her!" Jahmeen, waving his knife as if to make up for the fact that this was an afterthought.

The sheik's face turned wooden. He dropped to the girl's side and drew back the robe to expose her head. Tarelle chose that moment to sneeze and opened her eyes to fix her father with an unfocused stare.

"My child!" Sheik Malik drew his daughter to him, exposing enough neck and shoulder to give a Ha'tari apoplexy. He fixed me with cold eyes.

"The camels!" Tarelle pulled at her father's arm. "They . . . he saved me, Father! Prince Jalan . . . he jumped into their path as they charged and carried me clear."

"It's true!" I lied. "I covered her with my body to save her from being crushed." I shook off the brothers' hands with a snarl. "I got stepped on by the camel that would have trampled your daughter." In full bluster mode now I straightened out my robes, wishing they were a cavalry shirt and jacket. "And I don't appreciate having a damned knife held to my throat by the brothers of the woman I protected at great personal risk. Brothers, it must be said, who would currently be on fire at the Oasis of Palms and Angels if I hadn't been sent to save all your lives!"

"Unhand him!" The sheik shot dark looks at both sons, neither of which actually had hands on me any more, and waved them further back. "Go with Tahnoon and recover our animals! And you!" He rounded on the three retainers, ignoring their injuries. "Get this camp back into order!"

Returning his attention to me, the sheik bowed at the waist. "A thousand pardons, Prince Jalan. If you would do me the honour of guarding my daughters while I salvage our trade goods I would stand in your debt!"

"The honour is all mine, Sheik Malik." And I returned the bow, allowing my own to hide the grin I couldn't keep from my face.

◆ ◆ ◆

An hour later I found myself outside the sheik's second best tent guarding all four of his daughters who huddled inside, wrapped once more in the ridiculous acreage of their thobes. The girls had three ageing maidservants to attend their needs and guard their virtue, but the trio hadn't fared too well when the Builders' Sun lit the night. Two had burns and the third looked to have broken a leg when the blast threw us all around. They were being tended a short distance off, outside the tent sheltering the injured men.

The important thing about the injured was that none of them looked *mortally* injured. The sands are staggeringly empty: the Dead King might have turned his eyes my way, but without corpses to work with he posed little threat.

I heard my name mentioned more than once as the sisters discussed the calamity in low voices behind me, Tarelle sharing the story of my bravery in the face of stampeding camels, and Lila reminding her sisters that my warning had saved them all. If I hadn't been stuck outside in tribesman robes that stank of camel and itched my sunburn into a misery I might have felt quite pleased with myself.

The sheik, together with his sons and guards, had gone out amid the dunes to hunt down his precious cargo and the beasts it was tied onto. I couldn't imagine how they could track the camels in the night, or how they hoped to find their way back to us either with or without them, but that seemed to be firmly the sheik's problem and not mine.

I stood, leaning into the wind, eyes slitted against the fine grit it bore. During the whole day's journey a light breeze had blown in across us from the west, but now the wind had turned toward the explosion, as if answering a summons, and strengthened into something that might easily become a sandstorm. The fire in the south had gone, leaving only darkness and questions.

After half an hour I gave up standing guard and started to sit guard instead, hollowing the sand to make it more comfortable for my bruised arse. I watched the sheik's more able-bodied retainers salvaging additional tents and putting them back up as best they could. And I listened to the daughters, occasionally twirling a length of broken tent pole I'd picked up in lieu of a sword. I even started humming: it takes more than a Builders' Sun exploding to take the gloss off a man's first night in the living world after what seemed an eternity in Hell. I'd made it through the first two verses of *The Charge of the Iron Lance* when an unexplained stillness made me sit up straight and look around. Straining through the gloom I could make out the nearest of the men, standing motionless around a half-erected tent. I wondered why they'd stopped work. The real question struck me a few moments later. Why could I barely see them? It had become darker—much darker—and all within the space of a few minutes. I looked up. No stars. No moon. Which had to mean cloud. And that simply didn't happen in the Sahar. Certainly not during the year I'd spent in Hamada.

The first drop of rain hit me square between the eyes. The second hit me in the right eye. The third hit the back of my throat as I made to complain. Within the space of ten heartbeats three drops had grown into a deluge that had me backing into the tent awning for shelter. Slim hands reached out for my shoulders and drew me in through the flaps.

"Rain!" Tarelle, her face in shadow, the light of a single lamp hinting at the curve of her cheekbone, her brow, the line of her nose.

"How can it be raining?" Mina, fearful yet excited.

"I . . ." I didn't know. "The Builders' Sun must have done it." Could a fire make it rain? A fire that big might change the weather . . . certainly the flames reached high enough to lick the very roof of the sky.

"I heard that after the Day of a Thousand Suns there was a hundred years of winter. The winter of the north where water turns to stone and falls from the sky in flakes," Danelle said, her face at my shoulder, voice rich and commanding thrills down my spine.

"I'm scared." Lila pressed closer as the rain began to hammer on the tent roof above us. I doubted we'd be dry for long—tents in Liba are intended to keep out the sun and the wind: they rarely have to contend with the wet.

A crack of thunder broke ridiculously close and suddenly Prince Jal was the filling in a four-girl sandwich. The boom paralysed me with terror for a moment and left my ears ringing, so it took me a short while to appreciate my position. Not even thirty-six yards of thobe could entirely disguise the sisters' charms at this proximity. Moments later, though, a new fear surfaced to chase off any thoughts of taking advantage.

"Your father made some very specific threats, ladies, concerning your virtue and I really—"

"Oh, you don't want to worry about that." A husky voice close enough to my ear to make me shiver.

"Father says all manner of things." Softly spoken by a girl with her head against my chest. "And nobody will move until the rain stops."

"I can't remember a time when we weren't being watched over by Father, or our brothers, or his men." Another pressed soft against my shoulder.

"And we do so need protecting . . ." Behind me. Mina? Danelle? Whoever it was her hands were moving over my hips in a most unvirtuous way.

"But the sheik—"

"Gold plating?" A tinkling laugh as the fourth sister started to push me down. "Did you really believe that?"

At least two of the girls were busy unwinding their thobes with swift and practised hands. Amid the shadows thrown by so many bodies I could see very little, but what I could see I liked. A lot.

All four of them pushed me down now, a tangled mass of smooth limbs and long hair, hands roaming.

"Gold's so expensive." Tarelle, climbing atop me, still half-wrapped.

"That would be silly." Danelle, pressed to my side, deliciously soft, her tongue doing wonderful things to my ear. "He always uses silver . . ."

I tried to get up at that point, but there were too many of them, and things had got out of hand—except for the things that were now in hands . . . and, dammit, I'd been in Hell long enough, it was time for a spot of paradise.

There's a saying in Liba: The last yard of the thobe is the best.

　　　. . . or if there isn't, there should be!

"Arrrrgh!"

I've found that there are few things more effective at making a man's ardour grow softer than cold water. When the tent roof, weakened by

earlier traumas, gave without warning and released several gallons of icy
rainwater over my back I jumped up sharply, scattering al'Hameed women
and no doubt teaching them a whole new set of foreign curse words.

One thing that became clear as the water dripped off me was that
very little more was dripping in to replace it.

"Sshhh!" I raised my voice over the last of their shrieking—they'd
enjoyed the soaking no more than I had. "It's stopped raining!"

"ري خخ تنأ له ،ةقيش؟ع" A man just outside the tent, jabbering away
in the heathen tongue, others joining him. They must have heard the
screams. How much longer the fear of what the sheik would do to them
if they burst in on his daughters would outweigh the fear of what the sheik
would do to them if they failed to protect his daughters, I couldn't say.

"Cover yourselves!" I shouted, moving to defend the entrance.

I heard smirking behind me, but they moved, presumably not expecting to emerge unscathed if reports of "frolicking" reached their father.

Outside someone took hold of the tent flap. I'd not even laced it! With
a yelp I flung myself down to grab the bottom of it. "Hurry for Christ's
sake! And blow out the lamp!"

That set them giggling again. I grabbed the lamp and pre-empted
any attempt at entry by bursting out, setting the foremost of the sheik's
retainers on his backside in the wet sand.

"They're all fine!" I straightened up and waved an arm back toward the
tent. "The roof gave way under the rain . . . water everywhere." I did my best
to mime the last part in case none of them had the Empire tongue. I don't
think the idiots got it because they stood there staring at me as if I'd asked
a riddle. I strode purposefully away from the tent, beckoning the three men
with me. "Look! It'll all be clearer over here." I sincerely hoped those thobes
went back on as quickly as they came off. Two of the sheik's men were
bringing over one of the sisters' maids, urging her on despite her injuries.

"What's that over there?" I said it mainly to distract everyone. As I
looked in the direction I was pointing though . . . there was something.
"Over there!" I gesticulated more fiercely. Moonlight had started to pierce
the shredding clouds overhead and something seemed to be emerging
from the dune that I'd selected at random. Not cresting it, or stepping
from its shadow, but struggling through the damp crust of sand.

Others started to see it now, their voices rising in confusion. From the broken sand something rose, a figure, impossibly slim, bone-pale.

"Damn it all . . ." I'd escaped from Hell and now Hell seemed to be following me. The dune had disgorged a skeleton, the bones connected by nothing but memory of their previous association. Another skeleton seemed to be fighting its way from the damp sand beside the first, constructing itself from assorted pieces as it came.

All around me people started to cry out in alarm, cursing, calling on Allah, or just plain screaming. They began to fall back. I retreated with them. Not long ago the sight would have had me sprinting in the direction that best carried me away from the two horrors before us, but I'd seen my share of dead, both in and out of Hell, and I kept the panic to just below boiling point.

"Where did they come from? What are the odds we camped right where a couple of travellers died?" It hardly seemed fair.

"More than a couple." A timid voice behind me. I spun around to see four bethobed figures outside the women's tent. "Over there!" The speaker, the shortest so probably Mina, the youngest, pointed to my left. The sand in the lee of the dune had begun to heave and bony hands had emerged like a nightmare crop of weeds.

"There was a city here once." The tallest . . . Danelle? "The desert ate it two hundred years ago. The desert has covered many such." She sounded calm: probably in shock.

The sheik's retainers began to back in a new direction, retreating from both threats. The original two skeletons now seemed to sight us with their empty sockets and came on at a flat run, silent, their pace deadly, slowed only by the softness of the sand. That brought my panic to the boil. Before I could take to my heels though, a lone Ha'tari sprinted past me, having come through the camp. The sheik must have left one to patrol out among the dunes.

"No sword!" I held my empty hands up in excuse and let my retreat bring me among the four daughters. We stood together and watched the Ha'tari intercept the first of the skeletons. He hacked at its neck with his curved blade. Hearteningly, bone shattered beneath the blow, the skull flew clear and the rest of the skeleton collided with him, bouncing off to fall in a disarticulated heap on the sand.

The second skeleton rushed the warrior and he ran it through.

"Idiot!" I shouted, perhaps unreasonably because he'd acted on instinct and his reflexes were well honed.

Unfortunately sticking your blade through the chest of a skeleton is less of an inconvenience to the thing than it would have been back in the days when its bones were covered in flesh and guarded a lung. The skeleton ran into the thrust and clawed at the warrior's face with bone fingers. The man fell back yelling, leaving his sword trapped between its ribs.

I saw now, as the last tatters of cloud departed and the moon washed across the scene, that the skeleton was not as unconnected as I had thought. The silver light illuminated a grey misty substance that wrapped each bone and linked it, albeit insubstantially, to the next, as if the phantom of their previous owner still hung about the bones and sought to keep them united. Where the first attacker had collapsed and scattered, the mist, or smoke, had stained the ground, and as the stain sank away the desert floor writhed, nightmare faces appearing in the sand, mouths opening in silent screams before they lost form and collapsed in turn.

The Ha'tari warrior continued to back away, bent double, both hands clutching his face. The skeleton rotated its skull toward us and started to run again, the sword trapped in its ribcage clattering as it came on.

"This way!" I turned to do some running of my own, only to see that skeletons were closing on the camp from all directions, gleaming white in the moonlight. "Hell!"

The sheik's men had nothing better than daggers to defend themselves with, and I hadn't even filched a knife from the evening meal.

"There!" Danelle caught my shoulder and pointed at the closest of several lamp stands that had been set between the tents, each a shaft of mahogany a good six foot tall and standing on a splayed base, the brass lamp cradled at the top.

"That's no damn use!" I grabbed it anyway, letting the lamp fall and hefting the stand up with a grunt.

With nowhere to run I waited for the first of our attackers and timed my swing to its arrival. The lamp stand smashed through the skeleton's ribcage, shattering it like matchwood and breaking its spinal column into a shower of loose vertebrae. The dead thing fell into a hundred pieces, and the phantom that had wrapped them sank slowly toward the fragments, a grey mist descending.

The momentum of my swing turned me right around and the daughters had to be quick on their feet to avoid being hit. I found myself with my back to my original foe and facing two more with no time to swing again. I jabbed the stand's base into the breastbone of the foremost skeleton. Lacking flesh, the thing had little weight and the impact halted its charge, breaking bones and lifting it from its feet. The next skeleton reached me a moment later but I was able to smash the shaft of the stand into its neck like a quarterstaff then carry it down to the sand where my weight parted its skull from its body before its bony claws could reach me.

This left me on all fours amid the ruin of my last enemy but with half a dozen more racing my way, the closest just a few yards off. Still more were tearing into the sheik's people, both the injured and the healthy.

I got to my knees, empty handed, and found myself facing a skeleton just about to dive onto me. The scream hadn't managed to leave my mouth when a curved sword flashed above my head, shattering the skull about to hit my face. The rest of the horror bounced off me, falling into pieces, leaving a cold grey mist hanging in the air. I stepped up sharpish, shaking my hands as the phantom tried to leach into me through my skin.

"Here!" Tarelle had swung the sword and now pressed it into my grip. The Ha'tari's blade—she must have recovered it from the remains of the first skeleton I put down.

"Shit!" I sidestepped the next attacker and took the head off the one behind.

Five or six more were charging in a tight knot. I briefly weighed surrender in the balance against digging a hole. Neither offered much hope. Before I had time to consider any other options a huge shape barrelled through the undead, bones shattering with brittle retorts. A Ha'tari on camelback brushed past me, swinging his saif, more following in his wake.

Within moments the sheik and his sons were dismounting around us, shouting orders and waving swords.

"Leave the tents!" Sheik Malik yelled. "This way!" And he pointed up along the valley snaking between the dune crests that bracketed us.

Before long a column of men and women were limping their way behind the mounted sheik, flanked by his sons and his own armed tribes-men while the Ha'tari fought a rear-guard action against the bone hordes still being vomited forth from the damp sand.

A half mile on and we joined the rest of the sheik's riders, standing guard around the laden camels they'd recovered from the surrounding desert.

"We'll press on through the night." The sheik stood in his stirrups atop his ghost-white camel to address us. "No stopping. Any who fall behind will be left."

I looked over at Jahmeen, watching his father with strained intensity.

"The Ha'tari will deal with the dead, won't they?" I couldn't see mounted warriors being in too much danger from damp skeletons.

Jahmeen glanced my way. "When the bones rest uneasy it means the djinn are coming—from the empty places."

"Djinn?" Stories of magic lamps, jolly fellows in silk pantaloons, and the granting of three wishes sprung to mind. "Are they really as bad as the dead trying to eat us?"

"Worse." Jahmeen looked away, seeming less an angry young man and more a scared boy. "Much, much worse."

THREE

"So, about these djinn . . ." We'd travelled no more than two miles and somehow it was daytime among the dunes, scorching hot, blinding, miserable as always. As we left the time-river, rather than hasten into the next day we seemed to slip back into the one we'd escaped. The sun actually rose in the west in a reversal of the sunset we'd witnessed many hours before. The feeling was decidedly unsettling, and given my recent experiences "unsettling" is no gentle word! "Tell me more." I didn't really want to know any more about the djinn, but if the Dead King was sending more servants after the key I should at least know what I was running away from.

"Creatures of invisible scorching fire," Mahood said on my right.

"They will be drawn to the Builders' Sun." Jahmeen on my left. They had bracketed me the whole journey, presumably to stop me talking to their sisters.

"God made three creatures with the power of thought," Sheik Malik called back to us. "The angels, men, and djinn. The greatest of all the djinn, Shaytan, defied Allah and was cast down." The sheik slowed his mount to draw closer. "There are many djinn that dance in the desert but these are the lesser kind. In this part of the Sahar there is just one grand djinn. Him we should fear."

"You're telling me Satan is coming for us?" I scanned the dune tops.

"No." Sheik Malik flashed a white line of teeth. "He lives in the deep Sahar where men cannot abide."

I slumped in my saddle at that.

"This is just a cousin of his." And with that the sheik urged his camel on toward the Ha'tari riding point.

The ragged caravan continued on, winding its way through the dunes,

limited to the pace of the walking wounded, variously burned by the light
of the Builders' Sun, broken by the blast that reached us minutes later,
and torn by the bones of men long dead, emerging from the sands.

I hunched over my malodorous steed, swaying with the motion,
sweating in my robes, and willing away the miles between us and the
safety of Hamada's walls. Somehow I knew we wouldn't make it. Perhaps
just speaking about the djinn had sealed our fate. Speak of the devil, as
it were.

The Builders' Suns left invisible fire—everyone knew that. There were
places even in Red March still tainted with the shadow of the Thousand
Suns. Places where a man might walk and find his flesh blistering for no
reason, leaving him to die horribly over the next few days. They called them
the Promised Lands. One day they would be ours again, but not soon.

I half-expected the djinn to come like that, like the light of the
Builders' Sun, but unseen, turning first one man then the next into columns of flame, molten fats running. I'd seen bad things in Hell and my
imagination had plenty to work with.

In fact, djinn burn men from the inside.

It began with writing in the sand. As we snaked between the dunes
their blindingly white flanks became scarred with the curving script of
the heathens. At first, seen only where the sun grazed a slope at an angle
shallow enough for the raised letters to throw a shadow.

None of us knew how long before Tarelle noticed the markings we
had been riding between slopes overwritten with descriptions of our fate.

"What does it say?" I didn't really want to know but it's one of those
questions that asks itself.

"You don't want to know." Mahood looked nauseous, as if he'd eaten
one too many sheep's eyeballs.

Either the entire caravan was literate or the anxiety infectious because
within minutes of Tarelle's discovery each traveller seemed to walk or
ride within their own bubble of despair. Prayers were said in quavering
voices, the Ha'tari rode closer in, and the whole desert pressed in against
us, vast and empty.

Mahood was right, I didn't want to know what the writing said, but even
so part of me ached to be told. The lines of the words, raised against the

smoothness of the dunes, drew my eye, maddening and terrifying at the same time. I wanted to ride out and scuff away the messages but fear held me back amid the others. The main thing when trouble strikes is to keep a low profile. Don't draw attention to yourself—don't be the lightning rod.

"How much farther is it?" I'd asked that question a few times, first in irritation, then desperation. We were close. Ten miles, maybe fifteen, and the dunes would part to reveal Hamada, another city waiting its turn to drown beneath the desert. "How much farther?" I asked it as if repetition would wear away the miles more effectively than camel strides.

Finding myself ignored by Mahood, I turned to Jahmeen, and discovered that I was already the centre of his attention. Something in the stiffness of him, the awkwardness with which he rode his camel, gave me pause and my question stuck in my throat.

I met his eyes. He held me with the same implacable stare his father used—but then I saw it, a flicker of flame, glimpsed through the pupil of each eye.

"What . . . what's written in the sand?" A new question stuttered out.

Jahmeen parted his lips and I thought he would speak but instead his mouth opened so wide that his jaw creaked, and all that came forth was a hiss, like the sand being stripped from the dunes. He leaned forward, hand clasping around my wrist, and beneath his palm a fire ignited, trying to eat into me, trying to invade. My world became that burning touch—nothing else, not sight, or sound, or drawing breath, just the pain. Pain and memories . . . the worst memories of all . . . memories of Hell. And while I suffered and lost myself in them how long would it be before the djinn escaped Jahmeen and hollowed out my flesh, driving my own undernourished soul into Hell for good? I saw Snorri, standing there in my memory, standing there at the start of a tale I had no wish to follow, with that grin of his, that reckless, stupid, brave, infectious grin . . . All I had to do was hang on to the now. I had to stay here, in the now, with my body, and the pain. I just had to—

Snorri's hand is clamped about my wrist, the other on my shoulder, preventing me from falling. I'm looking up and he's framed against a dead sky from which a flat orange light bleeds. Every part of me hurts.

"The door got away from you, hey?" He stands me up. "Couldn't hold it myself—had to pull you through quick before it shut again."

I swallow the scream of raw terror before it chokes me in its bid for freedom. "Ah."

The door is right in front of me, a faint silver rectangle scratched into the dull grey flank of an enormous boulder. It's fading as I look at it. All life, all my future, everything I know lies on the other side of that door. Kara and Hennan are standing there, just two yards away, probably still staring at it in confusion.

"Give Kara a minute to lock it. Then we'll go." Snorri looms beside me.

Pretty soon Kara's confusion will turn into anger as she realizes I've picked Loki's key from her pocket. The thing just seemed to leap into my hand and stick to my fingers, as if it wanted to be stolen.

I cast a quick glance around me. The afterlife looks remarkably dull. They tell in children's tales that the Builders made ships that flew and some would soar above the clouds and out into the blackness between stars. They say the richest of kings once taxed all his nobles into the poorhouse and built a ship so vast and swift, hung beneath a thousand-acre sail, that it bore men all the way to Mars that, like the Moon, is a world unto itself. They went all those untold thousands of miles and returned with images of a place of dull red rocks and dull red dust and a dry wind that blew forever . . . and men never again bothered to go there. The deadlands look pretty much like that . . . only slightly less red.

The dryness prickles against my skin as if the air itself is thirsty, and each part of me is sore like a bruise. In the half-light the shadows across Snorri's face have a sinister cast, as though his flesh is itself a shadow over the bone beneath and any moment might find it gone, leaving a bare skull to regard me.

"What the hell is *that*?" I point an accusing finger over his shoulder. I tried this once when we first met and earned not so much as a flinch. Now he turns, bound by trust. Quickly I pull Loki's key from my pocket and jab it toward the fading door. A keyhole appears, the key sinks home, I turn it, turn it back, pull it clear. Quicker than a trice. Locked.

"I don't see it." Snorri's still peering at the jumbled rocks when I turn back. Useful stuff, trust. I pocket the key. It was worth sixty-four thousand in crown gold to Kelem. To me it's worth a brief stay in the deadlands. I'll open the door again when I'm sure Kara won't be waiting on the other side of it. Then I'll go home.

"Might have been a shadow." I scan the horizon. It's not inspiring. Low hills, scoured with deep gullies, march off into a gloomy haze. The huge boulder we're next to is one of many scattering a broad plain of fractured rock, dark and jagged pieces of basalt bedded in a dull reddish dust. "I'm thirsty."

"Let's go." Snorri rests the haft of his axe on his shoulder and sets off, stepping from one sharp rock to the next.

"Where?" I follow him, concentrating on my footing, feeling the uncomfortable angles through the soles of my boots.

"The river."

"And you know it's in this direction . . . how?" I struggle to keep up. It's not hot or cold, just dry. There's a wind, not enough to pick up the dust, but it blows through me, not around, but through, like an ache deep in the bones.

"These are the deadlands, Jal. Everyone's lost. Any direction will take you where you're going. You just have to hope that's where you want to be."

I don't comment. Barbarians are immune to logic. Instead I glance back at the rock where the door lay, trying to fix it in my memory. It's crooked over to the right, almost like the letter "r." I should be able to open a door out anywhere I choose, but I don't much want to put that to the test. It took a mage like Kelem to show us a door in and the chances are he's in the deadlands now. I'd rather not have to ask him to show me the exit.

We press on, stepping from rock to rock on sore feet, trudging through the dust where the rocks grow sparse. There's no sound but us. Nothing grows. Just a dry and endless wilderness. I had expected screaming, torn bodies, torture and demons.

"Is this what you expected?" I lengthen my stride and catch up with Snorri again.

"Yes."

"I'd always thought Hell would be more . . . lively. Pitchforks, wailing souls, lakes of fire."

"The völvas say the goddess makes a Hel for each man."

"Goddess?" I stub my toe on a rock hidden in the dust and stumble on, cursing.

"You spent a winter in Trond, Jal! Didn't you learn anything?"

"Fuckit." I hobble on. The pain from my foot almost unmans me. It's as if I've stepped in acid and it's eating its way up my leg. If just banging my toe hurts this much in the deadlands I'm terrified of being on the wrong end of any significant injury. "I learned plenty." Just not about their damned sagas. Most of them seemed to be about Thor hitting things with his hammer. More interesting than the stories Roma tries to feed us, true, but not much of a code to live by.

Snorri stops and I hobble two paces past him before realizing. He spreads his arms as I turn. "Hel rules here. She watches the dead—"

"No, wait. I do remember this one." Kara had told me. Hel, ice-hearted, split nose to crotch by a line dividing a left side of pure jet from a right side of alabaster. "She watches the souls of men, her bright eye sees the good in them, her dark eye sees the evil, and she cares not for either . . . did I get it right?" I hop on one leg, massaging my toe.

Snorri shrugs. "Close enough. She sees the courage in men. Ragnarok is coming. Not the Thousand Suns of the Builders, but a true end when the world cracks and burns and the giants rise. Courage is all that will matter then."

I look around at the rocks, the dust, the barren hills. "So where's mine? If this is your hell where's mine?" I don't want to see mine. At all. But even so, to be wandering around in a barbarian's hell seems . . . wrong. Or perhaps a key ingredient in my personal hell is that nobody recognizes the precedence of nobility over commoners.

"You don't believe in it," Snorri says. "Why would Hel build it for you if you don't believe in it?"

"I do!" Protesting my faithfulness in all things is a reflex with me.

"Your father is a priest, yes?"

"A cardinal! He's a cardinal, not some damn village priest."

Snorri shrugs as if these are just words. "Priests' children seldom believe. No man is a prophet in his own land."

"That sort of pagan nonsense might—"

"It's from the bible." Snorri stops again.

"Oh." I stop too. He's right, I guess. I've never had much use for religion, except when it comes to swearing or begging for mercy. "Why have we stopped?"

Snorri says nothing, so I look where he's looking. Ahead of us the air is splintering and through the fractures I see glimpses of a sky that already looks impossibly blue, too full of the vital stuff of life to have any place in the drylands of death. The tears grow larger—I see the arc of a sword—a spray of crimson, and a man tumbles out of nowhere, the fractures sealing themselves behind him. I say a man, but really it's a memory of him, sketched in pale lines, occupying the space where he should be. He stands, not disturbing so much as a mote of dust, and I see the bloodless wound that killed him, a gash across his forehead that skips down to his broken collarbone and through it into the meat of him.

As the man stands, the process is repeating to his left and right, and again twenty yards behind them. More men drop through from whatever battlefield they're dying on. They ignore us, standing with heads bowed, a few with scraps of armour, all weaponless. I'm about to call out to the first when he turns and walks away, his path close to our own heading but veering a little to the left.

"Souls," I mean to say out loud but only a whisper escapes.

Snorri shrugs. "Dead men." He starts walking too. "We'll follow them."

I start forward but the air breaks before me. I see the world, I can smell it, feel the breeze, taste the air. And suddenly I understand the hunger in dead men's eyes. I've been in the drylands less than an hour and already the need that just this glimpse of life gives me is consuming. There's a battle raging that makes Aral Pass look like a skirmish: men hack at each other with bright steel and wild cries, the roar of massed troops, the screams of the wounded, the groans of the dying. Even so I'm lunging forward, so desperate for the living world that even a few moments there before someone spears me seem worth it.

It's the soul that stops me. The one that punched this hole into death. I meet him head on, emerging, being born into death. There's nothing to him, just the faint lines that remember him—that and the howling rage and fear and pain of his last seconds. It's enough to stop me though. He runs over my skin like a scald, sinks through it, and I fall back, shrieking, over-written by his memories, drowning in his sorrow. Martell he's called. Martell Harris. It seems more important than my own name. I try to speak my name, whatever it is, and find my lips have forgotten the shape of it.

"Get up, Jal!"

I'm on the ground, dust rising all around me. Snorri is kneeling over me, hair dark around his face. I'm losing him. Sinking. The dust rising, thicker by the moment. I'm Martell Harris. The sword went into me like ice but I'm all right, I just need to get back into the battle. Martell moves my arms, struggles to rise. Jalan is gone, sinking into the dust.

"Stay with me, Jal!" I can feel Snorri's grip on me. Nothing else, just that iron grip. "Don't let him drive you out. You're Jalan. Prince Jalan Kendeth."

The fact of Snorri actually saying my name right—title and all—jolts me out of the dust's soft embrace.

"Jalan Kendeth!" The grip tightens. It really hurts. "Say it! SAY IT!"

"Jalan Kendeth!" The words tore from me in a great shout.

I found myself face to face with the thing that used to be Sheik Malik's son Jahmeen, before the djinn burned him hollow. Somehow the memory of that Hell-bound soul pushing into me, stealing my flesh had brought me back to the moment, back to fighting the djinn for control using whatever tricks I'd learned in the drylands.

The grip on my wrist is iron, anchoring me. And the pain! With my senses returned to me I found my whole arm on fire with white agony. Desperate to escape before the djinn could slip from Jahmeen and possess me in his stead I head-butted him full in the face and wrenched my arm clear. A heartbeat later I drove both heels viciously into my camel's sides. With a lurch and a bugle of protest the beast took to the gallop, me bouncing about atop, hanging on with every limb at my disposal.

I didn't look back. Damsels in distress be damned. Before I'd broken that grip I'd felt a familiar feeling. As the djinn had tried to move in, I in turn had been moving out. I knew exactly what Hell felt like and that was exactly where the djinn was trying to put the bits of me it didn't need.

◆ ◆ ◆

About a mile on, still following the channel between the two great dunes that had hemmed us in, my camel stopped. Where horses will frequently run past the limit of their endurance given enough encouragement, camels are beasts of a very different temperament. Mine just decided it had had enough and came to a dead halt, using the sand to arrest its progress. An experienced rider can usually pick up on the warning signs and prepare himself. An inexperienced rider, scared witless, has to rely on the sand to slow them down too. This is achieved by allowing the rider's momentum to launch him or her over the head of his or her camel. The rest takes care of itself.

I got up quick enough, spitting out the desert. Put enough fear or embarrassment into a man and he's immune to all but the very worst pain. Back along the winding route I'd ridden between dune crests a sandstorm had risen. Four main things worried me about it. Firstly, unlike dust, sand takes a hell of a wind to rise up into the air. Secondly, rather than the traditional advancing storm-wall, this storm appeared to be localized to the valley between two dunes, no more than two hundred yards apart. Thirdly, the wind was hardly blowing. And finally, what wind there was was blowing toward the sandstorm and yet it seemed to be advancing on me at quite a rate!

"Shit. Shit. Shit." I leapt toward my camel and scrambled up his side. Somehow my panic panicked the camel and the damn thing took off with me halfway into the saddle. I lay, sprawled across its hump for twenty yards, hanging on desperately, but it's hard enough to stay on a galloping camel if you're in the right place and sadly sometimes desperation isn't a sufficient adhesive. My camel and I parted company, leaving me with a handful of camel hair, an ill-smelling blanket, and a seven-foot drop to the ground.

The outer edges of the sandstorm were on me before I'd managed to get back any of the air that the impact sent rushing from my lungs. I could feel the djinn in there, more diffuse than it had been when confined inside Jahmeen, but there none the less, scraping sandy fingers across my face, burning around every grain the wind carried.

This time the invasion came indirectly. The djinn had tried to overwhelm me and kick my soul into Hell, but for whatever reason, perhaps because I'd just come from there, or perhaps due to the magic that runs in Kendeth veins, I'd resisted. Now it took away my vision and my hearing, and as I hunched there trying to snatch a breath that wouldn't burn my lungs, hoping not to be buried alive, the djinn prickled at the back of my mind, seeking a way in. Again my memories of the Hell-trip surged forward, Snorri grabbing me, trying to help me drive that stranger's soul out, trying to help me keep my body.

"No way." The words came through gritted teeth and narrowed lips. The djinn wouldn't fool me twice. "I'm Jalan Kendeth and I'm wise to your tri—"

But the sand is dust now, choking dust, and I'm being hauled through it by a big hand, fingers knotted in my shirt.

"I'm Jalan Kendeth!" I shout it then fall to coughing. The dust mixed with my saliva looks like blood on my hands—exactly like blood. "—alan" *cough* "Kendeth!"

"Good man!" Snorri sets me on my feet, slapping the worst of the dust off me. "One of the dead ran into you—almost took your body right off you!"

I feel I was somewhere else, somewhere sandy, doing something important. There was something I had to remember, something vital . . . but quite what it was escapes me even as I search for it.

"Take my body? They . . . they can do that?" More spluttering. My chest aches. I wipe my hands on my trousers. They've seen better days. "The dead can take your body?"

Snorri shrugs. "Best not get in their way." He waits for me to recover, impatient to follow the souls we saw.

"Dust and rocks." I'm not ready yet. I rasp a breath in. "Is that as scary as Norse storytellers can make the afterlife?"

Again the shrug. "We're not like you followers of the White Christ, Jal. There's no paradise foretold, no roaming in green pastures for the blessed, no everlasting torment for the wicked. There's only Ragnarok. The last battle. No promise of salvation or a happy ending, only that everything will end in blood and war, and men will have one last chance to raise their axes and shout their defiance at the end of time. The priests tell us that death is just a place to wait."

"Marvellous." I straighten. Holding out a hand as he tries to move off. "If it's a place to wait why be in such a hurry?"

Snorri ignores that. Instead he holds out a fist, opening it to reveal a heaped palm. "Besides, it's not dust. It's dried blood. The blood of everyone who ever lived."

"I can make you see fear in a handful of dust." The words escape me with a breath.

Snorri smiles at that.

"Elliot John," I say. I once spent a day memorizing quotes from classical literature to impress a woman of considerable learning—also a considerable fortune and a figure like an hourglass full of sex. I can't remember the quotes now, but occasionally one of them will surface at random. "A great bard from the Builders' time. He also wrote some of those songs you Vikings are always butchering in your ale halls!" I start to brush myself down. "It's just pretty words though. Dust is dust. I don't care where it came from."

Snorri lets the dust sift through his fingers, drifting on the wind. For a moment it's just dust. Then I see it. The fear. As if the dust becomes a living thing, twisting while it falls, hinting at a face, a baby's, a child's, too indistinct to recognize, it could be anyone . . . me . . . suddenly it's me . . . it ages, haggard, hollow, a skull, gone. All that's left is the terror, as if I saw my life played out in an instant, dust on the wind, as swiftly taken, just as meaningless.

"Let's go." I need to be off, moving, not thinking.

Snorri leads the way, following the direction the souls took, though there's no sign of them now.

We walk forever. There are no days or nights. I'm hungry and thirsty, hungrier and thirstier than I have ever been, but it gets no worse and I don't die. Perhaps eating, drinking, and dying are not things that happen here, only waiting and hurting. It starts to hollow you out, this place. I'm too dry for complaining. There's just the dust, the rocks, the distant hills that never draw any closer, and Snorri's back, always moving on.

"I wonder what Aslaug would have made of this place." Perhaps it would have scared her too, no darkness, a dead light that gives no warmth and casts no shadows.

"Baraqel would have been the best ally to bring here," Snorri says.

I wrinkle my lip. "That fussy old maid? He'd certainly find plenty of subject matter for his lectures on morality."

"He was a warrior of the light. I liked him," Snorri says.

"We're talking about the same irritating angel, yes?"

"Maybe not." Snorri shrugged. "We gave him his voice. He built himself from our imaginations. Perhaps for you he was different. But we both saw him at the wrong-mages' door. That Baraqel we could use."

I had to nod at that. Yards tall, golden winged with a silver sword. Baraqel might have been a pain but his heart was in the right place. Right now I'd be happy to have him in my head telling me what a sinner I was if it meant he would spring into being when trouble approached. "I suppose I might have misjudged—"

"What?" Snorri stops, his arm out to stop me too.

Just ahead of us is a milestone, old, grey, and weathered. It bears the roman runes for six and fresh blood glistens along one side. I look around. There's nothing else, just this milestone in the dust. In the distance, far behind us, I can just make out, among the shapes of the vast boulders that scatter the plain, one that looks crooked over to the right, almost like the letter "r."

Snorri kneels down to study the blood. "Fresh."

"You shouldn't be here." There's blood running in rivulets down the face of the boy who's speaking, a young child not much taller than the milestone. He wasn't there a moment ago. He can't be more than six or seven. His skull has been caved in, his blond hair is scarlet along one side. Blood trickles in parallel lines down the left side of his face, filling his eye, dividing him like Hel herself.

"We're passing through," Snorri says.

There is a growl behind us. I turn, slowly, to see a wolfhound approaching. I've seen a Fenris wolf, so I've seen bigger, but this is a huge dog, its head level with my ribs. It has the sort of eyes that tell you how much it will enjoy eating you.

"We don't want any trouble." I reach for my sword. Edris Dean's sword. Snorri's hand covers mine before I draw it.

"Don't be afraid, Justice won't hurt you, he just comes to protect me," the boy says.

I turn so I have a side facing each of them. "I wasn't afraid," I lie.

"Fear can be a useful friend—but it's never a good master." The boy looks at me, blood dripping into the dust. He doesn't sound like a boy. I wonder if he memorized that from the same book I used.

"Why are you out here?" Snorri asks him, kneeling to be on a level, though keeping his distance. "The dead need to cross the river."

The hound circles around to stand beside the milestone, and the boy reaches up to pat his back. "I left myself here. Once you cross the river you need to be strong. I only took what I needed." He smiles at us. He's a nice-looking kid . . . apart from all the blood.

"Look," I say. I step toward him, past Snorri. "You shouldn't be out here by y—"

Suddenly the hound is bigger than any Fenris wolf ever was, and on fire. Flames clothe the beast, head to claw, kindling in its eyes. Its maw is a foot from my face, and when it opens its mouth to howl, an inferno erupts past its teeth.

"No!" I screamed and found myself face to face with the djinn, at the heart of the sandstorm. Somehow I'd resisted its attempts to drive me out of my body again. Perhaps that child's hell-hound had scared it out. It certainly scared a whole other mess right out of me, double quick!

I saw the djinn only because each wind-borne grain of sand passing through its invisible body became heated to the point of incandescence, revealing the spirit shaped by the glow, trailing burning sand on the lee side where the wind tore through it. Here before me was a demon as I had always imagined them, stolen from the lurid imaginations of church-men, horns and fangs and white-hot eyes.

"Fuck." My next discovery was that being chest-deep in sand made running away difficult. And the discovery after that was worse. Through the storm I could make out a body, lying sprawled on the dune behind the djinn. A momentary lull allowed a better view . . . and somehow it was me lying there, slack-jawed and sightless. Which made me the one doing the watching . . . an ejected soul being sucked down into Hell!

The djinn held position, just before me, illustrated by the glowing sand tearing through its form. It just stood there, between me and my body, close enough to touch. It didn't even have to push me, the dune seemed eager to suck me down. Scared witless, I dug my arms down and tried to draw my sword but the sand defeated me and my questing hand came up empty. I grabbed the key off my chest, unsure of how it was going to help . . . or if it even *was* the key, since there had appeared to be an identical one hanging about my body's neck when I glimpsed myself during the lull. I clenched the key hard as I could. "Come on! Give me something I can work with here!"

In the instant of my complaint the sand about me fell away revealing a trapdoor incongruously set into the dune, with me two-thirds of the way through. And as the sand fell through it, I fell too. I managed to get both arms out and hold myself there, dangling over a familiar barren plain lit by that same deadlight. "Oh, come on!"

Finding little purchase on the dune, and still slipping into the hole by inches, I grabbed the only other thing there. Part of me expected my hands to burn, but despite its effect on the sand I'd felt no heat from the djinn, only the blast of its wordless rage and hatred.

Beneath my soul's fingers the djinn felt blisteringly hot, but not so hot that I was ready to let go and fall into Hell, leaving my body as its plaything. "Bastard!" I hauled myself up the djinn, grabbing horns, spurs, rolls of fat, whatever came to hand. With a strength born of fear I was two-thirds out of the trapdoor before the djinn even seemed to realize what had happened. Surprise had unbalanced the thing and though my soul might not weigh as much in the scales as some, it proved enough to drag the djinn forward and down whilst I climbed up.

Within moments the two of us were locked together, each trying to wrestle the other down through the trapdoor, both of us part in, part out. My main problems were that the djinn was stronger than me, heavier than me—which seemed deeply unfair given how the wind blew through him— and blessed with the aforementioned horns and barbs, together with a set of triangular teeth that looked capable of shearing through bones.

It turns out that when it's your soul doing the wrestling the sharp spikes and keen edges are less important than how much you want to win—or in my case, win clear. Panic may not be much help in most situations, but well-focused terror can be a godsend. I jammed Loki's key into the djinn's eye, grabbed both his dangling earlobes, and pulled myself over him, setting a booted foot to the back of his neck and pitching him further into the trapdoor . . . where his bulk wedged him fast. It took me jumping up and down on him several times, both heels mashing into his shoulders before, like a cork escaping an amphora, he shot through. I very nearly followed him down, but by means of a lunge, a scramble, and a good measure of panic, I found myself lying on the dune, the winds dying and the sand settling all about me.

Quickly I pulled the trapdoor closed and locked it with Loki's key, finding in that instant that it vanished, leaving me poking the key into the sand. I shrugged and went over cautiously to inspect my body. Re-inhabiting your own flesh turns out to be remarkably easy, which is good because I had visions of the sheik and his men turning up and finding me lying there and soul-me having to trek along behind while they slung me over a camel and subjected me to heathen indignities. Or worse still, they might have passed me by unseen beneath my sandy shroud and left me to watch my body parch, the dry flesh flaking in the wind until I sat alone and watched the desert drown my bones . . . So it was fortunate that as soon as I laid a soul-finger on myself I was sucked back in and woke up coughing.

I sat up and immediately reached for the key around my neck. How much of what I'd seen had been real and how much just my mind's way of interpreting my struggle with the djinn's evil I had no idea. I even harboured a suspicion that the key itself had drawn those scenes for me, calling on Loki's own twisted sense of humour.

The caravan outriders found me about half an hour later, crouched on the blazing dune, head covered with the ill-smelling blanket I snatched from my camel. The Ha'tari escorted me back to Sheik Malik, prodding me along before them like an escaped prisoner.

The sheik urged his camel out toward us as we approached, two of his own guards moving to flank him as he came. Behind him at the front of the caravan I could see Jahmeen, slumped across his saddle, kept in place by his two younger brothers riding to either side. I guessed the sheik would not be in the best of moods.

"My friend!" I raised a hand and offered a broad smile. "It's good to see there were no more djinn. I was worried the one I drew off might not be the only attacker!"

"Drew off?" Confusion broke the hardness around the sheik's eyes.

"I saw the beast had taken hold of Jahmeen so I pushed it out of the boy and then set off at once, knowing it would chase me for revenge. If I'd stayed it would have sought an easier target to inhabit and use against me." I nodded sagely. It's always good to have someone agreeing with you in such a discussion, even if it's only yourself.

"You pushed the djinn out—"

"How is Jahmeen?" I think I managed to make the concern sound genuine. "I hope he recovers soon—it must have been a terrible ordeal."

"Well." The sheik glanced back at his son, motionless on the halted camel. "Let us pray it will be soon."

I very much doubted it. From what I'd seen and felt I guessed Jahmeen had been burned hollow, his flesh warm but as good as dead, his soul in the deadlands enjoying whatever his faith had told him was in store for a man of his quality. Or perhaps suffering it.

"Within a few days, I hope!" I kept smiling. Within half a day we would be in Hamada and I would be rid of the sheik and his camels and his sons forever. Sadly I would be rid of his daughters too, but that was a price I was willing to pay.

FOUR

Hamada is a grand city that beggars most others in the Broken Empire, though we don't like to talk about that back in Christendom. You can only approach it from the desert so it is always welcome to the eye. It has no great walls—sand would only heap against them, providing any enemy a ramp. Instead it rises slowly from ground where hidden water has bound the dunes with karran grass. First it's mud domes, made startlingly white with lime-wash, half-buried, their dark interiors unfathomable to the sun-blind eye. The buildings grow in stature and the ground dips toward that promised water, revealing towers and minarets and palatial edifices of white marble and pale sandstone.

Seeing the city grow before us out of the desert had silenced everyone, even stopping the talk of the Builders' Sun, the endless whys, the circular discussions of what it all meant. There's something magical about seeing Hamada after an age in the Sahar—and believe me, two days is an age in such a place. I was doubly grateful for the distraction since I'd been foolish enough to mention that much of Gelleth had been devastated by one of the Builders' weapons and that I'd seen the margins of the destruction. The sheik—who obviously paid far more attention to his history lessons than I had—noted that no Builders' Sun had ignited in over eight hundred years, which made the odds against a man being witness to two such events extremely long indeed. Only the sight of Hamada had stopped him from carrying that observation toward a conclusion in which I was somehow involved in the explosions.

"I will be glad to get off this camel." I broke the silence. I wore the sword I had taken from Edris Dean, and the dagger I'd brought out of Hell with me, both returned on my request after the incident with the djinn. In Hamada I would swap my robes for something more fitting. With a horse under me I'd start feeling like my old self in no time!

There is a gate to the west of Hamada, flanked on each side by fifty yards of isolated wall, an archway tall enough for elephants with high, plumed howdahs on their backs. The Gate of Peace they call it and sheiks always enter the city through it, and so, with civilization tantalizingly close, our caravan turned and tracked the city's perimeter that we might keep with tradition.

I rode near the head of the column, keeping a wary distance from Jahmeen, not wholly trusting the djinn not to find some way back into him and escape the deadlands. The only good thing about that final mile of the journey was that the last of our water was shared about, a veritable abundance of the stuff. The Ha'tari poured it down their throats, over their hands, down their chests. Me, I just drank it until my belly swelled and would take no more. Even then the thirst the deadlands had put in me was still there, parching my mouth as I swallowed the last gulp.

"What will you do, Prince Jalan?" The sheik had never once asked how I came to be in the desert, perhaps trusting it to be God's will, proven by the truth of my prophecy and beyond understanding. He seemed interested in my future though, if not my past. "Will you stay in Liba? Come to the coast with me and I will show you my gardens. We grow more than sand in the north! Perhaps you might stay?"

"Ah. Perhaps. First though I mean to present myself at the Mathema and look up an old friend." All I wanted to do was get home, with the key, in one piece. I doubted that the three double florins and scatter of smaller coins in my pocket would get me there. If I could ride Sheik Malik's goodwill all the way to the coast that would be well and good— but I wondered if his approval would last the journey. In my experience it's never that long before any ill fortune gets pinned to the outsider. How many weeks into the desert would it be before his son's failure to recover soured the sheik and he started to look at events in a different light? How long before my role as the one who warned him of the danger twisted into painting me as the one who brought the danger?

"My business will keep me in Hamada for a month—" The sheik broke off as we approached the Gate of Peace. A twisted corpse had been tied above the archway—the strangest corpse I had seen in a while. Scraps of black cloth fluttered around the body: beneath them the victim's skin lay whiter than a Viking's, save for the many places where it was torn and dark with old blood. The true shock came where the limbs hung broken and the flesh, opened by sword blows, should have revealed the bone. Instead metal gleamed amid the seething mass of flies. A carrion crow set them buzzing and through the black cloud I saw silver-steel, articulated at the joints.

"That's Mechanist work," I said, shielding my eyes for a better view as we drew nearer. "The man almost looks like a modern, from Umbertide but inside he's . . ."

"Clockwork." Sheik Malik halted just shy of passing beneath the arch. The column behind us began to bunch.

"I'd swear that's a banker." I thought of dear old Marco Onstantos Evenaline of the House Gold, Mercantile Derivatives South. The man had taught me to trade in prospects. For a time I had enjoyed taking part in the mad speculation governing the flow of gold through the dozen largest Florentine banks. Banks that seemed sometimes to rule the world. I wondered if this could be him—if so, he hadn't governed his own prospects too well. "It might even be one I've met."

"That, would be hard to tell." Sheik Malik prompted his camel forward.

"True." A dozen or more crossbow bolts appeared to have passed through the banker's head, leaving little of his face and making a ruin of the silver-steel skull behind it. Even so, I thought of Marco, whom I'd seen last with the necromancer Edris Dean. Marco with his inhuman stillness and his projects on marrying dead flesh to clockwork. When his superior, Davario, had first called him in I had thought it had been to show me the dead hand attached to a clockwork soldier. Perhaps the joke had been that the man leading that soldier in was himself a dead man wrapped around the altered frame of a Mechanists' creation.

The Ha'tari remained at the gate, singing their prayers for our souls, or for our righteous damnation, while the sheik's entourage passed through. We left the ragged crowd of urchins that had followed us from the outskirts there too, only to have it replaced within yards by a throng of Hamadians of all stations, from street merchant to silk-clad prince, all clamouring for news. The sheik began to address them in the desert tongue, a rapid knife-edged language. I could see from their faces they knew that it wouldn't be good news, but few of them would understand yet quite how bad it would be. Nobody from the gathering at the Oasis of Palms and Angels would ever pass through this gate again.

I took the opportunity to slip from my camel and weave a path through the crowd. No one saw me go, bound as they were by Sheik Malik's report.

The city seemed almost empty. It always does. No one wishes to linger in the oven of the streets when there are cooler interiors offering shade. I passed the grand buildings, built by the wealth of caliphs past for the people of Hamada. For a place that had nothing but sand and water to its name Hamada had accumulated an awful lot of gold over the centuries.

Walking over the sand-scattered flagstones with my shadow puddled dark around my feet I could imagine it a city of ghosts, djinn-haunted and waiting for the dune-tide to drown it.

The sudden dip that reveals the lake is always a surprise. There before me lay a wide stretch of water taking the sky's tired blue and making something azure and supple of it. The caliph's palace sat across the lake from me, a vast central dome surrounded by minarets and a sprawl of interlinked buildings, dazzling white, galleried and cool.

I skirted the lake, passing by the steps and pillars of an ancient amphitheatre built by the men of Roma back in the days before Christ found them. The Mathema Tower stood back from the water but with an uninterrupted view, reaching for the heavens and dwarfing all other towers in Hamada, even the caliph's own. Advancing on it gave me uncomfortable recollections of the Frauds' Tower in Umbertide, though the Mathema stands half as broad and three times as tall.

"Welcome." One of the black-robed students resting in the tower's shadow stood to intercept me. The others, maybe a dozen in all, scarcely looked up from their slates, busy scratching down their calculations.

"*Wa-alaykum salaam.*" I returned the greeting. You'd think after all the sand I'd swallowed I would have more of the desert tongue, but no.

The exchange seemed to have exhausted both his words of Empire and mine of Araby and an awkward silence stretched between us. "This is new." I waved at the open entrance. There had been a black crystal door there, to be opened by solving some puzzle of shifting patterns, different each time. As a student it had never taken me less than two hours to open it, and on one occasion, two days. Having no door at all now made a pleasant if unexpected change, though I had rather been looking forward to poking Loki's key at the bastard and seeing it swing open for me immediately.

The student, a narrow-featured youngster from far Araby, his black hair slick to his skull, frowned as if remembering some calamity. "Jorg."

"I'm sure." I nodded, pretending to understand. "Now, I'm going up to see Qalasadi." I pushed past and followed the short corridor beyond to the stair that winds up just inside the outer wall. The sight of equations set into the wall and spiralling up with the stairs for hundreds of feet just reminded me what a torture my year in Hamada had been. Not quite walking-the-deadlands level of torture, but mathematics can come pretty close on a hot day when you're hung over. The equations followed me up as I climbed. A master mathmagician can calculate the future, seeing as much amid the scratched summations and complex integrations on their slates as the Silent Sister sees with her blind eye or the völvas extrapolate from the dropping of their runestones. Men are just variables to the mathmagicians of Liba, and just how far the mathmagicians see and what their aims might be are secrets known only to their order.

I got about halfway up to Omega level at the top of the tower before, sweating freely, I paused to catch my breath. The four grandmasters of the order preside in turn throughout the year and I was hoping that the current incumbent would remember me, along with my connections to the Red March throne. Qalasadi was my best bet since he arranged my tuition during my stay. With any luck the mathmagicians would organize my safe passage home, perhaps even calculating me a risk-free path.

"Jalan Kendeth." Not a question.

I turned and Yusuf Malendra filled the staircase behind me, white robes swirling, a grin gleaming black against the mocha of his face. I'd seen him last in Umbertide waiting in the foyer of House Gold.

"They say there are no coincidences with mathmagicians," I said, wiping my forehead. "Did you calculate the place and moment of our meeting? Or was it just the end of your business in Florence that brought you back here?"

"The latter, my prince." He looked genuinely pleased to see me. "We do of course have coincidences and this is a most happy one." Behind him a student came puffing up the stairs.

A sudden thought struck me, the image of a white body, black clad, broken and left hanging on the Gate of Peace in the desert sun. "Marco . . . that *was* Marco, wasn't it?"

"I—"

"Jalan? Jalan Kendeth? I don't believe it!" A head poked around Yusuf's shoulder, broad, dark, a grin so wide it seemed to hang between his ears.

"Omar!" As soon as I laid eyes on the grinning face of Omar Fayed, seventh son of the caliph, I knew my ordeal was over. Omar had been among the most faithful of my companions back in Vermillion, always up for hitting the town. Not a great drinker perhaps but with a love of gambling that eclipsed even my own, and pockets deeper than any young man I ever knew. "Now tell me that *this* was coincidence!" I challenged Yusuf.

The mathmagician spread his hands. "You didn't know Prince Omar had returned to Hamada and his studies at the Mathema?"

"Well . . ." I had to concede that I had known.

"They said you were dead!" Omar squeezed past Yusuf and set a hand on my shoulder. Being short, he had to reach up, which made a change after all my time standing in Snorri's shadow. "That fire . . . I never believed them. I've been trying to do the sums to prove it, but, well, they're tricky."

"I'm glad to have saved you the effort." I found myself answering his grin. It felt good to be back with people who knew me. A friend who cared enough to try to find out what had happened to me. After . . . however long it had been, trekking in Hell, it all felt suddenly a bit overwhelming.

"Come." Yusuf saved me the embarrassment of blubbing on the stairs in front of them by leading the way down half a dozen steps to the door onto the Lambda level and taking us into a small room off the main corridor.

We sat down around a polished table, the room crowding around us, lined as it was with scrolls and fat tomes bound with leather. Yusuf poured three tiny cups of very strong java from a silver jug standing in the window slit.

"I need to get home," I said, wincing as I knocked back the java. No point in beating around any bushes.

"Where have you been?" Omar, a smile still splitting his face. "You came south after escaping the fire? Why south? Why pretend to be dead?"

"I went north as it happens, in a hurry, but the point is that I've been . . . incommunicado . . . for a few . . . um. When is it?"

"Sorry?" Omar frowned, puzzled.

"It's the 98th year of Interregnum, the tenth month," Yusuf said, watching me closely.

"For . . . uh . . ." I'll admit to a little shame, struggling with subtraction in front of a master mathmagician of the Mathema. "About, well, damn it! Months, nearly half a year!" It hadn't been half a year, had it? On the one hand it *had* felt about two lifetimes, but on the other, if I considered the things that actually happened it seemed you could easily fit them into a week.

"Kelem!" I blurted the name out before deciding if that were a wise thing to do or not. "Tell me about Kelem, and the banking clans."

"Kelem's hold on the clans is broken." Yusuf's hands moved on the table top, fingers twitching as if he were struggling not to write down the terms and balance the equations with new information. "Calculations indicate that he has lost his material form."

"What does that mean?" I asked.

"You don't know?" Yusuf's left eyebrow suggested it didn't believe me.

I thought of Aslaug and Baraqel, remembering how Loki's daughter raged against Kelem when I set her free, and the look of hurt in her black eyes as I let Kara drive her back into the darkness. "The Builders went into the spirit world . . ."

"Some of them did," Yusuf said. "A small number. They used the changes they wrought in the world when they turned the Wheel. They escaped into other forms when their flesh betrayed them. Others were copied into the Builders' machines and exist there now as echoes of men and women long since dead. The Builders who left their flesh were as gods for a while, but when men returned to the lands of the west their expectations became a subtle trap. The Builder spirits found themselves ensnared by myth, each tale growing around the spirits, reinforced by them, weaving them into a fabric of belief that both shaped and trapped them until they could scarcely remember a time when they were anything other than what men believed them to be."

"And Kelem?" He was the one that worried me. "Can he come back? Will he remember . . . uh, what happened?"

"It will take him time to gather himself. Kelem was rock-sworn. If he has not died properly then in time he will go into the earth. And yes, he will remember. It will be a long while before he's snared into story. Perhaps never since he is aware of the danger."

I stared at the stone walls around us. "I need to—"

Yusuf raised a hand. "The rock-sworn are slow to act. It will take time before Kelem shows his face to the world again, and time is what he doesn't have, what none of us have. The world is cracking, Prince Jalan. The Wheel the Builders turned to change the world did not stop turning and as it runs free those changes will increase in size and speed until nothing that we know is left. We are a generation of blind men, walking toward a cliff. Kelem is not your worry."

"The Lady Blue . . . the Dead King." I didn't want to say their names. I'd done a good job of keeping both out of my thoughts ever since escaping Hell. In fact if that damned djinn hadn't sparked my memories then I might have managed never to think about the whole journey and poor Snorri ever again. "Those are the two I need to worry about?"

"Even so." Yusuf nodded.

Omar just looked more confused and mouthed "who?" at me from across the table.

"Well." I leaned back in my chair. "That's all beyond me. All I want to do is get home."

"It's a war your grandmother cares about." Yusuf spoke the words softly but they carried an uncomfortable weight.

"The Red Queen has her war and she can keep it," I said. "It's not the kind of thing men like me can change one way or the other. I don't want any part of it. I just want to go home and . . . relax."

"You say this, and yet you have been changing things at an astonishing rate, Prince Jalan. Defeating unborn in the northern wastes, dethroning Kelem in his mines, chasing the Dead King into Hell . . . and you hold the key, do you not?"

I gave Yusuf an angry stare. He knew entirely too much. "I have *a* key, yes. And you're not having it. It's mine." I'd be hanging on to Loki's key with everything I had until I got home. Then I'd hand it over to the old woman in a heartbeat and wait to be showered with praise, gold, and titles.

Yusuf smiled at me and shrugged. "If you want no part of shaping the future, so be it. I will arrange passage back to Red March for you. It will take a few days. Relax here. Enjoy the city. I'm sure you know your way around."

When someone lets you off too easily there's always that suspicion that they know something you do not. It's an irritating thing, like sunburn, but I know a sure-fire way to ease it.

"Let's get a drink!"

"Let's go win some gold." Omar jerked his head toward the grand library: a quarter of a mile past it the largest of Hamada's racetracks would be packed to bursting with Libans screaming at camels.

"A drink first," I said.

Omar was always willing to compromise, even though he kept to his faith's prohibition on alcohol. "A little one." He patted his well-rounded form and beneath his robes coins clinked reassuringly against each other. "I'm buying."

"A little one," I lied. Never drink small if it's at someone else's expense. And besides, I had no intention of going to the races. In the past two days I'd seen more than enough of camels.

The city of Hamada is officially dry, which is ironic since it's the only place to be found with any water in hundreds of square miles of arid dunes. One may not purchase or drink alcohol in any form anywhere within the kingdom of Liba. A crying shame given how damnable hot the place is. However, the Mathema attracts rich students from across the Broken Empire and from the deepest interior of the continent of Afrique and they bring with them a thirst for more than just water or knowledge. And so there exist in Hamada, for those who know where to look, watering holes of a different kind, to which the imams and city guard turn a blind eye.

"Mathema." Omar hissed it through the grille of iron strips defending the tiny window. The heavy door containing the window was set into the whitewashed wall of a narrow alley on the east side of the city. The wooden door was a giveaway in itself, wood being expensive in the desert. Most houses in this quarter had a screen of beads to dissuade the flies and relied on the threat of being publicly impaled to dissuade any thief. Though what horror "publicly" adds to "impaled" I've never been clear on.

We followed the door-keeper, a skinny, ebony-hued man of uncertain years clad only in a loincloth, along a dark and sweltering corridor past the entrance to the cellar where a still bubbled dangerously to itself, cooking up grain alcohol of the roughest sort, and up three flights of stairs to the roof. Here a canopy of printed cloth, floating between a score of supports, covered the entire roof space, offering blessed shade.

"Two whiskies," I told the man as Omar and I collapsed onto mounds of cushions.

"Not for me." Omar wagged a finger. "Coconut water, with nutmeg."

"Two whiskies and what he said." I waved the man off and sank deeper into the cushions, not caring what it was that had stained them. "Christ, I need a drink."

"What happened at the opera?" Omar asked.

I didn't answer. I didn't say a thing or move a muscle until five minutes had passed and a young boy in a white shirt had brought our drinks. I picked up my first "whisky." Drained it. Made the gasping noise and reached for the next. "That. Is. Good." I took the second in two gulps. "Three more whiskies!" I hollered toward the stairs—the boy wouldn't have reached the bottom yet. Then I rolled back. Then I told my story.

"And that's that." The sun had set and the boy had returned to light half a dozen lamps before my race through the highlights of my journey had reached all the way from the ill-fated opera house to the Gate of Peace in

Hamada. "And he lived happily ever after." I tried to get up and found myself on all fours, considerably more drunk than I had imagined myself to be.

"Incredible!" Omar leaning forward, both fists beneath his chin. He could have been talking about my method for finally finding my feet, but I think it was my tale that had impressed him. Even without mention of anything that happened to me in Hell and with talk of the unborn and the Dead King cut to a minimum it really was an incredible tale. I might think another man was humouring me, but Omar had always taken me at my word on everything—which was foolish and a terrible trait in a chronic gambler, but there it was.

For a long and pleasantly silent moment I sat back and savoured my drink. An unpleasant memory jerked me out of my reverie. I set my whisky down, hard.

"What the hell happened in the desert then?" As much as I like talking about myself I realized that in my eagerness to escape becoming part of Yusuf's world-saving calculations I'd forgotten to ask why, apparently for only the second time in eight centuries, a Builders' Sun had ignited, and why close enough to Hamada to shake the sand out of their beards?

"My father has closed the Builders' eyes in Hamada. I think perhaps they don't like that." Omar put his palm across the mouth of his cup and rolled it about its rim.

"What?" I hadn't felt drunk until I tried to make sense of what he said. "The Builders are dust."

"Master Yusuf just told you that they still echo in their machines. Copies of men, or at least they were copies long ago . . . They watch us. Father thinks they herd us, guide us like goats and sheep. So he has sought out their eyes and put them out."

"It took a thousand years for someone to do that?" I reached for my cup, nearly knocking it over.

"It took a long time for the Mathema to discover all the Builders' eyes." Omar shrugged. "And longer still to decide the time was right to share that information with a caliph."

"Why now?"

"Because our equations indicate the Builders may be done with herding and guiding . . ."

I didn't want to know what came after that so I took a gulp of my whisky.

". . . it may be time for the slaughtering," Omar said.

"Why for God's sake?" What I really meant was, *why me?* Do it in a hundred years and I wouldn't give a damn.

"The magic is breaking the world. The more it's used the easier it is to use and the wider the cracks grow. Kill us and the problem might go away." He watched me, eyes dark and solemn.

"But destroying Hamada is hardly going to . . . oh."

Omar nodded. "Everyone. Everywhere. They can do it too."

Footsteps on the stairs, a dark shape hurrying to Omar's side, a hasty whispered exchange. I watched, trying to focus, tipping my cup and discovering it empty. "Who's your friend?"

Omar got to his feet and I stood too, his steadiness making me realize quite how much I was swaying. "You're not off?" The racing finished hours ago.

"Father has called us all to the palace. This explosion of yours has changed things—perhaps turned theory into fact. We all saw it, then felt it. I was knocked off my feet. Perhaps Father will share with us how and why we were spared. Hopefully he will have a plan to stop it happening again!" Omar followed the caliph's messenger toward the stairs, waving. "So good to see you alive, my friend."

I half-sat, half-collapsed back into the cushions. Even though he never used it against me I always held the fact that Omar's father was the caliph of Liba, where mine was only a cardinal, to be a black mark against his name. Even a seventh son looks like a good deal to a man who is tenth in line. Still, when the caliph calls, you come. I couldn't hold that against Omar, though he *had* left me to drown my sorrows by myself. Not to mention added to those troubles with his talk of long-dead Builders lurking in ancient machines and wishing us ill. Even drunk I wasn't about to believe that nonsense, but there was definitely something bad happening.

I stared up at the stars through a gap in the awning. "What time is it anyway?"

"Lacking an hour to midnight."

I lifted my head and looked around. It had been a rhetorical question. I had thought myself alone up here.

"Who said that?" I couldn't make out any human figures, just low hillocks of cushions. "Show yourself. Don't make me drink alone!"

A black shape detached itself from the most distant corner, close to the roof's edge and the fifty-foot drop into the street below. For a moment my heart lurched as I thought of Aslaug, but it had been a man's voice. A lean but well-muscled figure resolved itself, tall but not quite my height, face shrouded in shadow and long dark hair. He walked with the exaggerated care of the quite drunk, clutching an earthenware flask in one hand, and flomped bonelessly into the cushions vacated by Omar.

Moonlight revealed him in a rippling slice, falling through the gap between one awning and the next. The silver light painted him, from a grisly burn that covered his left cheek, down a plain white shirt to the hilt of a sword. A dark eye regarded me, glittering amid the burn, the other lost behind a veil of hair. He raised his flask toward me, then swigged from it. "Now you're not drinking alone."

"Well that's good." I took a gulp from my own pewter cup. "Does a man no good to drink by himself. Especially not after what I've been through." I felt very maudlin, as a man in his cups is wont to do without lively music and good company.

"I'm a very long way from home," I said, suddenly as miserable and homesick as I had ever been.

"Me too."

"Red March is a thousand miles north of us."

"The Renar Highlands are further."

For some reason known only to drunkards, that angered me. "I've had a hard time."

"These are hard days."

"Not just today." I drank again. "I'm a prince, you know." Quite how that would get me sympathy I wasn't sure.

"Liba is straining at the seams with princes. I was born a prince too."

"Not that I'll ever be king . . ." I kept to my own thread.

"Ah," the stranger said. "My path to inheritance is also unclear."

"My father . . ." Somehow my train of thought slipped away from me. "He never loved me. A cold man."

"My own has that reputation too. Our disagreements have

been . . . sharp." The man drank from his flask. The light caught him again and I could see he was young. Even younger than me.

Perhaps it was relief at being safe and drunk and not being chased by monsters that did it, but somehow all the grief and injustice of my situation that there hadn't been time for until now bubbled up out of me.

"I was just a boy . . . I saw him do it . . . killed them both. My mother, and my . . ." I choked and couldn't speak.

"A sibling?" he asked.

I nodded and drank.

"I saw my mother and brother killed," he said. "I was young too."

I couldn't tell if he were mocking me, topping each of my declarations with his own variant.

"I still have the scars of that day!" I raised my shirt to show the pale line where Edris Dean's sword had pierced my chest.

"Me too." He pushed back his sleeves and moved his arms so the moonlight caught on innumerable silvery seams criss-crossing his skin.

"Jesus!"

"He wasn't there." The stranger pulled back into the shadow. "Just the hook-briar. And that was enough."

I winced. Hook-briar is nasty stuff. My new friend seemed to have dived in headfirst. I raised my cup. "Drink to forget."

"I have better ways." He opened his left hand, revealing a small copper box, moonlight gleaming on a thorn pattern running around its lip. He might have better ways than alcohol but he drank from his flask, and deeply.

I watched the box, my eye fascinated by the familiarity of it—but, familiar or not, no part of me wanted to touch it. It held something bad.

Like my new friend I drank too, though I also had better ways of burying a memory. I let the raw whisky run down my throat, hardly tasting it now, hardly feeling the burn.

"Drink to dull the pain, my brother!" I'm an amiable drunk. Given enough time I always reach the point where every man is my brother. A few more cups and I declare my undying love for all and sundry. "I'm not sure there's a bit of me that isn't bruised." I lifted my shirt again, trying to see the bruising across my ribs. In the dark it looked less impressive than I remembered. "I could show you a camel footprint but . . ." I waved the idea away.

"I've a few bruises myself." He lifted his own shirt and the moonlight caught the hard muscles of his stomach. The thorn scars patterned him there too, but it was his chest that caught my eye. In exactly the spot where I have a thin line of scar recording the entry of Edris Dean's sword my drinking companion sported his own record of a blade's passage into his flesh, though the scar was black, and from it dark tendrils of scar spread root-like across his bare chest. These were old injuries though, long healed. He had fresher hurts—better light would show them angry and red, the bite of a blade in his side, above the kidney, other slices, puncture wounds, a tapestry of harm.

"Shit. What the hell—"

"Dogs."

"Pretty damn vicious dogs!"

"Very."

I swallowed the word "bastard" and cast about instead for some claim or tale that the bastard wouldn't instantly top.

"That sibling I mentioned, killed when I saw my mother killed . . ."

He looked up at me, again just the one eye glittering above his burn scar, the other hidden. "Yes?"

"Well she's not properly dead. She's in Hell plotting her return and planning revenge."

"On who?"

"Me, you." I shrugged. "The living. Mostly me, I think."

"Ah." He leaned back into the cushions. "Well there you've got me beat."

"Good." I drank again. "I was starting to think we were the same person."

The boy came back, refilling my cup from his jug and moving the lanterns closer to us to light our conversation. The man said something to him in the desert tongue but I couldn't follow it. Too drunk. Also, I don't know more than the five words I learned in my year living in the city.

With the lamplight showing me the fellow's face I had a sudden sense of déjà vu. I'd seen him before—possibly recently—or someone who reminded me strongly of him. Pieces of the puzzle started to settle out of my drunken haze. "Prince you say?" Every other rich man in Liba seemed to be a prince, but in the north, where we both clearly came from, "prince" was a richer currency. "Where from again?" I remembered but hoped I was wrong.

"Renar."

"Not . . . Ancrath?"

"Maybe . . . once."

"By Christ! You're him!"

"I'm certainly someone." He lifted his flask high, draining it.

"Jorg Ancrath." I knew him though I'd seen him just the one time, over a year ago in that tavern in Crath City, and he hadn't sported such a burn then.

"I'd say 'at your service,' but I'm not. And you're a prince of Red March, eh? Which would make you one of the Red Queen's brood?" He made to put his flask down and missed the ground, drunker than he had seemed.

"I have that honour," I said, my lips numb and framing the words roughly. "I am one of her many breeding experiments—not one that has best pleased her though."

"We're all a disappointment to someone." He swigged again, sinking further back into his cushions. "Best to disappoint your enemies though."

"These damnable mathmagicians have put us together, you know." I knew Yusuf had let me go too easily.

Jorg gave no sign of having heard me. I wondered if he'd passed out. A long pause turned into midnight, as it often does when you're very drunk. The distant hour bell jolted him into speech. "I've made plenty of seers eat their predictions."

"Got their sums wrong this time though—I'm no use to you. It should have been my sister. She was to have been the sorceress. To stand at your side. Bring you to the throne." I found my face wet. I'd not wanted to think about any of this.

Jorg mumbled something, but all I caught was a name. Katherine.

"Perhaps . . . she never had a name. She never saw this world." I stopped, my throat choked with the foolishness too much drink will put in a man. I drained my cup. There's a scribe who lives behind our eyes scribbling down an account of events for our later perusal. If you keep drinking then at some point he rolls up his scroll, wraps up his quills, and takes the night off. What remained in my cup proved sufficient to give him his marching orders. I'm sure we continued to mutter drunkenly at each other, King Jorg of Renar and I. I expect we made a few loud and passionate declarations before we passed out. We probably banged our cups on the roof and declared all men our brothers or our foe, depending on the kind of drunks we were, but I have no record of it.

I do remember that I confided my problems with Maeres Allus to the good king, and he kindly offered me his sage advice. I recall that the solution was both elegant and clever and that I swore to adopt it. Sadly not a single word of that counsel remained with me the following day.

My last memory is an image. Jorg lying sprawled, dead to the world, looking far younger in sleep than I had ever imagined him. Me pulling a rug up across him to keep off the cold of the desert night, then staggering dangerously toward the stairs. I wonder how many lives might have been saved if I had just rolled him off the roof's edge . . .

Many men drink to forget. Alcohol will wash away the tail end of a night, erasing helpful advice, and the occasional embarrassing incident, whilst trying to weave a path home. Unfortunately if you've developed a talent for suppressing older memories, accumulated while depressingly sober, then alcohol will often erode those barriers. When that happens, rather than sleep in the blessed oblivion of the deeply inebriated you will in fact suffer the nightmare of reliving the worst times you've ever known. A river of whisky carried me back into memories of Hell.

"Jesus Christ! What *was* that thing?" I gasp it between deep breaths, bent double, hands on my thighs. Looking back I see the raised dust that marks our hasty escape from the small boy and his ridiculously vast dog.

"You did *want* to see monsters, Jal." Snorri, leaning back against another of the towering stones that punctuate the plain.

"A hell-hound . . ." I straighten up and shake my head. "Well I've seen enough now. Where's this fucking river?"

"Come on." Snorri leads off, his axe over his shoulder, the blades finding something bloody in the deadlight and offering it back to Hell.

We trek another mile, or ten, in the dust. I'm starting to see figures in the distance, souls toiling across the plain or clustered in groups, or just standing there.

"We're getting closer." Snorri waves his axe toward the shade of a man a few hundred yards off, staked out among the rocks. "It takes courage to cross the Slidr. It gives many pause."

"Looks like more than a lack of courage holding that one back!" The stakes go through the soul's hands and feet.

Snorri shakes his head, walking on. "The mind makes its own bonds here."

"So all these people are doomed to wander here forever? They won't ever cross over?"

"Men leave echoes of themselves . . ." He pauses as if trying to recall the words. "Echoes scattered across the geometry of death. These are shed skins. The dead have to leave anything they can't carry across the river."

"Where are you getting this from?"

"Kara. I wasn't going to spend months travelling to death's door with a völva and not ask her any questions about what to expect!"

I let that one lie. It's what I did, but then I never had any intention of ending up here.

We slog up a low ridge and beyond it the land falls away. There below us is the river, a gleaming silver ribbon in a valley that weaves away into grey distances, the only thing in all that awful place with any hint of life in it. I start forward but immediately the ground drops in a crumbling cliff a little taller than me and at its base a broad sprawl of hook-briar, black and twisted, as you'll see in a wood after the first frosts.

"We'll have to go a—" I break off. There's movement on the edge of the briar. I shift to get a better view. It's the boy from the milestone, lunging in among the thorns, leaving them glistening. "Hey!"

"Leave him, Jal. It is the way it is. It has been like this for an age before we came and will be like it after we leave."

If we leave!

"But . . ."

Snorri sets off to find an easier route down. I can't leave, though. Almost as if the briar has me hooked too. "Hey! Wait! Keep still and I can get you out." I cast about for a way down the cliff that won't pitch me in among the thorns.

"I'm not trying to get out." The boy pauses his lunging and looks up at me. Even from this distance his face is a nightmare, flayed by the briar, his flesh ripped, studded with broken thorns bedded bone-deep.

"What . . ." I step back as the ground crumbles beneath my foot and sandy soil cataracts over the drop. "What the hell *are* you doing then?"

"Looking for my brother." Blood spills from torn lips. "He's in there somewhere."

He throws himself back at the thorns. The spikes are as long as his fingers and set with a small hook behind each point to lodge in the flesh.

"Stop! For Christ's sake!"

I try to climb down where the cliff dips but it breaks away and I scamper back.

"He wouldn't stop if it were me." The words sound ragged as if his cheeks are torn. I can hardly see him in the mass of the briar now.

"Stop—" Snorri's hand grabs my shoulder and he pulls me away mid-protest.

"You can't get caught up in this. Everything here is a snare." He walks me away.

"Me? Hasn't this place had its hooks in you ever since you first held that key?" They're just words though, without heat. I'm not thinking about Snorri. I'm thinking about my sister, dead before she was ever born. I'm thinking about the boy and his brother and what I might do to save my own sibling. Less than that, I say to myself. Less than that.

I woke, still drunk, and with so many devils hammering on the inside of my head that it took me an age to understand I was in a prison cell. I lay there in the heat, eyes tight against the pain and the blinding light lancing in through a small high window, too miserable to call out or demand release. Omar found me there at last. I don't know how much later. Long enough to pass the contents of a jug of water through me and leave the place stinking slightly worse than I found it.

"Come on, old friend." He helped me up, wrinkling his nose, still grinning. The guards watched disapprovingly behind him. "Why do you northerners do this to yourselves? Even if God did not forbid it drinking is a poor bet."

I staggered out along the corridor to the guards' room, wincing, and watching the world through slitted eyes. "I'm never doing it again, so let's not talk about it any more. OK?"

"Do you even remember what happened to you last night?" Omar caught me as I stumbled into the street and with a grunt of effort kept me on my feet.

"Something about a camel?" I recalled some sort of argument with a camel in the small hours of the morning. Had it looked at me wrong? Certainly I'd decided it was responsible for the footprint on my backside and all other indignities I'd ever suffered from the species. "Jorg!" I remembered. "Jorg fucking Ancrath! He was up there, Omar! On that roof. You've got to warn the caliph!"

I knew there was bad blood between the Horse Coast kingdoms and Liba, raids across the sea and such, and that the Ancraths had alliances with the Morrow, which made Liba their foe. What I thought one man could do to the Caliph of Liba, especially if his head was like mine this morning, I wasn't sure. This was, however, Jorg Ancrath who had destroyed Duke Gellethar along with his army, castle, and the mountain they all sat upon. We had returned through Gelleth months after the explosion and the sky was still—"Christ! The explosion. In the desert! It was him, wasn't it?"

"It was." Omar signed for Allah's protection. "He has met with my father and they are now friends."

I stopped in the street and thought about that for a moment. "Starting his empire building young, isn't he?" I was impressed though. My grandmother had alliances in Liba—she'd reached out far and wide in the hope of good marriages—but her goal had been finding blood that mixed with her sons' would produce a worthy heir, someone to fill in the gaps in the Silent Sister's visions of the future . . . my sister. Jorg of Ancrath had other plans and I wondered how long it would be before they took him to Vyene to present his case to Congression and demand the Empire throne. "How far will it take him, I wonder . . ."

"What do you make of him?" Omar had come back for me, a caliph's son waiting for me in the dusty street. He seemed strangely interested in my answer. It struck me then that I'd never seen him as clearly as I did there that morning, burdened by my self-inflicted pain. Soft, pudgy, Omar, the bad gambler, too rich, too amiable for his own good. But as he watched me with an intensity he saved for the roulette wheel I understood that the Mathema saw a different man—a man who would not only insert my answer into an equation of unearthly complexity, but one who might also solve it. "Can he match his ambition?"

"What?" I clutched my head. I didn't have to fake it. "Jorg? Don't know. Don't care. I just want to go home."

FIVE

Omar and Yusuf came to the outskirts of Hamada to see me off, Omar in the black robes of a student, Yusuf in the fractal patterned grey-on-white of a master, his smile black and gleaming. They'd calculated me safe passage to the coast with a salt caravan. Travel with Sheik Malik, they told me, would not end well, though whether my downfall would have been at the sheik's instigation, or by djinn or dead man, or perhaps through indecency with his lovely daughters, they didn't say.

"A gift, my friend!" Omar jerked his head back at the three camels his man was leading behind them.

"Oh you bastard."

"You'll warm to them, Jalan! Think of the heads you'll turn in Vermillion riding in on camelback!"

I rolled my eyes and waved the man forward to add my trio to the laden herd browsing karran grass a short way behind me. Soon all four score of them would be trekking the dunes with just me and twelve salt merchants to keep order.

"And give the Red Queen my father's regards," Omar said. "And my mother's."

Omar's mother I liked. The second eldest of the caliph's six wives, a tall Nuban woman from the interior, dark as ebony and mouth-wateringly attractive. Funny too. I guessed Omar's sense of humour came from his father. Giving a man three camels after he's been locked up for assaulting one is mean-spirited, and not at all amusing.

I turned to Yusuf. "So, Master Yusuf, perhaps you have a prediction for me, something I can use." Tradition has it that nobody of consequence leaves Hamada without some numerology to guide their way. Most come from failed students who ply their trade in whatever way they can, be it as accountants, bookmakers, or mystics selling predictions on the street. A prince, however, might hope for an audit of his possibilities and probabilities to be issued by the Mathema itself. And, since I knew Yusuf from my days in Umbertide, there seemed no harm in trying to coax one from a master.

Yusuf's smile stiffened for a moment. "Of course, my prince. I'm afraid our halls of calculation are occupied with . . . notables. But I can do a quick evaluation."

I stood there, trying not to let my offence show, while Yusuf scratched away with startling speed on a slate taken from inside his robe. "One, two, thirteen." He looked up.

I pursed my lips. "Which means?"

"Ah." Yusuf glanced down at the slate again as if seeking inspiration. "First stop, second sister, thirteenth . . . something."

"Why can't these ever be like, on the third day of spring give the fifth man you see four coppers to avoid disaster? See, that's simple and useful. Yours could mean anything. First stop . . . on my way home? An oasis? A port? And second sister? My sister, the Silent Sister? Help me out here!"

"The calculation is done on the basis that you are told what I told you—if I wanted to tell you more I would have to do the calculation again and it would be a different answer, a different purpose. If I told you more now then it would disrupt the outcome and the numbers would no longer be true. Besides, I don't know the answers, that's where the magic comes in and it's hard to pin down. You understand?"

"So, do it again. It only took you a moment."

Yusuf showed me his black smile. "Ah, my friend, you have found me out. I have been processing your variables since we first met in that Florentine bank. I may have misled you when I implied that you were not important to the shape of things to come. I thought perhaps it would have been easier for you if you didn't know."

"Well . . . uh, that's better." I wasn't sure it was. I'd been happier being outraged about not being important enough to factor than I was knowing that my actions mattered. "I, uh, should be going. Allah be upon you, and all that . . ." I raised my hand in farewell but Omar was too fast for me and launched himself forward into a hug that, truth be told, was pretty much a cuddle.

"Good luck, my friend."

"I don't need luck, Omar! And I have the figures to prove it . . . one, two, three—"

"Thirteen."

"One, two, thirteen. That should see me safe. You come visit us in Red March when you're bored with balancing equations."

"I will," he said, but I know from experience it takes practice to lie when cuddling someone, and Omar had not practised.

I disentangled myself and set off toward the front of the caravan.

"Don't forget your camels, Jalan!"

"Right." And with reluctance I angled my way toward the rear of the group being lined up, already tensing to dodge the first barrage of camel-spit.

The desert is hot and boring. I'm sorry, but that's pretty much all there is to it. It's also sandy, but rocks are essentially dull things and breaking them up into really small pieces doesn't improve matters. Some people will tell you how the desert changes character day by day, how the wind sculpts it endlessly in vast and empty spaces not meant for man. They'll wax lyrical about the grain and shade of the sand, the majesty of bare rock rising mountainous, carved by the sand-laden breeze into exotic shapes that speak of water and flow . . . but for me sandy, hot, and boring covers it all.

The most important factor, once water and salt are covered, is the boredom. Some men thrive on it, but me, I try to avoid being left alone with my own imagination. The key if one wishes to avoid dwelling on unpleasant memories or inconvenient truths is to keep yourself occupied. That fact alone explains much of my youth. In any event, in the desert silence, with nobody but camels and heathens to speak to, none of them with much mastery of Empire tongue, a man is left defenceless, prey to dark thoughts.

I held out until we hit the coast, but that last trek along the narrow strip of sand between the wideness of the sea and the vast march of dunes broke me. One chill night we camped beside the skeleton of some great ocean-going ship that had floundered close enough to port for the irony to be more bitter than the seawater. I walked among its bare and salt-rimed spars rising from the beach, and setting a hand to one ancient timber I could swear I heard the screams of drowning sailors.

That night sleep proved impossible to find. Instead, beneath the bright and cold scatter of the stars, my ghosts came visiting and dragged me back to Hell.

"Isn't there supposed to be a bridge?" I ask, staring out across the fast-flowing waters of the River Slidr. It's the first water I've seen in Hell. The river lies at least thirty yards wide, the opposite shore is a beach of black sand sloping up to a set of crumbling black cliffs. The cliffs vault toward the dead-lit sky in a series of steps, and above them clouds gather, dark as smoke.

"It's the River Gjöll that has a bridge, not the Slidr. Gjallarbrú they call the bridge. Be thankful we don't need to cross it, Módgud stands guard."

"Módgud?" I don't really want to know.

"A giantess. The far shore of that river is corpse upon corpse. They build the Nagelfar there, the nail ship that Loki will steer to Ragnarok. And behind that bridge stand the gates of Hel, guarded by the chained hound, Garm."

"But don't we need to—"

"We're already past the gates, Jal. The key, the door, all that took us into Hel."

"Just the wrong bit of it?"

"We need to cross the river."

Thirst rather than a lack of caution draws me on, hurrying me down those last few yards of the shore.

I advance to the shallows. "Yeah. That's not going to happen." The riverbed shelves away rapidly and although the swift-flowing water lies unnaturally clear it soon becomes lost in darkness. Crossing a river like this would be a serious problem under any circumstances but as I kneel to drink I spot the real show-stopper. In defiance of all reason there are daggers, spears, and even swords being borne along in the current, all silvery clean and sparkling with sharpness. Some are pointed resolutely in the direction the current takes them, others swirl as they go, scything the waters all around.

Snorri arrives at my shoulder. "It's called the River of Swords. I wouldn't drink it."

I stand. Further out the blades look like fish shoaling. Long, sharp, steel fish.

"So, what do we do?" I stare upriver, then down. Nothing but miles of eroded banks stepping up to the badlands on either side.

"Swim." Snorri walks past me.

"Wait!" I reach forward to get an arm in his way. "What?"

"They're just swords, Jal."

"Yessssss. That was my point too." I look up at him. "You're going to dive in among a whole bunch of swords?"

"Isn't that what we do in battle?" Snorri steps into the water. "Ah, cold!"

"Fuck cold, it's sharp I'm worried about." I make no move to follow him.

"Crossing the Slidr isn't about bridges or tricks. It's a battle. Fight the river. Courage and heart will see you across—and if it doesn't then Valhalla will have you for you will have fallen in combat."

"Courage?" I know I'm sunk before I start then. Unless simply wading in constitutes courage . . . rather than just stupidity.

"It's that or stay here forever." Snorri takes another step and suddenly he's swimming, the water churning white behind him, his great arms rising and falling.

"Crap on it." I stick a foot in the water. The chill of it reaches through my boot as if it isn't there and shoots up the bones of my leg. "Jesus." I take the foot out again, sharpish. "Snorri!" But he's gone, a third of the way across, battling the waters.

I take the opportunity to put the key back around my neck on its thong. I find it hot in my grasp, reflecting nothing, not even the sky. I wonder if I call on Loki will the true God see and drown me for my betrayal? I hedge my bets by calling on any deity that might be listening.

"Help!"

The way I see it is that God must be pretty busy with people appealing to him all the time, so he probably appreciates it when prayers cut to the chase.

I pause to consider the injustice of a Hell that contains no lakes that drown heroes and let cowards float, but instead holds test upon test over which someone with nothing to recommend them save a strong arm may triumph. Then, without further consideration I run three steps and dive in.

Swimming has never been my forte. Swimming with a sword at my hip has always resulted in swifter progress, but sadly only toward the bottom of whatever body of water I'm drowning in. The Slidr, however, proves unusually buoyant when it comes to sharp-edged steel and Edris Dean's blade, rather than dragging me down, holds me up.

I thrash madly, my lungs too paralysed by the cold even to begin pulling back the breath that escaped me when I hit the river. The iciness of the water is invasive, seeping through blood and bone, filling my head. I lose contact with my limbs but it's not drowning that concerns me—it's keeping warm. Deep in my head, in the dark spaces where we go to hide, I'm crouched, waiting to die, waiting for the ice to reach me, and all I have to burn are memories.

I reach for the hottest memory I have. It isn't the blind heat of the Sahar, or the crackling embrace of Gowfaugh Forest engulfed in flame. The Aral Pass unfolds, dragging me back into that blood-soaked gorge packed with men at war, men screaming, men at cut and thrust, men fallen about their wounds, time running red from their veins, men dying, whispering beneath the cacophony, speaking to their loved and lost, calling for their mothers, last words twitching on blue lips, bargains with the Devil, promises to God. I see another man slide back from my sword, leaving it black with gore. By now it's too dull to slice, but a yard of steel is still deadly whatever edge it carries.

The Aral Pass carries me a third of the way across the Slidr. I find my focus and realize the river's sharp load has not yet cut me open but there's still too far to go and the opposite shore is slipping by too fast. In the distance I hear a roar, a low, steady, wet-mouthed roar. A long silver spear passes beneath me, too close. I start to swim again, pounding artlessly at the water, and this time it is the bloodshed at the Black Fort that drives me on. I remember the sick sound as my sword point pierces an eye, crunching through the bony orbit and into the Viking's brain. In an instant the fire is gone from him, a meat puppet with his strings all snipped. An axe cleaves the air in front of my face as I sway back. A high table catches me in the back and I topple onto it, twisting, throwing my legs into the spin. A broadsword hammers into the planks where my head was and I'm over the table, on both feet, swinging, shearing through the arm that held that sword.

The battle madness of the Black Fort releases me at last, panting amid tumbled corpses. I'm two-thirds of the way across the Slidr, still in the choppy, swift-moving clarity of the river. Downstream, in the distance, the valley is choked with mist. That roar has grown louder, filling the world, trembling in the depth of my bones.

I strike out for shore, desperate now. Something bad waits for me in that mist but I'm running out of fight and time. The coldness takes me and all I have to burn is my duel with Count Isen, the high, sharp crash of blade on blade as he tries to kill me and I weave my defence from desperation. It's not enough. I'm still ten yards from shore and going under. There's a sharp agony in my leg that reaches me even though the limb is frozen and numb. I've been hit. The waters close over me. I surface once more and see that before reaching the rising mist the whole Slidr vanishes as if itself cut by a massive sword. The thunder is louder than thought. I'm being dragged to the falls. I go under again and none of that matters: a shoal of knives is bearing down on me and I've no air to scream with.

Somehow, against all sense, my sword is in my hand. A fine way to drown. But then I remember it's not my sword and the heat that was in my blood in the moment I took it fills me once more. Edris Dean wielded this sword against me, seeking my life as he had sought that of my mother, and of my sister, warm in the womb. I battled him before Tuttugu's corpse. The corpse of my friend, a coward who died a hero's death. I remember how it felt to drive my sword between Edris Dean's ribs, to sink it into the meat of him, to feel it bedded in his flesh and to rip it out again, grating across bone. I open my mouth and roar, careless of the river, and there I stand, dripping in the shallows, sword in hand, and above me the mist from an endless waterfall rises in clouds that dare the sky. The Slidr plunges over a rocky lip just ten yards on. Swords leap from its clear waters as gravity takes the river and hauls it swiftly away.

I step forward on trembling legs, weak in every limb, three more steps, two more, and I'm on the wet sand. I've no injuries that I can see.

A figure is running toward me, Snorri, slowing as he draws near, panting. "I—" He raises a hand, draws in a huge breath, "thought I'd lost you there."

I look at the sword in my hand, the script etched into its blade, the water still dripping from it, diamonds turned rust red in the deadlight. "No. Not yet. Not today."

We climb up the riverbank in silence, both of us wrapped in memories. As the Slidr dries from me I feel that somehow its waters have left me more . . . connected. I remember my battle at the Aral Pass. I remember the fight within the Black Fort. For the first time Jalan the berserker has met everyday Jalan and we've come to some sort of agreement. I'm not sure exactly what it is yet . . . but something has changed.

Hell on the far side of the Slidr proves steeper than before. Hills of black rock replace the dust, hills in which everything is sharp and that offer a traveller no chance for rest. Everywhere the stone looks as if it were soup on the boil, frozen in the instant, bubbles bursting from it, leaving a myriad edges, all razored. Just touching the ground leaves my fingers bloody. How long the leather soles of my boots will last, and what will become of my feet after that, I can't say.

We see more souls here, grey clusters of them, flowing like dirty water along the dry valleys, men and women and children, heads down, unspeaking, drawn onward by some call I can't hear.

We follow, twisting and turning through the black hills, the valleys becoming deeper, broader, more thick with souls. The Slidr is less than a memory now, Hell has parched me again. I feel my skin dying, desiccating, flaking away.

"Wait." For no reason a gorge on our left catches my eye, high above us, emptying out of the valley side.

"This is the way." Snorri gestures after the departing souls ahead of us, more drifting by. His eyes are red with burst veins, like a man who has forgotten how to sleep. I feel worse than he looks.

"Up there." I point at it. "There's something up there."

"This is the way." Snorri repeats, starting off after the souls, head down once more.

"No." And I'm climbing over boulders, a dozen paper-thin cuts on my palm where I reach out to steady myself. "It's up here."

"I don't sense it." Snorri turns toward me, exhausted, the souls dwarfed as they flow around him.

"It's here." I keep climbing, drawing my sword to balance myself, to give myself some support that doesn't require touching the rocks.

It's a scramble to reach the gorge and my hand stings as if vinegar has been poured into each cut. I advance along the narrow path that leads up between the gorge's clifflike walls, Snorri a short way behind me, cursing.

It's silent here out of the wind, at least it is once Snorri stops complaining. A pervasive quiet, ancient and deep. Our footfalls sound like sacrilege. If it were water that carved these valleys it has been gone since before man walked here. In a hell built from loneliness this seems the most desolate and most lost place that the damned might ever walk.

"There's nothing here, Jal, I tol—"

The narrow walls draw back just ahead of us. There's a dell, perhaps a plunge pool where some long-dead river once fell. A single tree stands there, black, gnarled, the bare fingers of its branches stark against the dead-lit sky. Its trunk is mottled, a sickly white against the black, rising from the broad base toward the heights where the first branches divide.

Advancing, I see that the tree is both further away and more huge than I had imagined. "Help me up." There's a step in the gorge, taller than I am. Snorri boosts me to the top. I cut my leg through my trousers. More acid slices from the bubble-fractured rock. I reach for Snorri and help him join me.

Drawing closer we see that the tree, though leafless, is laden with strange fruit. Closer still and the diseased trunk reveals its secret. Bodies are nailed to it. Hundreds of them.

If this tree were the size trees are supposed to be then we would be ants. It must be some offspring of Yggdrasil, the world-tree that stands in the heart of all things and from which worlds depend. The branches which bear fruit droop like those of the willow, dangling almost to the ground. Some reach so low I could stretch up and touch them, but I've no wish to. The fruit are dark and shrivelled, some a couple of feet across, some no bigger than a man's head, all grotesque, unsettling in a way I can't define.

The low groaning of the tree's victims reaches us now. Men and women are pinned to its trunk, young and old, so crowded their limbs overlap, their splayed forms fitted together like interlaced fingers or the pieces of a puzzle.

We come amid the thick and sprawling tangle of the tree's roots to its trunk, as wide as the Mathema Tower and taller still. One patch of whiteness draws my eye, paler than the others and low to the ground.

"Hello, Marco." I step closer, sheathing my sword, looking up at him. There he is, nailed among the hundreds, hands and feet pinned by black spikes of iron. Scores of heads turn my way, slowly, as if it takes great effort, but only Marco speaks.

"Prince Jalan Kendeth." His gaze lifts. "And the barbarian."

"I'm glad you remember me."

"There are few curses worse than having your name spoken in Hell," he says.

That takes the wind from my sails. "W-well." I swallow and try to speak without stammering. "I'd rather have my name spoken in Hell than be nailed to a tree in Hell for all eternity."

Marco hasn't an answer to that.

"I remember you," Snorri says. "The man with the papers. You had Tuttugu tortured. Why are you on this tree?"

"Maybe this is where torturers go," I say.

"It would take a forest to house them," Snorri says. "This tree would not suffice."

"So some more specific crime . . ." I frown. This place scares me. All of Hell scares me, but this place is worse.

"A worse crime." Snorri's gaze wanders across the bodies, all naked, all pierced by nails, hanging on gravity's rack.

"Get me down and I'll tell you," Marco says, always the banker. I can see the desperation in his eyes, though.

"You put yourself there." Snorri turns to study the closest of the hanging fruit. He reaches up to touch it. "Ah!" And snatches his hand back as if stung. A flush of colour spreads across the wizened husk, a fleshy pink. We watch, Snorri still rubbing his fingers. The fruit swells, like a chest inflated with a deep breath. The thing's true shape resolves. We see limbs, coiled in tight, flesh tones mottling the previous lifeless black. The transformation lasts as long as the breath that Snorri drew in, and with his exhalation the "fruit" shrivels back to its dark dry husk.

"It . . . it was . . ."

"It looked like a baby," I whisper. Only too small, head too big, limbs too tiny, fingers webbed.

"An unborn." Snorri turns back to Marco. "That's the fruit of this tree? Your crimes?"

I'm not listening: my eyes have found another of the tree's fruit. Just one among hundreds, maybe thousands, but it draws me. I can't look away. Every other thing blurs, and I'm walking toward it.

"Jal?" Snorri calls me from somewhere distant.

I reach up with both hands and clasp the desiccated husk. The pain isn't in my fingers, it's in my veins, in the marrow of each bone as something is drawn from me. Thick arms wrestle me away and I'm on the ground looking up at the unborn, pink and tiny . . . wet and dripping with life.

"What are you doing?" Snorri hauls me to my feet. "Have you gone mad?"

"I . . ." I look at the pink thing, this almost-child. I draw Edris Dean's sword and the script along the blade has run crimson as if the symbols themselves are bleeding. "This is my sister."

Though some magic has drawn me to her our connection ends there. I've never met her—she has never grown—and I have had two brothers teach me that there's nothing holy in blood bonds. Given my elder brother, Martus, and a random stranger both dangling over a precipice and only time to save one of them, it would be my day to make a new friend. Especially if the stranger were young and female. All I have to link me to this . . . creature . . . is the memory of watching Mother die. Only sorrow binds us, and now she's been corrupted. This nameless child has been wrought into some terror, a terror that needs to kill me to escape into the living world and keep its place there . . .

I hold my bleeding sword and watch the thing before me, pink, ugly, wet and raw. Snorri stands beside me and says nothing. A cry escapes me, a harsh noise, as short and sharp as the arc of my blade: Steel slices. The unborn drops, and where she hits the ground there is only dust and small dry bones.

"Jal." Snorri reaches for my shoulder. I shake him off.

Above the dust something intangible is rising, ghost-pale, changing, growing, shifting swiftly through many forms. All of them her. My sister. A sleeping baby, a tiny child staggering as they do when taking first steps, a young girl, long-haired, pretty, a tall woman, slender and beautiful with Mother's looks, dark locks coiled about her shoulders. The images change more swiftly—a mother holding tiny hands, a woman, stern-faced, a power behind her eyes, an old woman on a tall throne. Gone.

I'm left standing there, tingles up and down my arms, across my cheeks, breath sharp and shallow, a pain in my chest. Why does this hurt me? Might-have-beens are lost every second of every day. Might-have-beens, plans that come to naught, pipe-dreams, they pour into nothing, swifter than the Slidr plunging over its cliff. I stand looking down at the tiny bones as they blacken and go to dust. Not might-have-beens: should-have-beens.

Marco laughs at me. An ugly sound, tight and full of pain, but laughter none the less, and from a man I never once saw smile in the living world. "It's not finished, prince. Not over." He groans, struggling to move but pinned by his extremities. "The tree bears what the lichkin leave behind."

"Lichkin?" I've heard of them, monsters from the deadlands, things the Dead King brought into the world to serve his purpose.

"What do you think rides the children taken from the womb? What moulds their potential and uses that power? It is fair exchange." He watches me dead-eyed. He could be talking of bargains made on the floors of Umbertide's exchanges for all the emotion he shows. "Where is the crime? The child that would not have lived gets to live, and the lichkin that has never lived gets to quicken and walk in the world of men where it may feed its hunger."

I look up into the distance above us, at the flesh-mottled trunk, tented by innumerable willow-like branches, each dangling its stolen life. Is Marco the worst man pinned there? It seems unlikely. I should hate him more fiercely. I should rush at him and hack him down. But this place burns emotion from you. In place of rage I feel hollow, sad. I turn and walk away.

"Wait! Get me down!"

"Get you down?" I turn back, the flame of anger guttering somewhere deep within. "Why?"

"I told you. I gave you information. You owe me." Marco heaves each word out over a chest being compressed by his own weight.

"This tree will not stand long enough for me to owe you, banker. Not if it stands ten thousand years and you save my life every day."

He coughs, black blood on his lips. "They'll hunt you now—the lichkin and what parts of your sister it has taken. A brother's death would open a door for them and let them emerge together, unborn, a new evil in the world. Your death would seal them into the lands above."

The thought of being tracked through Hell by some monster bound about my sister's soul scares me silly but I'm damned if I'll let Marco see it. "If this . . . thing . . . seeks me out I shall just have to end it. With cold steel!" I draw my sword for good measure—the thing has, after all, been enchanted to end dead creatures as effectively as live ones.

"I can tell you how to save her." He holds my gaze, eyes dark and glittering.

"My sister?" Saving her hadn't been on my list—that's Snorri's forte. I want to walk away but something won't let me. "How?"

"It can be done now that you've freed her futures from the tree." His pain is clear in his face for once, his desperation. "You'll get me down? You promise."

"By my honour."

"When you meet them in the living world, your sister and whichever lichkin wears her skin, any sufficiently holy thing will part them."

"And my sister will . . . live?"

Marco makes that ugly sound again, his laughter. "She'll die. But properly. Cleanly."

"Sufficiently holy?" Snorri rumbles the words beside me.

"Something of importance. It's the faith of all those believers that will make it work. A focus. Not some church cross. Not holy water from a cathedral font. Some true symbol, some—"

"A cardinal's seal?" I ask.

Marco nods, face lined with the pain and the effort of it. "Yes. Probably."

I turn to go again.

"Wait!" I hear Marco gasp as he tries to reach for me.

"What?" I glance back.

"Release me! We made a bargain."

"Do you have the paperwork, Marco Onstantos Evenaline of the House Gold? The correct forms? Are they signed? Witnessed? Do they bear the proper marks?"

"You promised! On your honour, Prince Jalan. Your honour."

"Oh." I turn away again. "That." And start to walk. "If you find it, let me know."

SIX

In the Liban port of Al-Aran I took ship on a cog named *Santa Maria*, the same vessel that took most of the salt my companions had spent the best part of the previous month hauling north from Hamada. They also found room for my three camels in the hold, and I'll admit to a certain satisfaction at the beasts' distress, having spent so long enduring my own distress on a camel hump.

"I warn you, Captain, God crafted these creatures for three things only. Passing wind from the rear end, passing wind from the front end, and spitting. They spit stomach acid so tell your men, and don't let anyone venture into the hold with a naked flame or you may find yourself the master of a marvellous collection of floating splinters. Also we'll all drown."

Captain Malturk snorted into the bushiness of his moustaches and waved me off, turning toward the masts and rigging to shout nautical nonsense at his men.

Travel by sea is a miserable business best not spoken about in polite company and nothing of any account happened for the first four days. Oh, there were waves, the wind blew, meals were eaten, but until the coast of Cag Liar appeared on the horizon it was generally distinguishable from all my other sea voyages only by the temperature, the language in which the sailors swore, and the taste of the food coming back up.

Also, never take a camel to sea. Just don't. Especially not three of the bastards.

Port French on Cag Liar, the southern-most of the Corsair Isles, is the first stop of many ships leaving the coast of Afrique. There are two ways to sail the Middle Sea and survive the experience. Firstly armed to the teeth, secondly armed with a right-of-passage purchased from the pirate-lords. Such things can be obtained from factors in many ports, but it bodes well for a ship to put in at Port French or one of the other main centres on the Corsairs. The code flags are changed regularly and it doesn't do to be sailing on out-of-date flags. Plus, for a merchant, once the painful business of "taxes" is concluded, there are few places in the world that offer as wide a range of goods and services as the corsair ports. They trade in flesh there too, the bought-and-sold type as well as the hired type. Slaves run mainly west to east and a trickle north to south. The Broken Empire never had a big demand for slaves. We have peasants. Much the same thing, and they think they're free so they never run off.

Coming into port it felt good to at last see the world I knew best, the headlands thick with pine and beech and oak in place of the scattered palm trees of northern Liba. And seasons too! The forest stood rust-speckled with the first crisp touch of autumn, though on a blazing day like this it felt hard to imagine the summer in terminal decline. In place of Liba's flat roofs the houses on the slopes above the harbour boasted terracotta tiles, sloped in a tacit admission that rain actually happens.

"Two days! Two days!" Malturk's first mate, a barrel of a man named Bartoli, who seemed incapable of wearing a shirt. "Two days!" A booming baritone.

"How many?"

"Two d—"

"I got it, thank you." I wiggled a finger into my half-deafened ear and proceeded down the gangplank.

The quays of Port French are like none I've seen. It's as though the contents of every brothel, opium den, gambling hall, and blood-pit have been vomited up onto the sun-soaked harbour, pushing out among the quays so that the dockhands have to weave their path among this bright and varied crowd just to tie off a hawser.

I immediately found myself swamped by maidens in all shades from jet through dusky to sun-burned, along with men trying to steer me to establishments where any vice might be indulged so long as it parts you from your coin. The most direct of all, and perhaps the most honest, were the small boys dodging in and out among the adults' legs and attempting to lift my purse before I'd gone ten paces.

"Two days!" Bartoli, on the rail, watching his crew and passengers disperse. The *Santa Maria* would sail with or without us once its business had concluded and the code flags were hung.

After Hell, the desert, and then the sea, Port French seemed as close to heaven as makes no difference. I wandered through the crowd in a state of bliss, paying no specific attention to any of the people trying to lure me this way or that, no matter how persistent. At one point I paused to boot a particularly annoying little cutpurse into the sea, and then at last I was off the quay and climbing into the maze of streets leading up to the ridge where all the finest buildings seemed to cluster.

Nothing paralyses a man so well as choice. Offered such a banquet after so long in the wilderness the decision stumped me. I settled at a table outside a tavern on a steep and cobbled street halfway to the ridge. I ordered wine and it came in an amphora cradled in a raffia jacket to keep it whole. I sat watching the world go by, sipping from my clay cup.

They call them the Corsair Isles and it's true that pirating defines them, but there are millions of hot dry acres in the interior where the sea can't even be spotted from a hill, and in those valleys they grow damned fine grapes. However cheap its container, the wine was good.

My travel-stained robes and Sahar tan made me more of an Arab than a man of Red March, only the sun-bleached gold in my hair told the lie. Certainly nobody would mistake me for a prince, which has its advantages in a town packed with robbers, thieves, pirates, and pimps. Anonymous in my desert attire I took a moment to relax. Hell, I took several moments, then two hours, then three more, and enjoyed the passing hustle and bustle of close-packed living while the sun slipped across the sky.

I considered my return to Vermillion, my fortunes, my future, but most of all I considered Yusuf Malendra and his calculations. Not just Yusuf though, not just the Mathema where a hundred mathmagicians scratched away at their algebras, but all of those who saw or told or lied about the future. The völvas of the north, the magicians of Afrique, the Silent Sister with her blind eye, the Lady Blue amid her mirrors looking for reflections of tomorrow. Spiders, all of them, laying their webs. And what did that make men like me and Jorg Ancrath? Flies, bound tight and ready to have our vital juices sucked away to feed their appetite for knowing?

Jorg had it worse than me of course. That boy prince with his thorn scars. He'd escaped that tangle of briars but did he know that he hung in a larger one now, its hooks long enough to eviscerate a man? Did he know my grandmother whispered his name to the Silent Sister? That so many conspired to either make or break him? Emperor or fool—which he would be remembered as I couldn't say, but he was one of those in the making, no doubt about it. Perhaps both. I remembered his eyes, that first night I saw him in Crath City. As if even then he looked past the world and saw all this coming his way. And didn't give a damn.

I knocked back my cup and tried to pour another. The amphora dribbled and ran dry. "I'm well out of that business." I had covered the Ancrath boy with a blanket and left him on that roof in Hamada. I should have done him the kindness of pushing him off. Still, *I* had escaped, and that, as always, was the important thing. A prophecy has to get up very early in the morning indeed if it wants to snare old Jalan!

"Rollas?" Looking up from my close inspection of the amphora's interior, in search of hidden wine, I saw a man turn from the main street into a side alley. Something about the square cut of his shoulders below the blunt and bristly back of his head put me in mind of my friend Barras Jon's man, Rollas. I stood, swaying somewhat, steadying myself with a hand to the shoulder of a man seated by the next table. "Your pardon." The words slurred over numb lips. "Just getting my land legs." And I stumbled out across the street. It hadn't just reminded me of Barras's man. It had *been* him. I'd followed the back of that head home to the palace after enough drunken Vermillion nights to know it anywhere. It was habit more than anything that made me set off after it this time.

I walked carefully, not wanting to step in anything unpleasant, and had to negotiate passage around an ill-smelling beggar even more drunk than myself. I emerged from the alley into another street leading from the docks to the heights, sure that I must have lost my quarry, but found myself just in time to see him enter a whorehouse. You can always tell the places: better presented than the drinking holes, more conspicuous than gambling dens, and if business is slow then girls will be leaning out of the upstairs windows. Besides, this one had "Hore House" painted in big red letters on a sign running the length of the eaves.

I crossed over and let the street-hook snare me.

"A fine-looking man like you shouldn't be alone on a nice afternoon like this now." The hook, a striking, dark-haired woman in her forties, took my arm, steering me toward the brothel door.

"And you'd like to keep me company, would you?" I leered politely.

She smiled, professional enough not to wince at my wine-sour breath. "Well, I'm a little old for a young man like you, but there are some beautiful girls inside just dying to meet you. Samantha has the b—"

"Do you know the man who went in just before me?" I held back against the tug of her arm, just shy of the doorway and the door-guard hulking in the shadows of its porch.

She released me and looked up, smile erased. "We're a very discreet establishment. We don't tell tales."

I held up a Liban bar between finger and thumb and let the rectangular coin catch the afternoon light. I'd borrowed ten bars from Omar the night before I left, each made of a touch more gold than an Empire ducat.

"I haven't seen him before. I would remember. Handsome fellow."

"What did he want?"

She rolled her eyes at that. "A whore."

"He came straight here. He wasn't wandering. He didn't hesitate . . . did he come to see a particular girl?"

"That's a pretty coin. Does it weigh much?" She held her hand out, palm up.

"Yes." I pressed it into her hand. It seemed a lot to spend on what was probably mistaken identity—and I didn't quite know why I hadn't just shouted out to Rollas. I considered walking away but Barras was my friend, albeit a treacherous, backstabbing one who had married the girl I'd been mooning over in the frozen north . . . at least when there weren't any other girls to keep me warm. And if it *was* Rollas I'd seen then something was very wrong. I couldn't think of any good reason that the man the Great Jon hired to protect his son would be hurrying into a Port French brothel. "I'm spending any change inside, so the better the story the less work this Samantha of yours has to do."

The woman bit her lip, considering the odds. She'd make a terrible poker player. She glanced at the doorman, at me, eyes finally coming to rest on the Liban bar in her hand. "Said he wanted to look the girls over. Wanted to know if we only used free workers, or if we bought chained skin. Asking after any new girls. White girls. My height, dark hair. Told him no, but he wanted to look anyway."

"Did he mention a name?"

"It doesn't do to ask questions like his on the Isles. It's an easy way to get a cut throat."

I took her meaning. Even drunk I knew it wasn't idle talk. Even so. "Did he mention a name?"

"Lisa?"

"DeVeer?"

"New girls only get one name. Do a good job and you might get another in a couple of years. DeVeer, though? That's not going to bring them in. DeLicious, maybe. Mine was FourWays. Serra FourWays."

Lisa? A corsair captive? I needed to think it through. I stepped away, almost crashing into a man laden beneath sacks. "Your pardon." Somehow I'd been reduced to apologizing to common labourers. "I . . ." I turned and started down the street.

"You don't want to use your credit?" Serra called after me.

"Maybe later . . ." I'd stopped turning but my head kept spinning, and it wasn't *all* too much afternoon wine. Lisa DeVeer a slave in Port French? How?

"You're still wondering what the fourth way is, aren't you?" She called the words at my back.

I didn't answer, but truth be told, even with thoughts of Lisa swirling in my head . . . I was.

The sun was setting as I walked back up the gangplank onto the *Santa Maria*. The quays were quieter, though far from quiet. There's a hush that settles as the sea turns crimson and the shadows reach. The shadow-masts stretch out from ships at rest, venturing farther and farther, across the docks, up the warehouse walls, meshing, merging until only the highest ridge is lit, the sun's last rays burning on the mansions where pirate lords and pirate ladies play at nobility.

"You back to water those fucking beasts of yours?" Bartoli loomed behind me as I stood at the rail looking out across the sea. Time was when a man took a risk interrupting me at sunset, but Aslaug no longer even whispered.

"They're camels, for Christsake. Camels don't drink. Everyone knows that." I held a hand in front of his face to forestall any reply. "Corsairs trade in flesh—but they don't raid for it . . . do they?" Asking questions in Port French might well get Rollas his throat cut. Me, I'd ask my questions on the *Santa Maria*. Much safer.

"You looking to buy? You can't even look after camels!"

"Where do they get their slaves from?" I stuck to my question.

"Slavers bring them in, obviously." Bartoli rubbed at the blackness of his beard and spat noisily over the rail. "Corsairs will sell on prisoners off a ship, but they don't snatch from ports or raid inland. Even pirates need friends. Don't shit where you eat. That's a lesson for everyone . . . except your fucking camels, apparently."

"So . . . where would someone buy a slave?"

"At a slave market." Bartoli gave me the same look he'd been giving me for days, the "you're an idiot" look.

"And where—"

"Take your pick. Must be a dozen of 'em. First one is just over there, general market, behind the Crooked Jacks warehouse, big one with the shingle roof, tobacco and such. Second one is a kids market, just past the King's Heart tavern at the bottom of Main."

"A dozen?" It seemed like a lot to check out just on a hunch and the back of a man's head.

Bartoli furrowed his brow and stared at his fingers. "Thirteen."

I felt the ripple run through me as the planets aligned. "Thirteen?"

"Thirteen."

First stop, second sister, thirteen . . . "Where's the thirteenth?"

"Way up, past the lords' houses, back in the hills." He waved a thick arm at the town. "They actually call it Thirteen. S'how I figured there's thirteen. Not so much selling goes on there. More of a . . . how'd you call it? School? Training up quality females. Not for the likes of us though. Sell 'em on to rich men in Maroc and the interior."

And so it was that on the following morning a hunch, the back of a man's head, the memory of Lisa DeVeer's many charms, and two devious math-magicians, had me toiling up through the streets of Port French nursing a hangover. I found myself drenched in sweat despite the cloud wrack burgeoning over the hills of Cag Liar. Storm coming. I didn't need to be a sailor or a farmer to know that.

Yusuf had set me up for this. I knew it. From plotting out my route home to handing over those three little numbers that he must have known I would ask for. I resolved to settle my scores with Omar and his master in due course. For now I kept on walking, manfully resisting the various taverns opening onto the street, the rattle of gaming wheels from low garrets, and the calls of commercially-minded young women from arched windows.

I'd slept on the *Santa Maria* the previous night. My afternoon's drinking had caught up with me and I'd settled on a big coil of rope by the forecastle steps just to rest my eyes. The next thing I knew seagulls were crapping on me and an unreasonably bright morning was in progress, with sailors shouting too loudly and the keenest salesmen already setting out their quayside stalls.

After forcing down a hearty breakfast I decided to do the honourable thing and see if I could find Lisa. I considered searching Rollas out—if it was Rollas—but at least I knew Lisa wouldn't be wandering about. And besides, the chances were that Rollas had already asked enough questions to get himself knifed and dumped in the docks. Or knowing Rollas, to have knifed his attackers first and then had to flee.

Port French peters out into a scattering of merchants' estates and vine-yards as you climb up into the hills that step their way into the country-side. It's pretty in its way, but I'd rather see it from the saddle. Or not at all. Especially not on foot, battered by a squally wind that couldn't decide on a direction in which to blow. I narrowed my eyes against the grit and dust and followed the conflicting directions of several locals, plotting the average path. Soon I found myself lost, pursuing dry tracks that snaked their way between drier ridges. I passed one slack-jawed yokel who gave me another bunch of lies concerning the route to Thirteen, his dialect so thick as to be barely distinguishable from the grunting of his hogs. After that I met only goats, and once, a surprised donkey.

"Bollocks."

I couldn't see the sea any more, nor the town, just rolling brown hills, studded with thorn bushes and rocks. Apart from the goats, the odd lizard sunning itself, and a buzzard circling overhead, possibly waiting for me to die, I appeared to be utterly alone.

Then it began to rain.

An hour later, sodden, muddy from several falls, and having already abandoned my quest—my goal now being to find Port French again—I scrambled over a ridge and there, on the crest of the next rise, lay Thirteen.

The place had the look of an old fortress to it, a high-walled compound with observation towers at each corner, facing out over a slate-grey sea. From my elevation I could make out a range of buildings within the compound: barracks, stables, officers' quarters—the only part of the edifice that looked vaguely hospitable—a well, and three separate exercise yards. Formidable gates of iron-banded timber stood closed to the outside world. Guards manned the towers, alongside bell-bars waiting to be given their voice in case of alarm. Other guards ambled around the walls, some resting on the parapet to enjoy a pipe or watch the clouds. It seemed unreasonably well defended until you realized that the concern was not the slaves escaping but that they might be stolen. They were, after all, a valuable commodity and this was an island ruled by criminals.

I could see small groups of women in sackcloth being marched from one building to another. At this range I couldn't make out the doors on the slave blocks, but no doubt they would be sturdy and well locked.

"Hmmm." I wiped the wet hair from my eyes and contemplated the place. The rain had slackened off and lighter skies promised in the east.

I've never claimed to be a hero, but I knew that a woman I had briefly intended to marry could well be incarcerated, destined for a life of slavery, most likely as a concubine in some harem far to the south. I drew Loki's key out from beneath my muddy robes. It glistened in the grey light. I could almost feel the thing laughing at me as I held it in my hand.

My gaze shifted from the consuming blackness of the key to the dark mass of the fortress they called Thirteen, glowering at me from the next ridge. Once before I'd stormed a stronghold to rescue a friend. The key twisted in my grip as if already imagining the locks that would surrender to it.

I didn't want to do it. I wanted to get back on the *Santa Maria* and ride her all the way home. But I was a prince of Red March, and this was Lisa, Lisa DeVeer, my Lisa, damn it. I knew what I had to do.

"You *bastard!*"

"What?" I stepped back sharply out of the reach of her fists.

"Camels?" Lisa shouted, and shuffled toward me, hampered by the rope still hobbling her legs. "You traded me for three camels? Three?"

"Well . . ." I hadn't imagined this reaction when I took her slave-hood off. We were only a hundred yards from Thirteen's doors. The men on the towers were watching and probably having a good laugh at my expense. "They were *good* camels, Lisa!"

"Three!" She swung at me again and I jumped back. Overbalanced, she toppled, cursing, into the mud.

No probably about it. I could hear the tower guards laughing.

"Lisa! Angel! I *rescued* you!" I thought it politic not to mention that it was actually just two camels. I traded the other one for five pieces of crown silver and a rather stylish leather jerkin with iron plates stitched to the chest and sides, nicely engraved. The factor had admitted after the deal that Lisa had been proving a pain to train in the duties of a harem girl and would likely have had to be whipped beyond the point of physical accept-ability in the role. "I saved you!"

"My *husband* should have done that!" Her shriek managed to make my ears ring.

"I'm sure Barras is . . ." I bit the sentence off and decided not to make excuses for the treacherous bastard. "Well, he didn't, did he? So you're lucky I found you." I drew my knife. "Now, if you'll stop trying to hit me I'll cut your legs free."

Lisa dropped her arms and let me kneel to slice the rope.

The moment the last fibres parted, she was off. Charging straight back at the doors, screaming bloody threats and dire promises, both hands raised in obscene gestures. Fortunately the circulation hadn't fully returned to her legs and I caught her before she got a third of the way back, wrapping my arms about her from behind and spinning her around bodily.

"Christsakes, woman! They'll take you right back off me and tear up the bill of sale. These are not nice men. Your mouth's going to get your nose cut off and find you doing tricks in a dark-house just to eat!" I was as worried for me as for her. We were a long way from town, and these were the Corsair Isles: they could do pretty much anything and get away with it.

I started to drag her away. It was actually slightly easier than dragging my three camels all the way up from the quayside. I got her back to where we started before she got her arm free and slapped me.

"Ow! Jesus!" I clutched my face. "What was that for?"

"They said you died!" Angry, as if it were my fault.

"They said you got married!" My turn to feel angry, and for more than being slapped, though I wasn't sure why. The ingratitude of it probably. I'd liked those camels. I grabbed her arm and pulled her on. "We've got to get out of here. If they see I know you they'll either want more money or just kill me so this never comes back to them." I set off, Lisa stumbling and jerking behind me. "How long before one of the men on the wall reports all this to someone important down below? I should have kept the hood on you till we were out of sight of the—"

I broke off as Lisa started sobbing, heaving in great lungfuls of air and shuddering them out as she walked. In other circumstances I might have said or at least thought something patronizing about the "weaker sex," but frankly I knew exactly the feeling—there had been too many escapes of mine where I would have been sobbing with relief too if I hadn't had a front to maintain before the company I was in.

I kept glancing back at Lisa as I led her down through those hills. Her sackcloth dress had got almost as muddy as my robes when I wrestled her to the ground, her hair stuck out at odd angles or hung in dirty straggles—slave-hood hair you could call it—and her eyes were red from too many tears.

Back at Thirteen I'd said I was after the least expensive beauty they had, and Lisa was in the line of eight they'd brought out from the discipline hut. None of them had been made presentable and some you had to look at pretty hard to see much beauty beneath the grime and bruises. Lisa, though, took my breath. Something in her eyes, or the shape of her mouth, or . . . I can't tell you. Maybe just because that mouth, those eyes, the curve of her neck, meant something to me, each part of her so overlaid with memories that it became hard to see what stood in front of me without our history crowding in. I didn't like the sensation at all—most uncomfortable—I put it down to the shock of my Hell-trek and having been so long in heathen climes. It gave me additional reasons to be grateful for the desert veil I'd put in place. I'd worn it of course to stop her recognizing me and giving away the fact I was there for her. At best that would have simply increased her price ten-fold. At worst it would have got me killed.

"What?" she asked, self-conscious for the first time. "Have I got something on my face?" She reached up to touch her cheek, unconscious of the action and smearing more dirt there.

"Nothing." I looked away, managing to stumble over a rock as I did. She looked gorgeous. Far too gorgeous for Barras Jon.

We reached the outskirts of Port French before Lisa gathered herself enough to ask, "You have brought a ship, haven't you?"

"Well. A ship brought me, that's certainly true."

Lisa shuddered. "I never want to sail again. I was sick the whole way to Vyene!"

"Ah. Well, we are on an island, so . . ." I fell back alongside her, stepped in closer, and put an arm around her shoulders. "Don't worry. I know a lot of people don't take well to boats. I'm a great sailor and even I felt a little rough during my first storm, but I took to the whole business with the ropes and whatnot immediately. Taught those Vikings a thing or two . . ."

"Vikings?" She looked up at me and frowned.

"It's a long story."

"And why are you dressed as a shepherd out of the nativity? Is it some kind of disguise?"

"Kind o—"

"And why." She shook my arm off. "Are you so muddy?" She poked at a particularly filthy part of my Bedouin robe. I didn't like to tell her it wasn't mud. Camels are disgusting creatures, a week at sea does nothing to improve them, and I've never seen the like before when it comes to projectile shitting.

Rather than explain my garb I diverted her with a question. "Why were you in Vyene?" I couldn't think what business she would have in the Empire's capital—or at least former empire's former capital.

"Barras was taking me to meet his family and settle on one of their western estates—"

"Barras, is he—"

"He's fine." Anger creased her brow. "He got held up with his father's business in Vermillion—the Great Jon went ahead of us to Vyene—so he didn't sail with me as planned, just sent me and my maids on with some more of the effects from the rooms in the palace . . . At least I think he's fine." Lisa put her hand to my arm. "He must be looking for me, Jal. He could have come to harm—you said the pirates—"

"I'm sure he's in good health." I may have snapped it. My momentary concern for Barras had vanished as soon as I heard he didn't sail with her. I wondered how many men he had out searching for his wife. Trust Rollas to come closest to the mark—a man of many talents. "Come on." I picked up the pace. "We need to get to our ship."

Lisa hiked up her sackcloth and hurried after me.

The *Santa Maria* lay where I left her, waiting for the tide, and we boarded without incident. Bartoli also remained where I left him, leaning against the ship's rail, scratching his hairy belly. He extorted two pieces of crown silver from me before allowing my guest passage to the port of Marsail, a price I paid without complaint, not wishing to seem cheap with Lisa watching on.

Before sailing we managed to secure Lisa a dress, negotiating with the rogues on the quays over the side of the ship. A short to-and-fro with some tailor's shop hidden back behind the warehouses and a dress was brought out, little more than an embroidered sack in truth, but better than the actual sack I'd purchased her in.

I stood guard outside the tiny cupboard that served as my cabin, defending Lisa's honour against the largely uninterested sailors whilst she changed clothes. She emerged, tugging at the sleeves but without complaint. She looked sick even in the gloom beneath decks.

"Are you all right?"

She put a hand to the door to steady herself. "It's just this rocking."

"We're still at anchor, tied to the quayside."

Rather than reply Lisa covered her mouth and made a dash for the steps.

When we set sail two hours later on the afternoon tide Lisa hung over the stern rail, groaning. I stood behind her, cheerfully watching Port French slip into the distance. I may have overstated my claim to being a good sailor, but in fine weather on the Middle Sea I can keep my footing and do a passable impression of enjoying the whole nautical affair. Lisa on the other hand proved to be a sailor who would make me look good on my worst day. I had thought I would never have shipmates messier, louder, or more given to complaint than the three camels Omar foisted on me, but Lisa outdid the trio. Like the camels the slightest swell emptied her from both ends. Only my robust objection prevented Captain Malturk having her kept in their former accommodation.

I learned on the second day of our voyage that Lisa's violent response to travel by sea had at least made her sufficiently unappealing to the corsairs who captured her vessel that she had remained unmolested during the long passage back to the Isles. Her maids were not so "lucky" and were sold into a different market at the corsairs' first port of call. Lisa's escape was not without cost though, since she had arrived in Port French so close to death that the slave master came within a hair's breadth of dumping her in the harbour rather than invest in her recuperation. At sea once again she went into a rapid decline and spent the three-day voyage curled up in my tiny cabin with two buckets. I kept to the deck and we saw little of each other until the blessed call "Land ho!" from somewhere up in the rigging finally coaxed her into the open.

She stood, pale green and shaking, as I manfully endured her stench and pointed toward the still-invisible coast as if I could see it. "The Port of Marsail! We'll charter a place on one of the cogs that sail up the Seleen and be in Vermillion within two days at most!"

Home! I couldn't see it but I sure as hell could taste it, and this time I'd be staying put.

SEVEN

In Marsail Lisa and I spent two days and a night recuperating incognito. We took two rooms—at her insistence—at a fine inn on the Prada Royal that runs below the various palaces of the old Marsail kings. I spent more of Omar's gold to get us both decently attired, a fine jacket for me with just enough brocade to hint at military connections without being vulgar, trews in a neutral grey, long black boots polished to a shine sufficient to see one's face staring back out of them. Lisa abandoned the soiled dress and selected some modest travelling clothes that would neither shame her nor draw too much attention.

A trip to the bathhouse, the barber, a fine meal at one of the better harbourside restaurants and we both started to feel a little more human. The conversation between us still ran in uneven and awkward bursts, skirting around talk of her marriage whilst still covering, again and again, her various worries about Barras and any trouble he might encounter on his search for her. Even so, I saw flashes of the old Lisa, drawing a few smiles and blushes as I talked about old times, carefully avoiding mention of her dead brother and father.

In the end Lisa's terror of yet another boat trip, even by river, saw us making the trip to Vermillion by express carriage, rattling along the various roads that track the Seleen's path east toward the capital. We passed several days side-by-side, opposite an old priest, and a dark-haired merchant from some distant Araby port. By night we jolted sleepily against each other as the carriage carried on, changing horses at various staging posts along the way. I was pleased to find that, asleep with her head against my shoulder, Lisa smelled as good as I remembered. Almost good enough to erase the memory of how badly she had reeked when staggering off the *Santa Maria* at Marsail. It occurred to me during one of those long nights as Lisa's head slipped from my shoulder to my lap, that although all three DeVeer sisters had married in indecent haste after my supposed death, Micha to my brother Darin, Sharal to the murderous Count Isen, and Lisa to my faithless friend Barras Jon—who I would never have let down—that it was really only Lisa I mourned the loss of.

All would be well. Home. Peace. Safety. The key would be secure in the palace. The Dead King might pose a threat to small bands of travellers in the depths of the desert or the wildness of the mountains, but he could hardly march an army through Red March and lay siege to the Red Queen's capital. And as for stealthier attempts—the Silent Sister's magics would surely not permit necromancy to function within the halls where she and her siblings dwelt.

Mile after mile vanished beneath our wheels and as my grandmother's lands rolled past, hypnotizing in their green and patterned familiarity, thoughts rolled through my head. The things I'd seen, people, conversations, all spooling out across the smoothness of my mind. Occasionally I would raise the shade screen and stick my head out through the window to enjoy the breeze. Only then did I feel any hint of worry. The road stretching out ahead, the parallel hedgerows to either side arrowing into the distance, growing closer, closer, never meeting, lost in the future. Only when looking ahead like that did my fears give chase, skittering along behind the carriage. Maeres Allus waited for me, there, in the midst of my city.

I had confided my problem to Jorg Ancrath that drunken night on a Hamadan rooftop. He'd given me some advice, that thorn-scarred killer, and there, in the hot darkness of the desert, it had seemed sound, a solution. Was he not, after all, the King of Renar? But then again he was just a boy . . . Also, whatever he'd said to me had been washed away by a river of whisky and all I could remember of it was the look in his eyes as he told me, and the completeness with which I had believed him to be right.

The carriage rocked and jolted, miles ran beneath our wheels and home grew ever closer. We overtook three long columns of soldiers marching toward the capital. Several times the road grew so crowded we had to edge along past idle baggage-trains, arguing teamsters, soldiers shouting commands down the line. And somehow amid all that rattle and clatter, the heat, the noise, the anticipation . . . I fell asleep.

I dreamed of Cutter John, grown vast and satanic, as if the reality weren't bad enough. I saw him reaching for me with his remaining arm, pale and hung about with the grisly trophies of his trade, lips he'd taken for Maeres Allus and worn as bracelets. I tried to run but found myself bound to the table once again, back in Allus's poppy halls. Those great white fingers quested for me, growing closer . . . closer . . . me screaming all the while, and as I screamed the walls and floor fell away, turning to dust on a dry wind, revealing a dead-lit sky, the colour of misery. Cutter's hand shrank back, and in that moment, knowing myself once more in Hell, I actually shouted for him to grab me and lift me back, not caring what fate awaited me—for the best definition of Hell is perhaps that there is nowhere, no place, no time to which you would not run in order to escape it.

"Something's wrong."

I look up and see that Snorri has stopped ahead of me and is eyeing the ridges about us. "Everything's wrong. We're in Hell!" Words won't shape it but even if all you're doing is walking down a dusty gully following the flow of souls, Hell is worse than everything you've known. You hurt, enough to make you weep, you thirst, you ache with hunger, misery weighs on you as if it were chains about your neck, and just standing there feels like watching everything you've ever loved die wretchedly before you.

"There!" He points toward a jagged collection of rocks on the ridge to our left.

"Rocks?" I don't see anything else.

"Something." Snorri frowns. "Something fast."

We walk on, bone tired. Here and there the earth is torn and fissured. Long tongues of flame lick out, flickering skyward, and the air is foul with sulphur, stinging my eyes and lungs. The gully broadens into a dusty valley, studded with boulders. The wind has carved them into alien shapes, many disturbingly like faces. I start to hear whispers, indistinct at first, becoming clearer as I strain to make sense of the words.

"*Cheat, liar, coward, adulterer, blasphemer, thief, cheat, liar, coward, adulterer—*"

"Are you hearing this, Snorri?"

He stops and lets me catch up. "Yes." He glances around, still spooked. "Voices. They keep calling me a killer. Over and over."

"That's it?"

". . . *blasphemer, thief, cheat, liar, coward, adulterer . . .*"

"You're not getting 'cheat' or 'thief'?"

Snorri frowns down at me. "Just 'killer.'"

I cup a hand to my ear. "Ah, yes, it's clearer now. I'm getting 'killer' too."

". . . *coward, adulterer, blasphemer . . .*"

"Blasphemer? Me? Me?" I spin around glaring at the rocky faces pointing my way. Every boulder for fifty yards seems to sport a grotesque set of features that wouldn't look out of place on the statues that decorate my great-uncle's tower.

"*Anger: you have committed the sin of anger . . .*" from a score of mouths.

"I'm not fucking angry!" I shout back, not sure why I'm answering but swept up by the tide of accusation.

"*Lust: you have committed the sin of lust . . .*"

"Well . . . technically . . ."

"Jal?" Snorri's hand settles on my shoulder.

"*Greed: You have committed the sin of greed . . .*"

"Oh come on! Everyone's done greed! I mean, show me a man—"

"Jal!" Snorri shakes me, spinning me to face him.

"Yes. What?" I blink up at him.

"*Lust: You have committed the—*"

"All right! All right!" I holler over the voices. "I lusted. More than once. I'll put my hand up to all seven, just shut up."

"Jal!" A slap and my attention is firmly back on the Northman. "These aren't things the gods care about. This is your creed. This is the nonsense churchmen rail against."

He has a point. "So what?"

"The deadlands are shaped by expectation, but there are two of us and our faiths don't agree." He lets go of me. "We were in Hel's domain, where she rules over all that is dead. But—"

"But?"

"Now I think we've strayed into your Hell."

"Oh God."

". . . *thou shalt not take the Lord's name in vain* . . ." Bishop James's voice, though my father's second had never sounded quite so much like he wanted to peel my face off.

The underworld that Snorri's twin-aspected goddess, Hel, rules over is a pretty horrendous place, but I have the feeling that my Hell of fire and brimstone, replete with sinners and with devils to roast them, might outdo it for nastiness.

"Let's get back." I turn around and start to retread our path. "How did we even end up here? You're the believer."

" . . . *unbeliever, unbeliever, burn the unbeliever—*"

"I mean you're the one with the strongest faith."

". . . *faithless, faithless, harrow the faithless—*"

"Not that my faith isn't really strong too, praise Jesus!" I cross myself, Father, Son, and Holy Ghost, and not that half-hearted wave of the hand that Father does but the deliberate and precise action that Bishop James employs.

"It might not be you, Jal." Snorri's hand on my shoulder again, arresting my motion. I glance back and he nods ahead.

Something flits across the gap between two of the larger boulders scattered across the valley floor. I catch only the edge of a glimpse—something thin and pale—something bad.

"This is our enemy's Hell. He's brought it with him on the hunt." Snorri has his axe in his hands now.

"But, nobody knows we're here . . ." I put my hand to the key, lying beneath my jerkin, just above my heart. Suddenly it feels heavy. Heavy and colder than ice. "The Dead King?"

"It might be." Snorri rolls his shoulders, blue eyes almost black in the deadlight and fixed upon the rock the creature has vanished behind. "If he's somehow been alerted to our presence he could just want revenge for us keeping the key from him."

"About that . . ."

The creature steals any further conversation, emerging from the shadows at the rock's base and starting to run toward us with appalling speed. It drives forward on bone-thin legs, the power of each thrust veering it to one side, only to be corrected by the next so that it threads an erratic path through the boulder-field, weaving around them and leaving the stone faces screaming their horror in its wake. The thing puts me in mind of the white threads you'll see in the muscle of a man laid open by a sword blow. Nerves, one of my tutors called them, pointing to the nightmarish drawings in some ancient tome on anatomy. It looks like a nerve: white, thin, long, dividing into limbs which in turn divide into three root-like fingers, its head an eyeless wedge, sharp enough to bury itself in a man.

"Lichkin." Snorri names the beast and takes three paces toward it, timing his swing. He roars as the head of his axe tears through the air, muscles bunching as they drive it forward. The lichkin blurs beneath the blow, surging up to catch Snorri by the neck, the other hand on his stomach, lifting him high off the ground and slamming him down with a sick-making crunch. Dust billows up around the impact and I can't see how he landed, though with so many boulders around it's unlikely to be well.

"Shit." At last I remember to draw my sword. It sings out of the scabbard, the deadlight burning along the runes that mark its length. My hand is shaking.

Snorri's axe rises, unsteady amid the billowing dust, and the lichkin snatches it, continuing the motion to bring it round and down in a circle that buries the blade roughly where I expect Snorri's head to be. The impact is dull and final. I can just make out the axe handle, pointing up unsupported as the lichkin abandons it and stalks toward me, the dust still rising smoke-like about it. Terror comes off the thing like heat off a fire.

"Oh crap." I thrust my off hand down the neck of my jerkin and bring out Loki's key. "Look, you can have it, just let me—"

The lichkin charges and it's so fast I think I must have been frozen in place. One moment it's there at the edge of the dust cloud and the next it has one hand wrapped around my throat and the other around the wrist of my sword arm. The thing's touch is foul beyond imagining. Its white flesh joins mine, seeming to merge. It feels as if innumerable roots are sinking into me, burrowing between veins, each afire with an acidic agony that leaves no space even for screaming.

I'm held, useless and immobile while that white wedge of a face inspects me and all I can do is beg to die, unable to get the words past a jaw locked so tight that I expect my teeth to break in the next moment, to just shatter all in one go.

The lichkin's head tilts down toward Loki's key, held between us, pointing forward, my arm rigid and paralysed.

I glimpse some large and smoking object, past the lichkin's head, rushing toward us. At the last moment I see it's Snorri, dust rising from him with each pounding step. He's empty-handed, as if he thinks to tear the creature apart by main force. The lichkin turns, faster than thought, and catches him by the shoulders. Despite its thinness the lichkin is rooted to the ground and absorbs all the momentum of the Viking's charge, needing just a single sharp step backwards.

I stand, still frozen in the moment. Edris Dean's sword has fallen from the hand the lichkin released but not yet hit the ground. My eyes follow its progress and see that in stepping back the lichkin has driven itself against the black shaft of Loki's key, the head of which has pushed an inch into the white flesh.

All I can do is turn it.

And as the key turns the blackness of it invades the lichkin's alabaster, darting along its length in ebony threads, each in turn forking and branching, staining, corrupting. Gravity reaches for me and I'm falling, pulling the key clear, but even as I hit the ground and the dust rises all around, I see the lichkin start to come undone, as if it were a thousand strands, a thousand thin white tubes, now grey and putrefying, each peeling apart from the next, the whole thing opening, spreading, falling.

"Vermillion!" A banging on the carriage roof, the rough voice of whatever lout currently had the reins. I sat up with a jerk, soaked in sweat.

"Oh thank Christ!" Shudders ran through me. I looked at my wrist, expecting to see the scald mark of the lichkin's hand still there. Lisa gave a sleepy murmur, face hidden by her hair, head in my lap. The old priest, Father Agor, narrowed pale eyes at me in disapproval.

"Did he say Vermillion?" I raised the shade and peered out, squinting against the brightness. The suburbs of Vermillion bumped past. "At last!"

"We're there?" Lisa, blinking, face creased where she lay on me, strands of hair stuck in the corner of her mouth.

"We're here!" My grin so broad it hurt my face.

Lisa gripped my hand and smiled back, and suddenly all was right in the world. At least until I remembered Maeres Allus.

Minutes later Lisa and I disembarked outside the courthouse on Gholloth Square and stood stiff and stretching, looking around with disbelief. Father Agor tossed a coin to a porter who received his luggage from atop the carriage and set off after the priest, a case under each arm. Our silent merchant friend departed, a boy with a mule carrying his trunk, leaving Lisa and me alone on a crowded street as the carriage rattled off to whatever stables would receive it.

On my journey south with Snorri I'd spent much of my waking day planning and anticipating my return to Vermillion. Travelling with Lisa, I had hardly spoken a word on the subject—perhaps fearing to jinx it, or unbelieving that after all I had endured our home would be waiting there to take us in once more as if nothing had changed. But here it was, busy, hot, wrapped around its own concerns and indifferent to our arrival. A large number of troops had been assembled on Adam Plaza, their supplies heaped against the side of the war academy.

"Will you take me home, Jal?" Lisa turned from the street and looked up at me.

"Best not. I've met your eldest brother, and he doesn't like me." Lord Gregori would have sliced me up himself if I hadn't hidden behind my rank and made him goad Count Isen into doing the job for him.

"I live at the palace now, Jal." She looked at her feet, head down.

"Oh." I'd forgotten. She had meant the rooms in the Great Jon's apartment in the guest wing. The ones she had shared with her husband. "I can't. I've got something really important I need to do straight away."

She looked up then, disappointed.

"Look." I waved my hands as if there were something to look at that might actually explain it. "You don't want me there. Not when you meet with Barras. And you'll hardly come to grief between here and the palace gates." She kept those big eyes on me, saying nothing.

"*I* would have married you, you know!" The words took me by surprise but they were out now and words can't be unsaid. Instead they hang between you, awkward and uncomfortable.

"You're not the marrying type, Jal." A tilt of the head, surprise touching her face.

"I could be!" Maybe I could. "You were . . . special . . . Lisa. We had a good thing."

She smiled, making me want her all the more. "Mine wasn't the only balcony you climbed, Jal. Not even within my father's grounds." She took my hands. "Women like to have their fun too, you know. Especially women born to families like mine, who know they're going to be married for their father's convenience rather than by their own choice."

"Your father would have jumped at the chance of a prince for one of his daughters!"

Lisa gave my hands a squeeze. "Our brother did jump at the chance."

"Darin." His name tasted sour. The elder brother. The one not to be seen staggering drunkenly from bordellos in the predawn grey, or gambling away other men's money. The one not past his eyes in debt to underworld criminals.

Suddenly I couldn't stand her kindness a moment longer. "Look. I've got this matter to attend to. It can't wait. I really have to do this. And—" I rummaged in my jacket's inner pocket. "I need your help." I withdrew Loki's key, wrapped inside a thick velvet cloth bound tight with cord. "Keep this for me. Don't open it. For God's sake don't touch it. Don't show it to anyone." I folded her hands about the package. "If I don't come to the palace within a day present it to the Red Queen and tell her it's from me. Can you do that? It's important." She nodded and I released her hands. And somehow, although that key was by far the single most valuable thing in the kingdom of Red March, something I had fought and bled for, literally walked across Hell to keep, I felt no pang at letting Lisa DeVeer take it. Only a sense of peace.

"You're scaring me, Jal."

"I've got to go and see Maeres Allus. I owe him a lot of money."

"Maeres Allus?" A frown.

I remembered that to most of my circle Allus was a merchant, a rich one to be sure, but nothing more, and who has time to remember the names of merchants? "A dangerous man."

"Well . . . you should pay him." She took my hand in both of hers. "And be careful."

The old Lisa might have laughed and told me to tell this Maeres fellow to wait—and if he had the temerity to lay a hand upon me, to draw my sword and have at him. The new Lisa was much better acquainted with the realities of swords meeting flesh. The new Lisa wanted me to swallow my pride and pay the man. There was a Jalan once who would have advised swinging the sword too—but that Jalan was eight and he and I had been strangers for many years.

I took myself first to the Guild of Trade, a great dome that may be entered by many archways about its circumference. Beneath the dome on a wide mosaicked floor merchants of a certain degree of wealth gather to make deals and swap the gossip that oils industry's wheels. A gallery runs around the dome, several storeys above the trade floor, and from it doors lead to offices that look out over the surrounding city.

I borrowed money on the trade floor first. I borrowed against my family name, leaving Edris Dean's sword as additional security—whatever evils tainted it nobody could deny the quality of the steel, ancient stuff melted down from Builder ruins: no smith today has the skill to match its strength. Whether word of my incarceration for debt in Umbertide had reached Vermillion yet I didn't enquire, but it seemed unlikely given that I walked out of the Guild with fifty pieces of crown gold.

With those monies and the remains of Omar's Liban bars I purchased clothing of sufficient quality to match my station, along with a blood-gold chain, a ruby ring, and a diamond ear stud. The garments had to be tailored to my build rapidly, adjusted from the dimensions of their intended recipients, but I paid handsomely enough and forgave any failings in the cut.

To borrow a lot of money you have to look the part. A king in rags will win no credit no matter what collateral he may own.

Penniless again, I climbed the stair to the gallery where Vermillion's richest moneylenders plied their trade. Maeres Allus would never be permitted an office in this circle, though he had the coin to sit among such men. Old money ruled here, merchant dynasties of good repute and long ties to the crown. I chose to approach Silas Marn, a merchant prince that Great-uncle Garyus had given good opinion of over the years.

The men at the door carried my petition inside and Silas had the manners not to keep me waiting. He saw me in person in his interview chamber, a vaulted room, marble-clad, with the busts of various long-dead Marns watching us from alcoves.

The old man, so ancient as to be practically creaking, rose from his chair as I entered, burdened by his velvet robes. I motioned for him to sit and he gave up on the effort before managing to fully straighten himself.

"Thank you for seeing me on such short notice." I took the seat he gestured to and we sat opposite each other across a span of gleaming mahogany.

"I would hardly turn away a prince of the realm, Prince Jalan." Silas Marn regarded me from murky brown eyes almost lost in the many folds of his face, his skin leathery and stained with age. I gave him a broad smile and he returned a more cautious one. Large ears and beak-like nose dominated his small head, though those seem to be the fate of any man who lives too long. "How may I help you?"

I pushed the relevant documentation across the desk. The crumpled parchment looked in no better state than old Silas, as stained and creased, the writing barely legible, the wax seal cracked.

"It looks like it's been through hell." Silas made no move to pick it up. "What is it?"

"Deeds to thirteen twenty-fourth shares in the Crptipa salt-mine."

"I am aware of your . . . misfortunes in Umbertide, Prince Jalan. There have been charges laid against you of a very serious nature. A murderer of children would find it easier to get credit than a bankrupt charged with multiple counts of fraud. I am sure that these charges hold no substance, of course, but the mere fact of them is a terrible impediment to—"

"I'm not seeking credit. I wish to sell. The Crptipa mine holds vast reserves of salt immediately adjacent to some of the largest markets and ports in the Broken Empire. It has the infrastructure in place to ramp up production now that the departure of Kelem has opened for exploitation areas that have for centuries been off-limits. Production from the mine could undercut the imported supply while still generating considerable profit on each ton. As a debtor I'm at liberty to conduct business in order to generate funds to cover my obligations."

Silas laid a withered hand across the deed of sale. "I see that your great-uncle's blood is not wholly absent from your veins, Prince Jalan."

I felt a pang of guilt then. "Is he all right? I mean . . . three ships . . ."

Those old eyes narrowed in disapproval, dry lips a thin line. The merchant watched me for a moment then relaxed into the smallest smile. "It would take more than three ships to put much of a hole in your uncle's concerns. Even so—and with the greatest of respect—it was not well done to lose them."

"How much will you give me?" I tapped the table.

"Direct." Silas's smile broadened. "Perhaps you think a man of my years doesn't have time to beat around the bush?"

"Make me an offer. The place is worth a hundred thousand."

"I am aware of its value. The mines have been the subject of considerable speculation. The legalities of your claim however would take some considerable clearing up though and run the attendant risk that Umbertide's duke might rule your assets forfeit given your unlicensed departure. I will give you ten thousand. Consider it a favour to your family."

"Give me five thousand, but allow me to buy it back for ten thousand within the month."

The old man tilted his head, as if listening to the advice of some invisible counsellor. "Agreed."

"And I need to walk away with the gold within the hour."

That raised his white eyebrows some considerable distance. "Can a man even carry five thousand in gold?"

"I've done it before. Your arms ache the next day."

And so it was that an hour later I left, carrying a small but extremely heavy coffer clutched to my chest. It took half a dozen senior underlings scuttling about beneath the dome of the Guild of Trade, calling in favours left and right, but Silas assembled the necessary coinage, and I handed over my controlling interest in the Broken Empire's richest salt-mine.

I walked through main streets, wishing I'd taken Silas up on his offer of a porter, whilst at the same time still agreeing with my own argument that nobody should miss the opportunity to carry that much gold. My passage drew a few looks, but nobody would be foolish enough to think I would carry such riches unguarded, and even knowing it few would be foolish enough to try to rob me in the broad thoroughfares at the heart of the city. In any event my new outfit came with a small knife in an inner pocket just above the wrist, ready for quick release to stab any thieving hands.

By the time I reached the great slaughterhouse a third of a mile from the Guild of Trade headquarters my arms felt twice their usual length and made of jelly. I stared up at the impressive edifice. It seemed a lifetime since I had last been inside. Just over a year by calendar reckoning. Two thousand miles and more by foot. Once a slaughterhouse for cattle, beef for the royal tables, and now a place where men carved man-flesh, the Blood Holes were one of Maeres Allus's more popular haunts.

The bruisers on the door let me in without question. Rich men came every day to watch poor men die and bet on the outcome. The elder Terrif brother, Deckmon, he recognized me sure enough, looking up from his cash table. He put a finger to the skin beneath his left eye and pulled it down, letting me know my entrance had been marked.

The usual crowd circulated around the four big pits, the numbers men at the margins with the odds chalked above their stalls. I took a moment to breathe it in, the colour, the noise, the aristocrats dogged by their toadies, a loose halo of hangers on, and moving here and there, wine-men, poppy-men, ladies of negotiable affection.

The stink of blood ran through it all, an undercurrent. I'd not noticed it in those years I spent here, betting on carnage. The smell brought back memories, not of the Blood Holes but of the Aral Pass and the Black Fort. For a moment I felt the icy waters of the Slidr enfold me and the red berserker heat rise to meet it.

I crossed over to Long Will, a trainer and talent scout, a thin strip of a man, crowned by a grey shock of hair. "Maeres here?"

Long Will jerked his head toward Ochre. Of the four big pits it lay farthest from the main doors. I eased my way through the crowd, sweating, and not just from the strain of carrying my treasure. The thought of Maeres Allus put a chill in me, making my legs feel as weak as my trembling arms—though an unexpected anger came with that fear, a rising heat that had been there beneath the terror, keeping me company all the long and rattling ride up from Marsail.

A pretty girl trailed her fingers through my hair, an oily wine-man thrust a pewter goblet at me. I glanced pointedly at the coffer occupying both my hands.

"Prince Jalan?" Someone recognizing me, unsure.

"Is that Jalan?" A fat baron from the south. "Damned if it is."

Underlings parted before me as I approached the tight knot of colour at the edge of Ochre. More than a year. Thousands of miles. Icy wastes to baking desert. I walked through Hell . . . and here I was again, back where it started. Fourteen months and they hardly knew me, here in the place where I'd spent so much time, and money, and other men's blood.

A murmur grew about me now: even if the crowd weren't sure of my name they recognized a man walking with intent toward the heart of things. The last few layers peeled back, men I knew by sight and name, Maeres's associates, merchants in his pockets, minor lords courting loans or being courted for this or that advantage. The business of business while twenty feet below, two men fought, each doing his level best to beat the other to death with his fists.

Two narrow-faced Slovs stepped aside, and there, revealed between them, stood Maeres Allus, small, olive-skinned, his tunic unostentatious—to look at him you wouldn't think he owned the place and much more besides. He registered neither surprise nor interest at my appearance.

"Prince Jalan, you've been away too long." A roar of triumph rose from the pit behind him, but nobody seemed interested any more. I imagined the victorious brawler looking up, expecting cheering faces, and seeing nothing but the wooden guardrail and the back of the occasional head.

Jorg Ancrath, that prodigy about whom so many prophecies seemed to circulate, that vicious and victorious youth on whom my grandmother's plans appeared to pivot, the young king who lit a Builders' Sun in Gelleth and another on the doorstep of Hamada . . . he had given me his advice on dealing with Maeres Allus. He had spoken his words in the hot and drunken darkness of a Hamadan night, and now, with Allus before me at long last, those forgotten words started to bubble from the black depths of my memory. "I've come to settle our business, Maeres. Perhaps we could go somewhere private." I gestured with my eyes to the curtained alcoves where all manner of Blood Holes negotiations were conducted, from the carnal to the commercial, not that the former wasn't the latter.

Maeres's dark eyes rested on the coffer in my arms. "I think perhaps too much of our business has taken place behind closed doors, Prince Jalan. Let us settle our accounts here."

"Maeres, it's hardly suitable—"

"Here." A command. He meant to humble me before witnesses.

"I really don't—"

"Here!" Barked this time. I don't recall Maeres Allus ever raising his voice before that. He glanced over his shoulder down into the pit. "A poor fight. Put the bear in."

If there were any people in the Blood Holes so taken with their own affairs that they weren't already staring in my direction then the mention of the bear soon changed that. A ripple ran through the crowds and as one they began to flow toward Ochre, drawn by the fighter's shouts for mercy and by the prospect of seeing him get none.

Maeres didn't turn to watch the spectacle, keeping his eyes on me instead. We stood there like that with the throng around us baying for blood, their voices competing first with the man's screaming and then with the grisly noise of the bear rending its meal.

"You had business to conduct, Prince Jalan?" Maeres cocked his head, inviting my reply. Two of his enforcers stood at my shoulders now, hard men who had survived the pits to climb to their current positions.

"I've come to settle my debts, Maeres. I borrowed in good faith and gave my word to repay in full. My father is the Red Queen's son and I don't give my promise lightly." I layered on the bravado. If I were going to spend thousands in gold I should at least enjoy the moment. "Remind me how much is due."

Maeres put out his hand and a hulking fellow in black placed a slate into his palm. I knew the man for Maeres's bookkeeper though with those big sausage fingers of his he looked better suited to wrestling trolls than pushing numbers around. "The debt stands at three thousand and eleven in crown gold." A sharp intake of breath ran through the onlookers, perhaps even the building itself sucked in its walls at such a figure. Many there would have difficulty imagining so large a sum, and none of the gentry were so rich that the loss of three thousand wouldn't hurt them.

Three thousand exceeded what I'd borrowed from Maeres by some considerable margin. Even with months of interest. I suspected I was being charged for the services of the men he sent after me, Alber Marks, Cutter John, and the Slov brothers who were tasked with returning me to the city for a secret and gruesome death. With a grunt of effort I supported the coffer with one aching arm and flipped open the lid with the other. "If you could have your man count out the required amount." I stepped forward so that the coffer almost reached Maeres, level with his head, the coins' glow lighting his face.

It took a while but each scoop of the bookkeeper's shovel-like hands lightened my load. He weighed the coins in his scales, calling the tallies aloud then spilling the gleaming heap into a leather sack. He quickly sent for two more, realizing that the one he had would prove too small to receive my payment.

"One thousand."

While the bookkeeper scooped and weighed, weighed and scooped, Maeres kept his gaze on me, eyes dark and unreadable. The madness I'd seen in them that day in his poppy halls lay hidden now.

"The repayment of a loan is always welcome—but tell me, what prompted this change of heart, from a man so keen to borrow to a man so keen to pay?"

"Two thousand." The bookkeeper tied off a second sack.

I stared back. Was Maeres inviting me to advertise his methods? Daring me? This killer with his vile tastes, murdering within the walls of Vermillion, dining so close to the palace that the shadows of its towers might brush against his mansion, richer than many a lord, making his own laws and dishing out his own justice. "I met a king and sought his advice."

"And he advised you to pay me?"

I thought of my meeting with Jorg Ancrath. When I had spoken of my problem he grew quiet at first, then serious as if not a drop had passed his lips all night. "He said to give you what you want." I set the coffer down between us and rubbed my arms.

"A wise king indeed."

"Three thousand." The bookkeeper tied off the last sack, then bent over the coffer once more and started to count out the last eleven coins.

"You seem a changed man, Prince Jalan. I do hope your travels in the remnants of our once great empire haven't soured you?"

"Six . . . seven . . . eight." The bookkeeper placed the coins into a pocket of his leather apron.

"I've been through Hell, Maeres."

"The roads *can* be dangerous." He nodded. "Still, I'm sure we'll see the old prince return, such a happy young man, so sure of his opinion, so ready to spend."

"Nine . . . ten . . ."

"I hope so too—but for now the prince you see before you will have to serve." I remembered how it felt to be tied to his table—the look on his face as he turned me over to Cutter John—how I'd shouted and begged. Snorri had mistaken that for bravery.

"Eleven." The bookkeeper straightened up, seeming reluctant to leave the coffer with gold still obscuring the bottom. "The debt is covered."

"Well and good." Maeres's smile told me he knew that despite the chains of debt being cast off he owned me now, more truly than he ever had before. A chill ran through me, the cold challenge of the Slidr, and the red heat that had seen me across the sharpest river in Hell now rose to burn away that chill. I remembered all the boy-king's words.

"Jorg Ancrath told me, 'Give him what he wants.'" I stepped forward, bending to recover my coffer.

"One more thing, Prince Jalan." Maeres's voice, arresting me as I bent before him. A cold hand closed around my heart and I knew there was only Jorg's path open to me.

"He said you would say that." I remembered all of it. I remembered the darkness, the heat, Jorg Ancrath's prediction: "When you've given, he will ask for more. Just one more thing, he'll say." And I remembered the look in the boy-king's eyes.

"He said, give him what he wants." I straightened, quick and smooth, without touching the box. "Then take what *you* want." A flick of my wrist brushed the back of my hand across Maeres's neck. The small triangular knife, once concealed in my sleeve, and now with its blade jutting between my fingers, slit his throat. I hardly felt it.

I caught him around the back of the head and held him close, spraying crimson and trying to speak. I had it done before any of his men even knew what had happened.

"I am the Red Queen's grandson." I roared the words out into the silence. "Maeres Allus is dead. His life was mine to take. There's nothing left to protect here." Hot blood soaked my chest while I clasped Allus against me, lifting my chin as one of his arms reached up weakly, scrabbling at my face. "I don't care how his assets are divided, but lift a hand against me and by God you will lose it."

The crowd had drawn back from us, aghast, as if the violence they looked down upon each day twenty foot below the level of their shoes was something different, a pretence perhaps, but a man in a well-tailored tunic bleeding among them was all too real and made them blanch and cringe.

Allus's guards had stepped away too. Their charge was dead, his heart would realize it in short order. They had nothing to gain by coming against me now. It had ended for them the moment I slit their boss's throat.

I pushed Allus away from me. He staggered back, pulsing crimson from his neck wound, fetching up against the wooden barricade. I followed and shoved him, two hands rammed hard into his chest. He went heels over head, plummeting backwards across the barrier. I peered after him. "Is the bear big enough for you?" Shouted at a volume that would reach the whole crowd, though Maeres himself was beyond hearing.

I spun around and picked up my coffer. I could see some of Allus's flunkies slipping away through various exits. The bookkeeper was clutching a wound in his side and the three sacks had vanished. Scuffles had broken out further back in the crowd. Half a dozen of the Terrif brothers' guards were closing in on me.

"He's dead!" I roared it at them. "I'm a fucking prince of the realm. Are you going to touch me?" I stalked past the first of them, paying him no heed. "Thought not!" I walked on, letting the onlookers part before me.

Just before the entrance I turned back. Several bloody fights were in progress and the richer elements had already started to flee the scene.

I used my royal shout to be heard. "My grandmother's troops will be burning the poppies by nightfall. Death warrants will be issued for Allus's captains. I expect to see Alber Marks's head on a spike by morning, Cutter John's too, and there will be leniency for any man who helped put them there."

I turned and left, exiting the main doors, with some of the lords who had wondered about my identity now sprinting ahead into the street, many others crowding behind me. I heard the mutter then, for the first time. "Red Prince." And looking down at myself as I stepped into the light of day I saw that few parts of me weren't crimson with Maeres Allus's lifeblood.

I walked twenty paces and leaned against one of the great buttresses that support the slaughterhouse walls, forehead to the stonework, cool in the shade. I saw my knife cut Allus's throat, again and again. On the third time I vomited until I was empty. At last I walked away, weak and shaking, wiping my mouth.

"Give him what he wants," Jorg had said. "Then take what you want. Nobody is more vulnerable than in their moment of victory, and you know that whatever you do this man will never let you go while he lives."

I walked away, coffer heavy in my arms, still a coward. Neither the old Jalan, nor the one who left Vermillion a year ago. Perhaps a little of each—still a coward, but when you've looked at your old life with eyes that have seen Hell you discover a new perspective and realize that you can only be pushed so far.

EIGHT

I walked to the palace. Three times city guards stopped me, concerned at the gore dripping from my finery.

"I'm Prince Jalan. A man tried to rob me. He won't try again." I said the same thing three times and passed on.

I met more soldiers than guards, units of them moving rapidly and offering me no more than curious glances. At last I came to the Errik Gate through which heroes enter the palace, and took instead the postern gate just as I had on my return from the North. The sub-captain on duty recognized me and admitted me without fuss once he'd established the blood wasn't mine.

On the far side of the wall the palace waited, unchanged, baking in the late Vermillion summer. "What's going on in the city?" I asked the sub-captain as I emerged. "Soldiers everywhere." It had been like this before we moved out for the Scorron border. That had been war in earnest and there hadn't been as many troops in the streets.

"It's a campaign against Slov, my prince."

"Why?" I cared little enough for politics but I was pretty sure Slov hadn't offered Red March even a hint of aggression in my lifetime. I seemed to remember half their royal family were honoured guests of the March, hostages against the good behaviour of the current regime— though quite how much the current Slov royals would care about people they hadn't seen in decades I didn't know. "What have they done?"

The man wrinkled his brow as if the act might produce an answer. "They're the enemy, sire."

"By definition if we're attacking them. But why are they the enemy?"

Again the frown, but this time relaxing into a smile as he remembered the fact he'd been hunting. "Harbouring a person of interest."

"Who?"

"I don't know, Prince Jalan."

"You're dismissed, sub-captain."

"But, my prince. We should escort—"

"I made it here from the deserts of Afrique, sub-captain. I should be able to negotiate the next three hundred yards in my own home without mishap."

The first two hundred and ninety yards went well. It was approaching the front steps of the Roma Hall that I ran into difficulty.

"Jalan? By Christ!" An angry roar from behind me. "It *is* you! Where the hell have you been you bankrupt little weasel?"

I paused. My big brother Martus. A man I'd not had to endure since that audience in the throne room the day I first laid eyes on Snorri. I made a slow turn and found myself in Martus's shadow as he loomed over me.

"Killing people, brother." I met his gaze squarely.

It took a moment for the words to sink in, another for him to take in the crimson state of me, one more for him to put the two together and take a sharp step back. "Dear God . . ."

"My debts have been paid in full." I turned back and walked on up into the house.

Not strictly true but the arm-aching weight of gold remaining in the coffer I held before me would pay off the various wine merchants, tailors, and bawdy houses still holding my credit notes. It would be good to be free of the burden.

I won't say the Roma Hall seemed small, because set against the places I'd been laying my head of late it was huge—but somehow it felt smaller than my memories of it. Fat Ned and young Double stood on guard at the front door, the former blanching at my approach and shaking so much the loose folds of his skin jiggled around his old bones.

"It's Prince Jalan, Ned." Double elbowed the old man, his dark eyes taking in more than just the gore drying across me. He bowed, the black locks of his hair falling across his face, eyes still studying me from behind this veil.

I favoured them with a brief nod and pushed on through, Fat Ned still gaping at me.

A couple of servants in the entrance hall ran off screaming murder, but Ballessa stood her ground, her expression disapproval and concern in equal measures.

"No errant peasant boys to take care of this time, Ballessa. Clean clothes will suffice."

A frown at the memory of Hennan's brief stay, then Ballessa gave a nod, rotated her matronly bulk, and set off down the corridor to order up a bath and fetch a collection of suitable garments from my wardrobes.

I washed off the blood and left the water pink, the last of Maeres Allus swirling around, diluted, sluiced away, and beneath it Jalan Kendeth, clean and without stain. I'd killed a man with intent, done it in cold blood, or as cold as any human's blood can be at such a moment. An evil son of a bitch, true enough, but it didn't feel good, it didn't feel right. No part of me felt the hero. I called for more water and washed again— though water will only take the stains you can see.

The clothes Ballessa brought still fitted me. They wrapped me, comfortable, familiar, rich, a second skin that completed my disguise—I stood before the mirror and Prince Jalan stared back at me, surprised. I looked the part, every inch of me, and every inch felt the impostor. Every step of my journey had taken me further from home, no matter the direction I took, and now, standing in my father's house, I was further away than I'd ever been.

I made to turn away and in the last moment caught a flash of blue that drew my gaze back to the mirror, staring past myself into the room behind, the doorways, the windows, the shadows. There'd been a flicker of motion. I was sure of it. I wanted to whirl around and check that nobody stood at my back. Instead I stood there, without motion, studying the reflected room, hunting it, looking for that blue.

Finally I turned the mirror to the wall then did the same for the three others hung in my rooms. I hadn't forgotten about the Lady Blue and much as I wanted her to forget about me that was unlikely to happen. She and Grandmother still had their war—and when the Red Queen crushed the witch the loudest cheer would come from me. She had the blood of my great-grandfather on her hands, a crime I could perhaps overlook, but the blood of my unborn sister, and the blood of my friend, Tuttugu, could not be washed away. Part of me, more than a small part, the pieces still burning with the memory of taking Maeres Allus's corrupted life, wanted to be the one to stick the knife into the Lady Blue, and twist it.

An hour later I stepped from the Roma Hall, fresh and clean, wearing my old clothes and my old smile. I doubted there'd be much to mark me from the Jalan who sneaked back from the DeVeer mansion at dawn on the day of the opera, though it felt like half a lifetime ago.

Walking away from my old home I felt a curious sensation of being watched. Not the adoration or curiosity a returning hero might expect but a crawling sensation on the back of my neck, as if I were the object of a close and cold scrutiny. Feeling distinctly uncomfortable, I picked up my pace and crossed the courtyard with a brisk stride.

I went to the palace. Not Grandmother's main doors, but to the guest wing, up the stairs to the Great Jon's suite. The guards at the ground floor informed me Barras still occupied the rooms, presumably now the headquarters for the search for his misplaced wife.

Knocking on the door I found my heart pounding harder than it had in the Blood Holes in the moment I realized I had murder on my mind.

"Good afternoon, sir." A short doorman, immaculately groomed, offered me his bow. "Who may I say is calling?"

"Jalan?" Lisa's voice calling from somewhere off the reception hall. She came running, holding her skirts at both hips to keep from tripping. Barras nearly as fast behind her, pale, dark lines beneath both eyes.

"Jalan . . ." Lisa pulled up short of throwing herself into my arms, hands going to her face as if I were still wearing all the gore I arrived at the palace with. "Are you . . ." She studied my face, leaving me wondering if perhaps I had changed rather more than I suspected.

"Jal!" Barras showed no such hesitation and threw himself into my arms with no pretence at a manly hug. "Jal! Thank you, Jal! Thank you!"

"Steady on!" I waited for a loosening of his grip then slipped free. "The bad news is you owe me two camels—" I caught Lisa's look of outrage. "Three! Three camels. Good ones!"

"Same old Jal!" Barras laughed, punching my shoulder.

"No, really. I'm not jo—"

"Thank you!" And he was back to the hugging.

When I finally untangled myself it seemed as if the moment to ask for my camels' worth had passed. Barras stood, running his hands back across the short brown shock of his hair and looking in happy amazement from me to Lisa and back again. "We have to celebrate . . . A feast!"

"I've been on the road too long to turn down a feast." I held up a hand to forestall him. "But right now I have an urgent meeting with our monarch." I looked to Lisa, lovely in her powders and jewels now, though I liked her looks just as much out in the wilds. "Do you have the package I gave you for safe-keeping?"

Barras looked confused and raised the tempo of his Jalan-Lisa-Jalan watching. Lisa nodded and pulled the velvet-wrapped key from some pocket artfully concealed in her skirts. She handed it over without even a twinge of hesitation, which meant something to me. I think perhaps it's not a key you can give to someone who isn't your friend without at least some measure of regret.

"Thank you." And I meant it. "Keep the feast warm for me." I slapped a hand to Barras's shoulder, finding it hard to hate him any more. "I'll come along later, if I can still walk when the Red Queen's finished with me."

"What have you done?"

But I was already striding away. "Later!"

Grandmother's court was not in session when I arrived beneath the great doors to her palace. Two lords, Grast and Gren, stood waiting on the steps along with a solid, dark-haired knight with an impressive moustache—Sir Roger, I thought. All three favoured me with dark looks. I don't think they recognized me but I had bad blood with Lord Grast's older brother, the duke, so I ignored the trio and went on up without a word.

Before the queen's doors the same plumed giant who had admitted me on my return from the North—or perhaps his cousin—tilted his head down at me and said he would see my request for audience carried to my grandmother.

I sat in the shade of one of the great portico columns and waited, watching the elite guardsmen swelter in their fire-bronze on the sun-drenched steps. The courtyard before us lay wide and empty, as blank as my future. I wasn't sure even what the night might bring. Could I really stand to watch Barras and Lisa's reunion? I briefly considered calling in on my father, but Ballessa informed me that the cardinal had taken to his bed a week earlier. Ill, she said. Ill on wine I suspected . . .

The door behind me slammed and turning I saw Uncle Hertet pushing aside the guardsman although the man had already stepped sharply out of his way. Lord Grast and Lord Gren were quickly by his side as the heir-apparent, or as he was more commonly known: the heir-apparently-not, stormed toward the steps.

"If she wasn't my mother . . ." Hertet smacked his fist into his palm. It might have looked menacing if he weren't a rather paunchy man of modest build in his fifties, gone to grey. His mother I was sure could still put him over her knee and deliver the soundest of spankings. Not to mention fell him with a punch that would leave few teeth for his dotage. "This city needs a king, not a damned steward. And it needs a king who will stay here and do his duty by it, not swan off on some wild expedition. These are troubled times, boys, troubled times. A queen who leaves her throne empty in troubled times is practically abdicating—" My uncle spotted me lounging in the shade. "You! One of Reymond's boys?" He pointed a ringed finger my way as if being his brother's son were an accusation.

"I—"

"Martus? Darin? Damned if I can tell you apart. All of you the same, and none of you like your father." Hertet went past me, flanked by the two lords with Sir Roger at his heels. "Still, what did Reymond expect ploughing such a foreign field? He wasn't the only plough, that's for sure." His voice carried back across the courtyard as he walked away, trailing off as the distance grew. "They can't help it, these Indus girls . . ."

I found myself on my feet, having got there swiftly and without conscious decision. My hand had found the hilt of my knife. The tide of angry words rising to defend my mother's honour had yet to leave my mouth only because they were still battling to organize a coherent sentence.

"Prince Jalan."

I looked up. The overly large guardsman loomed over me.

"The queen will see you now."

I shot a scowl at the retreating backs of Hertet and his cronies—one that in a just world would have lit them up like torches—and brushed myself down. You don't keep the Red Queen waiting.

Four guardsmen escorted me into the empty throne room, gloomy despite the day blazing through high windows, striated by their bars. Lamps burned around the dais and Grandmother sat ensconced in Red March's highest chair. Two of her advisors stood further back in the shadows, Marth, wide and solid, Willow, whip-thin and sour. Of the Silent Sister, no sign.

"You've changed, Grandson." Grandmother's regard could pin a man to the floor. I felt the weight of it settle on me. Even so I had time to be surprised by her acknowledgement of our relationship. "The boy who set out has not returned. Where did you lose him?"

"Some wayside tavern, highness." In Hell was the true answer but no part of me wanted to talk about that.

"And you have something to report, Jalan? I'm sure you didn't request an audience before the throne without good cause. Your northern friends eluded my soldiers. Perhaps you encountered them again on your travels?"

I glanced left and right, seeking the Silent Sister. Did Grandmother already know exactly what I'd been up to from the moment I left the city? Had my great-aunt's silence revealed it as prophecy before the march of days turned it into my personal history?

"I found them. I recovered the key. I returned it to Vermillion."

The Red Queen left her chair with remarkable speed for an old woman. Standing on the dais with the spars of her collar fanning out above her head she towered over me. Even toe to toe in our stockinged feet she would have overtopped me, and few men can say the same.

"You've done well, Jalan." She hadn't a mouth for smiles but she showed her teeth in a reasonable approximation. She stepped down and was before me in three paces. "Very well indeed."

I noticed her hand in the space between us, held out, palm up. The same hand I had seen wrapped around a crimson sword in my dreams of Ameroth. "I . . . uh . . . don't have it now." I took a quick step back, sweat running down my neck all of a sudden.

"What?" As short and cold a word as I ever heard uttered.

"I—it's not . . ."

"You left it somewhere?" Her eyebrows lifted a remarkable distance. "There's no safe place—" She glanced about and waved at the guardsmen around the walls, all hand to hilt. "Quick, all of you. Get to the Roma Hall and escort Prince Jalan back with the—"

"I gave it to Great-uncle Garyus," I said. "Your highness."

Grandmother raised both arms, one to each side, palms out, and every man in the throne room stopped moving, guards halfway to me now frozen in their tracks. "What?" I swear she could stab someone to death with that word.

I clenched my teeth and gathered my courage. "I gave it to my great-uncle."

"Why would you do that?" She took hold of my jacket, gathering two handfuls of the cloth, one just below each shoulder. "To." She hauled me closer. Far too close. "Me?"

We stood eyeball to eyeball now. Oddly—*worryingly*—that same red tide that had risen in me when standing before Maeres Allus in the Blood Holes rose in me now, curling my lip in a half-snarl. "I lost his ships. I gambled them away." Spoken too loudly. No highness. No apology. "I owed it to him."

I had gone from Lisa and Barras to the east spire above the Poor Palace and climbed the long stair. I'd told the old man of my failure and sat with bowed head for his judgment. Instead of raging he had struggled a little more upright against his pillows and said, "I hear you have a salt-mine."

"I have the option to buy the Crptipa mine from Silas Marn for ten thousand in crown gold. I am debt free and have two thousand to my name."

"So a man offering you eight thousand more might ask a high price?"

"Yes."

I left the tower room with a note for eight thousand and an agreement that Garyus would own two-thirds of the mine. As I left I set a black velvet package at the foot of his bed.

"It's Loki's key, Great-uncle Garyus. Don't touch it. It's made of lies."

I left then, though he called for me to come back. I ran down the stairs faster than any sensible man would, feeling something new, or at least something I'd not felt for a very long time. Feeling good.

"I'm paying the price for *your* failings!" The Red Queen thrust me before her and I staggered back as she advanced. "Your duty is to the throne! Your debts are not my concern." A roar now, her anger loose.

My own anger leapt from my throat before I could cage it. "I was paying *your* debts, Grandmother!" I halted my retreat. "I gave the key to Garyus. You took his throne. And *you*." I pointed without looking to the place where the Silent Sister stood. I could sense her now, like a needle in my flesh. "And you took his strength. I have given him something neither of you can take. You can ask and he may allow because he loves this land and its peoples, but you can't take. When you put a cripple in a high tower the message is clear enough. A hundred and seven steps are hardly an invitation to the man to join the world! I have put him at the centre of it." I exhaled and my shoulders went down, the anger gone from me, quicker than it came.

The Red Queen towered before me, sucking in her breath to roar again. But the roar never came. Something in her expression softened, just the smallest bit. "Go," she said. "We will speak of this another time." She dismissed me with a wave of her hand, and I turned for the door, willing myself not to run.

I saw the Silent Sister, standing where I had pointed. Rags and skin and glinting eyes. What she thought of the matter I couldn't tell. She remained as unreadable as algebra.

NINE

I returned to Roma Hall to find my brother Martus in a foul mood, waiting to pounce. "There you are. Where the hell did you vanish off to?" He strode out of an antechamber off the entrance hall.

"I had business with—"

"Well it doesn't matter. Glad to see you've cleaned up. You're lucky you weren't shot as a ghoul."

"A ghoul?"

"Yes, a damn ghoul. You don't know what's going on? Where the hell *have* you been? Under a rock?"

"Well yes, for some of the time. But more recently, Marsail, the Corsair Isles, the Liban desert, and Hell. So what is going on?"

"Trouble! That's what. Grandmother's marching the Army of the South off to Slov on some ill-conceived campaign. She doesn't even care about Slov—it's some damn witch she's after. Claims the Slov dukes are harbouring the woman. A whole army! For one woman . . . And the worst of it is my command's being left here."

"Yes, that is the worst of it." I made to walk by. I had an empty stomach and a sudden desire to fill it with something delicious.

"That damn Gregori DeVeer." Martus stuck a hand out and caught my shoulder, arresting my escape. "His army of foot-sloggers are forming up as the vanguard. He'll come back a blasted hero. I know it. He'll be acting this campaign out around the dining table at the officers' mess for years, lining the grapes up: 'The Slov line held the ridge,' pushing the cherries in: 'Our Red March infantry column attacked from the west . . .' God damn it. And that old woman's leaving me here to babysit the city."

"Well. It would be nice if you could keep it in one piece." I scratched my belly. "But does it really take . . . how many are you?"

"Two thousand men."

"Two thousand men!" I shrugged his hand off my shoulder. "What are you supposed to be protecting us from? This is Vermillion! Nobody is going to attack us."

"I just told you what, idiot!"

"You didn't say—Wait, ghouls?"

"Ghouls, rag-a-maul, corpse-men. We've seen them all in the city over the past couple of months. Nothing the guard can't handle, but it's made people jumpy. They're scared enough even with the Army of the South crowding the streets."

"Well . . . better safe than sorry, I guess. I shall sleep better in someone else's bed knowing that you're patrolling the walls, brother." And with that I turned and set off sharp enough to escape any restraining hand that might come my way.

Much as I wanted to leave matters of state to those who matter I found myself unable to shake off Martus's complaints. Not that I cared about his lost chances for glory—but I was worried by the idea that Grandmother was leading the army off into what seemed a fairly arbitrary war just as Vermillion was starting to see actual evidence of the kinds of dangers she'd been warning us about for years. The unanswered questions led me back up Garyus's stairs. I doubted the Red Queen would be particularly forthcoming, especially after our last meeting, and frankly I didn't know anyone else in Red March who might have both the information I was after and the inclination to share it with me.

The old man was where I left him, hunched over a book.

"Books!" I breezed in. "Nobody ever put anything good in a book."

"Grand-nephew." Garyus set the offending item to one side.

"Explain the Slov thing to me." There didn't seem to be any point beating about the bush. I wanted my mind set at ease so I could go and get drunk in good company. "She's starting a war . . . for what? Why now?"

Garyus smiled, a crooked thing. "I'm not my sister's keeper."

"But you know."

He shrugged. "Some of it."

"There are ghouls in the city. Other . . . things too. The Dead King has turned his eyes this way. Why would she rush off to fight foreigners hundreds of miles away?"

"What turned the Dead King's eyes this way?" Garyus asked.

Not wanting to say that I had done it, I said nothing. Though to be fair Martus's report indicated that the dead had been stirring within our walls for some while and I had only just returned.

"The Lady Blue steers the Dead King," Garyus answered for me.

"And why—"

"Alica says our time is running out, and fast. She says that the troubles in Vermillion are to distract her, to keep her here. The true danger lies in not stopping the Lady Blue. The Wheel of Osheim is still turning . . . how long remains to us is unclear, but if the Lady Blue is left unchecked to keep pushing it then the last of our days will run through our fingers so quickly that even ancients like me will have to worry."

"So it truly is a whole army, a whole war, just to kill one woman?"

"Sometimes that's what it takes . . ."

I came to my father's chambers also without knowing why. To learn more about his mother's war was the excuse that had led me there, but the Red Queen would rather share her plans with her court jester—if she had one—than Reymond Kendeth.

I knocked at his bedchamber and a maid opened the door. I didn't note which maid. The figure in the bed held my gaze, hunched in upon himself in the gloom, his form picked out only here and there where the daylight found a slit in his blinds.

The maid closed the door behind her as she left.

I stood, feeling like a child again, lost for words. The place smelled of sour wine, musty neglect, sickness, and sorrow. "Father."

He raised his head. He looked old. Balding, greying, flesh sunken about his bones, an unhealthy glitter in his eyes. "My son."

The cardinal called everyone "my son." A hundred dusty sermons crowded in on me—all the times when I'd wanted a father not a cleric, all those times since Mother died when I'd wanted the man she'd seen in him—for arranged or not she wasn't one to have given herself to a man she felt no respect or appreciation for.

"My son?" he repeated, a thickness in his voice. Drunk again.

The reason I'd come escaped me and I turned to go.

"Jalan."

I turned back. "So you recognize me."

He smiled—a weak thing, part grimace. "I do. But you've changed, boy. Grown. I thought at first you were your brother . . . but I couldn't tell which. You've both of them in you."

"Well, if you're just going to insult me . . ." In truth I knew it to be a compliment, the Darin part anyway. Perhaps the Martus part. Martus was at least brave, if little else.

"We—" He coughed and hugged his chest. "I've been a poor—"

"Father?"

"I was going to say cardinal. But I have been a poor father too. I've no excuses, Jalan. It was a betrayal of your mother. My weakness . . . the world sweeps along so fast and the easiest paths are . . . easiest." He sagged.

"You're drunk." Though that was hardly a judgment I could wield against anyone. We didn't talk like this, ever. Very drunk. "You should sleep." I didn't want his mawkish apologies, forgotten within a day. I couldn't look at him without distaste—though what part of that was just the fear that I looked into a mirror and saw myself old, I couldn't say. I wanted . . . I wanted that things had been different . . . I saw him from the other side of Mother's death now. Snorri had done that for me—shown me how a husband's grief can cut down even the biggest of men. I wished he hadn't shown me—it was easy to hate Father; understanding him just made me sad.

"We should . . . spend some time, talk, do whatever it—" Another cough. "Whatever it is we're supposed to do. My mother . . . well, you know her, she wasn't so good at that part of things. I always said I'd do better. But when Nia died . . ."

"You're drunk," I told him, finding my throat tight. I went to the door, opened it. Somehow I couldn't just leave—the words wouldn't go with me, I had to leave them in the room. "When you're better. We'll talk then. Get drunk together, properly. Cardinal and son."

Two days later the Red Queen led the Army of the South out of Vermillion, their columns ten thousand strong marching down the broad avenues of the Piatzo toward Victory Gate. Grandmother was astride a vast red stallion, her platemail gothic and enamelled in crimson as if she'd been freshly dipped in blood. I'd witnessed the Red Queen earning her name and had little doubt that she would soon be wearing a more practical armour and still be prepared to personally drench it in the real thing if need be. She paid the crowd no heed, her stare fixed on the tomorrows ahead. Her hair, rust and iron, scraped back beneath a circle of gold. A more scary old woman I'd yet to see—and I'd seen a few.

Behind the queen came the remnants of our once-proud cavalry, dropping a goodly tonnage of dung for the footmen to trudge through. Start as you mean to go on, I say.

I stood beside Martus, and on my other side, Darin, returned from his love nest in the country. He'd brought Micha back with him to Roma Hall, apparently with a baby, though all I saw was a basket hung with silver chains and loaded with lace. Darin kept threatening to introduce me to my new niece, but so far I'd avoided the meeting. I'm not partial to babies. They tend to vomit on me, or failing that, to vent from the other end.

"Hurrah . . . a parade . . ." The autumn sun beat down on us while we cheered and waved from the royal stand. The watching crowds had been issued with bright flags, the colours of the South, and many waved the Red March standard, divided diagonally, red above for the blood spilled on the march, black below for the hearts of our enemy. Martus bemoaned the state of the cavalry and the fact he'd been left behind. Darin observed that winter in Slov could be an ugly thing and he hoped the troops were equipped for it.

"They'll be back in a month, you fool." Martus offered us both a look of scorn as if I'd had something to do with the suggestion.

"Experience teaches that armies often get bogged down—no matter how dry the weather," Darin said.

"Experience? What experience have you had, little brother?" A full Martus sneer now.

"History," Darin said. "You can find it in books."

"Pah. All history has taught us is we don't learn from history."

I let their argument flow over me and watched the infantry march by, spears across their shoulders, shields on their arms. Veterans or not, few of them looked older than Martus and some looked younger than me.

Ten thousand men seemed a small force to challenge the might of Slov, though to be fair an army of well-trained and well-equipped regulars like the South can send five times its number of peasant conscripts running for their fields. Given Grandmother's objective, ten thousand seemed sufficient. Enough for a thrust, enough to secure the target area, and enough, when the Lady Blue was brought to ruin, to fight a retreat to defensible borders.

I wished them joy of it. My main priority remained unchanged. The pursuit of leisure—by definition a languid sort of a chase. I wanted to relax back into Vermillion and my newfound financial freedom, free from the threat of Maeres Allus and all those tiresome debts.

"Prince Jalan." One of Grandmother's elite guardsmen stood beside me, gleaming irritatingly. "The steward requires your presence."

"The steward?" I glanced round at Martus and Darin, who gave exaggerated shrugs, as interested as me in the answer.

The guard answered by pointing to the Victory Gate and raising his finger. There on the wall, directly above the gate, a palanquin, ornate and curtained, two teams of four men at the carrying bars to either side, guardsmen flanking them. Grandmother's own.

"Who—"

But the guard had already led off. I swallowed my curiosity and hurried after him. We threaded a path behind the crowd to one of the stairs leading up the inside of the city wall. After climbing to the parapet we made our way to the palanquin where the men ushered me along the treacherously narrow strip of walkway not occupied by the steward's box. Drawing level with the curtains I ducked through, not waiting for an invitation.

I shuffled in, bent low to keep from scraping my head, and squeezed into the seat opposite. Garyus couldn't sit in the seat but instead rested on a ramp of cushions heaped against it. "What the hell? Grandmother made you steward?"

He crinkled his face in a smile. "You don't think I'm up to it, Great-nephew?"

"No, well, I mean, yes, of course . . ."

"A resounding vote of confidence!" He chuckled. "Apparently she 'stole my throne,' so I'm getting it back for a few months."

"Well, I never said . . . Well, maybe I did but I didn't mean—I mean I did—" The heat in that little box was oppressive and the sweat left me at such a rate I worried I might shrivel and die. "It *was* your throne."

"Treason, Jalan. You keep those words off your lips." Garyus smiled again. "It's true that joined as we were, it was me that saw the light first. But I reconciled myself to the new order of things long ago. When I was a boy I'll grant you it stung. We dream big dreams and it's hard to let them go. I wanted to make my father proud—have him see past . . ." He raised a twisted arm. "This." He winced and lowered his arm. "But my little sister has been a great queen. History will remember her name. In these times she has been exactly what our nation needed. A merchant king would have served us better in peace—but peace is not what we have been given." He twitched the curtain open a little way. Down below us the martial pride of Red March came on rank after rank, gleaming, glorious, pennants rippling above them in the breeze. "Which brings me to the reason for my invitation." He reached into a basket at his side and fumbled something out. It fell to the floor as he got it clear.

I bent to retrieve it. "A message?" I lifted a scroll-case, ebony chased with silver, set with the royal seals.

"A message." Garyus inclined his head. "You're the Marshal of Vermillion."

"Fuck that!" My turn to drop the scroll-case as though it were hot. ". . . your stewardness."

"'Highness' is the correct form of address when the steward is of noble birth . . . if we're being formal, Jalan."

"Fuck that, your highness." I sat back and exhaled, then wiped the sweat from my brow. "Look, I know you meant well and all. It's nice that you wanted to do something for me by way of thanks for the key—but really—what do I know about defending cities? I mean it's soldiery—there must be dozens of better qualified people—"

"Hundreds I should think." Garyus said it a little too enthusiastically for my liking. "But since when was a monarchy about rewarding individual merit? Promote from within, is our mantra."

He had a point. The Kendeths's continued rule depended upon the carefully constructed lie that we were innately better at doing it than any other candidates, and also the idea that God himself wanted us to do it.

"It's a nice gesture, Great-uncle, but I'd really rather not." Being marshal sounded as though it might involve far more work than I was interested in—which was none at all. My plans involved mainly wine, women, and song. In fact, forget the song. "I'm hardly suited."

Garyus smiled his crooked smile and looked toward the bright slice of the outside world visible between the curtains. "I'm hardly suited to being steward now am I? Ruling Vermillion—all of Red March in fact— yet hidden away lest I demoralize our troops with my physical imperfections. But here I am, by your grandmother's command. Which, incidentally, is where your appointment comes from. I'm not so cruel as to separate you from your vices, Jalan."

"Grandmother? She made me marshal?" The last time I'd seen her she seemed so close to ordering my execution that the headsman probably had his whetstone out.

"She did." Garyus nodded his ponderous head. "There's a uniform, you know? And you'll be in charge of your brother Martus."

"I'm in!"

TEN

The uniform turned out to be a baton of office and an ageing sash of yellow silk with a number of worryingly bloodlike stains on it. Over the course of the next few days I came to appreciate the cruelty of Grandmother's revenge. After the initial joy of informing Martus that he was now my subordinate came an endless round of official duties. I had to inspect the wall guard, deal with engineers and their tiresome opinions about what needed repairing or knocking down, and officiate over disputes between the resident city guard and my brother's newly arrived infantry.

I would have told them all to go hang, but my assistant, Captain Renprow, proved annoyingly persistent, an example of the "raised on merit" class of energetic low-born types that the system needs in order to function but who have to be watched closely. Additionally, continued reports of rag-a-maul and ghouls in the poor quarter acted as an added incentive. If there's one thing that will get me to do half an honest day's work it's the conviction that doing so will make me safer.

"What are rag-a-maul, Renprow?" I leaned back in my chair, my feet in their shiny boots on my shiny marshal's desk.

Renprow, a short dark man with short dark hair, frowned, favouring me with a stare that put me uncomfortably in mind of Snorri. "You don't know? I've passed you a dozen reports . . . you attended that strategy meeting yesterday, and—"

"Of course *I* know. I just wanted *your* opinion on the subject, Renprow. Humour me."

"Well." He pursed his lips. "Some kind of malicious ghost. People describe them as miniature whirlwinds raising rags and dust. Whirlwinds so full of sharp edges they can flay a man, and when the wind drops the victim is possessed and runs around on a murderous rampage until they're put down." He puffed out his cheek and tapped two fingers to it. "That about covers it."

"And these incidents are peculiar to Vermillion?"

"We've had reports far and wide, but we do seem to have a higher incidence in the city. Perhaps just because the population is so much larger." He paused. "My father's people know them too. But they call them wind-stick devils, and they're very rare." Renprow had a heritage that began far south of Liba, giving him command of many odd facts.

"Well." I swung my boots off the desk and glanced around the room. The marshal's manse was a spacious building but had been unoccupied for so long that most of the furniture had wandered off. "If that concludes our business for the day?" The sun had passed its zenith and I had a flame-haired beauty to visit, a sweet girl named Lola, or Lulu, or something.

Renprow's mouth twitched into a short-lived smile as if I'd been attempting a joke. "Your next appointment is with the menonites in the Appan suburb. They're proving resistant to the idea of disinterring their cemeteries. After that—"

"We *still* have dead in the ground?" I stood up fast enough to knock the chair over. "Have the guard do it for them!" I'd seen what happened when the dead come clambering back from where they've been put. "Better still, have Martus's soldiers do it. I want every corpse burned. Immediately! And if they have to make more corpses to do it . . . that's fine. As long as they burn those too." I shivered at memories I'd been trying to bury—like the Vermillion dead they weren't buried deep enough.

Renprow picked up a weighty ledger from the shelf by the door and held it across his chest like a shield. "The menonites are unruly at the best of times and numerous. Their sect venerates ancestors to the ninth generation. It would be better if we could negotiate."

And there went my afternoon, just like the three before it. Smiling and performing for peasant stock, a bunch of ingrates who should be falling over themselves to obey my commands. I sighed and stood. Better to cajole the live ones than have to contend with the dead ones later on. The live ones may smell bad and have irritating opinions but the dead ones smell even worse and hold the opinion that we're food. "All right.

But if they don't listen I'm sending the soldiers in." I found myself still shivering despite the heat of the day, visions of the dead crowding in, patient, silent, waiting . . . until the Dead King woke their hunger.

"Jalan!" The door burst open without a knock and Darin stood there, pale and serious.

"My dear brother. And how have you decided to brighten my day? Perhaps some overflowing sewers need my attention?"

"Father is dead."

"Oh, you liar." Father wasn't dead. He didn't do that sort of thing. I took my cloak from its hook. The day outside looked grey and uninspiring.

"Jalan." Darin stepped toward me, a hand reaching my shoulder.

"Nonsense." I brushed his arm aside. "I've got menonites to see." A coldness sat in my stomach and my eyes stung. It made no sense. Firstly he wasn't dead, and secondly I didn't even like him. I walked past Darin, aiming for the doorway.

"He's dead, Jalan." My brother's hand settled on my shoulder as I passed him and I stopped, almost at the door, my back to him. For a moment visions of a different time replaced the square outside and rooftops beyond. I saw my father young, standing beside Mother, bending down, a smile on his face, arms open to receive me as I raced toward them.

"No." For reasons wholly beyond explanation the word stuck in my throat, my mouth trembled and tears filled my eyes.

"Yes." Darin turned me around and folded his arms about me. Just for a moment, but long enough for me to press the foolishness back where it came from. He released me and with an arm around my shoulders he steered me out into the day.

The cardinal died in his bedroom, alone. He looked small in the wideness of that bed, sunken, old before his time. If he'd been drinking then the maids had removed the evidence and tidied him up.

He'd gone into a decline following his trip to Roma. The pope's scolding was a thing to behold by all accounts, and accompanying Reymond Kendeth back to Vermillion, along with a heavy burden of shame, came the pope's own man, Archbishop Larrin, whose only job appeared to be making my father do his. Some men thrive on old age, others feel the world narrow around them and see no point in the path before them. A man's first taste of the poppy gives him something glorious and wonderful, something that he strives to recapture with each return to the resin, but in the end he needs to smoke it just to feel human. Life is the same for many of us—a few scant years of golden youth when everything tastes sweet, every experience new and sharp with meaning. Then a long slow grind to the grave, trying and failing to recapture that feeling you had when you were seventeen and the world rolled out before you.

The funeral took place three days later, Father's corpse under guard until then while the most pious of the faith filed past to honour the office if not the man. We gathered in the Black Courtyard, a sizeable rectangle between the Poor Palace and the Marsail keep, generally used for exercising horses but traditionally reserved for gathering with the coffin before the slow walk to the cemetery, or the church, depending on the deceased's station in life. Today, under a sullen and blustery sky, there was to be a cremation. Split logs of rosewood and magnolia, selected for fragrance, had been stacked into a pyre taller than a mounted man. Father's coffin lay perched atop the wooden mountain, polished, gleaming, chased with silver, a heavy silver cross placed upon the lid.

The entire palace turned out. This was the Red Queen's youngest son, the highest cleric in the land. In the tiered seating for the royals Garyus's palanquin sat highest, with Martus, Darin, and me in the row beneath, our cousins arrayed before us one row lower. Father's elder brother, Uncle Parrus, remained in his holdings in the east. The message hadn't had time to reach him, let alone allowed time for him to return, and in any event with Grandmother's thrust into Slov it would hardly be the time for the grandest lord in the east to abandon his castle on the border.

I had reports demanding my attention—disturbances in the outer city that morning—but I couldn't begrudge Father his due. Somehow, after Mother's death we never had anything to say to each other. I should have fixed that. You always think there's going to be time. Put things off. And then suddenly there's no time left at all.

"Here he comes." Darin to my left, nodding down at the courtyard. A crowd of the aristocracy emerged from the Adam Arch, chattering brightly despite their sombre blacks and greys.

"Grandmother's only been gone ten days and he thinks he owns the place." Martus on Darin's far side.

I could make out my father's eldest brother, my Uncle Hertet, at the centre of the crowd, not because of his height—which was modest—but by virtue of the shirt of brilliant yellow-and-green silk showing through the wide gap in his mourning robe, all of it stretched to contain an ample belly. His entourage swept before him, the phoney court he maintained as practice for when the throne would supposedly be his. To watch him you might imagine that he considered his mother gone for good—not merely on campaign but to her grave.

Hertet's sons, Johnath and Roland, peeled off to the lowest row to sit beside our other cousins along with the lords and barons. Their father, sweating in his finery despite the cool breeze, lumbered up the timber steps to the highest tier where he wedged himself alongside Garyus's palanquin. The heir-apparently-not gave no hint of a bow nor acknowledged his uncle's presence in any way other than that forced on him by having to squeeze in beside the curtained box.

"Hurry it along." Hertet raised his voice behind us. I turned to see him brushing a hand up through the damp straggles of his grey hair, plastering them back over his forehead. With sagging jowls and bloodshot eyes he looked a far more likely candidate for the reaper's scythe than my father ever had. "Reymond kept me waiting long enough in life with those damned masses of his. Let's not have him waste any more of our time."

Seeing Hertet's waving arm the archbishop down in the square began to read aloud from the huge bible held open for him by two choirboys.

"Damned nonsense all this pyre business." Hertet continued to grumble behind me. "Got better things to do with my morning than sit and smell Reymond cook. Should put him in the crypt with the rest of the Kendeths."

Since our family name passed down through the monarch we were all Kendeths despite Grandmother's three sons having three different fathers. I'd always taken pride in the name before, though sharing it with Hertet soured that pride somewhat there on the tiers. I hoped his opinions on cremating the dead didn't escape the palace. It was proving hard enough convincing Vermillion to exhume and burn her dead as it was, without Hertet Kendeth declaring it foolishness.

At length we were done with the Latin and the lies. Archbishop Larrin closed the huge bible with a thump that echoed around the Black Courtyard, and the finality of it sent a chill through me. Father's seal hung around the man's neck, catching the light. A minor cleric handed Larrin a burning brand and he duly tossed it into the kindling heaped at the pyre's base. The flames took hold, grew, crackled, found their roar, and started to devour the logs above them. Thankfully the breeze blew from the south and carried the smoke away from us, drifting in grey clouds across the Marsail keep, over the palace walls, and out across the city.

"Ballessa said an odd thing." Darin kept his eyes on the flames and I could imagine he hadn't spoken. "She said she passed by Father's chambers the afternoon he died and heard him shouting something about the devil . . . and his daughter."

"Father doesn't have a daughter," Martus said, with the kind of firmness that indicated if some bastard child were discovered she should be forgotten again pretty damn quick.

"Daughter?" I watched the flames too. Ballessa wasn't given to flights of fancy. You would have to look far and wide to find a woman more firmly grounded than the major-domo of Roma Hall. "He was just drunk and shouting nonsense. He was in his cups when I saw him a few days back."

Darin looked at me with a frown. "Father hadn't drunk for weeks, brother, not since he came back from Roma. The maids told me it was true. You can't hide anything from the people who clean up after you."

"I—" I didn't have anything to say to that. Father had said it for me. He wished that he had done a better job of being a father. Now I wished that I had been a better son.

"Jula was with him at the end," Darin said.

"He died alone! That's what I was told!" I looked at my brother but he kept his eyes forward.

"A cardinal shouldn't die alone with a cook, Jal." Martus gave a snort.

"She was there, even so," Darin said. "She brought him his broth personally. She's been his cook longer than any of us have been his sons."

"And Jula said?"

"That he faded quietly and she thought he'd fallen asleep. Then, seeing how pale and still he was she thought him dead. But he surprised her. At the end he was violent, struggling to rise—mouthing words but making no sound." Darin looked away from the burning pyre, up, past the smoke, into the blue heavens. "She said he seemed possessed. Like a different person. She said his eyes met hers and in that moment he reached for his seal beside the bed, and on touching it collapsed back to his pillows. Dead."

Neither Martus nor I had an answer for that. We stood in silence, listening to the crackle of the flames. The breeze rippled through the smoke and for a moment I saw shapes there, one moving into the next, almost a grasping hand, almost a face, almost a skull . . . all of them disturbing.

It took half an hour before the coffin fell in with a dull crash, a scattering of blazing logs and a maelstrom of sparks lofted toward the heavens. The heat reached us even on the upper tiers, red upon our faces. The archbishop signalled and the palace flag was lowered to indicate the start of mourning and that we could leave.

"Well, it's done." And Hertet levered himself up then stomped off down to the courtyard. Others took their cue and followed. Some lingered. My cousin Serah turned to offer my brothers and me her condolences for Uncle Reymond, Rotus shook our hands. Micha DeVeer waited for her Darin at the margins of the courtyard in her black dress, a milk-nurse beside her with my niece, pink and pudgy in her mourning cloth. Barras and Lisa said their words, kind ones, but they rolled off me. And finally it was just three brothers, and the possibly empty box on the tier behind us.

"I'm going to get drunk tonight." Darin stood. "We never saw the best of that man. Maybe our sons will never see the best of us. I'll say a prayer for him, then drink a drink."

"I'll join you." Martus got to his feet. "I'll drink to Uncle Hertet taking the forever nap before the Red Queen quits the throne. Christ, I'd see Cousin Serah take the crown before that old bastard." He slapped his hands to his upper arms. "You'll join us, Jalan. You're good at drinking at least." And with that he set off down the steps.

"Steward." Darin bowed to the palanquin, put a hand to my shoulder, then followed Martus.

❖ ❖ ❖

"How stand our defences?" Garyus's voice emerged from behind the curtains.

"The west wall is crumbling. Sections need to be underpinned. The suburbs need to be burned and razed. Martus's men are bored and picking fights with the guard. We're short a hundred crossbows and half our scorpions are in want of maintenance if they're to fire more than twice before breaking. Grain reserves are a third of what they should be. Apart from that we're fine. Why?"

"You've looked at the figures?"

"Some of them, certainly."

"Ghoul sightings inside the city walls in the past four days?"

He'd picked one I actually noticed when Renprow pushed it across my desk. "Uh, three, then seven, twelve yesterday, another dozen or so came in this morning before I left after lunch."

"They're scouting us," Garyus said.

"What?" I leaned forward and pulled his curtain aside. He looked like a monster in his shadowed den, an unwell monster, pale and beaded with sweat. "They're scavengers, half-dead corpse-eaters following the riverbanks. There have been dead floating downstream for weeks—some army of Orlanth laying waste in Rhone." I wondered if Grandmother would be clogging rivers with dead Slovs before the month was out.

"Have you mapped out the captures and the sightings?" Garyus asked.

"Well, no, but there's no pattern to it. Except more by the river than anywhere else. But they're everywhere." I tried to see it in my mind. Something about the picture I came up with worried me.

"All over. Never the same area twice?" Garyus looked grim.

"Well, occasionally. But not often, no. Once the guard see them off they don't come back. That's a good thing . . . isn't it?"

"It's what scouts do. Checking for weakness, gathering information to plan with."

"I should go," I said. "Had reports of corpse attacks in the outer city." It was the ones within the protection of the city walls that worried me most, but the recent messages spoke of a rash of attacks coming quite suddenly.

I made to turn away but something glinting on the palanquin's floor caught my eye. "What's that?" I leaned forward and answered my own question. "Pieces of mirror."

Garyus inclined his head. "The Lady is trying to open new eyes in Vermillion. She knows my sisters are coming for her—perhaps she's desperate. I hope so. In any event, I advise against using any mirrors. A handsome fellow like you shouldn't need to check his reflection—that's a pastime for us ugly people in case we forget our appearance and get to thinking that the world will look well upon us."

"I gave up mirrors a while back." A shudder ran through me: too many glimpses of movement that shouldn't be there, too many flickers that might have been blue. "Your sisters have left us to find the damn woman but what's to stop her stepping out of someone's looking-glass and murdering the lot of us while they're gone? Not to mention that the ghoul-problem hasn't gone away. Grandmother said that was a distraction to keep her here. Well she's gone now . . . but we're still finding bodies missing—dead ones and live ones. I don't like it. Any of it."

Garyus pursed his lips. "I don't like it either, Marshal, but it's what we have. I'm sure my twin has left enchantments in place to close this city to the Lady Blue—at least from physical intrusion. She learned that lesson at a very young age. The rest of it is for us to take care of."

I sighed. I would have rather heard a comforting lie than the frightening truth. "Duty calls." I glanced down at the Black Courtyard, preparing to go. The yard stood clear now of all but a few mourners, the clerics set to watch the pyre burn down, and of course Garyus's guard. The air above the embers rippled, reminding me of how Hell rippled when too many died at once and their souls came flooding through. I stared at the hot orange mound and through the heat shimmer I caught sight of a figure approaching. I watched, uncertain of what it was until it rounded the fire and I saw clear.

"Dear God! Guards! Guards!" I pointed a shaking hand at the thing walking calmly toward the stands. "It's a . . . a . . ." I had no idea.

The six men at the base of the seating tiers looked up at me and, following the direction of my finger, they seemed to see the flayed man for the first time. They recoiled in horror, but only for a moment, trained men these, hard men, Grandmother's elite. As one they reached for their swords . . . then, as one, they let their arms fall, looked away. A moment later they were standing as they had been before, as if for all the world there wasn't a hairless, skinless man in a black cloak walking calmly toward them.

"What?" I glanced back at Garyus in his palanquin. "What the hell? Garyus! Tell them! It's possessed! A rag-a-maul's had him!"

Two of the guards looked up at me, frowning as if offended by my tone of voice.

"Leave it be, Jalan. Luntar is a friend."

I moved quickly to the side of Garyus's box and drew my sword. I would have hidden behind the thing but it had been pushed back against the wall of the building that the stand rested against. "That thing is a friend? It's been fucking skinned!" I looked down at the palace guard who were scanning the courtyard, wary for any threat to the steward. "And what the hell is wrong with your bodyguard?"

"Burned. Not skinned." The black-cloaked man smiled up at me as he climbed the last few steps, his footprints wet behind him. "And the guards have merely forgotten what they saw. Memory is the key to any man. It's all we are."

I kept my sword up as he closed the last couple of yards. I'd seen burned men before and dearly wished I hadn't. Our visitor looked rather as if Father might have if he decided to clamber out of his coffin after the flames had taken hold good and hard.

"Luntar," Garyus twitched a hand up in greeting. "Good to see you, old friend."

"Well met, Gholloth. And this would be your great-nephew Jalan. A rare man."

I lowered my sword further than I wanted to and less than decorum demanded. "You know me?"

Luntar smiled again. For a man who should be screaming in horrible agony he seemed remarkably cheerful. Burned skin cracked and wept as he spoke. "I know far less of you than I know of almost any man. Which makes you a rarity. Your future is too twisted with that of Edris Dean to be seen clearly."

I frowned. The future-sworn don't see me—that's what Edris Dean had said about himself. The fact he loomed in my future as well as my past did not make me feel any better. I might want him dead but I didn't want to be the one tasked with the job.

"My condolences for the loss of your father, Prince Jalan." Luntar spoke into the silence where my reply should have been. "I met him once. A good man. The loss of your mother changed him."

"I . . ." I swallowed and coughed. "My thanks."

"To what do we owe the honour, Luntar?" Garyus asked.

"You know me, Gholloth. Always chasing probabilities and possibilities. Or chased by them."

Luntar looked out across the rooftops at the pale sky. The seared flesh glistened across his skull and I took a step back, or would have if I hadn't fetched up against the wall, banging my head. "Trouble is coming." Spoken to the heavens.

"Don't need a future-sworn to see that." I rubbed the back of my head. "Trouble's always coming."

"There's to be an attack? Here?" Garyus asked.

"Yes." Luntar faced us again. "But it runs far deeper than that. Your sisters have gone to stop Mora Shival, but it will not be enough. The world is broken, not just this empire, not just these lands, but the world itself, from mountain root to sky and out beyond. The armies of the dead are just the start of it."

I puzzled over "Mora Shival" then remembered that in Grandmother's memories it had been Lady Shival with the sapphire headdress that had come to kill the elder Gholloth. Somewhere after that she had become the Blue Lady.

"How long do we have?" Garyus again.

"Months."

"Months?" I asked. "Until the attack?" Grandmother would be back by then and it could be her problem.

"The attack will be very soon. Perhaps it has already started. It will be months until the end."

"Of?" I spread my palms in query.

Luntar echoed my gesture then spread his arms to encompass the palace and the sky. "Everything."

I laughed.

He stared at me.

I tried to laugh again. Grandmother had said her war with the Lady Blue was about the end of the world. I hadn't taken her literally. Or rather, I had understood the words but not absorbed them. Yes the Builders had cracked the world when they turned their wheel, yes mages like Kelem, Sageous, and the rest cracked it wider each time they worked their magics . . . but the end? I knew the Lady Blue's ambitions lay in whatever followed the ruin of everything we held, but that had always been years away, a problem for later. Even with Grandmother's departure for Slov I hadn't *really* thought everything was at stake. Not the whole world. Red March maybe or the lands around Osheim. But I'd always imagined that there would be somewhere to run to, somewhere to hide.

At least I understood now the urgency . . . or desperation . . . that had taken the Red Queen from her throne, leaving her beloved city in peril, to war in a distant land at an age when many grandmothers sit grey and wrinkled, knitting quietly in a corner and counting away the last of their days.

"Months!" I said the word again to see if it tasted any better. It didn't. I may have once said that six months was forever but right now it felt distinctly less than enough. For some reason Darin's baby popped into my mind, even though all I'd seen of her were plump pink legs waving and plump pink arms reaching for Micha's milk-heavy breasts. And frankly I hadn't been looking at the baby. Six months wouldn't take her very far.

"For you, less than a week if your walls don't hold." Luntar reached into his cloak and my sword came up between us. "Months for the world."

"A week!" I yelped. "*Less* than a week?" How far could I get on a fast horse in less than a week? "This isn't right! An attack here? Is an army coming? Is it the Dead King? Someone needs to do something! We need—"

"A gift, Gholloth." Luntar ignored my panic and drew out a white box, a cube six inches deep. "You once gave me a copper box in your possession and it proved very useful. Now I return the favour." Apart from the pale pink smears, where his burns had smeared the surface, the box was without design or ornament, a cube with rounded corners, made of white bone. Ivory perhaps . . . or . . .

"It's plasteek?" I asked. "A Builder thing?" I tried to keep my voice steady but the words "less than a week" kept running through my mind, along with images of my new horse, Murder, waiting for me in the stables.

"It is plasteek, yes." Luntar placed the box beside Garyus.

"What's inside?" I asked before my great-uncle could get the words past the twist of his mouth.

"Ghosts."

ELEVEN

We hurried into the throne room to interrogate Luntar within the protection of the Red Queen's strongest wards. All the way there I had to keep stopping to chivvy Garyus's bearers along as they negotiated the palanquin through the palace. I managed, at least when not looking at Luntar, to convince myself that I shouldn't take the predictions of some random soothsayer too seriously. Looking at the skinless horror of him it was hard to imagine him some charlatan. Even so, as a drowning man will clutch at floating straws, I still clutched at the idea he might be wrong, or at least lying.

The throne room had never been a place of crowds or colour. In the days since the Red Queen departed things had changed. With Garyus's palanquin set before Grandmother's high chair, the hall seemed to have taken on a new life. In addition to his nurses the old man had a rota of musicians come and go, filling the air with the songs and sounds of a dozen nations while he dealt with the petitions of his subjects. He spoke mainly to merchants both high and low, his thesis being that nations run on trade and produce, everything else being secondary.

He'd told me, "They say that money is the root of all evil, Jalan, and it may be so. But it is also the root of a great many things that are good. Clothe your people, fill their bellies, and peace may follow. Want makes war."

That relaxed atmosphere vanished on our hasty arrival, the scattering of courtiers sensing that a prince's funeral wasn't the worst this day had to offer.

Garyus's attendants laid him on a couch with a great many cushions supporting him in what looked to be the least uncomfortable position. I stood beside him, my foot tapping involuntarily as we watched the palace guards usher the last of the day's supplicants from the room. The day's players, a group of gypsies from the distant isle of Umber, packed up their pipes and music double quick.

"What news from the outer city?" Garyus asked.

Less than a week. Suddenly the perimeter reports seemed far more important.

"Trouble," I said. "Some graveyards we hadn't got to have emptied themselves. Occupants missing. A dozen corpse attacks reported. Two families . . . missing." I winced. The guard had led me to one house, close to the North Road. Blood on the floor, on the walls, broken furniture. Flies everywhere. No occupants. Except a baby in its crib. Or rather, the remains of one. "The neighbours saw nothing." That had been hard to imagine with the houses built shoulder to shoulder. I'd set the guard knocking on doors and hurried back to the palace to meet Luntar. Garyus had wanted the privacy of the throne room to conclude our discussion and Luntar had other people to see before he left. He'd mentioned Dr. Taproot as one of those, though I hadn't heard the circus had come to town. "I need to get back and oversee a series of sweeps." I turned back to face the throne room, and stopped in momentary surprise.

"I won't keep you long." Luntar stood before us, we two his only witnesses. He slipped from the memory of every other person even as they saw him. An invisibility of a kind. Whether there was something in the Kendeth blood that resisted the trick, or whether he simply chose to allow us to remember him, he didn't say, though even in the minute reporting to the steward with my back to Luntar I had forgotten that he was there.

"If you would all be so kind as to afford my great-nephew and me a little privacy." Garyus raised his voice to carry. The remnants of his court began to move toward the doors. "Even you, Mary." This to the most senior of his nurses, a solid matron who seemed to think herself indispensable. "And gentlemen—if you will." He nodded to the guardsmen flanking him. "All my guards."

The captain approached, boots heavy on the polished floor. "Steward, it's our place to protect you."

"If I die in your absence Prince Jalan is to be demoted to peasant. There, I should be safe enough now?"

The guard captain frowned, the word "but" struggling to get off his lips.

"And really, I insist," Garyus said.

Five minutes later, after the guard had double-checked each dark corner, we were alone.

"I had hoped to find the Red Queen here," Luntar said. "Now it seems I must follow her to Slov."

I resisted the obvious jibe that he should have foreseen this circumstance. No doubt he had interfered with Grandmother's fate in the past and denied himself further visions of her future. That or the Silent Sister guarded her from such foretelling.

"When must you leave?" The day before he arrived would have suited me. I still found Luntar deeply unsettling, the rawness of his burned flesh demanded a reaction and if it couldn't get one from him it certainly created something very close to pain in me. The Silent Sister had looked so far into our bright future that it had blinded her in one eye. Luntar had looked beyond even that and been burned head to toe by what he saw. To hear Garyus speak of it, somewhere not too far ahead of us the impossible brilliance of a thousand Builders' Suns consumed our all our futures.

"I will leave immediately we conclude our discussion here," Luntar said. "It's a long walk, and no horse will bear me."

"Tell me . . ." I glanced at Garyus, but he waved for me to continue. "Tell me, the future that burned you, that you say is coming, is this the end the Red Queen fears? The doom the Builders set upon us when they worked their science and changed the world?" I tried not to make it sound like an accusation—but it was. Luntar and his kind had been cracking reality for generations, driving us to the edge as they pulled more and more magic through the fabric of the world.

Beside me Garyus nodded his heavy head. His gaze rested upon the cube of white plasteek in his lap—the box of ghosts that Luntar had given him.

"There's nothing we can do?" I asked. Just somewhere safe to run to would be good.

Luntar set both hands to his face and slid them wetly toward his brow as if pushing away some weariness. "In some futures it's the cracking of the world that ends us, darkness and light, the elements taking on monstrous forms, the very substance of which we are made unravelling . . . In other futures it's the light of the Builders' weapons that scorches us from the earth."

"Shit." I had seen that light. I tried to take the whine from my voice and sound more like Snorri would. "Twice now in the space of a year Builders' Suns have lit. I heard of one in Gelleth on my trip north, and then in Liba I saw one with my own eyes, burning the desert. Who's using these dead men's weapons against us, and why?"

"Death isn't what it was." Luntar extended his skinless arm and studied it.

"The Builders are dead. They went to dust a thousand years ago." But as I said it I recalled Kara's words. The völva had told me on her boat that Baraqel and Aslaug were once human, Builders who had escaped into spirit when the world burned. She had claimed that others copied themselves into their machines before the end. Whatever that meant. "It can't be the Builders? Even if they weren't dead why would they wish us harm?"

"Do you recall how the Builders brought magic into the world in the first place, Prince Jalan?"

"Turned a wheel . . . I think that's how Grandmother described it. They made it so a man's will could change what's real. But the Day of a Thousand Suns came and the wheel kept turning with nobody to stop it—the magic getting stronger."

"That's more or less it," Luntar said. "But this wheel isn't just a figure of speech. It's not just words to paint a picture we can understand. There is a wheel. In—"

"Osheim." The word escaped my lips despite strict instructions not to emerge.

"Yes."

"These explosions in Gelleth and Liba though—"

"Ask the ghosts," Luntar said. "It's their work." And then he was no longer there.

"How?" I stepped forward, waving an arm through the space the burned man had so recently occupied.

"The same way any other man leaves," Garyus said. "He just made us forget it."

"Well damn that! Why couldn't he just stay and answer my bloody question? Why the hell be so mysterious about everything?"

With effort Garyus raised his head and smiled up at me. "I always felt those stories your Nanna Willow told you boys would have been a lot shorter if there had been some plain speaking in them. But perhaps you know the answer."

"Bloody future-sworn!" I almost spat on the floor but Grandmother's presence still haunted the throne room too strongly for that. Luntar saw a future that might be better than those that had burned him but if he steered us toward it, it would start to retreat, and if he answered our questions the whole possibility might evaporate like a morning mist. Even giving us the box would have blinded him to our paths now, making his vision less clear. Do nothing and see everything that will be with perfect and impotent clarity—or reach out to change things and like a hand touching water destroy the reflection of tomorrow. The frustration of it would drive me mad.

"Open the box?" Garyus placed the box in question on the small table I'd carried over. I placed a lantern beside it: afternoon had shaded toward evening and the shadows multiplied in every corner. "Open the box . . ." He tapped his fingers on the polished surface.

"That's been known to go wrong in the past," I said.

Garyus raised an eyebrow at that. "Pandora?"

"All the ills of the world." I nodded. "Besides, he said it's full of ghosts. That's the case made for burying it right there."

"He also said we should ask them our questions."

I looked at the box and found my curiosity had dried right up.

"Are you scared, Jalan?" Garyus looked up at me, the light and shadow conspiring to make a monster of him. His deformity had that character—innocent one moment, pitiable even, the next sinister, malign. At those times I had no doubt he was twin to the Silent Sister.

"Scared doesn't cover it." The plasteek looked more like bone in the lantern light. Visions of Hell bubbled at the back of my mind and I wondered just how much of that place the art of the Builders might fit into one small box. "Petrified."

"Makes you feel alive, doesn't it?" And Garyus opened the box.

"Empty!" A laugh burst from me, somehow small and hollow in the loneliness of the hall.

"It does seem to—" Garyus drew his hand back with an oath. One red fingerprint remained where he had touched the lid.

"Blood?" I asked, tilting my head to study the mark.

Garyus nodded, one finger in his mouth. "The thing bit me!"

As we watched, the crimson print faded, the blood drawn into the substance of the plasteek, leaving no stain. Something flickered in the air above the open box. A figure, there then gone, misty, as if formed and lost in a cold breath. Another came, flickering into being, a man's shape, maybe eighteen inches high, gone.

"Kendeth." The word came from the box, an ageless voice, calm and clean.

A host of figures now, men, women, young, old, each twisting into the next.

"Stop . . ." Garyus raised a hand toward the box and as he did so the flickering motion ceased, just one figure there now, a pale ghost, the lines of the table visible through his body.

"James Alan Kendeth," the ghost said, not looking at either one of us but rather at some distant point between.

"You're the ghost of my ancestor?" Garyus asked.

The ghost frowned, flickered, and replied. "I am a library entry for the data echo of James Alan Kendeth. I can answer questions. To access the full simulation requires access to a net-terminal."

"What's it saying?" I asked. Some of the words made sense, the rest might as well be another language.

Garyus shushed me. "Are you a ghost?"

The ghost frowned then smiled. "No. I'm a copy of James Alan Kendeth. A representation of him based on detailed observations."

"And James himself?"

"He died more than a thousand years ago."

"How did he die?"

"A thermonuclear device detonated above the city in which he lived." A moment of sorrow on the ghost's pale face.

"A what?"

"An explosion."

"A Builders' Sun?"

"A fusion device . . . so like the sun, yes."

"Why did the Builders destroy themselves?" Garyus stared at the little ghost, floating above its empty box, his great brow mounded above the intensity of his eyes.

The ghost flickered and for a split second I saw its skin bubble as if remembering the heat. "No reason that matters. An escalation of rhetoric. One domino falling against the next and in a few hours everything was ashes."

"Why would they do it again, now?" Garyus asked. "Why destroy us?"

"To survive." Our distant ancestor looked from Garyus to me and back to Garyus as if noticing us as people for the first time, not just voices with questions. "The continued use of will is unbalancing . . ." He paused, his gaze now on some distant thing in some other place. ". . . the Rechenberg equation—that's what they call it—it governs the change, what you people call the 'magic.' We called it magic too, to be honest. Maybe one person in ten thousand understood it. The rest of us just knew that the scientists had changed how the world worked and bang, magic became possible, superpowers! It wasn't like it is today though—it was harder to use—we had training and—"

"Our magics are unbalancing your equation." Garyus cut across him. "Why kill us?"

"If everyone dies there'll be no more magic used. The equation may balance itself. The change may stop. The world might survive and the data-echoes held in the deepnet would be preserved."

"You'd sacrifice us for echoes? But . . . you're not real. You're not alive," I said. "You're memories in machines?"

"I feel real." The ghost-James set ghost-hands to his transparent chest.

"I feel alive. I wish to continue. In any event, if we don't destroy you then you'll only destroy yourselves and us with you."

He had a point there but I had little sympathy for any point that might impale me. "So why are we still here? Why only two explosions?"

"There is disagreement. There isn't a majority in favour of the nuclear solution. Yet. Gelleth was an accident. Hamada was a test that went wrong."

"Why are you telling us all this?" I wouldn't have been so forthcoming in his position.

"I'm a library entry. Answering is my purpose."

"But somewhere . . . in the machines . . . is a full copy of James Alan Kendeth? One with opinions and desires?"

The ghost nodded. "Even so."

"Can the Wheel be turned back?" Garyus asked with sudden urgency.

A pause. "You're referring to IKOL facility at Leipzig?" James sounded as if he were reading from a book.

"The Wheel of Osheim."

James Alan Kendeth nodded. Another pause. "It's a particle accelerator, a circular tunnel over two hundred miles long. The idea of a steering-wheel for the universe is a simplified way of understanding the change that the IKOL facility effected and continues to drive. The engines at IKOL turn a hypothetical wheel, a dial if you like, changing the default settings for reality. The machinery in the collision chamber would dwarf your cathedrals. In short it is a machine, not a wheel that can be turned."

"It's a machine!" I seized on the idea. "You're a machine. You turn it off!"

"The system is isolated to prevent interference. To approach it physically would be . . . difficult. The Rechenberg field fluctuates wildly as one approaches."

"Oh well." I reached for the box, eager to shut it. Every bad story that ever began starts with Osheim, and I knew just how bad things grew as you approached it. I would put my faith in Grandmother to save us. "Nothing can be done then." My hand grew cold before my fingers even reached the box, as if I'd plunged it into cold water.

"Entanglement detected." The original voice of the box, neither male, nor female, nor human. Our ancestor's ghost flickered out of being to be replaced by an elderly narrow-faced man. He stood before us for a moment then faded into a younger woman with short hair and eyes ringed with dark circles, no beauty but striking. The man returned, then the woman. Both seemed familiar somehow.

"Stop," I said, and the woman stayed.

"Asha Lauglin," the ageless voice spoke and fell silent. The woman looked up and met my eyes.

"H . . . how did you die?" I withdrew my hand. Something in her gaze scared me.

"I didn't die," she said.

"You're just an echo, a story in a machine, we know that. How did the real Asha die?"

"She didn't die." Asha glanced at Garyus then returned her gaze to me.

"What happened to her on the Day of a Thousand Suns?"

"She transmuted by force of will. Her identity became mapped into negative energy states in the dark energy of the universe."

"What?"

"She became incorporeal."

"What?"

"A spirit."

"A dark spirit." I stared at the woman. "Aslaug?"

"She became trapped in the mythology of the humans who repopulated the northern regions, yes. The belief of many untrained minds proved stronger than her will."

I thought of Aslaug, Loki's daughter, lie-born, her spider-shadow and the monstrous form of her that day when she came through the wrongmages' door in Osheim. "I'm sorry."

The Builder-ghost shrugged. "It's not a unique fate. How many of us are trapped in the stories told about us, or by us?" She gave me a hard and quizzical stare that reminded me still more strongly of Aslaug.

I didn't much like the implication and started to bluster. "Well I'm not—"

"There's a story about a charming prince trying to snare you even now, Jalan. There's another story you tell yourself that might pull you along a very different path."

"You're very talkative for a library entry." I moved again to shut the box.

"I never liked to play by the rules, Jalan." She gave that dark smile I knew so well.

A pounding on the great doors of the throne room drowned out any reply I had and the head of the palace guard pushed through without waiting for a reply.

"Steward, Marshal, the city is under attack! The dead are in the river!"

TWELVE

The attack came along both shores of the Seleen, heralded by the arrival of a raft of corpses floating with the current. The bodies, more than a hundred of them, looked by the remnants of their colours to be war-dead from the Orlanth advance into Rhone. When the boat crews had gone out to intercept it, it quickly became apparent that mire-ghouls had insinuated themselves among the mass, hanging on to the edges, just their dark heads above the water, or lying flat on top of the tangled bodies, blowpipes held close and ready.

"Have the Iron Hoof join us at the Morano Bridge!" I shouted orders as I rode toward the Horse Gate to depart the palace. After being made marshal I'd secured a fine charger named Murder, a huge beast and fiery with it. Damned hard to control, though, and on the point of breaking into a gallop at every moment. "Tell Prince Martus to keep the Seventh at the palace gates until we know the situ—Whoa!" I wrenched Murder's head around and leaned forward as he tried to rear. "Tell him to send runners to all the wall towers."

"Yes, Marshal!" The palace guard captain had followed me from the throne room with five of his men, receiving, and hopefully remembering, the orders I reeled off as I collected Murder from the stables. Now, with Captain Renprow and ten message riders from the regular palace guard around me, I waved for the gates to be opened. We would make for the Morano Bridge, the best viewpoint from which to see a great length of the Seleen's banks, both east and west, upstream and down. The reports I had were already half an hour old: where the fighting might be now and what situation would greet us I couldn't say. The Iron Hoof was nothing more than a drinking club for the richest sons of the aristocracy these days, but they had all been officers in the cavalry before Grandmother disbanded it, and whilst lancers would be of little use in the city, they would at least be able to get where they were going in a hurry.

I spotted one of the house-guards, Double, heading off on some errand and sent him back to Roma Hall with orders to secure the place. He was the youngest of Father's house-guards and probably the only one still fit enough to give account of himself in a fight. "Don't let anyone you don't know in, dead or alive! Especially dead. Even if you *do* know them!"

Double set off back to the hall at a run and I took a last glance around. The shadows of Milano House stretched toward the Inner Palace, as if Hertet were reaching for his mother's throne. The sun burned low on the walls, without heat. The day was dying on me. "Let's go!"

Within moments we were clattering beneath the gate arch and racing off along Kings Way, our hooves striking sparks from the cobbles. For the next several minutes the business of riding at speed along roads variously packed, narrow, winding, or all three at once, occupied our attention. Flattening a peasant or two is all well and good, but if you're in a hurry to get somewhere it can slow you down. Also, in Vermillion peasants are thin on the ground and you're likely to have the injured party's father or guild or whatever camped outside the palace gates the next day seeking compensation. Or worse, justice.

I led the way as we galloped along the west bank toward the Morano Bridge. I didn't want to lead but everyone else deferred to me as marshal and Murder proved disinclined to let any other horse go ahead even when I tried to slow him. The lane along the west bank is broad in places, even paved in some stretches, but toward the bridge a strip of hard-trodden ground served, threading between stands of bulrushes leading to the water and a tangle of briar rising to the walls of the riverside merchants' houses. I saw figures ahead and shouted at them to clear the way.

"Marshal!" Captain Renprow hollering behind me. There was more to it lost in the thunder of hooves.

The people ahead proved too slow, and given the option of pulling up, veering left into swampy riverbank, right into briar patch, or simply mowing down muddy peasants, I opted for the princely solution and rode on. My disregard for public safety proved prudent as the figures turned out to be bloated and slime-covered river corpses that wanted to pull me from the saddle.

A dozen men of the Iron Hoof caught up with us as we turned onto the bridge, having taken an alternate route. Half of them looked as if they'd come straight from lunch. Lord Nester's son still had a napkin tucked into his collar, though Young Sorren had thought to strap on a breastplate.

"Iron Hoof, ho!" I led the charge up onto the Morano Bridge, a boyhood ambition, and we clattered to the middle of the span.

"The enemy don't appear to need bridges." Darin rode up beside me, having somehow joined our party unnoticed as we left the palace. "They're happy enough getting wet."

"It's me that needs the bridge." I stood in the stirrups, hoping that for once Murder would hold still. I never paid that much attention in our strategy and tactics classes but the one lesson that did seem to have been hammered in sufficiently deep to stick was that a commander needed to see his battlefield. When your battlefield was an entire city, in which seeing from one end of a road to the other could be difficult, that lesson came to haunt you pretty quickly. All I had to go on were brief reports now nearly an hour old. Any new intelligence not delivered by my own eyes would have to follow an increasingly long chain of directions to reach me.

I stared out across the city of Vermillion. Innumerable rooftops, spires here and there, mansions on the rises overlooking the river, starlings wheeling on high, the great blue sky above, dashed with cloud, the air crisp with that feel it gets when the leaves are colouring as they gather their courage for the fall. Somewhere amid all that the enemy was already at work. River-dead might be easily discovered at the end of a series of wet footprints, but necromancers were harder to find. Some Drowned Isles death-worker might have taken a room at a riverside tavern and be watching us even now through his shutters.

"Over there!" Darin, his steed perilously close to the bridge balustrade, pointed downstream toward the east bank.

"What?"

"It's still autumn and there's hardly a chill in the air," he said.

"So?" I hated him sometimes.

"People seem to be lighting their fires early . . ."

It was true. What I'd taken for smoke rising from a number of chimneys now looked more sinister.

"All that time spent seeing to our walls and the suburbs beyond might better have been spent here," Darin said. "The river's our weakest border."

"Marshal." Captain Renprow pointed upstream to the west bank, saving me from having to reply. A knot of figures, tiny in the distance, struggling on a boat dock, city guard units advancing down the river path.

Glancing to the opposite shore I saw more figures, some running away, some giving chase. Where the sun still lingered on the gabled rooftop of St. Mary-on-Seleen I saw shapes moving, just three hundred yards away: the black and spidery forms of mire-ghouls clambering over the tiled roof ridge.

"They're everywhere." Corpses must have lain hidden under the water where the current lagged, or been drowned in the river mud, waiting for the sign to attack. I couldn't tell their numbers—it didn't look like a vast army of them, but they were dispersing into the heart of my city, hunting for prey, and if the Dead King had his full attention on us then each kill might add to their numbers. "Send word to the watch garrisons at Taggio, Saint Annes, Doux, and LeCrosse. All city guard to advance toward the Seleen in groups of not less than twenty, clearing the streets as they go. All crossbow men to be deployed, with an eye to the rooftops for ghouls."

"Sire!" An Iron Hoof rider beside me, Lord Borron's younger son. He nodded to the far end of the bridge. A dozen or so figures had started to approach.

"The hell?" At first I couldn't make sense of it. Bloated river-men, black with slime, staggering our way with awkward steps; but city guard too, the dark red of their tabards clear, sun glinting on their helmets . . . those that had them.

"They're all dead." Darin, at my side. He was right: they weren't fighting each other, they were advancing on us.

"Well, what are you waiting for?" I asked. "Ride them down. Are you lancers or milk-nurses?" To be fair none of the Iron Hoof riders actually had lances with them, but they still had the advantage of being mounted on horses bred for war.

"I was just waiting to be led, Marshal Jalan." Darin managed a grin and gestured "after you."

"Ah." The odds were with us, but there were quite a lot of the bastards, and in war I like the odds stacked so heavily in my favour that the only danger to me is being crushed by them should they fall. "You see . . ."

Captain Renprow came to my aid. "The marshal is responsible for the defence of the entire city, Prince Darin. He cannot allow himself the luxury of actual combat. It would be a disaster were he to be incapacitated."

"That's right. Exactly right." I restrained myself from leaning across and hugging Renprow. "It kills me not to be allowed to get in there amongst them and swing my sword and whatnot, but duty is a stern mistress."

Darin rolled his eyes. "Get Martus down here with his men. It's madness to leave them by the palace." With that he raised his sword overhead and bellowed, "For the Red Queen!" Then, kicking in his heels, "Vermillion!" And he was off, the others streaming behind him. A deafening clatter of hooves and close on ten tons of angry beast hurtled toward the Dead King's creatures.

I managed to stop one of the palace guards from joining the charge by dint of grabbing his shoulder and demanding that he stay. In that moment of distraction Murder very nearly escaped me to set off after Darin, but if there's one thing I do well it's horses and I managed to turn him.

"Right," I said. "We need some sort of plan."

The man I'd held back slapped his neck, "Jesus!"

"Not a plan," I said. "What we . . ." I trailed off as he drew back his hand to reveal a small black dart sticking into the flesh just below his Adam's apple. "Jesus." I looked around wildly and spotted the mire-ghoul responsible, now clambering over the balustrade, blowpipe in one hand.

"I kept you back for exactly this kind of thing," I told the guard. "Kill it quick! Don't worry about the dart, it's just poison."

The man shot a very dark look at me from under the brim of his helm.

"I mean it just makes you weak—if you hurry you can kill the ghoul before—"

"Marshal . . . I can't see." He held one hand out before his face as if needing the confirmation. His eyes really had gone dark, the whites shading grey.

"Stay calm, it only lasts a few hours." I took his reins. Snorri had recovered from the weakness. "Renprow." I nodded to the ghoul that now had both feet on the bridge paving and was busy pushing another dart into its pipe.

"Marshal." Renprow drew his sword and cantered toward the ghoul ten yards closer to the riverbank.

"I'm fucking blind." The guard touched his eyes, forgetting all about princes and marshals now. His words came out slurred.

"You need to stay calm," I said. "It will get better."

At that the guard slid from his saddle with all the grace of a sack of oats. He landed on his head and shoulder with a rather nauseating crack and lay sprawled, his neck at an unnatural angle, one foot still in the stirrups.

"That might not get better," I acknowledged. I glanced up the bridge toward the melee where Darin and his fellows were now laying about themselves having trampled half the foe with their charge. Another glance at my fallen comrade and I put the boot into his horse, hard as I could. The dead man's eyes snapped open just before his horse lurched into motion and dragged him away toward my brother, head bouncing off every bump in the road.

A thud and the sound of a struggle returned my attention to Renprow and the ghoul. Somehow the thing had pulled him from his saddle, earning a slash in its side but now wrestling with the captain on the floor. Both had knives out, the captain's a long clean piece of steel, the ghoul's a curved and wicked-looking blade as darkly stained as its hide.

"Come on, Captain!" I offered moral support from Murder's back. Despite its wiry nature the ghoul seemed possessed of remarkable strength, its knife moving inexorably toward Renprow's neck against all the man's best efforts to stop it. "Ah hell." I slipped from the saddle and drew Edris Dean's sword. A moment presented itself so I hurried forward, and swung at the back of the ghoul's neck—not much more than dropping my arm really. With a blade that sharp and heavy I assumed anything more would risk decapitating the thing and carrying on through to the man beneath.

Actually it turns out that necks are tough as hell. My blade thudded in half an inch or so, becoming lodged in the ghoul's bony spine. Even so, between my wrenching it free and Renprow taking advantage to stab the creature repeatedly in the liver, we managed to triumph. The captain rolled to all fours then staggered to his feet, covered in filthy blood, while I looked over the balustrade and rapidly pulled my head back.

"Go get stones from the riverbank. Big ones!"

"What?" Renprow looked up from an inspection of his gore-spattered tunic.

"Big ones! Run!"

I risked a foolish glance back over the side and a ghoul dart nearly parted my hair for me. The bridge support was black with the things. Four, five, half a dozen? It was hard to tell as they clambered over each other, dripping, near naked, yet having no problem finding their grip.

I stood mid-span, aware that ghouls could climb up either side equally well. The sounds of combat still came from the far end. I couldn't risk a glance to see how Darin and the others were faring.

The first glimpse of the ghoul's blowpipe looked like a black stick poking up between the stone pillars of the balustrade. I ran, dived, slid, and ended up with my sword driven into the ghoul's eye socket as he raised his head to blow his dart. The creature fell away without a sound, nearly taking my blade with it.

By the time I made it across to the other side Renprow was closing on me, showing a decent turn of pace for a man burdened with four or five good-sized river stones.

"Take the other side." I dropped my sword and took the topmost of the stones with newfound respect for the small man's strength—the thing weighed a ton.

"Marshal." Renprow panted, letting another rock fall before lugging the rest to where I'd just killed the last ghoul.

Whatever venom the creatures coated their darts with proved remarkably water-resistant but coming from the marshes of Brettan that didn't seem too surprising. Just depressing. Advancing on the balustrade, I had few illusions about my fate if one of those darts hit me. I would have been running away but for the fact that my best chance lay in getting them while they were climbing rather than trying to dodge their missiles whilst sprinting down the bridge.

"I don't think so." I made a big last stride and managed to place my foot on top of the next blowpipe to edge into view.

With a grunt of effort I hefted the stone over the edge and, without looking over, let it drop onto the ghoul whose pipe I'd pinned. With even a modicum of luck it would strip several more of the creatures from the bridge support on its way down. As quickly as I could manage I grabbed the second stone and repeated the process a few feet to the right. There were no satisfying wails of despair or shrieks of agony, but the meaty thuds and accompanying splashes sounded promising.

"Got them, Marshal!" Renprow called over.

More men were approaching the bridge along the Morano Way, the route the Iron Hoof riders had taken. Soldiers, definitely the alive kind rather than the walking dead kind, filled the road from side to side, marching abreast, all in shadow, the sun gleaming only on the rooftops now.

"Check my side." I waved Renprow absently across the width of the bridge and started walking toward the advancing troops. By the time I got to the end of the bridge I could see Martus, four ranks back upon his horse, resplendent in breastplate, conical helm with faceguard and an aventail of chainmail spreading across his shoulders.

The sight of Martus and his army at least filled the citizenry with enough confidence for a few to open their windows and lean out to cheer whilst the men marched below. For my part I felt only a sense of nagging unease, which floated upon a sea of primal fear. I hadn't wanted the marshal's sash in the first place and it was beginning to look more like a noose by the minute.

Martus came to a halt fifty yards from the bridge with his soldiers streaming out to either side of him, heading in both directions along the bank.

"I left orders for you to stay at the palace!" I shouted, advancing on him.

"A good thing I ignored you!" He lifted his faceplate so he could bellow to full effect. "We've got a dozen or more incursions along both banks. Got to stamp these things out before they take hold. Like a plague these dead men. One makes the next and so on—"

"I'm the fucking marshal and you obey my orders!" I felt slightly foolish shouting up at him on the back of his stallion but I wasn't about to lose command to him, even if our audience were common foot soldiers.

Captain Renprow rode up behind me, leading Murder. Darin overtook him at the last, a good number of the men with him, battered, gore-splatted, but largely in one piece.

"You're to follow my orders, Martus," I said, not shouting now but loud enough for everyone to hear. "Or I'll see you hang."

"Hanging seems unlikely." Darin rode in between Martus and me, cutting off our brother's reply. "A week in the dungeons on the other hand . . ." He looked meaningfully at Martus, then glanced past him and frowned. "What's that?"

"Red smoke." I followed his gaze. "Shit. The walls." Red smoke had been my proudest instigation. Each wall tower now had a stock of a dozen paper-wrapped fire-powders that gave off copious red smoke when lit, the idea being that any emergency could be signalled swiftly across Vermillion in this manner, faster than messengers and with a longer reach than bells amid the cacophony of the city. As an added bonus the rare salts used in the fire-powder's manufacture were costly and dug from the Crptipa mines, leading to a nice profit that would come directly back to my pocket. Right now though, seeing a seven-tailed bank of red smoke rising from the towers of the east quarter, I would gladly have forgone all and any income resulting from the need to restock fire-powder.

"You're not making any sense . . . Marshal." Martus looked back at the smoke over the heads of his troops.

"We've got half the city watch and two thousand troops chasing less than two hundred dead along the riverbanks. Meanwhile at our city wall seven tower captains have seen something that made them scared enough to light the emergency signal . . ." Each tower stood sixty foot high, crenellated like a fortress and manned by a garrison of twenty-five with room for a hundred. I really didn't want to know what would be enough to cause seven of them to call for help at the same time. "This isn't the assault—this is the diversion!"

THIRTEEN

"I hope to God Grandmother named you marshal for a good reason."
Darin joined me atop the leftmost of the two towers flanking the Appan
Gate, his voice awestruck. "Most of our cousins thought it was a joke."

"Most?"

"The rest thought it was a punishment."

We looked out across Vermillion's overspill, the extended city reaching half a mile from the walls, still further where it followed the Appan
Way, as if desperate to wring a few more coins out of any traveller so
foolish as to leave. Dead people crowded the space before the gates—
men, women, children—the grey and flaking dead in the filthy remains
of their grave-clothes; the fresh dead, still scarlet with their murder, a
silent throng stretching out around the walls, back along the main road,
pressed tight in the alleys between houses.

Even sixty feet up with a light breeze the stench proved invasive,
tearing at the back of my throat, stinging my eyes. More than a few meals
had been splattered down the wall. The sight and smell of your first
walking dead is apt to do that to you.

"I gave standing orders for no archery." This to Renprow, the gore
drying on him now after our hurried ride from the bridge. A good number of the dead closest to the Appan Gate sported two, three, sometimes
five arrows, jutting from arms and chests—an elderly woman had one in
her eye. "It's a waste."

"I'll send out the order again, Marshal. It's hard for the men not to
shoot when the enemy advances on their positions."

I waved Renprow away. Soldiers of the wall guard packed the tower-top,
men of middling years in the main, many thick-waisted and gone to grey,

thinking to pace away their remaining years peacefully on the walls of the capital. The primary duty of a Vermillion wall guard is spotting fires. Apart from that they're basically a mobile reserve to the city guard and the only excitement they ever see is when they are called upon to descend into the city to back up their thinly stretched brothers in city red.

"Move!" Behind me Martus elbowed his way through the guard, blaring at any who didn't shift quick enough. "Get out of my way! I'm a bloody prince. I'll—Dear God . . ." Martus faltered in mid-bluster, squinting out across the dead horde against the setting sun. "Dear God." He grew pale. "I've never seen anything like . . . that."

"I have." I leaned out, hands on the battlements to support me. "I've seen worse." And in that moment I realized that while fear ran through me from head to toe, it wasn't the debilitating terror I'd known on so many other occasions. I thought then that maybe I knew why Grandmother had chosen me. "I've seen Hell." I raised my voice. "I've seen Hell and this isn't it. We're the Red Queen's men and we've all of Vermillion at our backs. A bunch of shuffling corpses isn't going to take it from us!"

A cheer went up at that, taking me by surprise. To be fair, Renprow did lead it, but the fact is the men around me had lost their courage and a few bold words from a frightened man had given them back some measure of it.

"How in God's name did . . ." Martus gazed across the multitude again, ". . . an army of three thousand dead reach our walls without any alarm?"

Darin rubbed at the stubble on his chin. "It's not as if you can't smell them a mile off! Didn't you send *any* scouts, Jal?"

I looked between my brothers. Some called them the twins, though Martus had a heavier build and Darin sharper features. No one ever called us the triplets, though in truth if I were two inches taller we might pass as such in a poor light. As much as I might profess to dislike them it actually felt good to have some family at my back—to have some people with me on the tower who genuinely didn't expect me to solve their problems or get it right.

"I have over a hundred men on wide patrol and no army could make its way through Red March without the word going out from towns and villages. That . . ." I pointed back at our enemy, ". . . was made here. Most of them probably killed in their homes within the last few hours while we were chasing ghouls around the river." I wondered how many necromancers might be out among those alleyways, or working in leafy squares, moving along rows of my people, fresh-killed and laid out on the cobbles side by side, one family at a time.

"What are we going to do?" Darin asked. The Darin I knew of old would have been telling me what we should do, laying it all out with a debonair swagger. I narrowed my eyes at him, wondering what ailed the man, before remembering the seven pounds of new pink flesh so recently arrived. Misha had put the baby in my hands when she and Darin had finally trapped me in the Roma Hall a few nights back. A tiny thing.

"We've called her Nia," Misha had said. I'd looked down at the child, named for my mother, and found my eyes stinging.

"Better take the little beast back before she wets my shirt," I'd said and thrust my niece back at her mother, but it had been too late. The old magic that babies weave so well had got in under my skin, contaminating me faster than piss or vomit or any of the other bodily fluids that newborns are so keen to share. Even a lifetime of evading all duties put upon me was insufficient practice to let this one slide off me like the others. How much worse to be the father?

Darin had taken Nia and lifted her up. "If my girl wants to soil her uncle's peacock feathers it's just testimony to her good taste." But he took no offence. He'd seen something come over me in the moment I held her, despite my trying to hide it, and had given me a knowing and very irritating smile.

"What are your orders, Marshal?" Captain Renprow asked, bringing me back to the horror of the tower-top and the Dead King's army.

"My orders?" I looked down at the dead again. "They don't seem to be much of a threat to the main city. No siege engines, no ropes, no bows. Are they planning to bore us to death?" It didn't make a lot of sense. I could hear faint screams, carried on the breeze from the outer city.

"My wife's out there." A man in the charcoal grey of the wall guard, a common ranksman. He pointed to a slight rise topped by a church, houses ringed around it like ripples. A muscle twitched in his jaw. "My sons and their children are down Pendrast way." He swung his arm to indicate another region, smoke rising above shingled roofs. "And over—"

"Hold your tongue, soldier!" A hefty sergeant, red-faced.

"Twenty-three thousand living beyond the city walls at the last census, Marshal," Renprow reported the number in a penetrating voice.

"I hope they're running." I hoped it for their sakes and for ours. If the dead horde were swelled by over twenty thousand new recruits they might ring the city so effectively that we would stand besieged.

"Can't we . . ." Darin didn't finish the sentence, he knew the answer was no. We couldn't go out there.

"We haven't the numbers."

Behind us a team of men struggled to position the scorpion, a hefty device of iron and timber and ropes, capable of hurling a heavy spear four hundred yards. At close range it could launch that spear through the front door of a house, put a hole through three men behind it, and punch its way out through the back door.

"We can't stand here staring at them all day," I said. "We've got dead in the streets, and mire-ghouls. They need to be stamped on, and hard."

Three of the four captains of the city watch had joined us on the overcrowded tower-top and now approached as I beckoned. Their commander, Lord Ollenson, would be overseeing the operation at the river— that or attending his own public beheading on the morrow—but the wall alarm had brought captains Danaka, Folerni, and Fredrico to my side.

"Danaka, I want you with three squads at the north watch." Two towers overlooked the Seleen where it entered the city, each of them standing with its feet in the water, terminating the wall. "Fredrico, three squads to the south watch." The fortifications overlooking the river's exit were less formidable. Any boats attempting to enter Vermillion that way would have to contend with the current, making them slow and cumbersome.

I turned to Folerni, a wiry goat of a man, his left eye milky, the brow above and cheek below divided by a scar. The look of him reminded me of the Silent Sister and I paused. Before I could find my words a dreadful howling overwrote whatever I might have said. The kind of sound that would set statues running the other way. I made a slow rotation toward the walls, though the sound unmanned me and no part of me wanted to look.

My eyes fixed on a disturbance past the dead crowding the Appan Gate. A few hundred yards back along the main road a change had come over the corpses shambling toward the walls. It almost seemed to be a wave, moving through their ranks. Their heads snapped up, they became horribly alert, and their mouths gaped wide to utter that terrible cry. Perhaps only the fresh-killed could scream but it sounded as though the noise came from corrupt lungs long past use, the voice of the grave, death itself speaking, and not softly. The undulating howl came full of threat, promising the worst kind of pain.

Every place where the change came the dead moved faster, with wild energy, scrambling up buildings to tear at the roofs, seeking any that might be left inside, hammering on doors, or rushing toward us with an enthusiasm that suddenly made the city walls small comfort. I heard bows creak beside me.

"Do not fire."

The wave of "awakenings" moved steadily toward the gates, a tight-packed knot of the quickened dead surging ahead. But I noticed something. Before my time in Hell my eye would have been too fascinated by the horror of the spectacle to pick up on details, but my time there had changed me. At the back of the surge I saw the dead return to their stumbling, once more closer to sleepwalkers than to wolverines.

"They're turning!" Martus, shouting beneath the death-call.

It looked at first as if he were right, but they weren't turning, the effect was turning. The area where the dead quickened veered off to the left a hundred yards from the gates. Those who had been howling for our blood fell silent and sullen once more and other dead men, and their wives, and their children, suddenly took up the cry in the streets to the left of the Appan Way.

"It's as if . . ." I spoke the words only for myself. It was as if they felt some awful heat that made them fierce, and the thing from which that heat radiated . . . was on the move. I tried to see where the focus of the effect lay . . . and saw it, a shifting point where it almost looked as if the world had folded around itself to obscure something the eye shouldn't see. "There!" I raised my voice, pointing now. "There! Do you see it?"

"See what?" Martus pushed to the wall beside me.

"There's . . . something." Darin on my other side, squinting. "Something . . . wrong."

"I can't see a damn thing! Where?" Martus shielding his eyes against the dying rays of the sun.

I stared, tracking the point, losing it behind houses, picking it up again. A space where the light seemed folded. A dead spot on the eye. And then, for just a moment, I did see. Perhaps it was the setting sun lending me a hint of the old dark-sight Aslaug used to bring, or maybe Hell had trained my eye to see what the men were not supposed to see. A flicker of motion, an impossibly thin body, nerve-white, clad in a shifting shroud of grey: soul-stuff perhaps, the ghosts of men haunting the lichkin's flesh like a garment.

"Shit."

"What? What is it?" Darin, still staring.

"A lichkin," I said. A lichkin, one of the parasites that Edris and his kind set riding the unborn children they slew. Such a thing held my sister and wanted nothing more than to wear her flesh into the living world. But here we had a naked one, broken into the world through God knows what crack, and scarcely less dangerous than an unborn from what I'd seen in Hell.

"Where's it going?" Martus asked. The sound of howling grew more distant as the lichkin moved away.

"Hunting," I said, and I felt Grandmother's gaze upon me as surely as if I stood before her throne, those eyes of hers, harder than hard, without any shred of compromise. I remembered finally opening that scroll-case Garyus had given me, seeing the Red Queen's seal, breaking it open to see the words in her own hand. *Marshal of Vermillion*. And a note: "*You say you saw the defence of Ameroth. Pray that you learned its lesson and pray harder that you will never have to show that you learned it.*"

A hundred men stood at my back, a city behind them, mine to wield, mine to protect. In all my adventures across the face of the Broken Empire I'd never want to be somewhere else quite as much as I did in that moment. I looked out across the rooftops, all in shadow now, the sky aflame, boiling red above the departed sun. "Burn it all."

The howling had passed almost beyond hearing, the dead below us stood silent. Nobody spoke. I heard the flutter of the flags, the wind's whisper, and far off behind the walls the cry of a street vendor singing out his wares.

I turned and walked toward the scorpion. The men parted before me. "Burn it all." I slapped a hand to the heavy spear loaded into the machine. "Rags and oil. Shoot for the rooftops. Send word to all the towers."

Martus wrenched me around. "That's madness! What the hell's wrong with you?"

"We can't defend the outer city. By morning they'll all be dead and added to the army at our gates."

"It's not sane! It's not right." Martus shook me, raising his voice, mutters from all sides adding to his protest.

"Would you lead the Seventh out there?" I cocked my head toward the darkening streets of the outer city. We could hear distant screaming, another house broken into.

"Well . . . I . . ." Martus screwed his face up, presaging one of his furious blusters. "It would be madness."

"I wouldn't let you." I shook him off and sought the guardsman who had pointed to his home out by the church on the hill. "You. Your name."

"Daccio, your highness." He had a subdued look to him, his anger gone, though it showed now on the faces of his comrades.

"Daccio. I'm sorry but your wife is dead, your sons too. Or they're hiding in their homes waiting to be saved." I looked about at the wall guard, grey in their ranks. "Are you going to save them? Will the wall guard descend these walls this last time and sally forth where the Seventh Army fear to tread? Or will the lichkin find them out? If we do nothing the dawn will show us your family standing bloody before our gates." I took a rag from the base of the scorpion, an oily thing used on the bow arms to keep them from rust. "Fire is clean. Better to burn than let those creatures have you. And what better chance will our people have to run than in the smoke and confusion of a great conflagration?" I slapped the rag into Daccio's hand. "Do it."

And he did.

FOURTEEN

The lichkin returned before the flames took full hold. I kept to the tower, needing to see though not wanting to. Darin remained at my side. Martus departed to direct the Seventh, dispatching them to the most vulnerable sections of the wall in hundreds, each squad led by a captain. At my direction five hundred men of the Seventh would stay with Martus in reserve at the palace. I told Martus to insist that the palace guard—some four hundred men, veterans in the main, be sent to join my command.

The dead had first mustered at the Appan Gate and the throng there grew steadily even as my order went out and the deep twangs of scorpions began to sound all along the walls. The fire took hold: a rooftop here, a covered wagon there, orange tongues licking up, hungry for new flavours, and a loose pall of smoke drifted over the dead.

"We're never going to be forgiven for this." Darin looked out over the fires with disbelieving eyes.

"It's me they won't forgive," I said. "And without this there will be no one left to do the forgiving."

"Never thought you had it in you, Jal." Barras Jon had sought me out, determined to do his bit for the defence. He looked ready for the tourney lists in his Vyenese armour, following the latest lamellar fashion, each iron plate embossed with the rose sigil of his house. "It looks like Hell down there."

"It's getting closer to it."

The night lay dark and moonless but the fires we'd started lit the scene in undeniably hellish tones. Barras wiped at his face, smearing an ash flake across his pale cheek. It seemed insane, the two of us here, staring out over an army of the dead lit by the growing inferno that had been Vermillion. I expected to see his face over a goblet of wine, or lit by the excitement of the races, not framed by an iron helm, eyes wide with fright. He lowered his perforated visor, becoming still more the stranger.

Through the smoke and flames we saw some of my prediction coming true, people moved by fear of the conflagration bursting out of the security of their homes and running for the open country. They stood a much better chance in this involuntary mass exodus than they did waiting for the dead to break in. When the lichkin came close the quickened dead would rip apart their doors and there would be no escape. Now although they faced hordes of walking corpses at least they were the shambling kind rather than the sprinting kind.

Additionally the sheer number of fleeing citizens, along with the leaping fire and thick smoke, confused the scene so much that many of Grandmother's subjects looked as though they might actually win free and get to watch the night's events from the comfort of some lonely cornfield or distant patch of woodland. Even so, as I saw them run I knew there would be others too paralysed by the horrors outside their walls to leave, even when the smoke crept beneath their doors and the flames started to peel back their roofs. If I had eaten more recently I might have added my own contribution to the vomit-stained walls.

"I just don't see how they can harm us," Darin said at my side, as if wanting affirmation. "They've got no weapons. They can't punch through walls or push open the gates. They can't climb . . . these ones are just shambling and even when they get angry they're not going to be scaling sheer walls. They've no ropes, no ladders, nothing . . ."

I hadn't an answer for him. Even so, the not knowing made me feel scared rather than confident.

"Christ, what's that?" Barras Jon spun around, clanking, nearly impaling a watchman on his sword.

"You'd see better if you took that thing off." Darin rapped his knuckles on Barras's great helm. Any further joking died on his lips as he too caught the sound of the death-cry.

"The lichkin is coming back." The roar, faint but still laden with enough threat to core a man, approached from the west. The dead below us had tripled in number since it departed, more crowding in by the minute. They had some rudimentary fear of fire, enough to make them press away from it, though with so little room to spare some of those closest to the burning buildings had started to smoulder. I saw one young woman in a blue dress—a merchant's daughter perhaps—with no marks of violence visible upon her, go up like a torch beside a burning tavern. I'd taken ale there once upon a time, though I couldn't remember the place's name. Her hair ignited in a fiery halo and she started to clamber over the backs of other corpses to escape the heat.

Getting a count of the numbers arrayed against us had proved difficult, what with the smoke, and the density of the buildings sheltering many of the streets from view, but no one who stood there with me argued that there were less than ten thousand dead before the gates of Vermillion. The noise came nearer, the speed of its approach terrifying.

"Here it comes! To arms! Your city stands behind you!" I shouted the words above the rising howl as somewhere out in the dark, amid the growing inferno, the lichkin raced toward us.

The lichkin swept through those thousands as fast as a horse galloping, veering toward the gates. I leaned out as far as I dared to track its progress but it raced out of view beneath the gatehouse into the space immediately before the doors of Vermillion.

When it struck the gates the dead there went berserk, hammering and howling at the timbers. I imagined fists striking the wood so hard their bones shattered. The pounding subsided and the nerve-splitting screaming intensified as the great mass of corpses behind them pressed forward, a slow but steady mounting of pressure. The gates began to creak, at first like a house settling at night, then louder, a series of high retorts as the timbers fought their battles against each other, and beneath that a deep groan as the locking bars took up the strain, three great iron-shod cores from the heart of thousand-year oaks. A sharp ping as somewhere a rivet shot out of its socket.

"Get men down there! Push back." My utter faith in the gates' strength lasted less than a minute. "Quick, dammit! I want three hundred men down there now!" I wanted to be down there myself, putting my shoulder to those doors, but I had to see.

I leaned out over the battlements to look down at the top of the gatehouse a short way below us. The soldiers there had two great caul-drons of oil set above a bed of glowing coals to boil.

Barras elbowed alongside me. "You think dead men are even going to notice boiling oil?" A mixture of pessimism and hope in his voice. I knew it well from long nights at the dice table, where he lost a fortune, and at the card table, where he won one back . . . mostly from me.

"It might inconvenience them . . . a bit." I shrugged. "The main thing is that the men have something to do." At times like these it's better to have something to do rather than let fear sink its claws into you.

"Burning oil now—that would be something!" Barras said. "They'd notice that!"

"Only an idiot starts a fire at the foot of his gates, Barras." Darin, joining us.

It's rare I'll support a brother above a friend but he had it right. "The oil won't burn, it's a mineral oil from Attar. You can put a bonfire out with that. Costs the earth but better pour money on your enemy than some-thing they can fire your gates with!"

Darin raised an eyebrow. "You know your stuff, little br—"

"I'm the fucking marshal, Darin."

"You know your stuff, Little Marshal." He grinned.

"I'm a good study when it comes to keeping safe." Darin had never bought into the whole hero of Aral Pass story and I didn't feel the need to pretend for his benefit.

The men by the cauldrons were looking up at me now, seeing they had an audience.

"Pour it!" I shouted. I'd seen no sign of necromancers but there was always a chance they were mingled among the dead, hiding in plain sight. Edris Dean had taught me that they weren't common men, but even so, a shower of boiling oil would certainly spoil their day.

At my order the men started to uncover the murder-holes and ready the supports that would tip the cauldrons.

The oil hissed down the murder-holes with a satisfying sizzle, but damned if I heard even a change in the tone of the screaming from down below.

"Damn." Somewhat deflated, I went back to watch from the front of the tower.

For ten minutes the howling dead threw their weight against the Appan Gate, each crack and groan of the timbers taking my guts in a cold fist and twisting them. The lichkin moved back and forth, in and out of the gatehouse, sending waves of surging fury against the doors. I heard splintering and bit my lip to keep from adding my own note of despair to the mix.

"The fire's really taking hold." Darin choked on the smoke as if to prove his point. I'd had my gaze fixed on the backs of the dead men pressing in, but now looking back out at the outer city I saw Darin had it right. The upper halves of several houses closest to the walls had collapsed, sending vast columns of flames roaring up higher than the walls, pluming sparks and embers into the air. All across the outer city fire leapt from roof to roof, chasing along fences, licking at doorways. Everywhere the dead stood scorched and blistered, some with their hair and clothing burned away. I could see the remains of others, coiled amid the spreading blaze. For a moment I thought of Father on his pyre.

I coughed and pressed the heels of my hands to stinging eyes. "They're moving!"

The lichkin flowed out through the corpse-ranks, abandoning the assault on the gates. The fire had removed the luxury of time from our enemy. A general might have retreated to the surrounding farms and waited in the olive groves before returning a day later, but I guessed that dead men and spirits were more elemental than strategic. What I knew of the Dead King himself, and it was precious little, painted him not as a planner but as a force of destruction unwittingly steered by the Lady Blue's machinations.

The dead did not withdraw and the lichkin didn't try to escape from the flames—instead it tracked away from us, around the walls, as if seeking a weakness.

Two hundred yards to the east the dead who had formerly been standing vigil before the walls now quickened and began to tear at the base of a tower standing so close that a man atop it might throw a spear at the watchmen with a good chance of hitting one.

I'd visited that same structure days before—a water tower to service the well-appointed homes of several merchants who could have afforded to live within the city bounds, albeit in considerably less grand mansions. The tower also supplied water to a prosperous smithy servicing the needs of various wheelwrights, cartwrights, and provisioners with outlets on the Appan Way just as it left the gates.

I had marvelled that Grandmother allowed the tower so close to her walls despite her oft-repeated threats to level the suburbs at even the hint of war. It turned out that licence had been granted on the basis that the structure was designed to fall. Sturdy wooden buttresses supported the tower wall and without them the thing would collapse. Rather than providing a platform from which archers might clear our walls, the tower was a death-trap. Targeting the buttresses with iron bolts fired from a scorpion would topple the tower, killing any enemy in it and hopefully no few of those close by.

"What the hell—" The tower came down before I could finish. A score and more of the dead shattered by the deluge of masonry and timber.

More quickened dead closed on the rubble, shrouded in dust now as well as smoke. Within moments they were on the move, hauling the broken stones to the wall, dead men hefting thick and splintered beams, dead children dragging smaller pieces. Others came rushing from nearby streets pushing carts, wagons, doors ripped from houses, all of it thrown in an untidy heap before the walls.

"They're building a ramp!" Darin gripped the battlements. "We've got to get over there."

The parapet at that section, like all the others, was well-manned, albeit by the old men of the wall guard, and more were converging on the spot from both sides. "We need to stop them is what we need to do, not stand there waiting for them to do it." I started toward the tower steps, but turned instead to the battlements overlooking the gates. The empty cauldrons stood beside the murder-holes, smoking gently.

"Fill those with fire-oil!" I gestured to the men on the scorpion that had been manoeuvred to the front of our tower. "Take it down to them." They had small barrels of the stuff, and tubs of tar, all used for the firing of the suburbs. "You! All of you." I pointed to the wall guard at the back. "Run to the other towers, fetch their fire-oil and tar."

"They're dropping rocks on them, Jal!" Barras hollered from the other side of the tower, looking back at me, visor raised, face flushed. "That should do it!"

I raced across to see. The guard were hefting stones over the top of the wall, some as big as a man's head, most much larger. Men with wheeled barrows hurried up with more ammunition from stockpiles along the parapet. Down below carnage reigned, dead men's heads shattering wetly as plummeting rocks hit them. Others, bent in the act of placing their own chunks of masonry on the heap, fell broken as stones hammered into their backs.

"It's working!" Captain Renprow beside me.

"Yes, but not for us," I said, narrowing my eyes at the heap, trying to pierce the shifting shroud of dust and smoke. None of the men around me understood the dead or their king the way I did. I turned to Renprow. "Stop them! Fast as you can. They're just helping to build the ramp for them." Their rain of stones, and the crushed bodies it created, were mounding up at the base of the wall. New dead just replaced the old, unloading their cargo of masonry and timber atop the twitching remains beneath their feet. "We need to reinforce that area. Get Martus's soldiers there." I didn't say it out loud but I didn't have much faith in the wall guard. Age may make a man a little wiser but it makes his sword arm a lot slower. It had never seemed likely that Vermillion would be attacked, certainly not without considerable warning. Having the wall guard as a retirement plan for old soldiers had seemed a sensible idea. Now it seemed less so.

The messages took forever to go out. The first load of fire-oil wasn't tipped into the first cauldron for several minutes. With the dead howling and their ramp building it seemed like a lifetime. Just to get the wall guard to stop raining rocks on the attackers took minutes when seconds felt too long.

"They'll never make it to the top," Darin said. He had a point. The walls seemed short from the elevation of a sixty foot tower, but they stood a good thirty feet above the outer city and the dead men's ramp was scarcely more than ten foot high, maybe twice that in width. The thing about a heap is that as it gets taller it grows more slowly, it spreads and requires ten times the labour and materials to double in height. "Never." Even so Darin's affirmation sounded more like a prayer.

For ten minutes we watched them build, while the fires beyond the ramp grew until the flames' roar became louder than even the rage of the dead. Perhaps necromancers watched us from the night, somehow enduring the inferno, but I saw nothing save corpse upon corpse, all driven toward the wall and their mound of broken rock and broken bodies. I glimpsed the lichkin from time to time, and regretted even looking for it. Once it turned the narrow, eyeless wedge of its head toward our tower and the cold horror of its regard settled upon me like a great weight of ice. I backed rapidly, then half-crouched, half-collapsed, and dropped out of sight below the level of the tower wall.

"Marshal?" Renprow followed, reaching down for me.

"Here you go, Jal." Barras grabbing my arm to haul me to my feet. "Can't have our glorious leader fainting. Bad for moral."

"I dropped something." I pretended to shove some item hidden in my fist into a pocket beneath the chainmail I'd donned. There'd been no time to get my armour from the palace so instead the Marshal of Vermillion stood in an ill-fitting chainshirt from the gatehouse stores. "Where's that damn oil? Aren't the cauldrons full yet?"

"Something coming!" An archer at the front of the tower.

"Something big!" The man beside him, clutching his spear as if it were the only thing keeping him on his feet.

Renprow let go of my arm and elbowed his way forward to see.

"Lots of them!" A large, bearded man, backing away from the wall in what looked suspiciously like retreat.

"Marshal!" Renprow beckoning me.

Dread nearly pushed me back on the floor but I walked forward to join him, squinting into the stinging smoke. The approaching shapes, dark against the blaze to either side of the Appan Way, were the kind to give you nightmares. They had something of the spider about them, but also something of the hand, or perhaps a mutilated dog, hollowed out and walking on the stumps of its legs. I could make out the figures of men behind them, and realized in that moment that each of the half dozen monsters was larger than two carthorses strapped together.

"Get that scorpion forward again!" I turned back. "Do it fucking now! And signal the other towers to open fire. Archers on the men behind! Every man with a bow." I prayed that these at last were the necromancers and that filling them full of arrows would put them down. "And, for the love of God, get those cauldrons over to the ramp. I don't care how full they are!"

The men around me started to volley arrows into the sky. Whether they were hitting or not I couldn't tell until at last one of the men toward the rear of the column fell, clutching his face.

"Target the men! Target the men! They're necromancers!"

The initial scorpion shot went wide. It impaled three dead men shuffling along just in front of the foremost monstrosity, passing through and skimming off the road behind them. The three turned like lazy tops turning once, twice, and falling. All of them had regained their feet before the next shot sounded. The things advanced and the smoke blew aside for a moment to let the fire's glare reveal them. Each of them crafted along similar designs, shaped like a hand missing the two middle fingers, walking on three legs, the limbs made from the thighbones of half a dozen men, glistening with the remnants of muscle and bound together with yards of sinew. Several arrow shafts jutted from the first one's limbs and back, causing it no obvious inconvenience. Red flesh wrapped the construct like thick ivy vines and a glutinous white mass of fat obscured the vertex where the three limbs met.

"Jesus." Barras still had his sword out for some reason but now let his arm drop limply to his side.

I'd known necromancers for raiders of the grave, practitioners of arts that would stand the dead back up, full of violence and hunger. This was a fresh horror. Here they had become flesh-mongers, sculpting corpses into new and grotesque forms. It reminded me of the unborn, shaping themselves nightmarish forms from whatever carrion might lie within reach. The only small comfort lay in the fact that where the unborn creations possessed deadly speed and coordination, the things that the necromancers had built moved slowly and without grace. So awkward in fact that it was hard to see how they might be a threat. The first of them looked as though it might be hacked apart by three men with greatswords before it managed to mount an attack. I turned away. "Shoot them down."

Archers bent their bows and lofted more shafts. Four men laboured at the scorpion's winding wheel, drawing the great crossbow arm back, another waited with the spear, ready to load it. The howling at the ramp reached new heights now and the dead threw themselves forward in frenzy, locking arms, sinking their teeth into each other, holding tight while new corpses clambered over them. I'd seen something like it before when ants bridge a tiny stream, building the span out of their own bodies, hundreds of them locked tight while others run across.

"Where's that fire-oil?" Darin hollered, looking out over the back of the tower.

I rushed to join him, rediscovering in the act just how hard it was to rush anywhere in chainmail. Two teams of men had reached the steps to the wall, each team carrying a cauldron between them, hanging from a sturdy wooden pole. "Hurry up!" I shouted, though it was doubtful they could hear anything but the howling dead and the voice of the fire.

Returning to the tower front I saw that the men driving the monsters had vanished, though another body lay in the road, trampled by more oncoming dead. The constructs themselves had veered toward the ramp and were moving with greater speed, jolting and swaying as they came.

The dead on the ramp now reached to within six foot of the top of the wall and the guard there had resumed pelting them with rocks. Almost nothing held them to the wall—here and there dead fingers jammed into gaps between the stones where the mortar had fallen out, shattered away by a hard frost one winter and not maintained. There were parts of the wall in worse repair where it would be easier to swarm over, but the dead had collected here for their attempt on the gate and with the outer city alight any reorganization of the attack would probably cook half of their number. I'd had men working on the sections of wall around us only the week before. If they'd done a better job the attempt to scale the walls would be going rather more slowly. On the other hand, if I'd not assigned them to the task at all then we'd be overrun by now.

"We won't last!" Barras pointed to where yet more corpses clambered up the tower of bodies. One wall guard leaned out to thrust down at them with his spear. He lunged for his target, an old woman in a soot-streaked smock, her hair white and wild, left arm flame-seared. The spear took her in the neck and she seized it, falling back. The guardsman fell with her, too surprised to release his weapon.

"It's a race," Darin breathed beside me. The men with the cauldrons had gained the parapet and needed to navigate fifty yards of crowded wall top. The monsters were closing on the ramp with maybe twice that distance to go, moving faster and with more surety now they approached the lichkin's orbit and they too were quickened by its presence.

Several scorpions spoke in quick succession. The leading monster, already pierced by one spear, now sprung two more, one tearing through a leg, shattering bones. It fell, scrabbling, sending dead men flying with wild kicks of its raw legs, and, unable to get up, began to inch toward the ramp. Another of the monsters lost balance when hit by a scorpion bolt and veered out of control into a blazing stable block, collapsing the weakened structure around it.

I scanned the scene, trying to force some meaning from the chaos. Something caught my eye. Not monster nor lichkin nor the flames roaring up between rafters. A single figure among the thousands. Sometimes it's not the way a man moves that gives him away: rather it's the way he's still. The only thing that drew my eye was the current of the crowded dead as they flowed around the point where he stood. Other than that, nothing marked him. Smoke and ash stained him as it stained so many others, colouring his tunic and trews a dirty grey. Old blood covered half his face and ran down his neck in dark trickles. Both his hands were crimson to the elbows. He held his neck at an odd angle and a dark scar ran across it. At first I thought the scar must have been from the blow that killed him, and that the dark streak across the crown of his grey hair was just ash from some burnt timber. Then he glanced up at the tower, at me, and I knew him.

"Edris Dean!" I shouted, though none around me would know his name. "Shoot him! Shoot that bastard, right there!" I pointed, and seizing a bow from the man behind me demanded an arrow so that I could follow my own order. "Necromancer!" I yelled—and that got them going.

Where my arrow fell I have no idea. I very much doubt I emulated my grandmother's feat at Ameroth, but she was aiming at her sister and we Kendeths seem to do rather better under such circumstances. Of the dozen or more shafts launched at Edris two hit him and a few more sprouted from corpses walking by, scarcely causing them to break stride.

One of the two to strike him took him in the shoulder, the other, and I'm claiming it no matter what the odds, jutted from his chest. Having seen Edris Dean escape Frauds' Tower in Umbertide despite being cut so deep that only his neckbones prevented decapitation, rather than punch the air I started to order a second volley. Before I finished shouting out the command Edris shattered—as if he were a reflection on a pane of glass. The pieces of him fell from view, lost in the tide of walking corpses.

"Hell." I thrust the bow I'd stolen back at its owner.

"What . . . was that?" Barras asked.

"A necromancer," I said.

"Did we kill him?" Darin used the royal we: he hadn't a bow, but he probably would have got nearer the mark than me if he'd had a try.

"I wouldn't bet on it." I'd seen too much mirror-magic to think him destroyed. I wondered instead how many other reflections he might have scattered among our foe and how I might avoid meeting any of them. The Dead King's hand might be behind this army of our fallen and he may have bound the necromancers to his cause, but one at least had a blue hand on his shoulder. The Dead King spent his power here hunting Loki's key to let him out into the world, but the Blue Lady no doubt had still more pressing aims—with Grandmother and her Silent Sister bound for the Blue Lady's stronghold in Slov, perhaps she sought to turn Alica Kendeth from her path with a direct strike at the heart of her kingdom. If that was the case then she clearly didn't know my grandmother very well. The Red Queen would sacrifice us all to win this war of hers and go to her bed that night to an untroubled sleep.

"Load faster! Load faster!" Captain Renprow's panicky commands brought me out of my own panicky thoughts. He directed the scorpion toward the base of the ramp, invisible now beneath the weight of dead citizens swarming over it.

I could see terror on the faces of the men at the wall above as they struggled to get the two heavy cauldrons in place. No single man would be able to lift either, and with dozens of gallons of fire-oil and tar inside, the four men who could fit around each were hard-pressed to position them.

Just below the guards battling the cauldrons' weight a sea of dead men surged, howling, washing up around the ramp of broken stone, broken timber, broken bodies. The scaffold of human corpses reached to within a yard of the wall top, hundreds in the construction, dozens more clambering up, screaming their awful hunger. And out beyond that scaffold, stepping through the dead horde, crushing some, knocking others aside, came the monsters, the tripods, raw, bloody, scuttling like spiders. And yet the wall guard held their ground. Those old men I'd doubted, they kept their place, bound by their oath and by their duty, where I would have run.

"Yes!" Darin, Barras, in fact every man around me, calling out as two torches were set to the mouths of the cauldrons and each began to tip.

Twin streams of fire started to splash down onto the pyramid of dead, flattened against the wall. A cheer went up from all the guards. And yet the dead men below held tight even as they burned, their skin withering before the heat, hair and clothes burned away, flesh sizzling.

The first of the great three-legged monstrosities began its climb, anchoring its legs into the burning corpse-tower and scuttling up toward the wall. A wave of blazing oil broke across it but still the thing came on, new dead men ascending in its wake. The tower scorpions could no longer target the thing, so close to the guards, and with a last lunge it hooked two of its legs over the lip of the wall. Burning dead men scrambled over its back, howling, and threw themselves at the cauldron crews, who fell back in panic. The remains of the fire-oil spilled from the dropped cauldrons, setting the parapet afire.

"Get more men down there! Now!" I waved my sword unnecessarily. "Sound the breach!"

Trumpets blared, an alarm that no one alive in Vermillion had ever heard except in wall-drills. The city had been breached.

FIFTEEN

For half an hour it looked as if we might hold the Dead King's forces on the wall, and perhaps even beat them back once the soldiers of the Seventh reached the fray to relieve the old men of the guard. On the narrow parapet the dead could come at the wall guard only two or three abreast. They threw themselves forward with alarming speed, accepting the thrust of sword or spear to close on their opponents and lock hands around a man's throat.

"It's always strangling with these dead men. What's the point of it?" I couldn't see it was a very efficient way to kill anyone, especially in the midst of a pitched battle.

"What other options do they have?" Darin asked.

"Thumbs in eyeballs? Head smashed against the wall?" I'd spent entirely too much time with Snorri.

"And there's that too!" Barras pointed to another pair struggling, the attacker a young woman, seared with fire-oil and still smouldering, now with a spear through her guts. She grappled the guardsman who speared her and both pitched off the walkway, a twenty-five foot drop headlong onto the cobbles below.

We watched from the tower as the fighting progressed. Given the narrowness of the battlefront there wasn't much else to do. In those first moments the breach had seemed a complete disaster but ten minutes later the dead had pushed the wall guard back maybe twenty yards on each side for the loss of scores of their own number.

"They throttle them because an undamaged corpse is easier to stand up again," Darin said. On cue back along the parapet two gauntleted hands reached up over the wall and a guardsman stood up, his neck livid and the dead-scream bursting from his lungs.

"They've no intelligence though," Barras said. "Look. Half of them just fall straight off the other side as soon as they scramble over the wall. It must be a bloody mess down there."

I watched for a moment. He was right. The stream of corpses, on climbing their blackened and smoking scaffold of dead, lunged over the wall as if expecting immediately to find someone to grapple with. At least half of them failed to arrest themselves on the oily stonework before reaching the edge of the parapet and plunging to their doom.

"Shit!" My blood ran cold. "Follow me!" It would have taken too long to explain or issue orders. I snatched one of the oil-rush torches by the scorpion and hurried down the spiral stair that led through the tower. "Follow, damn you!"

Hundreds of citizens watched from the streets behind the gates, fifty yards back or so, huddled in nervous crowds. Young men mostly, carrying spears, butcher knives, the occasional sword, whatever they could arm themselves with, but there were older men too, and boys, even young women and grey-haired mothers, all drawn by the thought of spectacle. They say people are dying to be entertained and here stood an audience who seemed ready to do just that. Hawkers walked among them, bearing lanterns to display their wares, pastries and sausage, sweet candy and sour apples. I doubt they had much business, what with the stench of death, the wafting smoke, and the stomach-turning death howl. The fact the crowds were still here stood testimony to their faith in our walls but if any of them truly understood what waited on the other side they would have been running for their homes screaming for God's mercy.

"What?" Darin caught up with me at the base of the tower.

I looked back to check we weren't alone. Renprow, Barras, and now a steady stream of guardsmen emerged behind us, two more bearing torches. "All those dead men falling . . ." I said. "Do you hear them landing?" I led the way into the utter darkness along the base of the wall, then slowed so that guardsmen overtook us. I'd no intention of being in the front rank. "Renprow! Get more men down here. And send for Martus's reinforcements." I felt sure I'd already ordered them forward to the wall. "And where are the palace guard, damn it?"

"But why are we down here?" Darin repeated.

"The dead from the wall. Can you hear them hitting the ground?" I asked, eyes roaming the darkness, wishing I had Aslaug here to help me.

"Can't hear anything but you shouting," Barras said, clanking along in his fine tourney mail.

It was there though, beneath the din of men fighting and dying, beneath the death-howl, a dull thudding, with no rhythm to it, like the first heavy raindrops presaging a downpour.

"What's got you spooked?" Darin held his long blade before him, catching the torchlight. "It's nearly a thirty-foot drop onto hard ground. That's more than broken ankles, its broken shins, knees, hips, the lot. I don't care if they don't die—they won't be chasing anyone." He stepped slowly, despite his words, as if he didn't trust the flagstones not to bite.

"It was thirty foot onto hard ground for the first dozen. We've seen more than a hundred go over. By now they're landing on a nice soft pile of broken bodies."

We could hear it clearly now, a rapid and irregular beat, flesh thudding into flesh, an erratic heartbeat in the dark behind the wall.

The torchlight showed figures up ahead. Lots of figures, standing there in the blind dark, unspeaking. A few steps closer and the shadows yielded still more. They looked up as one, eyes catching the flames and returning them. Then they charged. And the screaming started.

Close up, the ferocity of the quickened dead was a shocking thing. Their utter fury and lack of regard for sharp edges made defence feel a futile business, a momentary delaying of the inevitable. The first rank of guardsmen went down in moments, borne to the floor, dead hands closing around their necks. The second rank fell apart in short order, with more dead streaming around the flanks of my band of some thirty men, which left me surrounded and being leapt upon by a fat man in rags who looked to have spent a couple of weeks in the grave before being roused to join today's festivities. I didn't have time to complain that his burial was in direct contravention of the Red Queen's orders, not to mention mine as marshal. I barely had time to scream.

The thing about dead men who won't die again, and who need to be dismembered if you're to stop them, is that it's all very well telling your-self this information, but when one of the bastards jumps on you scream-ing unholy rage . . . you run them through. It's instinct. They should have put that on my tombstone. "Killed by instinct."

In defiance of reason however, the hunger fled the corpse-man's eyes in the moment my sword hilt met his chest above his corrupt, unbeating heart. The weight of him threw me back into the guardsmen behind me but with their help I kept my feet, and managed to haul my blade clear as my enemy—now a simple corpse of the type that lies still and waits to be a skeleton—fell to the side. The next dead thing came at me in the same instant. Repeating my mistake, I slashed at its neck, and repeating the miracle it fell clutching at the cold blood welling from the ruin of its throat. Edris Dean's blade seemed to vibrate in my hand as if alive. I risked a glance at the blade as I stuck it through the howling mouth of the dead woman next in line to kill me, a slightly-built young thing who might have been pretty under all that soot and blood and murderous hunger. Along the length of my sword dead men's blood clung to the script that had been etched into the steel. A necromancer's weapon—the tool of his trade—seemingly as adept at cutting the strings that animate a corpse as at cutting those that lead a living man through the dance of his days.

"Watch out!"

I didn't have time to contemplate my discovery. A man who'd died in the athletic prime of his life threw himself at me, pinning my blade, and took me to the ground. I've not been savaged by a hound but I imag-ine the experience is similarly terrifying. The sound of the thing's roaring filled my world. Its strength wholly over-matched mine and without the chainmail surcoat it would have been tearing the flesh from my bones. Other hands seized me and I felt myself dragged across the flagstones, though I'd lost my bearings and couldn't say in which direction. I almost hoped it might be into the mass of the dead where I could at least expect a quick death.

In the next moment I discovered what it might be like to be on the butcher's block. Swords rose and fell above me. I heard and felt the thudding of blades in flesh. I struggled as the cold blood washed over me, and after what seemed a lifetime, strong hands hauled me to my feet.

"Marshal!" Renprow, seizing my head, inspecting me for wounds while my now-limbless assailant twitched on the ground before us. The sounds of the battle raged close by, not the clash of steel on steel or the thrum of bowstrings, just the screaming, of both the living and the dead, and the dull chopping of meat. "Marshal? Can you hear me?"

"What?" I looked around. Men of the guard packed in close on every side, reserves brought in by the long circular road that the wall parapet constituted. Up above us the war of attrition was still being waged, the dead pushing slowly out from the point where they overtopped the wall, but the real battle lay before me. More dead continued to spill over the wall in a steady rain, landing on the mound of those too injured by the fall to move on. The drop would probably still kill a man, but it didn't break enough bones to slow the Dead King's army, and now guardsmen recently throttled were facing their old comrades. "Where are our reserves? Damn it! We need the Seventh! We need the palace guard!"

I let Renprow lead me back through the ranks. Our presence had drawn the dead but we didn't have the numbers to contain them. A necromancer's orders could see them scatter out into the city. Perhaps only their masters' desire to see the officers and commanders of Vermillion's defence dead kept them here.

"Darin? Where's Darin?" I shook Renprow off. "Where's Barras?"

Renprow looked up to meet my gaze, jostled as more guardsmen hurried past to join the fray. He held me with the dark intensity of his gaze. "Marshal, all that stands between this city and disaster is your command. You need to concentrate on the bigger picture—"

I had him by the throat in a moment. "Where is my brother?" I shouted it into his face.

"Prince Darin fell." The captain choked the words out. "While he was helping to drag you clear."

I let Renprow fall and bent forward, doubled up by a blow to the stomach—though nothing had hit me but the truth. "No."

There's a red rage that runs deep in me, so deep you wouldn't catch even a hint though you kept my company month after month. Even so, it is there. Edris Dean ignited it the day he ran his sword through my mother's belly. He took that young boy's bravery, his anger, his despair, and with one blow he set it apart from me, bound tight into something new, something darker, more bitter, and more deadly. And in the years of my life I've lived on a surface below which this crimson outrage ran unknown and unsuspected, stolen from me, leaving a different man.

"No!" That old rage rose then, surfaced from its depths, and I welcomed it. As I ran back through the ranks of my men I roared a welcome to it that Snorri himself would have been proud of—greeting an old friend.

Edris Dean's sword, the same blade that shaped my life, sent dead men back to the grave as easily as it sent live ones on their first visit. There was a crucial difference though—the dead had no fear of men with swords. It made them easy for me to kill. I ran among them, swinging with every ounce of skill that my old swordmasters had beaten into me at Grandmother's insistence, and every lesson that unwanted experience had taught me since. The men of Vermillion followed in a wedge behind me, and at every slash and slice I bellowed my brother's name. I kicked corpse-men from their victims, chopped away the arms fastened on men's throats, hacked and slew until my blade began to weigh like lead and my traitor limbs betrayed me, the strength running from them.

A corpse-woman grappled me about the legs, another grabbed my left arm, trying to sink its teeth into the inside of my elbow. The chainmail foiled the bite, and a spearman drove his shaft through the dead woman's head, though she didn't loosen her grip. Strong arms wrapped me from behind and pulled me back among my men. Unable to fight them, I collapsed into the embrace. For a moment the world went darker, the light of torch and lantern dimming as the thunder of my heart filled my ears.

"Darin?" I gasped the question between great lungfuls of air drawn through a raw throat. "Barras?"

I blinked and cleared my vision. The men around me were of the Seventh. Renprow stood looking down at me, making me realize I lay on my back. I'd passed out but had no idea how long I'd been unconscious. I blinked again. Cousin Serah stood beside Captain Renprow, her face soot-streaked and framed by a close-fitting chainmail hood; her eldest brother, Rotus, loomed behind her, his lean frame armoured, his customary sour expression in place.

"Where is my brother?" I demanded, sitting up, gasping at the pain from bruised ribs.

The captain tilted his head, face torn in three parallel furrows across his cheek. I followed the gesture and saw Darin, propped in a sitting position against the Appan Gate, more pale than I'd ever seen him.

"Barras?" I asked as I got up.

"Who?" Serah reaching down to help me

I shook her off.

"Barras Jon, the Vyene ambassador's son. Married to Lisa DeVeer," Rotus supplied, always full of facts—even in the midst of battle.

"My sword!" I shouted, before finding it in my scabbard. "And where's Barras, damn it?"

Captain Renprow shook his head. "I've not seen him."

I reached my brother's side and knelt down opposite the chirurgeon examining him.

"How—" My voice stuck, so I coughed and tried again. "How are you, brother?"

Darin raised a hand, as though it were the heaviest thing, and set it to his neck, torn by the nails of dead men, the crushed flesh livid with blood both above and below the skin. "Been . . . better." A pained whisper.

I looked to the chirurgeon, a grey-headed battlefield practitioner in studded leather armour bearing the crossed spears of the Seventh. He shook his head.

"What do you mean, 'no'?" I stared at him in outrage. "Fix him! He's a bloody prince. His elder brother's in charge of your whole army . . . and I'm the fucking marshal!"

The man ignored me, as used to battlefield hysteria as to battlefield wounds, and tapped at Darin's chest, above his ribs. "Ruptured a vessel in his windpipe. His lungs are filling with blood." He set his fingers to my brother's neck to count his pulse.

"Damn that!" I made to grab the so-called healer. "Why don't you—" Darin's hand on my wrist stopped me mid-flow, even though there was no strength in the grip.

"You . . . came back . . . for me." So faint I had to lean in to hear it. I heard the bubbling then, of blood in lungs.

"I wish I hadn't now!" I shouted at him, the smoke stinging my eyes so I could hardly see. "If you're just planning to lie there and die on me." Something caught in my throat, more smoke perhaps, and I choked on it. When I spoke again it was quiet, meant only for him. "Get up, Darin, get up." More than a hint of a child's whine in my voice.

"Nia." I thought for a moment he was speaking of Mother—just for a moment, then I remembered his new daughter, small and soft in Micha's arms. She would never know him.

"I'll protect her. I swear it."

Darin's head lolled to the side and my heart seemed to stop inside me though I'd never claimed any love for my brothers, not even my favourite one. But he raised his brows and I followed the line of his gaze to his fingers, glistening with some clear liquid.

"Oil," Darin said.

It was true, we were crouched in the stuff, thankfully cool now: it must have leaked under the gate after being poured through the murder-holes. Darin brushed slippery fingers across the back of my hand.

"Stopped . . . them."

I puzzled on that for a second. The oil hadn't stopped them. I set my fingers to it and slid them over the cobbles. "It did!" I understood, passing from confusion to clarity in one instant. The dead beneath the gatehouse hadn't been able to push, they had no traction on the ground. All they could be was a plug of flesh to transmit the shove from outside. The doors had only just held. The oil saved them. A moment of triumph lit me. "I knew if I—" But Darin had gone.

The chirurgeon kept his fingers on Darin's neck a moment longer, feeling for that beat. He shook his head. And, blinded by tears that had never been from the smoke, I drew my sword.

Something moved beneath my brother's skin. Large enough that even with my eyes misted I could see it. Like a small hand sliding up his neck. His body jerked as if a blow had been struck from inside his chest.

"What in God's name?" The chirurgeon jumped back aghast, clearly not fully acquainted with the nature of our foe.

Darin's lips writhed. With a curse I slid my sword up through my brother's sternum into his heart, and without a sound he relaxed into a true death.

"It's not enough." Serah behind me. "You need to bind him—"

"With *this* sword it's enough." I pulled the blade clear, red with my brother's blood, and stood to face my cousins.

"That wasn't the same as the others—what happened to him . . ." Rotus leaned in, peering.

"No." The dead had always woken in an instant, hunger in their eyes, ready to do murder. Darin had been different. As if . . . as if something were trying to break out of him. Or through him. "I—" Then I noticed it. "The dead howl . . . it's gone." It struck me that since I'd come to my senses after that insane charge the dead had fallen silent. The shouts and screams I could hear now came from living throats, some full of rage, others terror, or pain, but the chilling and unending scream of the attacking dead had . . . ended.

"The dead have slowed," Renprow reported, eyeing me as if worried I might collapse again, or throw myself back into the fray. "But we're barely holding them and they keep coming—they must have a usable ramp to the top of the wall now."

"Get back on the tower, Captain. We need eyes on this." Beyond the walls the roar of the fire sounded like a river in full tumult.

Cousin Serah stepped closer, raising her hand to my upper arm. A light touch. "I'm sorry about Darin, Jalan. He was a good man."

I'd put him out of my head. Just like that, my own brother, lying dead on the floor behind me, bleeding from the wound I gave him. Suddenly I needed to fill myself with something else. Right then I was even grateful for the attack. I stepped past Serah. "These can't be all the Seventh! Where's Martus?" Barely a hundred men in the chain surcoats of the Seventh stood around us and the battle-line held against the dead lay just twenty yards away. The citizens who came for the show had fled long ago, hopefully spreading necessary panic throughout the city. "Where in hell are the palace guard? We might hold them with all our forces here."

Serah set herself before me once again. "I came from the Victory Gate. We saw the fires starting and brought these men to help." She glanced over her shoulder at the battle, pale but with her mouth set in a grim line of determination.

"I came from the palace," Rotus said, looming over his little sister. "Uncle Hertet has commanded Martus to keep the Seventh close to the walls—"

"Why isn't he fucking here then?"

"The *palace* walls," Serah said. She looked as young as her seventeen years.

"He has ordered the palace guard to remain at station and defend him at all costs," Rotus said.

"Oh. That. Bastard." I sheathed my sword, still red with my brother's blood. "What the hell is Garyus doing letting Hertet give orders? I'm going back. You'll have to hold here. I'll get the reinforcements."

"We'll hold." I expected Rotus to make the pledge, but it was Serah who spoke. She held my gaze for a moment and I saw something familiar. Something I last saw in her grandmother's eyes on the walls of Ameroth.

"I know you will." And I began pushing my way through the troops, aiming for the main street from the Appan Gate, lit only by a scatter of dropped lanterns.

SIXTEEN

"Marshal!" Renprow at my shoulder. "You can't go alone!"

"We need every man here." I really didn't want to go alone, but we really did need every man at the breakthrough.

"I'll come too. Just let me gather a squad." He caught hold of my arm.

"A squad who can ride? And have horses?" My stallion and the mounts of the men who had ridden from the Morano Bridge had been stabled at a tavern a hundred yards along the Appan Street. It would take an age to gather those riders together, if they still lived, and many of the horses weren't the sort to take kindly to a new rider.

"I'll come." He reached out and took two soldiers by the shoulder. "And these men can ride with us. There are messenger horses in the stables."

"You know more about this city's defences than anyone else, Captain. You're needed here. These two I'll take."

Coming to the edge of the press of soldiers and wall guards I found myself suddenly reluctant to leave. Stepping beyond the crowded bodies, out into the dark, seemed like a very bad idea indeed. The men huddled together as sheep will in the pen, so tight I'd had to force a path through them. Fear bound us close, herd animals before the predator, though it appeared that only I had truly appreciated the nature of the threat haunting this night. The dead had fallen silent. That meant the lichkin had left. I would have liked to think it had retreated back over the wall to some devilry outside amid the firestorm. But looking at the dark I knew. The lichkin was in my city now. Out there in the streets. Loose among the innocent, and believe me when I say that before the ancient malice of the lichkin we are all innocent.

Leaving the shelter of the men took all my meagre reserves of courage. Once out in the open, with the pair of guards following, pride kept
me moving. Pride has always been my most lethal character flaw. Worse
even than being cursed through my grandmother's blood with the tendency to infrequent berserker rages when pushed to the edge. Pride lets
a man be skewered on the point of other people's expectations. How often
had I walked into the proverbial, and sometimes literal, fire with Snorri
watching on, my justifiable instinct to run in the opposite direction
crushed under the weight of his confidence in me?

I collected a lantern hanging from a pastry stall abandoned when the
crowd panicked and led the way across toward the stables, the light jitter-
ing in my grasp. I hurried across Appan Street in the dark with the two
soldiers at my back.

Appan Street lay eerily quiet, no sounds but the distant cries from
the fighting at the wall. Tell-tale cracks of light at upper windows and
the occasional shadow moving behind closed shutters were all that
betrayed the fact the city hadn't been abandoned.

"Easy now." I held up a hand to stop the soldiers and drew my sword.
The stables' door stood ajar. I could hear the stamps and whinnies of the
horses inside. "Something's got them spooked." Any number of dead men
could have broken away from the battle by the gates—one of them could
be lurking in the darkness behind the door, bloody and silent. I raised
my lantern. "You go in first." A nod to the larger of the two soldiers, a
sturdy fellow though still lacking a good few inches and pounds on me.

"Sir." He gave me a "why me" look but since it wasn't actually possible to find two men in Vermillion whose military ranks stood further
apart than mine and his, he stepped forward. I handed him my lantern
and he prodded the door open with his sword. He edged in, reluctant as
a man dipping a hand into a jar full of spiders.

"All clear, Marshal."

"You're sure?"

"Just horses. Must've been the smoke that spooked 'em."

I followed him in. He wouldn't be safe to lead Murder out, otherwise
I'd have stayed in the street.

Within two minutes we had Murder and two of the messenger horses out in the road. I swung into the saddle, feeling slightly better as I always do with four legs under me. It was probably a good thing for my honour that the city was besieged on all sides, because if I'd known there was a gate open then I might well have been overwhelmed by the temptation to gallop out of it and ride off until I found somewhere safe.

"The palace!" I pointed my sword in the appropriate direction, gripped the reins in my lantern hand, and clattered off.

Even in dire straits there's a certain joy in riding hard through the empty streets of a city that is never empty. In my whole life, no matter how late the hour, I had never been able to let a horse have its head along Evening Way or the West Star Parade. I'd never once seen Evening Way without at least a dozen drunks, a city watchman or two, perhaps a young lord in pursuit of a young woman who was no lady . . . and by day there was never room enough to pass without scraping elbows with half of Vermillion. The din of Murder's hooves echoed off the walls as we shot through.

By Thread Needle Corner a woman's cry caught my attention. I looked up to see her at a high window, the uppermost floor of Melican's, a fine tailor's in which I've disposed of at least a modest fortune.

"Prince Jalan!"

I pulled on my reins. I'd out-distanced the two sluggards Captain Renprow had picked to accompany me and being hailed at least gave me an excuse to let them catch up. A quick glance around for lurking dead men or mire-ghouls creeping along the rooftops, and I called out, "Yes?" I'd expected to have more to say but "yes" seemed to cover it.

"You—you're going to the palace? Take me with you . . ." She seemed to know me. She did look vaguely familiar—at least young and pretty.

"I'm in haste . . . good woman." My lips wanted to say "Mary" but I settled for "good woman" rather than guess. I hoped that was how marshals talked.

My escorts clattered up, reining their steeds in with a distinct lack of expertise.

"Wait for me!" The good woman pulled back from the window then, as if in afterthought, thrust her white face back out. "There's a horror in the Shambles. Killing people and making their bodies dance." With that she withdrew, presumably headed for the stairs.

"Ride!" I set my heels to Murder's ribs and he leapt forward. I didn't even feel bad about it. I'd been charged with saving a city, not each citizen individually. And besides, Mary—I dimly recalled something about squeezing into a fitting room with the girl and finding her most accommodating—would likely be far safer hidden above an anonymous tailor's than in the palace.

We rode on through dark streets, occasionally breaking into squares where the moon, now edging above the rooftops, washed the flagstones with silver. In Reymond Square, less than a quarter of a mile from Grandmother's iron gates, a sharp wind blew up suddenly about us, whipping dust and stinging grit into the air. Dry leaves spiralled around in the dust-devil's grip, old rags too, grey tatters lifted in the gyre.

"Rag-a-maul!" The man behind me.

"Ride!"

Something sliced at my cheek. I dipped my head and galloped, hearing the scream of one of my soldiers, and the thud as he hit the ground. More screaming, a torn and hideous gabbling, growing fainter as we pulled away. Thundering toward the mouth of the street opposite I saw a man walk out into the road, and turn toward us, arms wide. What remained of his skin hung in tatters from wet and dripping arms. Closing the last yards, I saw the faintest outline of what rode him—a skeletal thing, some awful grinning devil with more than a touch of insect in its mix. The man opened his mouth to speak, grinning in an echo of the devil's mirth, but I rode him down before his first word.

A cold shudder ran the length of me even as Murder bore me away. The spirit from the whirlwind had been riding its victim much like a lichkin must ride its host, though the lichkin achieve a far more intimate union, burrowing within the unborn flesh to release its potential in hideous new ways. I dug my heels in and we reached ridiculous speed, hooves nearly slipping out from under us as we took the next corner. I couldn't be away from that thing quick enough.

A minute later and I rounded a corner to the sight of the palace walls. The moon rode on the shoulder of the Genoa keep now, a blood moon, reddened by the smoke of ten thousand burning homes. I cantered on, my remaining soldier far behind. The palace walls, ever my sanctuary, had never been such a welcome sight. Nor, sadly, had they ever looked so low. For once I shared my grandmother's disappointment that history had fur-nished the Red March monarchy with a luxurious seat, steeped in arts and culture, rather than a grim fortress menacing the surrounding city.

Almost immediately I spotted Martus. His command pavilion, pitched just a few yards before the walls, sagged drunkenly, there being few places a tent peg could be driven between the flagstones. A force of a hundred or so soldiers stood arrayed in the street, wide eyes searching the night as if they knew just how haunted it was. A couple of grooms stood with Martus's horse close by the pavilion, along with two message-riders in their saddles and a trio of drummers bent under the weight of their instruments. Two minor officers stood at the pavilion's entrance.

"Martus!" A roar as I rode through the infantry ranks. "Martus!"

"The general—"

"What?" Martus cut off his adjutant as he ducked out of his tent, helm under one arm, old gore drying on his breastplate. He saw me as he straightened, belligerence warring with guilt—unusual for Martus: normally there was just belligerence.

I jumped down from Murder's back and pushed through to confront him, immediately regretting losing the height advantage. "What the hell are you doing here? Didn't you get the messages? You can see the fucking smoke!" I pointed just in case he'd missed it rising above the fire-glow in the distance. "There's a full-fledged battle at the gates . . . and we're *losing*!" I glanced around. "And where in God's name are the rest of your men? Get them moving to the Appan Gate—right now!"

Martus squared up to me as he had so often before, normally a pre-lude to flattening me if I proved too slow on my feet to escape. "Hertet has ordered that we stay." Angry but with the tone of a man caught doing something that he shouldn't be doing. "My command is patrolling the streets around the palace, in eight squads of fifty."

"Who gives a bucket of elephant dung what Uncle Hertet has to say?" An anger rose in me, one I hadn't felt in years . . . perhaps since I was seven and Martus used a head-butt to take me out of the last battle where

I stood my ground. "I'm the Marshal of Vermillion—I have command of its armed forces, and you, General, answer to me!"

Martus surprised me then. He let out the air swelling his chest in a sigh, first exploding from behind teeth clenched in his own rage, then trailing off into a long slow exhalation. "There's word the Red Queen has fallen. Some report about the army in Slov being encircled . . . an arrow . . . Hertet has declared himself king."

As Martus's shoulders slumped I remembered Darin, lying pale against the Appan Gate. They could almost have been twins: of a height, Martus a little broader, his features less fine. I saw Darin dying and his name fought to escape the tight line of my lips. I saw, perhaps for the first time, Martus as both man and boy, not a rival, not a bullying brother, but a son like me, competing for the affection of a father who had nothing left to give. When Mother died it had been as if the stopper had been drawn from Father and all that she had seen in him had run out, any drive, passion, that vital interest in the world that makes us alive, leaving him empty.

"Gather your men, Martus, and get to the Appan Gate. If we fall there, we fall everywhere. If we can't hold the city walls then the palace walls will not hold. If he truly is king then better an angry king than a dead one?"

Martus nodded. "I'll send runners."

"Have my man." I gestured at the surviving soldier who'd come with me from the Appan Gate. "He can ride as fast as your soldiers run. Almost."

Martus gave an absent nod, looking out along the dark length of Kings Way, barely a crack of light from any shutter. "But king or not, idiot or not, I don't think our uncle is entirely wrong—there *is* something out there, coming this way . . . I can feel it. And close. Not your battle at the gates . . ."

"Maybe." I felt it too. "But we can't let the city fall." I set off walking toward the main gates. "We need the palace guard too!"

"He'll never let you have them!" Martus called at my back.

"Got to try!" I waved him off and strode on toward my meeting with Vermillion's new king.

SEVENTEEN

I approached the great portcullis. Along with the gatehouse it sat in, it was perhaps the only military element of the palace. The main wall stood barely twenty feet high and no thicker than a sword-length. Further from the gatehouse it dipped to fifteen foot in places.

Martus had said Hertet would never release the guard.

"I know cowards! I'll find a way!" Spoken to myself, my brother now beyond earshot.

I hadn't spoken of Darin. Perhaps I wasn't brave enough. The words hadn't wanted to come and even if they had I wouldn't have trusted myself to speak them. Maybe none of us would survive the night. If we did there would be time to mourn in daylight.

Closing on the main gate, I saw no guards on the walls, none in the sentry boxes to either side of the gates, no sign of activity at the arrow slits or murder-holes. I drew my sword and banged its pommel against the metal boss where two timbers in the portcullis intersected.

"Open the gate!"

Nothing for a long moment, then a shape broke from the deep shadow on the far side of the entry tunnel and ambled across to face me through the grid of oak and iron, unhooding a lantern as he came. A scrawny fellow in the grey-greens of the Marsail keep, toting a spear over his shoulder, on his head an iron skullcap that looked older than the Red Queen.

"Open the damn gate." I banged again.

"Don't rightly know how, yer worship." He didn't seem too bothered by the fact, and given that he should properly be stationed out of sight guarding prisoners in the Marsail's cells he was likely telling the truth.

"Your name, guardsman." A demand, not a question.

"Ronolo Dahl, if it pleases you." He clicked his heels together—albeit without any actual click.

"It doesn't overly please me. Now, Guardsman Dahl. Open. The. Gate." These fellows rarely had contact with royals and had little notion how to conduct themselves. How Ronolo came to be guarding the main gate to the Red Queen's palace, apparently all by himself, I had no idea, but it didn't bode well.

"Can't, yer worship. King's orders. Nobody in, nobody out."

"Sorry?" I cupped my hand to my ear, and leaned in close to the heavy timbers.

Ronolo echoed me, leaning in and raising his voice, "Nobody in! Nobody out!"

I snaked an arm through the small square hole between verticals and horizontals, catching him around the back of the head and hauling him up against the portcullis. With my other hand I reversed my blade and set the point against his neck.

"I am the marshal of this city's armed forces. I am a prince of Red March, grandson to the Red Queen, and I have lived in this palace for over twenty years. Believe me, Ronolo, when I say that I have walked the paths of Hell itself, and the things I will do to you if you fail to obey me will make Satan's devils weep." I let him go. "Now. Open the gate."

Fear can be an excellent tutor and, although Ronolo had no real cause to fear me given that he was out of reach of my sword, he scuttled to acquaint himself with the complexities of the winding gear. The two minutes that passed before the gate began to rise were very long ones, in which I considered the highly probable eventuality that Ronolo had just kept running. Staring into the darkness of the courtyard beyond the gates I found myself haunted by visions of a baby, soft and pink in her crib, fast in sleep while with slow intent a mire-ghoul crept through the nearest window. Foolishness, of course. Darin's little Nia would be safe in Micha's arms with the household guard tight around her in Roma Hall. I thought of Lisa too. Pacing her rooms in Grandmother's guest wing, waiting for Barras to return. I wondered if I saw her—would I have the courage to tell his fate? *I know cowards.* I knew I wouldn't.

The portcullis lurched into motion, making me flinch. It ratcheted up a whole inch before stopping. Then another one. I imagined Ronolo labouring at the great winch all by himself. Another inch. I sheathed my sword. Carrying bare steel within the palace compound would be foolish at the best of times. That said, I felt instantly vulnerable the moment the hilt hit home against the leather of the scabbard.

I rolled under the gate as soon as the gap would admit me. My armour colluded with gravity to make rising to my feet quite a struggle. Reminded just how cumbersome a chainmail shirt can be, and lacking Murder's four swift legs beneath me, I decided to lose the extra weight. I pulled the mail over my head, taking a knife to the straps rather than wrestling with buckles in the gloom. I let the chain shirt fall to the ground, a heavy metallic slither.

Without waiting for Ronolo's reappearance I hastened into the compound. Several of the lanterns that should light the archways leading from the grand courtyard had burned out and those passageways yawned like dark mouths. My feet made too loud a noise on the flagstones. I felt like an intruder in a mausoleum rather than a prince returning to his home. Many nights I'd staggered through this compound while the palace slept, almost too drunk to stand, but tonight the Red Queen's house held a different quality.

"Fuck it." I drew my sword and ducked into the inky passage that led to Victory Square. I drew breath again once I emerged. Across the breadth of the square the lanterns burned on their poles before the steps to my father's house. Lights showed in several of the upper windows and I thought of Micha with her child. I quickened my step, hoping she had bolted her doors.

To my left I passed the Adam Barracks, home to the grounds guard, the structure dark-eyed and silent. To my right the guard stables, looking equally deserted though I could hear the nervous whinnies of the beasts within, the chargers stamping as if sensing the night's tension. I could smell the smoke of the outer city even here. The moon rode higher, still bloody with the burning. My boots rang out too loud on the flagstones.

The east and west wings of Roma House both lay quiet and unlit, the servants' quarters and kitchens on one side, the palace church, St.

Agnes, on the other. I focused on those lanterns, the pool of light about the doors of my home. I could gather some guards together there and get a fuller picture of events. I started to run.

The dead men came from the church. The great oak doors slammed open on their scrolling hinges of black iron, and bursting from the inky interior came the corpses of two priests, three young novices behind them. Swift as the quickened dead at the city walls they saw me immediately and started to sprint. I glanced at the sword in my hand, the image of Darin's child in my mind, and for a moment I held my ground.

The thing that followed in the clerics' wake had been a man once—a huge one. A necromancer must have been at work on it for hours, perhaps hidden away in the crypts beneath the church. How long had death-sworn been waiting within Grandmother's walls? A week, a month, years? Hidden in plain sight, no doubt. Maybe even as one of Father's servants or guards, maybe the serving maid who had brought hot water for my bath . . .

Slamming my sword into its scabbard once again, I turned on a heel and ran for my life. The man must have stood taller than Snorri in life and near as broad. Now he wore additional muscle, heaped atop his own, the raw meat of other men somehow tied into his own flesh and bone. The glistening red slabs over his arms looked like both the thigh muscles of a grown man.

All of them ran swift and silent, the only wailing coming from me as I rocketed by the Adam Barracks, keeping well clear of any doors for fear of what might burst out of them as I passed.

My main rule of running, after "don't stop" and "go faster" is "go high or go to ground." Hiding is always good, unless you've got somewhere you really need to be, but if you can't hide—go up. I've occasionally met a runner whose foot speed exceeds my own, but I've yet to meet one whose eagerness to catch me exceeds my eagerness to escape. Once I get to the rooftops I inevitably find a leap that my pursuer is not prepared to make, or a ledge along which they are not prepared to run. As always, it helps to know your ground, and fortunately the palace had been my playground for years.

I skittered around the back of the barracks block, hopping at the extremity of the turn, and spotted a cartload of water barrels standing close to the outer wall. I made directly for it. The sound of pounding feet behind me told me my pursuers were just as fast as I'd feared.

The stays of the cart provided a ramp and at the top I vaulted onto the tall stack of barrels. The walkway around the outer wall is supported at regular intervals by square beams which stand up from the ground rather than being braced lower down the wall as they would be if it were taller. Halfway up each beam are two brackets for torch or lantern, one to a side. I leapt toward the nearest beam, aiming a kick at it, my foot hitting just above the bracket. Kicking off as I started to slide, I boosted myself up and leapt at full stretch for the edge of the walkway, making it by fingertips, and hung, gasping and dangling. Given that the walkway stands about sixteen foot off the ground my feet were at a tempting height for any dead man down below wanting to jump up and grab my ankles.

"Fortunately" the corpses running me down had followed my path. The first priest threw himself off the barrels, his face twisted with awful silent rage. I tried to swing out of his path. Fingernails scraped my side as he shot past me, his priests' robes fluttering like the wings of some great crow. I hauled myself up as the second priest leapt. It's no easy thing to gain a ledge that only your fingertips have hold on, but terror lent me strength. I drew my chin level and swung a foot up onto the parapet. Somehow fear propelled the rest of me over the lip. The second priest brushed the sole of my trailing boot as he passed by on his short trip to the flagstoned yard.

I took off at speed, preparing to congratulate myself, when a glance back—seldom advisable when running along a narrow walkway lit only by the light of the moon—revealed the white-robed form of a novice half on the walkway, boosting himself up with both arms.

"How . . ." Then I saw. Revealed by the curve of the wall I could just make out the huge form of the giant, balanced on the cart and already lifting a second novice toward the parapet. Cleverer dead men than any I'd yet encountered!

I ran counter-clockwise, up over the deserted gatehouse. An ancient scorpion sat toward the front gatehouse wall and for a moment I considered wrestling it round and skewering my pursuers. Sanity prevailed—it would take four men five minutes to do the job, and in any event a spear through the chest might not make a noticeable difference to the corpses chasing me. Instead I sprinted on and out the other side.

The roaring of a great wind or fire turned my head as I ran. Over the wall I could see the streets leading away from the palace and, despite my extremity, something caught my eye. A gyre of dust and rags scoured its way over the broad, empty space before the palace. Like the rag-a-maul I'd seen on my ride from the Appan Gate this one had hollowed and hag-ridden victims around its margins, but that one had been little bigger than a man and had just a couple of possessed in thrall to it. This whirl-wind blew taller than the gatehouse, the moonlight glittering on broken glass braided through its storm-cone, and scores of citizens, torn and flayed, wandered about it, bright-eyed, their riders visible as faint and ghostly forms upon each back, devilish and horrific in their variety.

Perhaps twenty soldiers of the Seventh emerged from the cover of the wall, Martus at their head. Where the rest had gone in so short a time I couldn't say. Martus had his sword drawn and looked to be about to lead the charge.

I glanced back, and seeing the swiftest of the novices still a hundred yards back, stopped. You can't hurt rag-a-mauls. You keep the path clear and let them blow out. The small ones last an hour or so. I had reports of a nine foot one blowing for half a day . . .

I snatched a breath. "Run, you moron!"

Martus looked back, finding me on the walls. Even at a distance his face told the story I knew it would. He was General Martus Kendeth, head of the house now that Father lay in ashes. He stood before the walls of the Red Queen's palace and—though fear might knot like a cold fist in his guts—he would not be running in any direction except toward the enemy.

"You can't hurt it, you stupid bastard!" The novice had cleared the gatehouse and now sprinted toward me, careless of the drop to his side. Two more ran behind him, and then the giant himself.

"Shit." Without letting myself think I pulled Edris Dean's sword clear and with an oath flung it over the wall. "Use that! It destroys the dead!" And I was off and running. I regretted the gesture before I'd taken two paces—not that I had any intention of standing and fighting. Damned if I liked

Martus but we had both loved my mother and there's a bond there . . . something . . . I wasn't going to lose two brothers in one night. Besides, one can run away all the faster without the encumbrance of a longsword.

About three hundred yards on from the gatehouse the wall curves close to a building where cured hams and other smoked meats are hung, ready for the kitchens. I know this because I once had occasion to battle my way through the main store after falling through the roof. It's a hell of a leap from the wall, but if you get a good speed up and manage to convert it into the required direction then you'll make it.

An important element of landing on roofs is knowing where the rafters run so they can take the impact of your arrival. I landed sprawling and immediately started to slip. A spot of frantic kicking while trying to heave some air into my evacuated lungs saw me gaining traction while showering the ground below with terracotta tiles. I had a hand on the roof ridge when the first novice slammed home behind me. I pulled myself up as he slid and fell without a scream, taking more tiles with him. The second novice went straight through the roof as I gained my feet on the roof ridge and started to advance along it, arms spread, fast as I dared and faster than advisable. The third novice hit the roof above a rafter and managed not to slip.

The building I was on adjoined another taller building whose contents, by virtue of a stronger roof, were a mystery to me. I jumped, caught the next roof ridge, and hauled myself over it, losing all my buttons along with considerably more skin than I had to spare. The leading novice almost caught hold of my dangling foot. I had the satisfaction of hearing his fruitless charge smack him face first into the wall. A quick glance revealed the giant halfway along the first roof ridge, showing an unreasonable degree of balance for something so large and crudely made. One priest trailed in his wake, his left arm at a broken angle. I knew the man, one of Father's more regular assistants, but his name eluded me—doing a better job of escape than I was managing.

Whilst running away is a great strategy, a good coward always takes the unfair advantage. I backed along the higher ridge, staying low, and swivelled around, drawing my dagger, already missing Edris's sword. Two pale hands grasped the roof edges to either side of the capping tiles. I brought my dagger down on all four fingers on the right, gripping the hilt with both hands and applying my weight. A moment later the novice's snarling face thrust into view over the ridge, his eyes empty of any holy intent and full of that unmanning hunger that drives the dead. I left off the attempt to trim his fingers and swung my doubled fist into his face. He dropped away and I took off running again.

Any man fool enough to run to the end of the second building's roof is met by a yawning chasm and the possibility of leaping it to the broad, sloping roof of the royal stables. Forewarned, I sped up and left the roof with a mighty scream, legs still kicking, arms pinwheeling. I hit the stables' roof with the sound of cracking tiles and possibly cracking bones, smacking my face and, by the feel of it, breaking my nose yet again. It took a moment before I regained enough of my wits to realize that I was rolling. I splayed my limbs starfish style and slid to a halt a few inches from the guttering.

Fifty yards back I could see the giant vaulting onto the roof ridge that I'd thrown myself from. The broken-armed priest had the lead now, the novice with the sliced fingers behind, both presumably lifted up in advance by the augmented corpse. I scrambled up the side of the stables' roof, blood falling from my nose in a steady stream of fat drops.

Escape needs to be a pure and solitary goal. Images of Micha and her infant kept complicating the current chase, and as I gained the roof ridge it occurred to me that in times of trouble the DeVeer sisters would seek each other out. Had Lisa joined Micha in the Roma Hall? Because if so then whatever butcher had put together the thing chasing me was undoubtedly beneath the same roof as both women. Slowly my "escape" route had been curving around on itself, back toward Roma Hall, and leading me to a series of increasingly death-defying jumps that the dead seemed to be defying better than I was.

I lay panting for a moment, exhausted. The priest crashed into the roof a few yards below my position, thrown bodily by the giant. Somehow he clung on with one hand and looked up at me, moonlit. He snarled, with a depressing amount of energy for an elderly cleric who I recalled as walking with the aid of a thick stick or thin choirboy. Up close his name came to me at last. Father Daniel.

The novice crashed home beside him, failed to keep a grip with his bloody hand, and fell away to the distant ground. My cue to run again.

Ten yards shy of the end of the stables' roof I veered left, racing down the incline at an angle. Five yards from the lowest corner of the roof I put on the brakes, going into a prolonged skid. By the time I reached the corner I'd slowed from breakneck to breakleg and dropped off with a wail that was half-prayer and all hope.

The trick to hitting the ground is to roll. Well, mainly it's not to break. But rolling helps. My legs crumpled beneath me, resisting my momentum as manfully as they could and pitching me forward, already rolling as I fell. I smacked into the flagstones far harder than anyone should and went arse over elbow, coming to a halt in a groaning heap several yards on.

Father Daniel landed a short distance back from me, shattering both ankles. He continued to crawl after me, sparking memories of several old nightmares, but now reduced to an even slower pace than he managed in life.

I staggered up and limped away. The thud behind me as the giant landed nearly stopped my heart. With a groan I increased the tempo of my limp, cursing my right knee, which seemed to have become filled with broken glass. By the time I reached the side of the Poor Palace, gasping out cries for help, I still hadn't seen a single person other than Ronolo who wasn't dead and trying to kill me.

I followed my childhood route to the roof of the Poor Palace, windowsill to window arch, two gargoyle heads—mouths gaping and ready to vomit foul water from the privies within—another sill another arch and the tricky matter of clambering over the lip of the roof from an underhang. That had been a lot easier when I weighed a quarter of what I do now and had yet to realize that I wouldn't just bounce if I fell.

How the giant was following me I didn't understand. It sounded rather as if it were tearing handholds out of the sandstone walls. I gained the dark slate slope of the roof with the dead thing reaching for my heels.

Running up a forty-five degree slope feels like climbing a cliff at the best of times. After the chase I'd been through the best I could manage was a steady crawl. Behind me it sounded as if the monster was breaking through the eaves of the roof rather than attempting to circumnavigate them. I found a loose slate and turned to hurl it at the dead man's head. It sliced past his ear and arced out into the night.

I reached the base of the west spire as the giant pulled itself onto the roof, its skinned face glistening in the light of the rising moon. My brain had no advice to offer but "up" and I followed it. There's a point where exhaustion settles in so deep that it leaves no room for new ideas. I climbed by instinct, hands finding the familiar holds that had led me up and down these spires for a decade and more. It's an easy climb and one that offered little hope of defeating my pursuer, but I'd run out of places to go. I grabbed the first of the gargoyles and drew myself up. Technically they're grotesques, given that they don't spout water, but large ugly stone monsters will always be gargoyles to me; also I'm not one to care about the niceties of architecture when being hunted down by a skinless horror. Or when I'm not.

I climbed and the monster climbed beneath me.

In truth, though I had climbed down this particular tower I had never ascended it. I relied on the fact that it was twin to the east spire that stood on the other side of the grand portico, which I had scaled many times when visiting Great-uncle Garyus. The window directly above me was in fact, of all the palace's many windows, the last one I would choose to clamber through. Only the certain knowledge that the Silent Sister was in Slov, combined with the presence of a huge and gory corpse following me up the wall, gave me the impetus to keep going.

I got one hand on the windowsill, one foot on the back of the last gargoyle's head, one moment when I thought I might make it, then the monster's fingers closed on the heel of the boot on my dangling leg.

"Oh, *come on!*" It seemed so unfair.

I braced my leg against the gargoyle and heaved with all my might to break free. I hadn't a chance but I'd try anything in desperation.

The gargoyle gave way with a shockingly loud crack. The dead giant hung on for a split second even as the man-sized statue hit him square in the face. In the next heartbeat both were falling. A second gargoyle interrupted the drop to the roof of the main entrance far below. The dead thing became momentarily impaled on stone horns before the weight of the first statue tore it free and both punched a hole through the flat roof of the portico and, slamming down to the entrance steps, created a stone-dead flesh-stone sandwich.

I hung there, gasping, so nearly torn away with the pair as they fell. Time passed and at last the thunder of my heart ceased to fill the world. I stared at the raw stone where the gargoyle had broken away from the wall. It had been waiting to fall since before I was born. Sometimes the difference between saving a life and taking one is just a matter of timing— the right moment and the wrong.

Dry-mouthed, I struggled up through the Silent Sister's window, trembling in every limb.

I saw nothing until I stepped to the side and let the moonlight flood in after me. A small and empty antechamber. The dark steps spiralling down to the foyer below. The door to the Silent Sister's room stood closed, one tall-backed chair beside it. A second chair, twin to the first, had been moved to the middle of the antechamber, halfway between the door and the arch to the staircase. On it rested a goblet, moon-washed and silver, a strip of linen, and a boot.

"What the hell?" I staggered forward, my left leg hurting unaccount-ably and my right foot cold against the stone floor. I looked down. The giant hadn't released his grip on me—the sole of my boot had torn off in his hand. Blood ran freely down my left leg from a gash above the knee— one of the gargoyle's horns must have torn me as it came free.

I took the linen and bound my leg. The boot looked suspiciously like a new version of the one I was wearing. Ridding myself of the remnants of the old boot I slipped the new one on. A perfect fit. The goblet stood three-quarters full of water. Some must have evaporated in the two weeks since my great-aunt placed it there. A black fly floated in it.

"I'm not *that* thirsty!" A hoarse dry whisper. I took the goblet and flicked the fly corpse clear. I wasn't even fooling myself, and I'm good at that. I drained the cup and wiped my mouth, wondering if the old witch had weakened the joint that held the gargoyle to the wall. I felt weak and dizzy, sweaty with exertion and fear.

How much had she seen? "Do you ever get it wrong, old woman?" A short laugh burst from me as I wondered if there were other such tableaux set against foreseen events that never happened. If I'd never climbed the tower I wouldn't know she got it wrong . . .

At that point another wave of dizziness swamped me and my legs gave out. I collapsed into the chair, placed in just the right position to receive me.

"Show off."

EIGHTEEN

I came to myself with a start, bewildered for a second, then guilty, hoping I had only rested in the chair a few moments. I stood and patted the empty scabbard at my hip. The room held no replacement sword.

"Surprised you there, you old witch!" I couldn't manage a smile over the victory. It'd been a moment of madness, regretted almost immediately. Still, I hoped Martus had survived. How else would I take the credit for it at every opportunity for the rest of our lives?

"Lisa!" I meant Micha and Nia as well, but it was Lisa's name that broke from me as the sudden realization hit me and I was off and running. If Hertet had gathered every guard in the compound to his side then the Inner Palace would be the place to go for safety. The DeVeer sisters would be there, sheltering under the new king's wing with Darin's child.

Nobody in the dark hall of the Poor Palace foyer, no guard on the door. I took the front steps in one leap. The landing reminded me how badly my knee hurt. A sprint-hobble took me across the courtyard, through a passage, and across another courtyard bringing me to the Inner Palace. I angled for the guest wing.

"Stop!" A booming voice. "Stop right there!"

I halted ten yards shy of the entrance to the guest wing and turned to see a tall palace guardsman approaching, a squad of a dozen wall guards at his back, spears over their shoulders.

"I need to see—"

"Nobody can break the curfew." The man's voice was the kind of deep that sounds as though it must hurt. "By order of the king!"

I eyed him. Young, thick-thewed, a gleaming breastplate, his face the variety of handsome that declares an unabashed lack of imagination. "Your name, Guardsman?" I tried to sound in charge. Technically I was.

"Sub-captain Paraito."

"Look, Sub-captain, I'm *Prince* Jalan." I hadn't the energy to put on my royal roar. "I need to check on my family, then I'm going to see Hertet so—"

"Put him in the cells with the other dissidents." Paraito waved his men forward. Four of the chain-armoured wall guards came forward. I reached for my absent sword, something that was becoming both a habit and a liability.

"Look!" I found my roar as the four men reached for me. "I'm the marshal of this entire fucking city, appointed by the Red Queen *herself*, and in case you hadn't noticed—Vermillion is under attack. Half of it's burning and there are dead things stalking this very palace." I slapped away the closest hand. "So if you plan on living to see the dawn I strongly advise you to bring me before my uncle. Right now!"

The sub-captain stared at me as two of his minions took my arms. The frown on his handsome brow suggested that I might perhaps have put a small dent in his surety. "We'll take him to the court and let the king decide if he wants to see him." He turned and led off.

"Wait!" I dug in my heels but started to walk as it became clear they would drag me. "Wait! Where are we going?" The palace man had set off back across the courtyard, directly away from the Inner Palace.

"The king has made court in Milano House."

"But . . . that's insane." The palace was compromised and Hertet had set up as king in his old house? The Inner Palace had been the seat of kings for generations. Spells and wards layered the place thicker than any rugs or tapestries: it was a place of safety against dark magics. For all I knew any dead thing crossing its threshold would burn or turn to dust . . . or simply become the more traditional kind of corpse, cut free of the necromancer's strings. I very much doubted Milano House enjoyed the same protections. Still, Uncle Hertet had been practising to be king beneath that roof for longer than I'd been alive. Perhaps he felt safest there. Perhaps the Red Queen's throne scared him. It would me. Especially if my claim were premature . . .

Passing by Scribes' Row I saw the wiry form of a mire-ghoul, stark against the moon, just for an instant as it crested the roof.

"There!" I twisted to free an arm and failed. "Up there, a ghoul!"

"Don't see it." Sub-captain Paraito glanced upward without breaking stride.

"Aren't you at least going to send men to investigate?" I managed to shake off one of the guards. "Unhand me, you buffoon, my uncle is exactly who I want to see. I don't have to be dragged there!"

"The king has ordered all men-at-arms to defend Milano House. Our patrols are to round up traitors and forewarn of any attack. We're not to go chasing shadows."

I shook my head and carried on walking. In all honesty the shadows would probably eat Paraito and his squad if they ventured into them.

I didn't make another break for it until we passed within sight of Roma Hall. In one of the upper rooms a faint light escaped the shutters. I twisted free and took a stride. One more stride and I would have made it clear, but one of the wall guards, either by accident or design, got the haft of his spear tangled between my legs and I went down with two men piling on top of me.

They dragged me up, spitting grit from the flagstones.

"Bind the prisoner!" Sub-captain Paraito nodded to one of his squad.

"I wasn't trying to escape, you idiot!" An echo of berserker rage rang through me and more guardsmen stepped in to help hold my arms. "Prince Darin's wife and child are alone in Roma House with a necromancer." I took a deep breath as they looped the rope about my hands. "I'll remind you again. I'm a prince, and the marshal of this whole damn city! If you let my sister-in-law die . . . Wait! The necromancer! He's a threat to Hertet—the king, I mean. It's your duty to—"

"It's my duty to enter the information in my report." The sub-captain motioned his men on, and on they went, dragging me while I fought my bonds.

As we approached Milano House I saw a host of armoured men drawn up around its walls, torches burning in such profusion as to light the entire courtyard. I saw members of the palace guard, the throne-room elite, the wall guard, the grounds guard, the aristocratic remnants of the

Red Lance, Long Spear, and Iron Hoof cavalries, prison guards from the Marsail keep, even house guards from the noble houses.

"Alphons!" I spotted one of Father's men in the host gathered before the front steps. "Alphons! Is Lady Micha safe? Lady Lisa?"

He shouted something but I only caught the word "double" before my captors forced me up the front steps along a narrow corridor of armoured knights. The great bronze doors opened a begrudging two feet, allowing us to file into the crowded entrance hall.

"Keep a tight hold on him." And Paraito left us, presumably to file his report.

I stood there, sweaty, hurting, and above all furious. Every person crammed into the entrance hall appeared to be talking at once, the tide of conversation making only the slightest of dips when I was brought in. The antechamber held a dozen clusters of lords, the occasional lady, a few barons, an earl, even merchants plumped up in their most expensive finery, all talking at each other, some jovial, some worried, some heated. I saw Duchess Sansera wearing her age tonight, along with all her diamonds; Lord Gren, my old adversary in matters of gambling on both horses and men, looking more nervous here than he ever did at the pits; a score more highborn who might be expected to speak for me. A few glanced my way but the ropes on my wrists discouraged any from coming forward.

"We can't just stand here!" I looked around at the four men detailed to guard me, a distinctly dowdy presence amid the silks and gold of the high and the mighty. "You saw what it's like out there . . . You—"

"Cousin Jalan!" Hertet's second-eldest son, Roland, came in through the main doors, spotting me immediately. Martus called him "the Chinless Wonder," and to be fair the growing of a sort of beard to hide that fact, and siring the Red Queen's first great grandson, did rank highest among his few notable achievements. "Father will want to see you!"

I met his watery blue eyes, he seemed oblivious to the fact I was under guard. I managed a smile and nodded. "Lead on." And with a swirl of his emerald cape, embroidered with the trefoils that Uncle Hertet had adopted for his branch of the Kendeth family tree, Cousin Roland led on.

"A moment, cousin!" I stopped Roland as we approached the doors to the great hall. "You know the DeVeers? Everyone does." I didn't give him pause to answer. "A necromancer has taken St. Agnes. I fear Lisa and Micha DeVeer may still be in the main house with my infant niece. It would be a great favour to me if you could dispatch a squad of men to ensure they have escaped and to bring them to safety if need be."

"A necromancer?" Roland mangled the "r"s and left his mouth open in surprise. "In the palace?"

"In the church. At Roma Hall. A baby in peril!" I nodded and kept it simple. I hoped mention of the baby might stir him, as a father. "You could send some guardsmen."

Roland blinked. "Most certainly." He raised his hand and beckoned. "Sir Roger! Sir Roger!" A short knight in the shiniest armour I'd ever seen clanked awkwardly toward us. "Ladies in distress at Roma Hall, Sir Roger!" Roland made a "Woger" of each "Roger."

"I shall attend to the matter, Prince Roland." Roger, pockmarked and sporting a thick black moustache, gave a curt bow, all efficiency and purpose.

"Take a dozen men, Sir Roger." All the advice I could offer as Roland continued toward the doors. "Good ones!"

Cousin Roland elbowed past the elite guardsmen at the entrance to his father's court, four of them in the queen's fire-bronze armour beneath her scarlet plumes. He set both hands to the towering oak panels and pushed into the great hall.

I hadn't been into the great hall at Milano House since Roland's wedding when I was thirteen. Father and his eldest brother had fallen out over some matter concerning the disciplining of the house-priest. It wasn't really about the priest, of course—it was about who got to boss who around, as are most disputes among brothers. In any event, heavy words were lightly thrown and Father led his brood from the hall in high dudgeon, Martus forcibly detaching a slightly drunk young Prince Jalan from a pretty young bridesmaid whose name I forget.

In the subsequent decade the hall had changed beyond recognition. Dozens of bejewelled lanterns joined to cast a brilliant light across what was undeniably the most splendidly appointed room I'd ever laid eyes on.

The tapestries behind Hertet's mahogany throne were of gold-and-silver wire, the rugs of Indus silk, colours so vivid they assaulted the eye. Suits of gilt armour stood around the perimeter of the hall, intermixed with Grandmother's guard, so immobile that it was hard to say at a glance which armour stood empty and which held men.

The throne room proved less crowded than the chamber before it, with thirty or so of Uncle's favourites gathered around, wine goblets in hand, servants hovering. I saw a dozen familiar but anonymous lords, Sir Grethem all in armour as if prepared for one of the tourneys that made his reputation, Lady Bellinda, stood close to the centre, the most recent and youngest of Hertet's long string of mistresses. And beside her, perhaps Hertet's most powerful supporter, the Duke of Grast, a burly fellow sporting a thick grey beard, a man I might have spread the odd cruel rumour about over the years after he caught me with his sister.

Hertet's ebony chair stood on a dais and rose above him, the back spreading in a dramatic scroll, the lines of it tracked with inset rubies, returning the lantern light and turning to glowing drops of blood.

None of this splendour exerted quite such a draw on my eye as the crown upon the new king's head. Grandmother's imperial crown, a heavy thing of iron, honouring the bloodiest of her ancestors and the days of the Red March when we were warriors one and all. Centuries had softened the thing with a wealth of diamonds and a tracery of red-gold, but it still spoke of power won by the sword and the bow.

Hertet looked lost in the dark grip of his throne, swamped by a voluminous robe of cloth-of-gold, worked all over in elaborate whorls and spirals of the Brettan kind. I followed in Roland's wake, noting my uncle's unhealthy pallor as he sweated beneath the crown, more haggard than he had been at Father's funeral that morning.

"Father!" Roland's slight speech impediment managed to put a comic edge on most words. A kinder sire would have changed his son's name to John when the problem with "r"s became apparent. Roland pushed past another couple of lords and raised both his hand and his voice. "Father! I've found Prince Jalan, come to swear to you!"

Roland stepped aside to present me, his gaze falling to my bound wrists for the first time, with some confusion, now taking in the torn and blood-spattered clothes.

"Nephew. I commend you for being the first of Reymond's boys to bend the knee . . . but you've come before me in rags and ropes? Some new fashion perhaps? Heh? Heh?"

His barked laughter sparked the court-in-waiting into sycophantic echoes, tittering at the state of me. I supposed they might now just be called "the court" since the waiting appeared to be over.

Hertet raised both hands, a tolerant call for quiet. "So where are those brothers of yours? Martus should be offering his fealty. He's head of your house now, no? Until the pope's new cardinal evicts the lot of you at least!" More laughter at that.

"Martus holds the enemy before the palace walls at your command . . . Uncle." I couldn't call him king, not yet. "I last saw him about to charge a rag-a-maul. I don't know if—"

"A what?" Hertet asked.

The Duke of Grast stepped in before I could reply, cold eyes upon me. "A rag-a-maul, majesty. The peasants' word for the dust-devils that blow up from time to time. They hold them to be haunted."

"Heh! Heh! That boy! I always said he'd fight wind if he hadn't anyone else to battle! Didn't I say that, Roland? Didn't I?" Hertet wiped the grey straggles from his forehead as the dutiful laughter followed.

"I don't know if Martus survived." I raised my voice. "And Darin is dead, killed behind the city walls by dead men who over-ran the Appan Gate. The outer city is burning. We have—"

"Yes. Yes." Hertet's brow furrowed beneath the crown, irritation showing in his voice. "Aren't you the marshal, Nephew? Shouldn't you be out there putting a stop to all this? Or are you unequal to the task?" He looked nervous as much as angry, twitchy in the throne.

I sensed a weakness in him. I would never get the help needed at the gate if I let them laugh me from the court, so I attacked. "How did you get the crown, Uncle?" The sparkle of the diamonds captured my eye. "It was locked in the royal treasury." My father had told me about the iron vault. The first Gholloth spent a small fortune to defend a large fortune. Turkmen master smiths travelled from the east to build it in situ. In time the vault might be breached—but so quickly? "The Red Queen keeps the key."

Silence followed the scattered gasps at my temerity. Hertet reached into the golden collar of his robes and drew forth Loki's key, making slow rotations on the end of a twisted silver chain. "It didn't take any effort to wrest this from that ugly old man she keeps in the tower. Much safer with me, and so good at opening doors! You wouldn't believe the secrets I've found or how much gold dear Mother had stashed away . . ."

"You took it?" Of course he had. Garyus wouldn't give it to an idiot nephew, not while he was steward. "It's a bad idea to *take* that key from anyone. It needs to be given."

"Nonsense." He twitched, then forced a smile. "I'm king and I'll take what I like. It's mine by right. And none of your concern. Take those silly ropes off and bend the knee. Then you can get back to what you're supposed to be doing. Or shall I appoint somebody more competent?"

Every instinct tried to put me on my knees but one question kept me standing. "Is Garyus . . . alive?"

Hertet frowned. "Of course he is. I'm no monster. He's locked up safe until he sees things my way. Some—" He shot a glance into the glittering line of courtiers closest to the throne. "Some advised a sudden and sharp solution. But those times are behind us now. I am not my mother."

I'd been on one knee from the moment I heard Garyus was alive. I've always been happy to abandon my pride if it gets in the way of ambition, whether that be escape or a tumble in a lady's bed. Hertet could have my allegiance, it really wasn't worth much. "My king, I need the palace guard at the Appan Gate, and all the men that can be rounded up from the Seventh. A battle is raging there and we are not winning. If the gate falls the palace will fall—it's not built for defence. Our men-at-arms will serve you better at the city wall."

Hertet tucked Loki's key away and frowned. "You would leave your king unguarded? At the mercy of any dissenters who can gather a mob? That's hardly a demonstration of your loyalty to the crown, Marshal!"

Voices rose in agreement on several sides, not just the sycophants but genuine self-interest. Sending your guards out of sight while the city burns and battle rages is never an easy sell. Rather like throwing away your sword whilst being chased, it feels like a damn stupid thing to do.

I returned to my feet, awkward with my hands still bound. "Majesty, you fail to understand the scale of the threat. Thousands of dead men crowd the city wall, ten thousand perhaps. If they are able to take the Appan Gate and enter in force then Vermillion is lost. The palace, this house, would fall within an hour. The city wall is our only defence and it is the only place where our numbers can tell. The men outside your door are wasted—at the gate they may yet turn the tide. Prince Rotus and Princess Serah are with our forces there. They need support." I saw a measure of conflict on Hertet's face. He might be stupid, but not entirely stupid. I suspected most of his current measures were the result of paranoia, the possibly valid belief that his family, or the city, or both, would reject his claim to the throne and set some younger and more capable Kendeth in the Red Queen's seat.

"Tell Father about the necromancer, Jalan!" Roland at my shoulder, helpfully muddying the waters.

"Necromancer?" Hertet shifted forward, hands gripping the arms of his throne.

"There's a sub-captain in the foyer claiming there are dead men roaming the courtyards and ghouls on the rooftops!" Some newly-arrived lord far behind me at the main doors.

I spread my hands as far as the ropes allowed. "It's only a hint of what's coming if we don't hold the Appan Gate. These are just scouts and still the palace walls mean nothing to them!"

"Necromancers and dead men on my very doorstep!" Hertet rose from the throne, colouring crimson, voice rising toward a shout. "And you try to send away my personal guard?"

"Vermillion will fall! You must—"

"*Must*?" Hertet swung his head left then right as if seeking echoes of his outrage. "Must? I am the king of Red March, from sea to sea, and there is no 'must'!"

"Listen to me!" I shouted to be heard.

"Put Prince Jalan in the cells. Let him cool his temper and find his reason." Hertet fell back into his chair, anger spent as quickly as it came.

"Marshal Roland, gather fifty men of the grounds guard and take the situation at the Appan Gate in hand. I expect a report in the morning."

"This is insane!" I made to climb the dais, but strong arms already had me, dragging me toward the exit. "You'll all die here if you follow this idiot—" A heavy fist took the treason from my mouth and the rest of the world followed into darkness a moment later.

NINETEEN

As tyrants go, Uncle Hertet proved not to be too terrible. They dragged me dazed and disoriented into one of his grand drawing rooms where the "cells" proved to be a collection of large, comfortable armchairs to which eight or nine well-dressed men were lightly chained. I looked a beggar next to them and a housemaid rushed to get a dustsheet before the guardsmen thrust me into my own comfy chair.

"Hertet likes to keep his enemies close," I said, reclining with a groan. Few parts of me didn't hurt.

"Prince Jalan?" A concerned voice from just behind me. "Are you injured?"

"I'm fine. The worst of the pain is in my . . . body." I craned my neck to see who addressed me. Squinting against the remnants of double vision I made out a thin and balding man in the latest Rhone fashions, yellow buttons on a black velvet jacket. The two images joined to reveal him sharp featured, sporting a port-wine stain below one eye. "Bonarti Poe!" On my list of likely rebels Bonarti Poe would be keeping me company in the weasel section at the very bottom. "What did you do? Rush my uncle screaming death threats?"

Poe gave a high-pitched and flustered laugh. "No! No, never!" He coughed into a lace-edged handkerchief. "The king considers me Count Isen's man and mistrusts me." Another cough and he raised his voice. "But there's no man more loyal to the throne of Red March than Bonarti Poe!"

"Isen is against my uncle?" That sounded promising. Count Isen was madder than a bag of ferrets but very capable and with a standing army of his own.

"I'm sure the count's loyalty is beyond reproach," Poe replied. "But he cannot yet have expressed an opinion on the matter. Even with the swiftest of messengers and leaving his hall immediately the count can't be anywhere near Vermillion. I fear the king has simply anticipated defiance where I'm sure none exists."

I was far less sure, but the count's opinion didn't matter one way or the other if he was still down at his holdings in the south. "So we're doomed to live out the rest of our lives in this damn awful dungeon then?" I sunk further back into the chair and smiled at the maid standing attendance between two guardsmen at the door. A pretty girl with red curls.

"They'll move us to the Marsail cells come morning." An ancient, crumbling lord I recognized but couldn't name. "That silly boy's too scared to spare the men right now."

"Hmmm." I tested my chain. It turns out that heavy chains are just for show. A light chain will hold a man. I had more chance of breaking off the chair leg that the other end was wrapped about. Actually, if not for the half dozen guards stationed around the walls, I could just turn the armchair over and slip the chain free. But with my sword gone, my knife confiscated, and the fact I had no intention of pitting myself against six trained guards, with or without a sword, my options were limited.

"They seem to be having fun." The sounds of conversation just reached us from Hertet's court, a low continuous rumble interspersed with the occasional shriek of laughter or outburst of applause.

"Scared out of their wits, most of them." The Baron of Strombol, a portly but fierce little man governing a sizable territory in the mountains to the north. "Terrified of whatever is at our gates, frightened that the Red Queen won't come back to save them, frightened that she will."

"She isn't dead?" I hadn't believed it, not truly. I didn't think she could die. Not a woman that tough. And the Silent Sister . . . she always seemed too old for death to bother with.

The baron threw up his hands, chain clattering. "Who knows? Hertet says she is, but I've had no word of it save his. Wishful thinking?"

I pursed my lips. It was perhaps the best chance the heir-apparently-not was ever going to get to wear the crown. Maybe he just decided to gamble. We both shared that weakness. I understood gambling.

We sat and time passed. I took a goblet of wine and picked at a bowl of olives. I smiled at the maid and earned a scowl for staring. A few parts of me even stopped aching, though I knew I'd be walking like an old man tomorrow, if I could even stand. It would have been quite pleasant but for the nagging of an unwelcome conscience. I'd left Darin's wife and child in the care of a necromancer and sent just a dozen men under the command of a shiny knight to save them. Along with a barbed conscience I also had "overwhelming terror" to spoil the evening for me. The certain knowledge that the forces at the Appan Gate would soon crumble if they hadn't already, and the tide of dead citizenry would then swamp the palace walls and kill us all.

I had less than an hour's uneasy rest before the screaming started. I recognized it immediately despite the sound reaching only faintly through the curtained windows. The death-scream, issuing from the mouths of corpses all across the palace compound.

"What the?" The baron shifted his bulk around in the narrow confines of his chair.

"The lichkin is here." I'd intended it to be a resigned announcement but it emerged more as a squeaking whisper.

"The what?" Bonarti Poe looked as frightened as a man could be of something he knew nothing about.

"A bad thing," I said.

By the sound of it the lichkin hadn't come at the head of a break-through from the gate. The death-scream was too scattered and too quiet for that. Even so, there were many of the dead and the lichkin on its own was a thing to fear. In Hell a single lichkin had defeated Snorri ver Snagason in moments.

My chair seemed suddenly less comfortable, more like an anchor holding the lamb for the slaughter. The illumination from the new king's candles and lamps seemed to grow more dim by the moment, as if a second sunset were upon us, one that cared nothing for the works of men, only that the light must die. Shadows lengthened and grew darker, twitching with possibility.

And then the lichkin drew near. I could almost taste it through the outer wall of Milano House, stalking the night. Colours died, shade by shade, leaving the room subdued, and a great sorrow fell across us, blacker than the blackest of black dog days—the certainty that joy had fled and nothing would ever be right in the world again.

It lasted an age, but at last the sensation lifted by degrees. Poe's weeping quieted to a deep heaving. The oppression eased enough for me to wonder how bad it must have been for the men out there in the dark with just the feeble illumination of torch and moon between them and that stalking horror. It had been terrible even when safe in the light, comfort, and security of the house.

A death-scream right below the window answered my question and made me lurch in my chair so badly it nearly tipped over. Men had died out there from sheer terror, and now they tore at their living comrades, spreading horror and panic.

Glancing about me, I saw that the curtains had developed grey patches where the material had rotted. The brass handles on the doors held a tarnished look. All of us, prisoners and guards alike, looked aged, as if we'd spent a week without sleep.

"We need to get out of here. We need to get out of here. We need—" A skinny lord with a wispy moustache leapt to his feet, yanking at the chain restraining him. He'd turned the chair over and had managed to tug the chain from the leg before the guards beat him down.

"Shut it! Just shut it!" One of the guardsmen in the struggle gained his feet, raw-knuckled from punching Lord Wispy in the jaw. He looked more scared than the fallen prisoner, the deep-set eyes in his piggy face as haunted as if they'd seen the butcher coming for his bacon.

The sounds of fighting and panic reached us from outside. Screaming, both from the hungry dead and the terrified living, rang out toward the front of the house. We heard shutters splinter in the chamber next to us.

"The windows! Barricade the windows!" I stood up, lifted my chair, releasing the chain from around its leg, and walked with it toward the curtains. None of the guards moved to stop me: instead they looked about for anything that might aid the effort.

I reached to help two guardsmen struggling with a heavy cabinet, the treasured pottery within spilling from its many shelves. Nobody commented on the fact that the chain on my wrist now hung loose, no longer tethering

me to my seat. I helped with a suit of armour and its stand then moved off
to get something else to use . . . and carried on going.

The sounds of the fight outside were terrifyingly familiar. If I closed
my eyes I could have been back at the Appan Gate. New sounds close
by of breaking glass and splintering wood lent a little more pace to my
escape. I wasn't sure quite how far I'd been dragged after being taken
from the throne room, nor in which direction to head in order to leave
the building. I wasn't even entirely sure I wanted to go outside. I opened
one door onto a library, not huge, but lined with books from floor to
ceiling. The windows were uncurtained—half a dozen tall, narrow arches,
each sealed with a dozen plates of puddle-glass, leaded together. As I
moved to pull the door closed blood splattered the entirety of each window, save the top-most panes. A wave of it breaking against the building.
Despair washed over me, then lessened as the lichkin moved away again,
tracking down more victims outside the house.

I slammed the door, turned, and saw Hertet hurrying down the
corridor toward me, the crown askew upon his head. A group of knights
followed at his back. His gaze slid across me unregistering, his face
deathly pale. I noticed his cloth-of-gold robe bore a scarlet splatter across
the middle as if someone had been gutted in front of him. I flattened
myself to the door to let them by.

"It wants the key!" I shouted as he passed me. I'm not sure why I said it.

Hertet stopped, seeing me for the first time. "Jalan. Reymond's boy."
He reached out and patted my hand. "You were always a good boy." His
other hand drew the key from beneath his collar. He tugged it and it came
loose, though the chain looked too strong to break like that. "Here. You take
it. You'll know what to do." He folded my hand around Loki's key and moved
on without a pause or a glance back. "We can go to the cellars and . . ." I
lost his voice beneath the tramp of mailed feet as the knights swept by.

I stood for a moment in the corridor, sounds of chaos from the direction of the throne room, screams and howls ringing out at intervals from
random directions. The blackness of the key held my gaze, cold and heavy
in my hand. I managed to tear my attention from Loki's gift and check
both directions along the corridor, absently noting a long dark smear of

blood along the wall panelling opposite and a painting, knocked from the wall, its frame splintered: the young Hertet staring out at me with heroic intent, footprints all over his face. At the far end of the corridor three women hurried by in silken finery, one old, two young, there one moment, gone the next.

The screaming from the throne room grew more desperate. Something struck the doors leading from it with enough force that the echoes trembled through my chest.

The key. The key had ended a lichkin in Hell. But that had been pure chance. Luck. My gaze returned to the blackness of it, unlocking the memories of that victory, and in an instant they had sucked me in.

Snorri stands before me, a monotone giant clad in the blood-dust of Hell. A fissure behind him gouts tongues of crimson flame and the air is thick with the stink of sulphur. I'm holding Loki's key before me at waist height and the lichkin has gone, just a black stain lingering where its corrupted remnants fell to the ground. The key undid it. The lichkin took a step back when it blocked Snorri's charge and impaled itself, just an inch, but it was enough. I turned the key and the lichkin came undone.

Snorri's gaze is on my hand. He thought the key was safe with Kara, back in the living world.

"Well look at that," I say, opening my fingers to reveal the key fully. "The thing is . . ." I struggle to come up with an explanation. "The thing to remember is that . . . without this we would both be dead." I hold up my other hand to forestall him. "And not the good kind of dead. The really, really nasty kind." I shudder, remembering the pain as the lichkin held me. I've never experienced anything close, and never want to again.

"You brought *that* key into Hel?" Snorri appears to have heard none of the words I so carefully brought up in my defence. "Into Hel?"

"You heard the bit about saving both our lives?"

Snorri looks scared. It's one of the more worrying things I've seen in a life that lately has been more or less one worrying thing joined to the next. "We have to get it out of here. You have to take it back, Jal. Now!"

I look around. A wide and dusty valley dead-lit by a sky the colour of old sorrow. Fiery vents, a scattering of disturbingly shaped rocks. "How?" I'm not going to argue about leaving. I was doing my best not to come in the first place.

Snorri frowns, concentrating but unable to hold in his thoughts. "What were you *thinking*? This whole time you've being carrying . . ." He looks so disappointed in me that I almost see his point.

"The Ancient Greeks had a hall of judgment . . ." I say, mainly to distract him.

"The Greeks? What have the Greeks got to do with anything?"

"Well . . ." I often come up with my best plans by opening my mouth and listening to the words that come out. This time it doesn't seem to be working. "Well . . . we've been trekking through your underworld, Hel's domain. And now we're in my Hell, or the Dead King's Hell—"

"But the Greek mythology we've both known our whole lives! So both of us can shape it. Brilliant!"

The truth was I'd had ancient Greek mythology beaten through my thick layer of disinterest in my early teens by a detested tutor named Soros using a blunt cane and sharp sarcasm. I still have no idea why it was considered necessary, even if some in those regions have taken up the worship again. I did, however, learn it well enough to avoid the cane, if not the sarcasm.

"Anyway. The Greeks had a hall of judgment with three judges to direct the souls of the dead to their various rewards and punishments." I start walking again. The lichkin might only be a stain on the ground but it's a stain I don't wish to stand next to any longer than I have to. I spit to clear the sulphur taste from my mouth. It doesn't work.

"You're thinking to leave the deadlands that way?" Snorri asks. "Because after the hall of judgment there's a big dog named Cerberus, and if you don't get eaten by him then it's the River Acheron and the River Styx, that's the rivers of woe and hate. The ferryman is supposed to be a—"

"Doesn't matter," I say. "I'm not dead. I shouldn't be here. As soon as I reach the judges they'll see that I'm in the wrong place and send me back home. It's what they do—send people where they belong."

"You think so?" Snorri looks doubtful, which is the opposite of what I need.

"I *believe* so," I say. "And that's what counts." It strikes me that in this Hell a man of sufficient will, a man willing to sacrifice anything, might bend the world itself around his desire and create of himself whatsoever he wished. It also strikes me that I am not such a man.

Snorri's long stride brings him level with me. "So all we need to do is to get you to the judges' hall."

"That *is* one of the weaker parts of the idea," I admit, slowing to look about for clues, but of course there aren't any. Just dust and rocks.

Snorri keeps walking. "You haven't figured this place out yet." He calls it over his shoulder. "Direction doesn't matter. It's like in dreams. The things you want come to you. The things you don't want as well."

I hurry to catch up. "We're just going to walk in this direction?"

"Yes."

"Until we find it?"

"Yes."

"Kara said the door would be everywhere," I say, always eager to avoid a long walk.

"If you see it before we get there let me know." Snorri snorts. "Now what do you think this hall is going to look like? What are the judges' names?"

We walk through a valley that slowly becomes a plain, beneath a sky that darkens by degrees, settling shadows upon us. All the while we talk about the underworld of Hades and the gods of Olympus and the legends that the ancients set about it all. After the Thousand Suns many lost faith with the God of Rome and turned to older gods whose failures lay too far back to recall. As we remember the shape and history of Hades we find ourselves walking into it, or rather that part of the deadlands shaped by the faith of those who believe such tales.

"What is it with pagan hells and dogs?" I ask. "And rivers?"

"What do you mean?" A defensive tone enters Snorri's voice.

"The Greeks have the River Styx, crossed by a ferryman who dumps you on a shore guarded by a huge dog named Cerberus. The Norse have the River Gjöll, crossed by a bridge that takes you to a shore guarded by a huge dog named Garm."

"I don't see your point."

"It's like you copied them item by item, just changing the odd detail and using your own names."

The ensuing argument takes my mind off the unrelenting misery of walking the deadlands. Hell is hell, whatever mythology you dress it up in. Every part of me is dry. Every part hurts. Famine and thirst have set up home in me, bone deep. As the darkness grows, any hope in me wanes and my tongue lacks interest in conversation . . . but arguing, baiting the Northman, that still holds enough appeal to stop me lying down in the dust and waiting for my turn to blow on the wind.

Jalan.

It's just the breeze, speaking my name into a pause in the conversation. *Jalan.*

But when the wind speaks your name in the darkness of Hell there's a chill that comes with it.

In time even the pleasure in enraging Snorri fades and I stagger on beneath a burden of unbearable pain and exhaustion. My surroundings might be only darkness and dust and a low but endless headwind, but in my mind I've returned to the singular hell that was our trip across the Bitter Ice. I'm there once more, with the Norsemen dying beside me step by step, Ein and Arne and Tuttugu, all of us trailing along in that white wasteland with nothing to draw us forward but Snorri ver Snagason's broad back always moving on.

"Up!"

I find I've fallen to my knees, head bowed, unmoving.

"I got you." Snorri's hand closes around my upper arm and he lifts me to my feet.

"I'm sorry." I stumble on.

"This place will wear any man down," he says.

"I'm sorry." I'm too exhausted to explain, but I'm sorry for everything. I'm sorry I had to be dragged through that door before I could live up to my promise, sorry to be leaving Snorri alone in Hell, sorry for his family, sorry I can't believe in his quest, sorry I know he'll fail. "Sorry for—"

"I know," he says, and catches me before I fall again. "And no man who walks through Hell for a friend has anything to apologize for."

"I—" A sound in the distance saves me from more foolishness, faint, then gone. "What's that?"

"I heard it too."

Having heard nothing but the wind for so long the strange cry seems full of portent.

It sounds again, a touch louder.

Jalan.

Louder than my imagination this time. A voice, speaking my name, or at least making the sound of it, making something unfamiliar of it.

"Run?" I find I have more energy left than I thought. Not enough to run, that's just the fear talking, but enough to stagger along at a decent rate.

"Let's keep going." Snorri leads the way.

"But what is it?"

"What do you think it is?" he asks.

Jalan. It's almost the way my Mother used to speak my name. The way a child might struggle to reproduce both syllables. I don't want to say, as if naming my fear might make it real, but somehow I know what's coming, what's hunting us down. In Hell with its peculiar lack of directions, all your fears will find you soon enough. It's my sister and the lichkin that has bound itself to her to make a corruption of her soul. If they kill me here my death will punch a hole through which they can emerge into the living world. The unborn queen, the rider and the ridden, birthed into dead flesh so many years after her conception. All my sister's potential unleashed onto the world in the hands of a lichkin . . . To be honest, all that other stuff is just icing on a deeply unpalatable cake—I stopped caring after the "killing me here" bit. "Is that a light?" I point.

"Yes." Snorri confirms that I'm not hallucinating through sheer terror.

JALAN! The howl comes from behind us, distant but by no means distant enough. *JALAN!* It turns out I can run.

Snorri jogs alongside me and with agonizing slowness the light resolves from one into a multitude, outlining the roof and many supporting columns of a towering building, all carved in white stone, just as we described it to each other.

Souls cluster in the darkness near the court. From time to time a new soul will run down the steps, a translucent recollection of a man or woman, not keeping a single shape but moving through memories of their life, moments of terror mostly. None of them lingers where the light falls, rather they run until the darkness takes them, as if the judges' light burns them. They move away from Snorri and me too. Perhaps the life that still persists in us hurts to look upon with eyes where none remains.

We stop a hundred yards from the many-pillared hall. Walls rise behind the pillars, white and broad, every inch carved with scenes from legend. A doorway stands open, allowing the judged souls to flee their guilt. Our faces are cast into sharp relief by the slanting illumination. Even at this distance that light promises running water, warm air, green things growing.

The air seems brittle here, alive with possibility. I get that same sensation when the souls of the dead break through from the living world and I glimpse blue sky through the tears they make. This is a place of doors. I can feel the key on my chest, cold then hot, vibrating at some pitch beyond hearing. When Kara said the door between life and death lay everywhere, that was just words. I could no more spot that door in the midst of Hell than I could in a market square on a warm day in Vermillion. But here . . . here it seems that home is just a touch away. Here it seems that the door I need might just fracture out of nothing and stand before me. The living world is tantalizingly close, it just needs . . . some small thing to happen, like a lost word finally tripping off the tip of my tongue, and I would see the door . . .

My name rings out again, a howl, loud now, echoing off the walls, an undulating noise empty one moment, violent the next, full of hunger and malice. I take another step into the light. "You should come with me, Snorri." The words are hard to say. "You've seen this place. Nothing good can be brought out of it."

I wait for the anger, but there's none in him. He hangs his head, refusing to look at the glow before us. "Arran Vale."

"What?" I want to go, but I stay.

"Do you remember Arran Vale?" he asks.

"Um." I should be running but Snorri's bravery won't let me. His image of who I am pins me here. I should be sprinting for the hall— instead I stand and try to answer him. Arran Vale? My mind races through names and faces and places, dozens, hundreds, all encountered on our long travels. "Maybe . . . a valley in Rhone? Near that little town with the one church and three whorehouses, where—"

"Hennan's grandfather, the grandson of Lotar Vale."

"Who could forget Lotar Vale? The hero you'd never heard of until the moment that old man said his name!"

"Doesn't matter." Snorri raised his head to fix me with that steady blue gaze of his. "What matters is that Arran Vale had a history, roots, something to live for, something to make a stand over."

"All I remember is that you and Tuttugu were about to throw your lives away beside some old farmer you'd met only moments before, and all to defend his hut and its worthless contents from Vikings who probably wouldn't have even bothered taking it anyway." The ground is trembling now, the dust starting to dance. My sister is close and coming fast.

"A life lived well is one you're not prepared to compromise just in order to draw it out for another day."

"Well . . ." Reading out the list of things I would do to live another day would consume all of the extra day in question.

"The point is that there are things I'm prepared to die for. Times when it is right to make a stand, whatever the odds. And if Tuttugu and I would do what we did for Hennan's grandfather—an old man we didn't, as you rightly say, know. Then what do you think I'm prepared to do for my children? For my wife? Whether I can win is not a factor."

We have had this conversation before. I didn't expect him to have changed, but sometimes you owe it to a friend to try.

"Good luck!" I slap a hand to Snorri's shoulder and I'm off. The dark behind him looks thicker as if a storm is rolling down on us. She's there at the heart of it, the one whose mouth knows my name—my nameless sister and the lichkin who wears her soul.

I'm five yards away when he says, "Show me the key."

I stretch out my hands, one toward Snorri, the other toward the door into the judges' hall. "I've got to go!" The hell-night is boiling blackness behind him, the howl coming again so loud it drowns out my objections. Every hair I own tries to stand on end.

Even so, I pull the key from my shirt on the thong about my neck and run back to him. Snorri takes the knife from his belt and puts the blade to his palm.

"Jesus, no!" I wave my hand in what I hope is a negative pattern. "What is it with you northmen and cutting yourselves? I remember what happened last time you tried this Viking shit on me. How about we just shake hands?"

Snorri grins. "The key will be our link. You back in the world. Me here. Blood will bind us." He cuts his palm and I wince to see it done, the blood welling up where the point of the knife passed.

"How do you know any of this?" I'm still hoping there's a way out of this without having to slice myself open. A dark mist is rising now, pushing back the light. The souls scatter. They know a bad thing is coming. Suddenly I find myself ready to cut my damn hand off if it means I can leave. Even so, I stay, Snorri's friendship holding me just the same way it very nearly pulled me through the door into Hell. "Blood will bind us? You're just making it up as you go, aren't you?"

Snorri meets my gaze, a slight shrug in his shoulders. "If I learned anything from Kara it's that in magic it is will that counts. The words, the spells, scrolls, ingredients . . . it's for show, or perhaps better to say they're like a warrior's weapons, but it's the strength of the warrior's arm that is what truly matters. He can kill you with his hands, weapon or no weapon." He reaches out and folds his bloody hand about the key. "This will be our link. When you open the door you'll find me."

The dark has grown thick about us, and cold. It's as if Snorri doesn't see it, though: there's no fear in him. Me, I have enough for both of us. A howling rises with the midnight, the sort a thousand wolves might make . . . if you set fire to them. Close now. Close and closing fast.

"How will I even find the door? How will I know you're ready to return? Christ, look, I've got to go—"

"You need to will it to be so." Snorri takes his hand back. There's no blood on the key though it drips scarlet from his clenched fist. "It will work—or it won't. Kara was to open the way for my return. Kara, or Skilfar, if she had taken the key back to her grandmother as she promised her. Now all I have is you, Jal. So keep the key safe and listen for my call."

I tuck the key away. "I'll listen." It's not much of a lie. I don't even know what "listen" means. On my chest the key grows warmer as if falsehoods please it. I try to think of some last words for Snorri. "Farewell" sounds pompous. "Stay safe" is obviously not going to happen.

"Give them hell."

The howl sounds so loud and close it's like a punch. I'm running, running toward the light, that marvellous, living light, my sights set on the doorway.

"Be careful!" Snorri shouts after me. "They will test you."

I don't like the sound of that, but test or no test, I'm going home.

I close on the doorway racing past the soul of a young woman just coming out. I can see her terror in the faint lines of her. She runs, cowering, as if some great eagle might swoop upon her at any moment. I do pretty much the same thing, only in the opposite direction.

The darkness washes after me like a wave racing up the beach, outpacing me to either side, freezing my heels. I fly through the doorway, contriving to trip on the doorstep, and sprawl headlong into the corridor beyond. Looking back in terror I see the blackness slam into the building, the doorway becomes a rectangle of night and a tremor runs through the floor, but not a wisp of the dark enters the passage where I lie and no hint of the horror outside can be seen. If she's howling out there—I can't hear her.

I stand up, brushing the dust off me, still eyeing the darkness outside nervously. Steeling myself I risk a glance away, into the judges' hall. It's not what I expect. No courtrooms, no souls queuing for the verdict on their lives, no trio of Zeus's bastards sitting in judgment. There's nothing but a long corridor, too long to fit within the building, though the structure is huge. At the far end something burning and bright—a blue, a green, a promise. All I need do is walk forward and I'll be home. I sense it in my bones. I don't even need the Liar's key. This is a true path, one the just may walk.

I take a step forward and doors appear along both walls. A plain wooden door every ten yards, scores of them. I take another step and each one swings open, the closest ones first, then the next an instant later, and so on, creating a wave rippling off toward the distant blue-green promise.

It's easy to pass by the rooms behind the first doors. The first to the left is empty save for a discarded purse in the middle of the floor, to the right also empty but for a scattering of silver coins. The next pair are empty save for a discarded sword and a small closed casket.

"Are you trying to tempt me?" The laugh comes easy and I pick up the pace, not even looking in the rooms as I pass.

A hundred doors on and I stop as if I'd hit a wooden post. The most delicious smell ever in the history of aromas has fastened itself to my nose and turns my head without permission. A table has been set in the room to my left. A simple table without cloth or silver, and on it rests a wooden plate where half a roasted chicken sits and steams. Instantly my mouth is full of drool, my stomach a tight and demanding knot. Every part of me screams with desire for that hot roasted meat. I've lived with famine in Hell for so long that my body literally howls in answer to the call of a good meal.

Sobbing, I turn away, only to see in the room opposite a simple goblet of clear glass, brimming with water. I know in the moment I lay eyes upon it that this will be the purest of spring waters, gurgling free from beneath ancient rocks, and that gulping it down, letting it flow into my parched and death-touched throat, would take the thirst from me in a moment. To anyone who has not known the desiccation of death's drylands the idea that a man might sacrifice himself for just a glass of water may seem insane. But it must be experienced to be understood. I have been dry in the desert of the Sahar. It is a small thing compared to the thirst that a day in Hell will put in a man.

Even so, I tear myself away and stumble on, my body aching with the life awakened in it so suddenly by the proximity of the world after so very long walking the deadlands.

More scents assault me, each more delicious than the one before. Apples, caramel, fresh baked bread . . . beer. Young beer, fragrant with hops, the sound of it pouring from the spigot . . . that nearly turns me. I catch glimpses of the rooms: one a meadow in sunlight, another a horse ready to ride, a magnificent beast, muscles bunched under dark hide, ready to gallop all day. There are rooms where treasure lies in drifts, gold enough to buy kingdoms whole. I focus my vision on that distant rectangle of green grass and blue sky, coming closer with each stride. My will is iron. I understand the test and will not be turned.

I'm twenty yards from the end door. I can see the blue sky, the green of a garden, a wall behind it. It looks like the royal herb garden behind the messenger stables. I break into a run.

"Come back to bed, Jal."

One sideways glance and I stumble to a halt, turn, take three steps back. I recognize the room, a bedchamber. The light slants through shuttered windows dividing the bed into parallel lines of light and shadow. Each bright line rises over her, describing her contours, tawny skin smooth across warm flesh. She lies naked, just as I left her, silken sheets rising halfway up her back and following her curves as faithfully as the light does.

"Lisa?"

She doesn't speak, just makes that languid stretch that's only possible in the moments between waking and sleeping.

This is a doorway into the past. The air itself shimmers with doorways, fractures in the world, each leading to new possibilities, new versions of my life. If I had stayed with her that morning, if I had turned at the door when she called to me, still half-tangled in her dreams, if I had slid in beside her once more . . . none of this would have happened. I would have missed Grandmother's address. I would never have seen Snorri. He would have made his own way home. I would have lived on as I always had. Perhaps I would have asked Lisa to marry me and spent her dowry buying off Maeres Allus, and the idle, easy, soft days of my life would have carried on.

That one thought overwhelms me. Go back. Turn it back. Do it over. That one thought and the glorious aliveness of her after so very long in the deadlands. Lisa DeVeer, long, lean, lovely, warm, soft, vital. Go on along the corridor and return to the now, to the palace of Vermillion where she is married and the world stands against me . . . or turn here at the last moment and step back into that first morning where it all went wrong and could so easily have been avoided.

One step is all it takes. The rest I don't even remember. I lay a hand on her hip and sit at her side. I start to kick off my boots. Lisa reaches up to draw me down to her, turning slowly, dark hair cascading over her shoulder.

She hasn't any face, just a funnel of flesh from which a score of cobra fangs jut, venom dripping from their sharpness. I fall off the bed with a shout of horror, my shirt ripping, most of it still hanging in her clawed fist. I pull the key and would run for the door but there is no door. I scrabble backwards across the bedroom floor as the thing that isn't Lisa rises from the bed. Trapped in a corner, I reach up to throw the shutter wide but all it reveals is the dead sky of Hell—damnation waits for me out there. In the deadlight the shimmers where the worlds brush against one another show more clearly and Not-Lisa looks more like something made rather than grown, unclean flesh on old bones. She moves from the bed, awkward, limbs jerking, and steps my way.

In desperation I shove the key toward the closest place where the light fractures. It's not a door but it might almost be. It's a half-chance and I take it. I feel Loki's key engage with something, locking its teeth into the stuff of being . . . and I turn it.

A moment later I'm tumbling out into the oven of the Sahar, scaldingly hot sand, blind white heat, a place that eats hope and buries the bones . . . and it feels *great*.

"Marshal?" Someone shook my arm, hard. "Marshal!"

It's Bonarti Poe, white-faced and trembling. The key released my gaze and I found myself sitting in the corridor exactly where I was when Hertet first pressed it into my hands.

"How long have I—"

"I think everyone's dead!" Poe looked back along the passage. A hideous scream rang out to contradict him—the kind of howl heard in torture chambers.

"We should leave." I got to my feet, using the wall for support. It was dark, just one lamp guttering in a niche between us and the door to the throne room, its oil nearly spent.

"T-they said you know about . . . this thing that's attacking us?" Bonarti had yet to relinquish my arm.

"I've seen one in Hell."

"Oh Christ." His grip started to hurt so I shook him off. "But you know how to beat it, right?"

The door at the end of the corridor burst into pieces, saving me from a reply. The lichkin stood there like a wound on my eye, there but invisible, glimpsed the next moment, not as the raw white nerve but shrouded in ghosts, wearing the grey souls of men as a skin.

The air between us rippled, fault-lines and fractures seen in an instant then gone, some brilliant, some dark. This was the doom Luntar had warned us of. Not the lichkin dealing out deaths by the score, or thousand, but the breaking of creation. I'd seen the same fractures where the judges' hall stood on the boundary between worlds, and here the Dead King's creature caused two worlds to collide, leading the denizens of Hell back into their bodies and into the lands of the living. It's in the nature of any crack to spread and, with the slow turn of the Wheel driving them, the fractures would spread ever faster and further. The Wheel of Osheim might lie untold miles away but its influence reached into the heart of every place, driven by the vast unslumbering machinery of the Builders, still pulsing with their energy though they lay dead a thousand years.

The lichkin came on slowly as if daring us to run. I knew how fast the thing could be and made no move that would spark it into action. Instead I hung on to those last few moments of life remaining to me. Bonarti, lacking my understanding, ran for it. He got two steps before the lichkin hit him in the back. It flowed into him like a string of sinew sucked up by a hungry mouth. I caught a nerve-white flicker as the last of its thin body vanished beneath the skin to wrap his spine. The lichkin's shroud of ghosts peeled away as it found flesh, winding themselves smoke-like about the paralysed man.

Bonarti's scream was thankfully short, but his pain didn't end with it. A moment later a hundred razor cuts opened all across him, no more than skin deep. With the lichkin anchored in Bonarti's flesh I would have run, but he blocked my path away from the throne room and at the doorway corpses crowded, hungry-eyed, held back only by the lichkin's desire to toy with its food. I had nowhere to go, nowhere to hide.

Bonarti faced me, eyes wide, mouth twisted into a grin he didn't own. His skin began to peel away, a dozen broad strips flayed out slowly between parallel cuts. There comes a point where you get so scared that it really doesn't matter where you're running to as long as you *are* running. I knew that the half-doors and broken chances that lay behind the fractures all around me each led straight to Hell, but frankly Hell had already come visiting and terrible as every part of it was I would rather be running toward some part that didn't contain a lichkin. The creature reached for me with Bonarti's raw red hand, flayed skin dangling. With the same scream a man uses when steeling himself to some awful task, like cutting off a limb to escape a fire, I drove Loki's key into the nearest fracture. The closest fault-line shimmered through the wall beside me and had nearly faded to nothing before my hand reached it. The key found its socket and held there, anchoring the fracture. Bonarti's wet fingers found my neck and, still screaming, I turned the key.

It seemed in that moment that the world broke. Rather than falling through the hole I'd made I flew back as something big burst out of it, barging me aside. Something big, hard, and fast.

Snorri swung overhead, his axe shearing through Bonarti Poe's collarbone and deep into his chest. A heavy boot, shattering ribs, gave the leverage to wrench Hel's blade clear. The Norseman's next blow swept in from the side before Bonarti's corpse hit the floor, taking off his arm at the elbow and carving toward his spine.

Snorri followed the corpse, roaring, reddish dust smoking from his hair and clothing. Behind him the fractured window into Hell started to close, reality still able to heal itself. Just.

The lichkin forced Bonarti's body to crawl beneath the rain of axe blows. The ghosts rose to blind and tear at Snorri but he scarcely noticed, hewing deep into the meat of the man beneath him. White tendrils reached out, questing for other bodies, for dead flesh to inhabit, but the Northman struck them off with swift efficiency. Properly bound to a host as the lichkin are in the form of unborn, the thing could have drawn more effectively on the dead and the living to repair itself, but this unbound lichkin had become reckless, thinking to toy with its food, and in winding itself so tightly about Bonarti had become vulnerable.

The butchery continued unabated. Snorri knew his foe was buried deep inside the flesh before him. I glimpsed the whiteness of the lichkin where Snorri's axe shattered Bonarti's spine. A second later the creature began untangling itself from the ruin of the corpse. But, like me, Snorri seemed able to see it, his time in the deadlands lending something to his sight. His axe became a blur, hacking at the lichkin, somehow finding it solid in these moments where it tried to rid itself of flesh. Perhaps so long a time in Hell had given Snorri's axe an edge that could find even the lichkin, or being wetted in the blood of devils had enchanted the blade—either way . . . it bit.

In Trond they hold contests to ward off the boredom of winter. One such requires the Norse to take an axe to the trunk of a fir tree about as thick as a man, and the first of them to chop entirely through it is the victor. Snorri's assault on the lichkin held much of that contest in it, and before the thing escaped Bonarti's ruin it came dangerously close to being cut through. In the instant that the last nerve-white tendril of it withdrew from the bloody remains before us the lichkin folded the world around itself and fell away into the deadlands. With an animal howl Snorri threw himself after it. If not for my strategically placed leg he would have vanished back into Hell in pursuit of his prey. As it was he sprawled, face-first, on Hertet's sumptuous, though soiled, hall rug. The air rippled where the lichkin had punched its hole through the world, and lay still, the portal gone.

I glanced back at the dead men watching from the entrance to the throne room. Perhaps if I hadn't they might have continued to stand there watching vacantly for another five minutes. My gaze seemed to animate them, and as one they surged forward.

"Get up!" I leapt to Snorri's side and tried to raise him. Just touching him gave my hands back that death-dry feeling, making paper of my skin, sucking the vitality from my flesh. "Get up!" I'd have more luck lifting a horse.

Snorri got his arms beneath him and launched himself to his feet as the dead men reached us. They had lost their speed now that the lichkin had fled, but they still had numbers.

Numbers didn't seem to matter. Snorri went through them like a scythe. It reminded me of my glorious victory over the bucket-boys back at the opera house. Snorri waded through the dead like a prince of Red March wades through terrified street urchins. The axe is truly the weapon for such work. A sword is a tongue: it speaks and gives eloquent voice to violence, seeking out a foe's vitals and ending him. An axe only roars. The wounds it gives are ruinous and in Snorri's hands nearly every blow seemed to take a head or limb.

Two minutes later the Norseman stood amid the carnage of his work, perhaps a score of corpses now divided to the point at which necromancy could make nothing dangerous of them. I followed him into the throne room, casting nervous glances over my shoulder against the possibility of new foes advancing along the corridor. Many of the dead had swords, still scabbarded at their hips. I took one that looked to have been forged for service rather than show.

"Are . . . are you all right?" I looked about the hall. Snorri stood, head down, coated with other men's blood, breathing heavily. He held his axe across his hips, one hand just below the head, the other at the far end of the shaft. He didn't look all right. Neither did the hall, every surface soiled, the throne cast down, tapestries trampled, the whole place stinking of death and decay. "Snorri?" He seemed almost a stranger.

He raised his head, staring at me beneath the black veil of his hair, unreadable, capable of anything. "I . . ." His first word to me since we parted in Hell. It had been months for me—how many lifetimes would it have felt like in that place?

From the darkest corner of the hall a dead man rose from beneath a tapestry—some victory picked out in silver thread, now smeared with blood and foulness. He charged toward Snorri's back, trailing the embroidered cloth like a banner. Snorri lashed out to the side, almost without looking, his axe an extension of his arm. The man's head flew clear; his body stumbled, and collapsed.

"I am at peace," Snorri said, and walked over to clap me in a warrior's embrace.

TWENTY

"Lisa!" I broke away from Snorri, nearly tripping over one of the butchered corpses littering Hertet's great hall. "Lisa!"

"The girl you wanted to marry?" Snorri stepped back, taking in his surroundings for the first time.

"We have to go!" I started toward the main doors. "I have family in trouble."

Snorri shouldered his axe and followed, stepping over scattered pieces of armour and the occasional twitching corpse.

The great doors to Hertet's throne room crossed each other at drunken angles, each clinging to the frame by a single hinge. I kicked the left one and sent it swinging back. The antechamber was a well-dressed charnel house.

"Christ." Someone had put up a fight here—probably Grandmother's elite. Dismembered bodies littered a floor awash with blood, a dozen or more mire-ghouls in the mix, many of the dead bloated and still smeared with stinking river mud.

"What country are we in?" Snorri at my shoulder.

"This is the palace in Vermillion. My uncle had a go at playing king. It didn't work out very well."

The front doors of Milano House lay in fragments, the wood grey with dry rot, corrupted by the lichkin's touch. We went down the steps, Snorri holding up a shield he'd lifted from a fallen guard.

"Not your style?" I looked back, raising a brow.

"Ghoul darts are even less my style." He followed me out onto the steps.

Enough torches had kept burning when dropped to surround the house in a loose halo of faint illumination. The story here ran similar to that inside. Broken corpses, scattered gore, half a dozen dead men in sight, wandering aimlessly, at least until the first of them spotted us.

"Run!" I shouted and took to my heels.

I stopped about ten yards later, realizing that Snorri wasn't following me and that it was dark where I was going. I turned back toward him. "Run?"

Snorri gave me that grin that shows all those white teeth in the blackness of his beard. "I haven't been walking all this time in Hel—" he paused to behead the first dead man to reach him, a savage and perfectly timed swing, "—to run from these sorry remains." He didn't so much decapitate the next man as swing his axe through the fellow's head. Then two were on him together. I hadn't time to see how he dealt with those because a serving woman in a torn dress had singled me out. She came on at an awkward, urgent lumbering, her grey hair fanned out in disarray, purple bruises around her neck where dead hands had choked the life out of her. I stuck my sword through her mouth and out the back of her head. A grisly business. I was still wrestling my blade out when Snorri strode past me. Even with her head a ruin she still clutched at me blindly. I had to dodge back and leave her flailing on the ground.

"Come on then," he called over his shoulder. He held a pair of burned-low reed torches in one hand, at arm's length to light his way, the flames guttering over the last of the pitch.

I led the way, expecting some or other horror to leap at us from the night—the further we went without assault the worse the feeling of anticipation—but at last we stood before Roma Hall, unchallenged by anyone, living or dead.

"Who's inside?" Snorri asked. "Just Lisa?"

"I don't know for sure, Lisa, her sister Micha, my baby niece." As marshal of the city I should be gathering men and making for the walls. Lisa would be as dead as the rest of us if the main force outside gained the city. Whatever the logic, I had to know she was all right, that they all were. Or at least to see their end and know that nothing now could save them.

The front doors stood ajar, the hall behind them dark. As I led the way up the steps I saw blood, just a smear, where perhaps someone had fallen and hit their head.

I opened the door on the left using the point of my blade. The light of Snorri's dying torch hinted at the long hall beyond, Father's Indus statuettes and vases in their niches at measured intervals. Fat Ned's head lay a few yards in, staring up at the ceiling with an expression of mild surprise, perhaps at having died on guard duty and meeting a quick and violent end after such a slow battle against whatever was eating him inside. Proof that none of us really knows what to expect. I glanced about for his bony carcass but saw no sign of it.

At this point I remembered the small cone of orichalcum buried in the depths of my deepest pocket. I considered digging for it. Snorri loomed behind me raising his torch, and when I stepped aside, he walked on through. Not carrying any source of illumination proved such a good excuse for sending the Northman in ahead that I left the orichalcum firmly where it was.

"Lisa!" Snorri boomed. "Lisa!"

"Shhhh!" I motioned frantically down with my hand.

"What?"

"They'll know we're here!"

"That's the idea. LISA!"

I supposed it was the idea, but the notion of calling out the enemy ran opposite to a great many deeply ingrained instincts and half of me still wanted to slap my hand over Snorri's mouth.

Snorri led the way down the entrance hall. The place didn't smell like home, it held a sour odour, the stink of death, old rather than fresh. There should be men at the door but I'd seen Alphons back outside Milano House, conscripted to Hertet's guard, and Double could have been drafted too.

"Lisa!" Another booming announcement. Snorri glanced back at me. "It's big!"

"It's not like I haven't been telling you I'm a prince all this time." I waved him on. "Turn left past the next doors. And try not to kill any servants." If we met Ballessa while carrying a smoky torch it might be Snorri who was in danger. Dirtying up the cardinal's ceiling was not allowed. I remembered then that we'd made smoke of my father that morning and an unexpected sadness settled on me—something all my own rather than a lichkin's gift.

It's an odd thing to be sad about someone in death that you never really cared for in life and a thing that chooses its own moment to sneak up on you—usually a damn inconvenient one—but there it is . . . perhaps we hurt for the lost opportunities, for the conversation that would have released all the unspoken words, for the way it should have been.

"Where now?"

I paused. It *was* a big place. "Upstairs. We'll check Darin's old rooms."

As we climbed the staircase I caught the distant sound of banging, something pounding on a door? The place seemed silent apart from that hammering, though silent is the way of corpses and necromancy—right up to the moment they leap out at you from the dark.

"Left at the top."

Snorri's torch guttered and the shadows danced, the untouched darkness crawling with horror. "Trouble." He used a small word to understate a large disaster. Blood had congealed in sticky waterfalls down the top four or five steps. The landing was scattered with body parts, dark smears of blood reaching further up the walls than seemed reasonable.

"Palace guardsmen." A few chunks bore large enough pieces of uniform to identify them. The men must have been killed then reanimated and finally hacked apart.

At the margins of the torch's illumination a dark figure crouched on an armoured one. Snorri pressed the torch into my hand. Moving slowly, he let his axe slide until he gripped it just below the head and did the absolute last thing I would have recommended. He set it down.

"What?" I could see the black figure pause in whatever had occupied it and look our way, a tension in it as if poised either to attack or run.

Snorri ignored me, instead gripping the rim of his round shield and easing his other arm from the straps. Two things happened at once. The figure in the shadows sprang away and Snorri hurled his shield like a discus, the iron rim catching the creature in the back of the head and felling it.

We rushed forward, Snorri grabbing his axe. A mire-ghoul lay sprawled beside a gory torso in very shiny armour. I couldn't say who it was—the face had been eaten away. Snorri turned the ghoul over with his foot. A dark and bristly moustache was stuck in the thing's teeth, along with several unpleasant gobbets of flesh.

"Sir Wodger," I said, understanding at last who had inhabited the gleaming armour. "My cousin sent him and these men to recover the DeVeer sisters."

The ghoul opened an eye. Snorri sank his axe into its chest.

The hammering sounded louder, close at hand. Snorri put his boot on the ghoul's neck, wrenched his weapon free with a wet sound.

"Lisa?" I pushed past, sword before me, torch to the side. A priest stood before the door to Darin's suite, fists raw from banging against the wood. He turned to face me. Bishop James, I thought . . . the choked purple of his face made it hard to tell. Stout, ageing, and stern, Bishop James had spent many futile hours trying to teach me the error of my ways as a child, with either the rod or the bible, both wielded as a weapon. I never liked him but I wouldn't have wished this end on him.

Bishop James ran at me with the recklessness of dead men. I knew enough not to let him impale himself and trap my blade, and swung instead, taking off one of his reaching hands somewhere between wrist and elbow. I ducked at the last, shoulder down, and let him tumble over me. A wet crunch from behind indicated an ungentle meeting with Snorri's axe.

"Lisa?" I rapped on the door. "Micha?"

"Barras? Is that you?" A woman, voice muffled.

"Darin? Thank God!" A second woman.

"It's Jal," I said.

A moment of silence. "How many men have you got with you?"

"Enough." I felt mildly insulted. "Open the door. We need to leave, quickly."

"We've barricaded it. It will take a while to move all this stuff." Lisa's voice, rather faint.

"Leave it shut." Snorri came up to stand beside me. "We need to clear the place first."

"Leave the barricade!" I called out more loudly, trying to make the idea sound like my own. "We're going to make sure it's safe first."

"It's Double, Jal!" Micha called from behind the door. I heard a cry of complaint from little Nia.

"What?" I shouted back. Either I'd misheard or she wasn't making sense.

"Double!"

I turned to look up at Snorri and shrugged. "Double?"

"She means me." The voice came from behind us on the landing.

Turning, I saw a thing built of body parts. Not a man like the augmented giant who had chased me across the rooftops, but something closer to the monstrosities that had bound together to form the scaffold by which the dead had overtopped the city wall. To my eye it was a gory spider made from the severed limbs of the men Sir Roger had led to their deaths. Arms and legs fused one to the next to make crude and gangly spider-limbs, with the dripping upper half of a torso at the apex where six or seven of these limbs converged.

"Hasty work and crude, I apologize." I focused on the man behind it, holding a lantern aloft.

"Double?" He wore the household uniform though the arms of it were thick with gore past the elbows.

"Not really my name of course, but you've been using it for the past year so why not let's keep it that way for the last night of your life."

"But . . . you're . . ." When I thought about it Double seemed an unlikely name. I'd met him for the first time escorting Snorri to the Marsail keep the day Grandmother set him to be freed after telling his story in the throne room.

"I would stay to chat but I've things to do in the church. I just came in to see what the noise was." Double lifted his lantern a little higher. "And you brought the Northman back, I see. Where *has* he been? I see death all over him."

"Yours," Snorri said and moved toward the flesh-spider, a grimace on his face as if the distasteful shape of it worried him more than the actual combat.

Double reached his hand toward Snorri, extending his fingers around the rounded black object he was holding. Snorri stopped, distaste turning to surprise.

"What?" Snorri tried to move but it seemed as if his body had frozen into one solid piece. Even forcing the question past his lips took effort.

"This really is quite remarkable." Double showed a smile wholly at odds with my memories of his bland and friendly face. "You're clearly alive and yet death has seeped into you almost bone deep. We really will have to have a discussion before I kill you."

And that left just me guarding Lisa's door against a treacherous necromancer and his pet horror.

"It was you who searched my room when I came back from the North!" The main thing about not fighting someone is to not let the fight start. In some circles this is known as stalling.

"There's no point trying to stall me, Prince Jalan." Double focused on his creation and it scuttled forward a yard or so. "But yes. Me. If you'd had the decency to leave Loki's key with your other possessions then all this unpleasantness might have been delayed." He returned his attention to the flesh-spider and it jittered forward another yard, the head in the middle of it all watching me with the same avid attention the hawk reserves for the mouse.

"What is that thing?" I pointed at the object in the hand Double had extended toward Snorri.

"Oh please." Double advanced his creature a few more steps.

"No, really, it looks familiar." At first I'd thought his hand wrapped about some kind of necromantic blackness—but it was something solid and real and I'd seen it somewhere before.

"This?" Double inverted his hand so the object rested on his palm. "A young woman threw it at me while I was organizing things in the church."

"A holy stone!" Father's holy stone, to be precise.

"Yes. One of the DeVeer sisters threw it. I'll return it to her soon." Again that stranger's smile. "I suppose she thought one of the cardinal's symbols might hold some power over me? What is it they say? Let she that is without sin cast the first stone? But the DeVeer sisters are hardly innocents now, are they? And your father never was very much of a cardinal . . ."

"Why don't you give it to me instead?" I needed Father's seal to defend me against my sister if she broke through—when she broke through. Darin's death had nearly given her the doorway she needed and with so much dying in the city it could only be getting easier for her. I needed a cardinal's seal, Marco had said, but the other symbols of his office were almost as holy—they might be enough.

"This?" Double set his lantern on one of the support posts for the railings that ran alongside the landing. He passed the holy stone from hand to hand, like the lichkin enjoying his moment of power. I guess it had grated on him serving my father's house in such a lowly capacity while all the time hiding such talents. "You think I don't know why you want it?" He held it by the dark metal handle that followed the curve of the stone's black iron body. "Sister," he said. "Sister . . ." Drawing out the word into a taunt. "Your father's seal would serve you better against her, but Archbishop Larrin made off with that. The one that got away. If I'd caught him I would have had the whole set from choirboy to archbishop."

In the corner of my eye Snorri struggled against the bonds holding him. He'd been too long in Hell, steeped in the dryness of the deadlands, and necromancy would have a hold on him until the living world fully accepted him back. Double's monstrosity began to advance again.

"Wait!" I shouted. You'd be surprised how often that works.

The flesh-spider paused and Double raised his eyebrows, inviting me to elaborate.

"If you could put down my father's holy stone. I don't want to damage it when I kill you." I lifted my sword. Bravado is as good a delaying tactic as begging. I just needed to buy a few minutes for Snorri to shake off the necromancer's spell.

"I might take my time with you, Prince Jalan." Double examined the holy stone. "You've no idea how dull it is waiting on your family. How difficult it is to nod and bow before such a collection of pompous morons puffed up on their own misplaced sense of self-importance . . ." He banged the stone against the banister, hard, examined it with a scowl, then waved his creation on to finish me.

"On second thoughts, keep the stone. I don't think you *can* damage it." Although I wanted the thing myself I would rather spend the next minute watching him smashing it against the banisters than spend it with me going man to men against his ugly monster.

Double rose to the bait. I didn't expect him to. Still, I played along, shouting out an agonized "no!" as he beat the thing against the wall. Bullies are to be avoided but often their cruel streak does allow them to be manipulated. "No!" I cried, as if he were swinging my child against the doorposts. When he finally did manage to pull some minor piece free, a metal pin of some kind, nobody was more surprised than me to see the whole side clasp come away in his hand. I'd always thought of the holy stone as an iron pineapple, impervious to any harm.

"There!" He grinned. "I doubt that's holy any more. It's not even whole. What do you think of that, Prince Jalan?"

I don't recall making any reply. In fact the next thing I recall is finding myself horizontal, on a bed, in a room with an oak panelled ceiling.

"What?" I've never been very creative with opening lines when recovering consciousness.

Lisa DeVeer's face swam into focus above me. I jerked into a sitting position, narrowly missing breaking her nose with my forehead. Micha stood at the foot of the bed, clutching Nia to her breast. Snorri occupied the doorway, his back to us.

"Double!" I patted my hip, hoping to find the hilt of my sword. "Where's Double?"

Lisa pointed to the left and slightly up, Micha to the right and down. Both of them seemed to be speaking at once but I couldn't make out the words through the ringing in my ears. I lurched off the bed, found my sword on the dresser close by, and pushed Snorri aside.

An acrid smoke hung over the landing outside. Ten yards of the banister had vanished, splintered stumps of the railings punctuating the gap. The flesh-spider appeared to have been returned to a scattered collection of ill-matched limbs, and I could see that the sisters had technically both been correct about the location of Double. Some pieces of him were sticking to the wall on both sides of the doorway.

Snorri said something but the only word I caught was "exploded."

"Holy hell!" I turned back into the room. "Let's get out of here!"

"Where to?" I could see that Snorri was shouting though I had to struggle to make out his words.

"The Inner Palace. That's the safest place. Garyus might be there too." I could hardly hear my own voice through the ringing in my ears. I took one of the lanterns from the mantelpiece and ushered Lisa and Micha out of their sanctuary. "Quickly. Quietly." And I led the way out of a place I couldn't ever imagine would feel like home again. We walked through the scattered remains, a red lesson in how the church rewards an abundance of curiosity in its clerics. Clearly dismantling your holy stone against strict orders results in it reducing you to several hundred small and bloody lumps.

TWENTY-ONE

"How many men have you?" Garyus sat in Grandmother's throne, propped by cushions, flanked by two of the elite guard in their fire-bronze mail. He had another ten such men arrayed around the hall, some bloodied from their night's work.

"Sixty or so." I stood before the dais with Snorri at my shoulder. "There are dozens more scattered about the palace. I've sent officers to gather them by the gates."

Garyus regarded me with one dark eye. The other had been closed by Hertet's fist. Uncle Hertet had come to Garyus's tower room after nightfall. A week before I had asked my great-uncle why he didn't move his quarters into the Inner Palace now he was steward but he had shaken his head and told me that he thought more clearly in a high place. "Also, people only bother you if it's important. A hundred steps put a different perspective on what matters and what is just time-wasting."

"Hertet?" I asked. "Has he been found?" He would be among the dead. The slaughter at Milano House had been thorough.

"Not yet." Garyus touched the swelling around his eye. "There were fires at the house, and part of the rear wall collapsed. It may be that even counting the dead proves beyond us. But I've had no word that he escaped." He shook his head, the sorrow seemingly genuine. "Foolish boy." Perhaps he remembered the child and not the man that replaced him.

"I should take what men we have and get back to the Appan Gate." The sentence didn't sound like something I would say, but then again, if the dead broke through in numbers none of us would see the next sunset.

"I've a more important task for you two," Garyus said.

I raised a brow at that and wondered if Hertet's fist had scrambled his uncle's wits. "What could be more important? Christ! They were over the wall hours ago. For all I know they've taken the gate by now. We need—"

Garyus raised a hand. "I have more recent reports. Marshal Serah is—"

"Marshal Serah? How many marshals is this city to have in one night? And Serah's a child for godsake!" Though if I were honest she had been doing an efficient job of organizing the defence when I left.

Garyus waited, pursing his lips to see if I had any more complaints. I held my tongue. "The breakthrough is reported to have been contained. The dead remaining outside the walls grew less . . . vital . . . and proved unable to follow the others over the ramp and scaffold. Reinforcements arrived: a mercenary force in my employ together with armed citizenry, including a number who formerly made their living in the Blood Holes and other illegal fighting dens . . ." Here his eye wandered in Snorri's direction, letting me know the story of the Northman and the bear had reached his ears. "And these reinforcements ensured the destruction of the dead that made it into the city."

"They'll strike somewhere else! The walls by Tannery Square are hardly standing as it is. I—"

"The firing of the outer city cremated a large number of the corpses raised against us and has severely curtailed the ability of those remaining to move around the walls. My reports indicate that the dead host lacks leadership or direction."

"But there were necromancers . . . I saw Edris Dean myself! They must be planning something . . . The sewers!"

"You saw to that weakness yourself, Jalan, and there are no indications of attack. It seems that the Dead King has lost interest in this assault."

"But . . . why? Because we sent his lichkin back to Hell?" It didn't make sense. He almost had us. Why give up?

"A merchant would ask what profit our opponent sought to make." Garyus eased himself back, wincing. "Why did he spend his strength here, against this city?"

"Because the Red Queen left us. What better time to attack Vermillion?"

"You're thinking about what we value, Jalan, not what the Dead King values. What does he care for Vermillion? Or all of Red March? There are many cities, many places where the living can be converted into the dead far more easily than in the heart of Red March, wherever the Red Queen might be."

"All this for the key? All this?" It didn't seem possible, though as I said it Loki's key turned to ice against my chest.

"What other thing would profit him more?"

"But." I clapped my hand over the key. "He doesn't have it. Why give up now?"

"I don't know, Jalan. But I do know his power is not limitless and the prospect for a victory of the sort he would need in order to claim the key became slim when the lichkin fled and our defences proved more formidable than perhaps he anticipated."

"Or he found some other treasure," Snorri rumbled at my shoulder.

"Indeed." Garyus showed no irritation at a barbarian interrupting. "I have considered the possibility. But what other compensation might have satisfied?"

A horrible thought unrolled itself and try as I might to pack it back into a small neat dot of possibility it wouldn't go. "Why did they come here in the first place?"

"Who?" Garyus shifted his gaze from Snorri to me.

"The unborn." So many miles had passed beneath my feet and still I found myself back at the start of it all. Me and Snorri together in the Red Queen's throne room again, talking about the dead once more. And on the evening of that same day I had bumped shoulders with the Unborn Prince, at the opera, a place where no good thing ever happened. "Why did the unborn come here in the first place?"

"They came to bring another unborn into the world. A powerful one." Garyus watched me with peculiar intensity. "It must have been powerful to risk the Dead King's two greatest servants within Vermillion's walls with the Red Queen in the city."

"My sister."

"You don't have a sister, Jalan . . ."

"Edris Dean killed her in Mother's womb the night he came to the palace. I saw Mother test her belly with your orichalcum just before the attack. The light . . . it was as if the sun had come to Earth . . ." Snorri's hand gripped my shoulder in a moment's sympathy, then fell away. "My sister chased me out of Hell. If she had caught me I would have been her gate into the world. I think she tried to come through Father when he died. And again, when Darin fell at the walls. Something tried to come through him."

"But it didn't succeed?" Garyus frowned. "So why did the Dead King withdraw his strength . . ."

"Martus!" A cold certainty tightened in my chest. "Send for word of my brother!"

Garyus lowered his head. With effort he lifted a hand and motioned, two fingers extended. A bloodied soldier stepped out from beside one of the royal guards, the smaller man hidden by the larger until now. He stopped five yards from the throne. The tattered uniform announced him an officer of the Seventh. Numerous thin cuts on his hands and face suggested a recent encounter with a rag-a-maul.

"Captain Davio was to report once our business had concluded," Garyus said. "Speak what you know, Captain." Garyus motioned for the man to step closer.

"General Martus . . ." The captain choked, and grabbed his jaw as if to wring the emotion from his voice. "Prince Martus, your highness . . . he . . ." Davio pulled his hand away, leaving both cheeks blood-stained. "He led the charge. There wasn't any fear in him. Ran straight into that unholy windstorm. I saw him cut two ghosts in half as the wind tore at him. We were battling the possessed, but General Martus just made straight for the centre of it. I lost sight of him . . . and then it was over. The wind died. Rags and glass and stones falling out of the sky . . . and the possessed running wild, no organization to them any more."

"And my brother?" I knew the answer.

"We found him in the middle of it, sir, your highness. Cut and torn. I looked for a pulse but I could see he was gone, sir. I called for men to carry him to the palace, and I saw his sword close by. It happened while I was picking the blade off the ground." He fell silent, staring at some memory, and I thought Garyus would have to ask, but just as we reached the point at which one of us must speak, the captain jerked his head toward Garyus and continued. "His eyes opened. General Martus's eyes opened and I thought he would rise like the others we'd lost, crazed and dead and needing to be cut down. The lads all raised their swords and axes . . . we'd set aside our spears and found whatever we could that would cut. Them without swords had woodsmen's axes, butcher knives, whatever we could find . . . Nobody wanted to be the first to strike him. Not with him being a prince, and our general.

"But he didn't leap up. His body . . . moved . . . but it was like something was eating him from the inside. His bones . . . we heard them snap and it looked like he was full of serpents, writhing. All his flesh sunk in . . . only his eyes didn't change." Davio choked back a sob. "They kept watching us. And then . . . and then . . ."

"Just tell us the facts, Captain," Garyus said, not unkindly. "They'll leave fewer scars the quicker you speak them."

"Yes, Steward, sir." He drew a breath. "And then the thing escaped him. A red bloody mess it was, like a skinned dog, only with his eyes, with General Martus's eyes. It ripped out of him like he was a sack they'd put it in to drown, and it ran, quick as quick. Batran Deens tried to stop it. Fast hands, that man. He threw himself at it as it passed. Got both arms round it. But the thing slipped through and left him screaming. Everywhere he'd touched it the flesh was melted off him, gone . . . I saw bones in his arms." The captain dropped his head, staring at the floor.

"There's the Dead King's compensation," I said. My sister was in the world at long last. I felt nothing—only hollow.

We stood in silence for a moment, contemplating the depth of the shit we stood in. I'd burned my father, burned half the city I lived in, lost two brothers, and gained a homicidal unborn sister all in the same day. I doubted it was possible to fit more misfortune between two sunrises.

Garyus spoke first. "You need to take the key north."

"That's madness. The Dead King will catch us and take it!" I didn't feel safe behind Vermillion's walls any more but I felt a damn sight safer than I would outside them.

"The Dead King didn't catch you all the time you spent travelling from Trond to Umbertide. You were months on that journey." Garyus looked to Snorri as if seeking confirmation. "It's when the key is still that he finds it. While it is here the whole city is at risk."

"Where would we take it? You want us to just keep running until we fall off the edge of the world?"

"The dead outside our walls are not the greatest threat we face, Jalan." Garyus studied his palm. The Red Queen had the same mannerism when thinking.

"There is a greater threat?" I felt rather than saw Snorri turn to watch me. His question seemed to burn unspoken on the back of my neck.

I raised my hands. "I will concede that the imminent end of the world is a bigger problem. And . . ." I swivelled sharply to stare up at Snorri. "I don't want to hear a damn thing about Ragnarok. It's not like that at all. It's that stupid wheel of yours, it's going to crack the world open. Or rather it's allowing us to do so. Or rather it's allowing people like the Lady Blue and Kelem and the Dead King to do so. So yes, we're all going to die. And we may not even get a chance to destroy the world because the machines the Builders left behind are probably going to ignite a whole bunch more suns and burn us off the face of the Earth to stop that happening . . . Either way, it's not good."

Snorri stared back at me with an intensity he usually reserved for men he was about to swing his axe at. "We will go to Osheim and stop the Wheel's turning."

"That's just Viking talk." I turned back to Garyus. "What should we do really?"

"You need to take the key to the Wheel of Osheim," Garyus said.

"Take—" I had doubted it was possible to fit more misfortune between two sunrises. I had been wrong. "What? Why?" I'd been intending to just say no but when I opened my mouth questions came out instead.

"The key has to be taken to the centre. Nobody has ever escaped from that place. It's one of the few locations that should be secure. If the Dead King, his servants, or anyone else goes hunting it, they won't return."

I cleared my throat. "I think you're missing an important point here. Nobody has ever escaped from that place."

"That *is* the point, Jalan. I didn't miss it."

"I—" I had dug myself into Hell by not having the bravery to admit my cowardice. I resolved not to get into a similar situation again. "Look.

I'm just going to say it. I'm not in favour of any plan that doesn't see me coming back again, and that's that. I'm sure there are far more capable volunteers ready to do . . . this thing."

"I will do it," Snorri said. We both ignored him.

Garyus kept his gaze on me. "The rest of the point is that you're not just going there to put the key in a safe place—you're going there to use it. The Wheel is the source of our problems and the key is the one thing that might stop it. You're going there to turn the Wheel back. If you fail then the key will be in a place that is dangerous to reach and impossible to escape from, but if you succeed then the world won't split open, you'll be able to return, and we will all live whatever lives were laid out for us."

I breathed a sigh of relief. The old man was mad. Someone would need to replace him as steward and then we could all sit tight until the Red Queen came back to save us. If she was still alive.

"Yes." Snorri didn't sound like he needed any convincing. "We should leave today." We both ignored him.

"Great-uncle." I tried for a sympathetic voice. "The Wheel of Osheim . . . it's not an actual wheel, you know? It's a tunnel deep underground that runs in a circle miles wide. It can't be 'turned.'"

"It's a machine. That's what Kara told me," Snorri said. "It's a machine that changed the world a thousand years ago and is still changing it. It was started—so it can be stopped."

"Interesting," I said, by which I meant "shut the fuck up." Why the hell Snorri was so keen to rush off to Osheim I had no idea. I stroked my chin as if contemplating his words and tried not to sound too tetchy. "Tunnel, machine, whatever, it's huge and we can't turn it back."

"You could turn it off though," Garyus said. "If you had the right key."

TWENTY-TWO

And so I found myself down at the river docks about to flee Vermillion by boat with a Viking once again. Same Viking, different boat.

I had argued long and hard that I should at least take a crack squad of troops, by which I meant a small army . . . or, if it were up to me, a large one. Garyus pointed out that any infantry would slow me down and were needed at the walls. The horde of dead men wandering the embers of the outer city still posed a substantial threat and there was no certain knowing that the Dead King would not return his attention to them or send another lichkin or unborn to focus their efforts.

"A fast horse will serve you better than two hundred men, and the queen took what little cavalry remains to us to Slov with her. Any riders we have left in Vermillion are needed as swift reserves to react to possible incursions."

Garyus had directed that we should begin our journey by following the line of Grandmother's advance into Slov. The trail of destruction should allow for relatively unhindered passage. He had had no word of his sister and reports of her death appeared to be wishful thinking on Uncle Hertet's part. With any luck Grandmother would already have levelled the Lady Blue's stronghold and killed the witch with her bare hands.

This of course led me to suggest that I then deliver the key into the Red Queen's hands and let her see to its future, whether that lay in the Wheel of Osheim or around her neck. If it were to be the Wheel she would surely do a better job of it than me.

Garyus had contradicted me again. "You have qualities she lacks, Jalan. Necessary ones. You will run away. You will lie and cheat. My sister is more likely to fight and die. The only sure way this key is getting to Osheim is in the hands of someone as flexible and resourceful as you."

Garyus's talk of his sister had returned my thoughts to my own. In Hell Marco had revealed that the holiest of items might separate an unborn into the child's soul and the lichkin that rode it. But Father's seal was gone, his holy stone too, and a search of the Inner Palace had turned up nothing more holy than a gold cross blessed by the cardinal. I took it anyway. It was made of gold! But truth be told I suspected that being blessed by my father would probably have rendered it less holy rather than more.

All of which left me standing on a cold and misty riverbank thinking that if I really were flexible and resourceful I would have found a way out of this. It also left me clutching the side of my face.

"I think she loosened one of my teeth." I probed with my tongue.

"You look fine to me," Snorri said, his gaze on the water.

I'd had a guard bring Micha to me in one of the palace's waiting rooms. She had come with Nia bawling in her arms, wearing the worn-through look of a new parent overlayered with the long horror of the night.

"Jalan?" She had been surprised to see me.

"Sit down, Micha." I nodded to the couch opposite, an overstuffed confection from some Florentine master.

"What is it? It's Darin! Tell me!" She stood, rooted to her mark, even Nia's howls fading away to underscore the moment.

The words dried up in my mouth and I desperately wanted to be able to play deaf again. "He was very brave," I said. I had plenty more I planned to say. I knew how I was going to declaim it, words regarding my brother's heroism, words of comfort, words of encouragement for the future. But when it came to saying them to her—all I had were those four.

She had crumpled then, folded and gone to the floor, Nia still safe and silent in her arms. I had expected rage, questions, denials, but her grief just reached up and took her voice.

I had Alphons, from my father's guard, lead her away to the ballroom where a number of soldiers watched over a growing collection of survivors from around the palace. Next I sent for Lisa. She walked in white-faced, cold-eyed, proud, as if I were the invader and she my captive.

I tried to deflect her toward the couch but she kept on coming until we stood almost nose to nose. My instinct has always been to deliver bad news at a distance and be ready to run.

"Two teeth, I think."

"What?"

I took the fingers out of my mouth and repeated myself more clearly. "Two teeth, I think." I should have stuck with my instincts. Being honest and compassionate just gets you slapped so hard your teeth rattle. I didn't even say Barras was dead, just that I'd lost sight of him in the battle and it didn't look good . . .

"There's the boat." Snorri pointed to a darker patch of mist.

The blur resolved itself as it drew closer to the shore. A flat-bellied riverboat of the sort used to ferry livestock and goods across the Seleen or a short way up or downstream. Currently it held my stallion, Murder, and three other horses chosen for their endurance, the pair not immediately intended for riding laden with provisions and a tent.

Two boatmen leapt ashore and pulled the craft into the shallows so Snorri and I could board. The plan was to take us downstream beyond any danger from the city's besiegers and put us on some safe stretch of riverbank so we could follow my grandmother's trail to Slov. From there our path would take us through Zagre, north into the kingdom of Charland, and eventually back to Osheim.

Strangely, despite all the terror and the hopeless nature of our journey, the actual being on the move part felt pretty good. I'd missed Snorri. Not that I'd ever go as far as showing it. And now he was back and the world was slipping past us, I thought of Kara and the boy again. We'd spent so long travelling together as a four that being a two once more seemed to make their absence more palpable. As if it should be the völva's hand on the tiller, and Hennan messing about with the ropes.

I joined Snorri in the prow as the boatmen pushed us back out into the current with long poles. "I told you the Wheel draws everyone back in the end." That was how Nanna Willow had it. The Wheel would pull you in. Quick or slow, but in the end you'd come, thinking it was your idea, full of good reasons for it. And here we were, hundreds of miles away, full of good reasons, and aimed for the Wheel.

"Maybe so." Snorri nodded. "Some things can't be avoided."

He said it lightly but I felt a weight behind it. Perhaps a lesson learned in Hell.

"Osheim has its teeth in you, Snorri. Deep. The old man just had to mention it and you were packing your bags. If it's got this much of a hold on you across hundreds and hundreds of miles . . . what use will you be when we're actually there?"

"I will do what needs to be done."

He looked so grim, so determined, that I let the matter drop. Perhaps he knew something I didn't. I didn't ask. Snorri could keep his secrets— I had no appetite for stories from the deadlands—but maybe they waited for me anyway in the days to come; perhaps like the Wheel they stood in my path and could not be avoided.

Snorri still had a strangeness about him, that mixture of death and legend he'd carried with him back from beyond death's door. We both stood, watching the dark waters of the Seleen escape the mist and vanish beneath our prow, neither of us talking.

The events of the past day unfolded themselves across the blank page offered by the river fog. The whiteness at first the smoke of Father's pyre, twisting and rising, then the hot clouds billowing over the Appan Gate, thick with the screams of the dead and the dying amid an inferno of my making. I saw Darin's face, shaped across the mist. Barras appeared too and I realized I couldn't remember when I saw him last. Had he been with me when I led the charge to save Darin? I didn't know. I had an image of him, wild-eyed, swinging his bloody sword amid a crowd of dead, but where and when it came from, and what happened after, I couldn't say. Lisa told me I'd let Barras die, abandoned him to his fate because he'd married her. I saw Martus there too, his face raised to me, as he was when I threw him my sword. He hadn't been the best of brothers, and not the best of men either, but damn it, he was *my* brother, my mother's son, and knowing he was gone left me hollow. The sword hung again at my side, the last point of contact between us.

What Snorri saw in the mists I couldn't say, but neither of us spoke until the autumn sun unravelled the last white thread from the river-banks. By that time the current had borne us ten miles and we'd seen no trace of the Dead King's army at any point.

Murder, sensible horse that he was, proved to be terrified of boats and the process of getting him onto dry land without anyone getting kicked to death proved tricky. It wasn't far off noon by the time all four steeds had been assembled ashore and we'd checked our gear. Garyus had foisted Luntar's "box of ghosts" on me, saying it might prove useful in Osheim. I suspected he just didn't want a box of ghosts any more than I did.

"What *is* that?" Snorri asked as I carried it away.

"That," I said. "Holds the ghosts of a million Builders. Aslaug's in there too."

"I thought you locked her back in the dark place?" He didn't look as worried as he should be.

"Well, not *Aslaug*, the woman who became Aslaug. Her ghost. It's complicated."

"Aslaug was human once? What about Baraqel? Is he in there too?"

"Probably. Don't know. Don't care. The thing gives me the creeps. None of them have anything useful to say anyway."

I buried the box deep in a saddlebag on my back-up mount, a chestnut mare with the unreasonable name of Squire, and did my very best to forget about it.

Half an hour found us riding at a measured pace along the road to Verona, two gentlemen about their business on a day as pleasant as any autumn has to offer. The fields lay empty, the richness of their harvest gathered in, each farmhouse stood undisturbed, quiet in the fastness of the land, the honest folk of Red March about their duties. We passed a charcoal yard, a wagon at its gates filling up with sacks, a yellow dog on the step of the owner's shack, too lazy to chase us. It seemed amazing that life passed so gently here, undisturbed by the horror at Vermillion. Looking back, I couldn't even see the smoke of the outer city.

"I could almost feel safe out here." The road wound past a copse of trees all burning with autumn's fire, only the oaks held to their green against the distant threat of winter and even they were touched with gold. "Almost safe. At least with a good horse under me." I slapped Murder's neck. The night's terror nibbled around the edges of my imagination but sunshine and open country helped me to do what I do best—lock all the bad stuff away and forget it for the moment. "There's a good inn along this stretch of the road. I'm sure of it. We should stop and get some lunch. Roast pork and ale would do nicely." The loss of a night's sleep started to weigh on me, combining with the day's warmth, and the thought of a good meal, to make me dozy. I fought to keep my eyes open, yawning wide enough to click my jaw.

The next turn of the road brought a sight so unexpected that every ounce of sleepiness dropped away, along with every trace of the sense of security that had been winding around me.

"A very little man on a very big horse, with a sword that's too long for him," Snorri stated the obvious.

"And a lot of friends." I already had Murder turned most of the way around. Why Count Isen might be sat in our path at the head of a column of several hundred men I couldn't say. The important thing was that I really didn't want to know. Our duel might have been behind us, but I'd had extensive carnal knowledge of his wife, the eldest of the DeVeer sisters: no doubt the little bastard would find some new way to twist the fact against me.

Snorri leaned from his saddle and caught my reins. "This is your country, Jal. Aren't these men yours to command?"

"He's a count," I said. "His loyalty is to the queen." I tugged at Murder's harness, trying to free us from the Northman's grip. "He's also a madman who hates me. So I plan on circumnavigating him with the help of some of the local lanes—cross-country if we need to—trust me, it's not going to end well otherwise. Present ourselves and at the very best we're delayed, more likely he murders us both."

Snorri let go with a shrug. "When you put it like that . . ." He started to turn too, then paused. "Kara?"

I glanced back over my shoulder. There was a blond woman standing in front of the first rank of foot soldiers, Isen on one side of her, four mounted knights to the other side. It couldn't be Kara, though. "It's not her." I set off back along the way we'd come, Squire following dutifully on her rope.

"Prince Jalan!" Count Isen's voice carried well on the still air. "I have two northlings here that claim to know you."

"Hennan?" Snorri called out.

"Ah hell." I turned Murder back. Making a break for it still seemed like the best idea but I knew I wouldn't be taking Snorri with me, and I had a long, dangerous path ahead. "What do you want, Isen?"

"Perhaps you could do me the honour of approaching so we don't have to shout down the road at each other like peasants."

I had a bad feeling about the whole affair but advanced reluctantly, pulling up five yards shy of him. The infantry lining the road behind the count and his knights wore the Isen livery over light chainmail, their spears making a thicket above hundreds of iron skullcaps. Kara and Hennan stood in the shadow of the knights' horses, both of them travel-stained but in better shape than when I left them. It's hard to look pleased and worried at the same time but the völva and the boy were doing a fine job of it.

Kara opened her mouth but Isen spoke before she got a word out. "I've been east, protecting the queen's supply lines into Slov." The little count kept those unforgiving beads he'd been given instead of eyes pointed firmly my way. "But word reached me that the city is under siege. Burning, even? I would have cursed the riders for liars but I could see the glow myself last night as we drew nearer." A tight little smile flickered across Isen's lips. "I must have been mistaken though. A prince of Red March would not be riding away from the city in its hour of peril!"

"The steward has sent us on an urgent mission." I indicated Snorri since Isen had singularly ignored him. Perhaps he felt the very existence of so large a man an insult to the short measure allocated to him despite his high station. "And you have been correctly informed—Vermillion stands besieged and the outer city has been burned."

"By God!" Count Isen stood up in his stirrups as if the news were too galling to take sitting down. "Who the hell would dare? Rhonish coming down the river is it? No! An Adoran revolt! I told Queen Alica a dozen times to watch her back. Any adventure to the east begs treachery in the west. And how in God's name did they get to the capital so swiftly? Are our border guard so lightly thrown aside?"

"It's the Dead King who attacks us," I said. "The troops didn't cross our borders—they're the dead of Vermillion, risen from their graves, or from where they were slaughtered yesterday." Isen opened his mouth, his expression telling me that it would be to object to what would have sounded like nonsense to me as well a year previously. I forestalled him with a raised hand. "Just believe it, Isen, I'm really too tired to argue. Or if you can't believe then reserve your judgment until you get there—either way, you've seen the fire for yourself, so believe that your help is needed and get these men there as quickly as possible." I drew a deep breath and redirected the conversation by pointing at Kara and Hennan. "So tell me: why is so high a man keeping such low company?"

"Come down off your horse, Prince Jalan, and we'll discuss the matter."

"Perhaps I didn't stress the urgency of—"

Isen started to dismount as if I were just flapping my lips to pass the time.

"—urgency of my mission. I didn't leave a city in the middle of an assault, a city I should add of which I happen to be marshal, so I could pass the time of day with every acquaintance—"

"Get off your horse, Prince Jalan, this won't take long." Count Isen beckoned Hennan forward, and finding him reluctant, went to the boy and set a hand to his shoulder. Hennan appeared to have grown a foot taller since I last set eyes on him and now stood a couple of inches taller than the count. "This young man seems to think rather well of you, my prince. You wouldn't want to disappoint him, would you?" Isen steered those mad black insect's eyes of his my way. Unlike his men he went unarmoured, his fur-trimmed cloak too warm for the weather. Leather gauntlets lay one across the other over the pommel of his saddle.

With a sigh I dismounted. Murder could surely outrun Isen's knights but there's something about being stared at by people who expect more of you . . . it's rather like an anchor, a damned inconvenient anchor. Ignoring Isen, I strode across to Kara, looking rather fine in a plain linen road-dress, her hair in braids as it had been when we first met. The sun had finally darkened her skin and it suited her. "Kara." I offered her my best smile.

"Thief!" Her slap caught me off guard.

"Ow! For godsake, Kara!" I reeled back, clutching my face. I could feel her handprint burning there in red, thankfully on the opposite side to the one Lisa had chosen. "Jesus!" Isen whacked me around the "Lisa's side" of my face, swinging one of his heavy gauntlets—he had to stretch to reach but he put enough power in it to snap my head around, sending out a spray of spit and surprise. "Oh come on!" I bellowed, staggering away, hands raised in defence. "What the hell was that for?"

By way of answer Isen held up his thumb and forefinger, pinched together as if presenting something for my inspection. Through the tears in my eyes I could see something tiny and golden.

"What is it?" I wiped my mouth, finding my fingers bloody.

"A reason," Isen said.

"It's a fucking small reason!" I shouted.

"It looks like a sharp little piece of gold," Snorri offered. I'd rather he just divided Isen into two even smaller pieces.

"It's a splinter," Isen said, speaking through gritted teeth. "I had it gold plated. Care to guess where I found it?"

"I'm thinking . . . when they stuck that stick up your arse." The pain in my face made me temporarily forget that he had several hundred men lined up behind him—though I was gratified to see quite a few of them battling to keep a smile from their lips.

"I discovered it under my scalp a month after you hit me from behind with a tree branch. Finding it returned the memory of the incident to me. And now, sir, we shall conclude the matter that should have been settled at the roadside many months ago." He drew the gleaming length of his sword. Seeing him there with that same mad look in his eye, his lips pressed in a thin and murderous line beneath his grey moustache, made me remember just how fast he was with a blade and how much I didn't want to face him again.

I drew myself to my full height, keeping my hand well clear of my sword hilt, and tried for haughty dignity. "I'll grant you that some blow has scrambled your wits, Isen, but it was none of mine. I've no time for your games and no intention of being side-tracked from such urgent business."

"Speechify all you like, Prince Jalan, but by God you will not leave this spot until I have had my satisfaction."

By which the lunatic clearly meant dead and slung over a horse. I racked my brains while stepping backwards.

"If he tries to run ride him down, Sir Thant!" The little count knew me too well.

Even if Snorri cut one knight down he couldn't get them all. Plus he expected me to fight Isen. He probably thought my reluctance was on account of the man's stature.

"Since I'm challenged I get to choose the weapons." An extensive knowledge of duelling might save me yet.

"Swords!" Isen replied, both eyebrows elevating to quite a remarkable degree. "What else is there? No gentlemen would have at each other with peasants' weapons like the axe or scythe!"

Snorri growled, but made no move. I rubbed at my aching jaw a moment. Isen would refuse any weapon beneath his station and be within his rights. I could feel the imprint of his gauntlet on my cheek, and it gave me an idea. "Fisticuffs!" I said, balling both hands and raising them.

"What?" Isen leaned forward, craning his neck as if he thought he'd misheard.

"Fisticuffs! The sport of kings," I said. "No gouging, no biting, no blows below the belt." I knew from painful experience that they taught the art to young princes, and I imagined young countlings were not excused the rigours of such an education either.

"I'm not going to brawl on Her Majesty's road like some drunken commoner—"

"Have a care, Isen. My grandmother encourages the pugilistic art in the very highest of circles—I trust you aren't going to criticize her judgment any more than you would deny the challenged party the age-old right of choosing his weapons." I brandished both fists. "And here they are!" I didn't exactly relish the prospect but I'd beaten a few opponents into the dust in my time, and Isen fulfilled one of my acceptance criteria, standing no taller than your average twelve-year-old boy.

Isen scowled. "If I must beat you to death with my bare hands, Prince Jalan, then that is exactly what I will do." He passed his sword up to Sir Thant, of whom I could see little but a beard bristling below his pot helm and fierce eyes glinting in the shadows behind a visor.

"Well and good." He had big balls, I gave him that. I'd expected him to bluster and call the whole thing off.

I passed my sword to Snorri in its scabbard. "Your dagger too." Snorri motioned with his eyes to my other hip. "I've seen men stab each other in brawls without meaning to—once the blood gets up instincts take over."

I clenched my teeth and managed to thank him through them whilst handing over my knife.

The knights rode into position so as to mark out the four corners of a fighting ground and the front ranks of Isen's command filed around to watch, completing the square. Snorri loomed over the soldiers on one side, frowning.

"Well . . . all right then," I said, squaring up to my opponent and feeling slightly embarrassed. Somewhere in the sea of faces Kara and the boy would be watching. I wasn't sure that flattening a half-crazed midget would raise me in their estimation.

Isen came at me, fists raised, ducking and bobbing like some enraged chicken. Somewhat embarrassed for both of us, I took a swing at him, knowing I had at least a foot more reach, not to mention two or three decades and seventy pounds. The little maniac ducked under my arm and surged up to loose a flurry of blows at my stomach and ribs. It felt rather like being struck by small iron mallets. Iron mallets, small or large, are incredibly painful. Yelping, I leapt away, only to find him bearing down on me immediately.

"Steady on . . . I don't want to hurt you." The jab I threw his way had everything I could muster behind it. Isen blocked the punch on both his fists, just before his face, then hit me in the wrist with a vicious uppercut before I could pull my arm back. It hurt like fuck and left my wrist aching.

I glanced at Snorri for inspiration. He mimed a punch, and I turned back to find Isen doing exactly that. At nearly full stretch he struck me on the jaw. It felt as if my head had exploded: I saw lights flash, the world spin, and a bone-rattling reunion with the ground allowed me to deduce that some falling had been involved too. Lifting my head and squinting I could make out two smaller figures advancing on me. Was I really going to end my illustrious career by being beaten to death by midgets?

A shake of my head reunited the two images of Count Isen as he closed on me. All the parts of me hurt and I lay still while he paced around me.

"Confess your crimes, Prince Jalan!" he roared. "You pressed your unwanted and degenerate attentions on my sweet Sharal!"

I stared up at the sky, hoping his theatrics would let me get some much-needed air into my lungs. Around the periphery of my vision I could see Isen continue to stalk around me as if I were some trophy kill, an eighteen point stag he'd brought down on some hunt perhaps.

"Confess your crimes! You forced yourself on my innocent—"

I swept my arm out taking Isen's feet from under him. He fell backwards, landing heavily as I sat up.

"I fucked her!" I got to my feet as Isen rolled to his front. "But she wasn't an innocent." I stooped down and grabbed the back of Isen's belt in one hand, the back of his collar in the other. "And she liked it!" The last with a roar as I hoisted him above my head, holding him firm despite his struggles.

Isen bucked like a fish on deck but I held him. "Yield!"

"It's to the death, you fool!"

He might have been a small fellow but already it was starting to feel as though I had a full-grown man held above my head.

"Death is a permissible outcome but either party may still choose to accept if the other party yields." I quoted from my extensive knowledge of duelling regulation.

"Well I don't yield!" Isen shouted. I could imagine the froth around his moustache.

"I can drop you on my knee and break your back. You realize that?"

"Do your worst, despoiler!"

I was sure someone must have swapped Isen for Snorri: it was the only way to explain how heavy he had become. I had to rest some of his weight on my head to relieve my arms. "Two of the DeVeer sisters have been widowed since the last sunset," I said, through teeth gritted with effort. "I'm loathe to widow the third." Then, too quietly for the crowd to hear, I hissed, "And if you don't yield I'm going to put you over my knee and spank you before your troops."

A deathly silence followed, during which I barely managed to keep him aloft. If he'd struggled he would have broken free and I would have been too weakened to fend him off—but in the end it was the threat to his dignity rather than his life that scared him.

"I yield."

I did my best not to drop him but the effect was pretty similar. "Isen yields!" I shouted it loud enough for everyone to hear and stepped away sharply while two of his captains hurried forward to help him up. I would have lifted my arms in victory but right then even reaching up to scratch my nose would have been a labour of Hercules.

Isen shook off his knights and came striding toward me. I tried not to flinch or beg him not to hit me again. Instead I played on the role of bold, brave, bluff Jalan, hoping that a sufficiently convincing performance would erase the memory of me being flattened by a single punch and lying at the count's mercy.

"Honour is settled, Isen, and at least one of the DeVeer sisters still has a husband. Count your blessings, and remember that Sharal is the greatest of them."

Count Isen's mouth twisted with all the harsh words he wanted to let loose in my direction, but like old nobility he bit down on it and followed protocol. "Settled."

Lowering my voice for just his ears. "Do your duty. Vermillion needs you. Play your cards right and you could come out of this a hero. You might find the dead wandering close to the city—in small numbers it would be a chance to let your men adjust to the idea and to develop your tactics. Spears are not the best weapon."

"The dead are truly risen?" Isen chewed at his lip, staring into the distance over the heads of his men.

"You need to get messengers into the city to coordinate with the new marshal. Send them in by river—watch out for mire-ghouls, they swim and use envenomed darts. Your men will be more useful inside the walls so getting them in will be the first task . . ."

Isen favoured me with a hard stare, perhaps reevaluating me, though from his expression it could be in either direction. He raised his hand and shouted, "Move out!" He walked briskly to the roadside and men hurried out of his path. From the embankment he beckoned the Norse to him then waved his knights on. Snorri, Kara, and Hennan came to stand beside us as the spearmen started to march past. Sir Thant led the count's steed over, Murder immediately snorting a challenge at the larger horse.

"I'll leave these foreigners in your care, Prince Jalan. My agents found them on the Roma Road heading north and since they were the only link I had to finding you after your remarkable disappearing act." He shot me a dark look. "I extended the hospitality of my house to them. The woman mumbles a lot of heathen gibberish." He nodded toward Kara as if she were incapable of understanding Empire tongue. "Claimed you and the other had descended into the underworld!" Isen managed to combine disgust and amusement in a single snort. "But she knows some tricks and said she would be able to find you when you got closer . . . and she did! In any event, they're your responsibility now. Release them, have them incarcerated as spies, or turn them over to the inquisition—whatever you choose."

Isen turned and mounted his monstrous horse, a feat that required several more steps than is traditional. He turned in his saddle and regarded us all from on high. "We won't speak of this again."

A shake of reins and the count left us, Sir Thant trotting after him toward the head of the column. We watched him go, silent for a long moment.

"So." I turned back to Kara and Hennan. "Did you miss me?"

TWENTY-THREE

Half a mile down the road we found the inn I remembered, The Jolly Marcher, a long timber-framed building with stables and outbuildings, set up to feed, accommodate, and if necessary repair, any traveller with sufficient coin in their pockets.

We chose a table outside. It pays to take advantage of the last warm days of a year when and where you find them. And autumn days, when the sun shines, are made for outdoor dining. Once a few cold snaps have wielded the scythe through the ranks of the bugs that traditionally try to add themselves to your meal, the pleasure in taking your fill beneath the roof of the sky increases immeasurably. And of course the thing that really puts the "great" in the Great Outdoors . . . practically any direction you care to run off in is an escape route.

"So, you led Count Isen right to me?" I gave Kara an accusing look and rubbed my jaw, possibly on the side she slapped me—my face had been so battered of late I couldn't tell any more.

"Why should I not?" Kara returned my accusatory stare with one of her own. She was better at it. "You had never mentioned the man in my hearing and he's a noble who swears fealty to your grandmother. Also, he was holding us prisoner and intended to do so until he found you."

"Well . . ." I took a gulp of wine to buy time in which to think of a riposte. "It's . . . disloyal! Not the sort of thing friends are supposed to do."

"But stealing from them is fine?" Kara tore a chunk from the crusty loaf, using the same violence that someone might throttle a chicken with.

"That's rich coming from a woman who spent three months trying to steal Loki's key off Snorri!"

"I was trying to stop the key going into Hel. You think what happened

to your city was bad? If the Dead King got hold of that key he could do
the same to a hundred cities in a year!"

"And how *did* you lead him to me?" I turned the conversation in a
less damning direction.

"Loki's key leads all sorts of people to it." Kara turned her angry stare
from me to her bread and soup. "Particularly once it settles in one place."

The speed with which she looked away caught my attention. A practised liar gets good at noticing the failings of those with less practice. I
glanced at Snorri, then back at Kara. "Snorri put his blood on the key to
bind it to him. That's why when I used it to open the door there he was
standing on the other side." I rested my chin in my hand, noticing how
stubbly it was. A day in Snorri's company and I was already starting a
beard. "But originally it was you who was supposed to help him return,
you who tied your piece of string to his toe . . . or whatever it is witches
do when they want to find something. And I've been in Vermillion for
the best part of a month . . ." I pointed a finger at her. "It was Snorri
turning up that made you get old Isen to abandon his post, wasn't it?"

She looked up, scowling and without an answer, but the colour in
her cheeks said enough. I looked back at Snorri but he was concentrating
on his food and I couldn't see what expression he wore. "Well." I paused
to finish my wine and wave at the table-boy for some more. "It's been
lovely. And it was nice to see you again, young Hennan. But Snorri and
I are on a very dangerous mission where speed is of the essence, so we
will have to take our leave." I snagged a leg from the cold roast chicken
set at the middle of the table. "Once we've finished our meal." I let the
table-boy fill my goblet. The local red proved highly palatable. "So we
must bid you adieu and let you make your own way to your destination."

"Where are you going?" Hennan asked. It had been less than half a
year but he'd sprung up like a summer weed, his face taking on the
longer, more angular shape it would keep as a grown man, providing the
world didn't fall to pieces first. "We could come too."

"Absolutely not," I said. "I'm not taking a child into mortal danger."

"But where are you going?" Kara repeated the boy with the same lack
of decorum.

"That, I'm afraid to say, is a state secret." I gave her my best princely smile.

"Osheim," Snorri said.

"That's where I was taking Hennan," Kara replied, not missing a beat. "He has relatives not far from the Wheel." She nodded to where I'd tied up Murder and Squire. "You have four horses."

"You don't know how to ride." It seemed easier than "no."

"We've spent a rather tedious summer as Count Isen's prisoners. Though he did insist on referring to us as guests and allowed us some freedoms. Sir Thant taught us both to ride."

I looked over at Snorri, not expecting any support after his rapid and treacherous disclosure of our destination. "You see? It's the Wheel. It even gets to völvas in the end. She even thinks it's her idea . . ." I faced Kara again. "No. You'd slow us down. Besides, we may be hunted—you'd be much safer on your own."

Kara's jaw took on a familiar determined set. "You don't think you'll have more chance with us? You think we're useless?"

"Hennan's just a boy!" I spread my hands. "I don't think you quite understand what's at stake—"

"Hennan lived his whole life a day's walk from the centre of the Wheel. His family lived in that valley for at least four generations, probably forty. Any sons of that line who felt the draw of the Wheel walked in a century ago. What could be more valuable to you than someone who can resist the glamours there when you might be losing your reason?"

"We should take the boy home, Jal." Snorri said it in the tone of voice that meant the matter had been decided. Combined with Kara's underhand use of logic, and the fact that I was too exhausted, beaten up, full, drunk, and generally traumatized to want to argue, I let the Northman have his way.

For the next five days we rode east. Autumn continued to do a passable impression of summer, the mornings came crisp and the sunsets flowed warm and golden. Red March unfurled her beauty, dressed in the traditional colours of the season, and while we kept up a sharp pace the opportunity to bed down in good inns and dine at open houses along the roadside took much of the sting from the exercise. In truth there are few better ways to spend time than riding through the March on a fine day in the fall of the year.

The four of us renewed our acquaintance with various degrees of hesitation. Hennan proved shy at first, keeping his mouth closed and his ears open, but when he finally did reach the point of asking questions they came in a deluge.

Kara kept her reserve longer, clearly not having forgiven me for stealing the key and denying her a triumphant return to Skilfar. I did point out that Count Isen would likely have taken it off her with potentially disastrous consequences, but that logic didn't seem to placate the völva.

Snorri, true to his word back at the palace, appeared to be at peace, enjoying our company though showing no signs of wanting to talk about what had happened to him. I'd been terrified every moment I spent in Hell: to be left there alone lay beyond my imagination. I was quite happy for it to stay there too.

It didn't take long though for Hennan's questions to turn to what happened to Snorri and me when we passed through the door in Kelem's cavern. I soon found myself sharing Snorri's desire to let things lie.

"What did you see?"

"I . . ." I really didn't want to think about it. I certainly didn't want to put it into words. Somehow saying it out loud would stop it being a nightmare, something unreal and belonging wholly to that other place. Speaking of it in the light of day would bring it firmly into the realm of experience, a real and concrete thing that had to be dealt with. I might have to start thinking about what it all meant: the idea that after a short span on Earth an eternity in such a place might be waiting for us was a deeply depressing one. It's all very well when death is a mystery that churchmen fritter away the best part of Sunday droning on about. Seeing it for yourself at first hand is a profound horror and not something I wished to inflict on a child, or myself. "It's too nice a day, Hennan. Ask a different question."

Try as I might to bury the memories of Vermillion my old talent proved unequal to the task and they kept pace with me on the road, haunting each hedgerow, ready to spring into any quiet moment, or paint themselves across any blank canvas, be it sky or shadow.

My mind kept returning to Darin's death, to the lichkin in Milano House, to my last glimpse of Martus. Each of those a stepping stone to the cold and ugly fact that my sister had at last emerged into the world so long denied to her. My sister, unborn, ridden by a lichkin, and still hungry for my death to further anchor her against the relentless pull of Hell.

I sought Kara's wisdom on the subject, hoping the völva might have made some study of our enemy in the time we'd been parted.

"A man in Hell told me it took some holy thing to break an unborn," I said, nudging Murder up close to Kara's mare.

She shrugged. "It's possible. It would have to be something very special. Some relic maybe. Perhaps in the hands of a priest. Sometimes faith moves more of the mountain than magic."

"Wouldn't Loki's key be the best thing to unlock one thing from another? My sister from the beast that wears her? It's holy—a god made it!"

Kara gave me a bleak grin. "Loki is a god, but who has faith in him?"

"But the key works! It could unlock—"

"The lichkin are monsters of many parts. Not born, not made, but accumulations of the worst parts of men, the filth that falls from souls purged in Hel." Though the day was bright around us it seemed colder and more brittle as Kara spoke of such things. "When old hatreds sink to the deepest rifts of the underworld sometimes they fit together and interweave, perversions of the most twisted kind, detached from their owners, drift until they become entangled, and slowly over generations, something awful is built. But what is tangled together can be unravelled. Use the key and the lichkin will be undone, but your sister will be torn apart, shredded, still bound to the pieces of its crimes. You need something less destructive—something that will persuade the lichkin to release its hold and let her go."

I remembered how the lichkin I had inadvertently stabbed with the key in Hell had fallen apart. Kara had it right. Besides, the chances of me driving the key into an unborn on purpose were too remote to bother considering. I needed something sacred and I had nothing. Father's seal had been reclaimed by Rome and his holy stone had consumed itself in the violence that destroyed Double and his necromancies.

Kara proved no help and my fears continued to stalk me toward the border.

On the fifth day we crossed into Slov. No battles had been fought here, though the passage of so many men of the March had left scars of a different sort. The arrival of Grandmother's ten thousand must have taken the little fort of Ecan by surprise—certainly the place bore no signs of conflict and the small garrison of Red March soldiers left to hold it looked bored rather than worried.

King Lujan probably heard of the incursion a day or two later. I would not have liked to have been in the same room when he did. I'd never met the man but the stories painted him as possessing the disposition of a wolverine with belly-ache, and a tendency when angered to lash out at those within reach using whatever happened to be handy, be it his dinner plate or a flanged mace.

The Slovs' unpreparedness could be forgiven to a degree. Invasion is usually preceded by months of bad blood and the progressively loud rattling of sabres. Armies first gather along borders, defences are reinforced against counterattack. Sometimes a battleground is even agreed upon to stop two large armies missing each other and marching in circles for days or months.

Grandmother's strike, aimed as it was at one target—the fortified town of Blujen—and more specifically at the tower housing the Lady Blue in the city's eastern quarter, followed none of the rules of war. There had been no threats, no discontent, no border incidents. Her army had been gathered in the midst of Red March, drawing on forces from the western regions, and had then headed east without delay. A sudden and direct blow from deep cover, unexpected and deadly. Perhaps if she had struck at Julana City the Red Queen might have taken Slov's capital and already have the king's head on a spike—but what value is there in shading another kingdom red on the war-room chart if the whole map is about to burn?

Any army will make a ruin of the land as they pass through. Grand-mother's army had left its marks on the borderlands of Slov, not through

malice or conflict but through sheer numbers. In places where the road
could not contain them the troops had marched through fields, though
luckily for the farmers the harvest no longer stood there to be trampled.
Less luckily however any travelling force of thousands picks the countryside clean as it goes and a newly gathered-in harvest simply makes it
more convenient to pick up and take.

"The people will starve come winter. Even in these green lands." Kara
seemed disgusted with me, waving her arm at the hollow-eyed peasants
who watched us pass.

"They're lucky to have homes still standing," I said. "Hell, they're
lucky to be alive." Snorri and I had passed through the border region
where Rhone and Scorron meet Gelleth—towns there had been reduced
to fields of hot embers, others had been left to ghosts and rats, the people long fled. But Kara didn't seem placated, instead eyeing me as if I'd
personally led the invasion.

"Starvation has a crueller edge than any sword, Jal." Snorri watched
the road with a grim set to his mouth.

"I think we're missing the big picture here." Ragged children watching us from a roadside tree didn't help put me in a sympathetic light. "If
the Blue Lady isn't stopped, and if we don't succeed in Osheim nobody
is going to have time to starve: there won't be a winter, and being hungry
will cease to be an option."

None of them had a reply to that and we rode on in silence, with me
still feeling guilty despite my flawless logic. It struck me belatedly that I
should have added the way the pair of them made me feel guilty for all
sorts of things I normally wouldn't give a damn about to the case for not
taking Kara and Hennan with us.

The next dawn came with a bite, crisp, leaving the hedgerows heavy with
dew and us in no doubt that winter was sharpening its teeth.

We rode more cautiously now, scanning the woods and hedgerows for
signs of ambush. An invading army leaves dangerous ground in its wake.
Add to the desperation of the surviving populace the removal of their ruler's
yoke and you get the perfect mix for armed bands of looters and raiders.

Fortunately Grandmother's plan called for a quick exit once her goal was accomplished and this required that she keep the roads back to Red March clear. We passed half a dozen checkpoints before the sun set on our first day in Slov, and at each of them I had to argue my case, the volume and confidence of my delivery seeming to be more of a factor in getting us through than Garyus's ornately worked scroll of authorization.

At Trevi we saw our first true signs of battle. I smelled it first, the bitterness of smoke lacing an evening mist as we rode along the Julana Way, weary and feeling the miles where we sat. The scent of Vermillion's burning still haunted my nostrils but that had been an inferno billowing out hot clouds that quenched the stars. This was the stink of old fires hiding among ruins, smouldering, chewing slowly through the very last of their fuel beneath thick blankets of ash.

The sun descended toward the western hills, throwing our shadows before us and tingeing the mists with crimson before we saw the ruined fort. The mound it stood upon was too small and isolated to make it a convincing foothill, too large for me to easily believe that men had heaped up so much earth. A small town had grown at the foot of the mound to service the fort's needs. Little of those homes remained: most lay in ashes; here and there a standing spar. The fort itself had lost a large part of its gatehouse in some devastating explosion, masonry scattered the slope, reaching down to the blackened ribs of the closest buildings. What magics or alchemy the Red Queen had employed I couldn't guess but she had obviously not been minded to mount a long siege or to leave the garrison secure to threaten her supply line.

"Impressive." Snorri sat tall in his saddle, eyes on the scene ahead of us.

"Hmmm." I'd be glad when it was all behind us. The road led on into a tangle of forest a quarter of a mile or so past the fort. It looked like the sort of place survivors might gather and plot revenge. "We'll steer well clear of it. Stay alert. I don't like this place."

The words were scarcely off my lips before Squire started beeping. It wasn't something she'd done before. The noise was like no sound any horse could make, or any human or instrument for that matter. It held an unnatural quality, too precise, too clean. Hennan looked around in surprise, trying to locate the source. As far as I could tell what he was sitting on was making the sound.

"It's coming from the saddlebags," Kara said, nudging her mount closer to the boy's.

"Ah." I guessed then what was making the beeps and all at once the day seemed colder than it had a moment before. "Hell."

Snorri gave me that two-part look of his, the first part being: *tell me what you know*, and the second part being: *or I'll break your arms*. I dismounted and started to undo the straps on Squire's left saddlebag. It took a bit of digging to get the package out, and then some wrestling with twine and rags to unwrap it. The beeps came every four seconds or so, the gap long enough so you might imagine the last one was the end of it. A few moments later I pulled away the last of the wrapping and held Luntar's box of ghosts in my hands. In the light of day it looked every bit as unnatural as it had back in the throne room. It seemed as if it were a piece of winter viewed through a box-shaped hole, and it weighed far too little for what I knew it to contain. It beeped again and I nearly dropped it.

"What is it?" Kara and Hennan almost in unison, the boy a fraction ahead.

"A funeral urn," I said. "Containing the ashes of ten million dead Builders." I opened the lid. A fan of light spread out above the open mouth and coalesced into a pale human figure. A gaunt man. I realized two things simultaneously. Firstly, that I recognized the man. Secondly, that the shock of the first realization had made me drop the box.

Hennan moved as fast as I've ever seen another human react. He'd been fleet-footed when I'd tried to catch him the first time we met in Osheim, but half a year had quickened him. He dived forward and, at full stretch, caught the box an inch above the ground. The air left his lungs in a sharp "oooof."

"Thank you." I scooped the box from his outstretched hands and set it on a marker stone beside the road. Snorri leaned down to help the boy up. I crouched to stare at the ten-inch ghost standing in the air above the box. The phantom wore a long white tunic, buttoned at the front and coming down past his knees, a lean, one might say scrawny, man of about my age, a narrow, owlish face beneath an unruly mop of light-coloured hair, a frame hooking over his ears and holding two glass lenses, one immediately before each eye. He looked far too young but I knew him.

"Taproot?"

"Elias Taproot, PhD, at your service." The figure executed a bow.

"Do you know me, Taproot?"

"Local data suggests you are Prince Jalan Kendeth."

"And him?" I held the box so he would get a good view of Snorri, now standing in the road, hands resting on Hennan's shoulders just before him, both of them staring our way.

"Big fellow. Name unknown." Dr. Taproot frowned, one hand coming up to stroke his chin, fingers sliding toward an absent goatee.

"You don't remember, Snorri?" I asked.

"I am simply a library record, dear boy. This unit has not been connected to the deepnet for . . . oh my, nearly a thousand years."

"Why do you look like Dr. Taproot?"

"Who else would I look like? I am Elias Taproot's data-echo."

I frowned and considered shaking the box to see if it held more intelligible answers.

"Why have you popped up out of all the ghosts in this box? And—" *beep* "And why is it beeping?"

Taproot frowned for a moment, flexing his hands rapidly in the space between us as if trying to wring out a reply. "A narrow bandwidth emergency signal, broadcast using residual satellite power, has activated all devices in this immediate area."

"Say that again in words that have meaning or I'm closing this box, digging a hole, and leaving it here under five foot of soil." I meant it too, except for the digging part.

Taproot's eyes widened at that. "This is a level 5 sanctioned emergency broadcast. You can't just walk away from that—it contravenes any number of regulations. You wouldn't dare!"

"Watch me!" I turned away.

"Wait!" The thing had Taproot's voice down pat, I had to give it that. He'd had the same mix of outrage and nervousness when dressing me down for bringing an unborn into his circus. "Wait! You wanted to know why I was projected rather than any other record?"

I glanced back. "Well?"

"It's me that's in trouble. My flesh. Somewhere close by. The location system is corrupt, orbits have decayed—" He caught my deepening frown and amended his language. "The box will beep more rapidly as you get closer, but it's only a rough guide."

I reached over and snapped the box shut. I don't like ghosts. "So, let's go." I picked it up, straightened, and turned toward Murder. "While we still have the light."

"He said Dr. Taproot is in danger." I could tell without looking that Snorri wasn't moving.

"The circus man?" Hennan piped up. I must have told him stories at some point.

"There might be more wonders with him . . ." Kara sounded like a starving woman describing a hot roast with gravy. I glanced her way but the box in my hands held her gaze. It beeped again. "That was truly his likeness?"

I shrugged. "Like him, but thirty years younger." In Grandmother's childhood memories Taproot had been there at the palace, a man in his forties, head of Gholloth the First's security. What in hell's name he was, or what gets a man like that in trouble, I had no interest in discovering.

"Which direction shall we try?" Snorri asked.

I sighed and pointed up the hill without looking at it. "It's pretty obvious. Where else would it be? A fortress full of corpses, laced with the remnants of some horrendous magic or Builder weapon . . . it's got to be there, doesn't it?"

None of them bothered to deny it.

TWENTY-FOUR

The sun set, leaving us to climb up to the fort in the day's afterglow. We beat the rising mists up the slopes, and glancing back I could see nothing of the burned village, just a white sea, all a-swirl, flowing into the woods, coiling around each trunk before reaching up to drown the trees.

In the west the sky glowed red; in the east darkness threatened, and somewhere a screech-owl lifted its voice to greet the night. Just great.

beep "We could wait until morning, you know." *beep* I wrapped the box in my cloak, trying to muffle it. The thing had been annoying from the start, and the irritation increased with the increasing tempo of the beeps. "Or I could stay here with the box—we don't want it to give us away."

"We need the box to find Taproot," Snorri said. "And I never saw your Red Queen as the sort to leave survivors. Certainly not armed and dangerous ones."

Large chunks of masonry littered the upper slope, some pieces so big we had to track around them. Hennan leapt from one to another, clearly oblivious to the growing sense of dread that any reasonable person should feel in such circumstances. Just above us the breach in the walls yawned wide, still jagged with the violence of the event that had obliterated the gatehouse.

"Is that . . . smoke?" I pointed to a white cloud hanging across the breach.

"The memory of smoke." Kara reached up to snatch something from the air. Opening her palm she revealed a small seed hanging below a scrap of downy fluff. "Fireweed. Always the first green among the black."

And as we gained more height I could see she was right. Among the tumbled and blackened walls the stuff grew knee-high, the seeds floating away in white profusion. Even so, something seemed wrong.

"Doesn't it look odd to you?" I asked.

Ahead of me Snorri stopped and looked back. "What?"

"It's too still," Hennan said, coming up behind me.

That hadn't been what I was thinking, but he was right. The seeds had been drifting around us lower down the slope, but above the fireweed they hung in a great motionless cloud as if the air were wholly without motion.

"Grandmother came through here . . . what, two weeks ago at the very most?"

Snorri shrugged. "You tell me. You saw her leave—I was in . . . another place."

Kara frowned. "Two weeks isn't long enough for fireweed to grow and go to seed. Not even if it sprang up the moment the fire went out." She kept her gaze on the false and unmoving smoke. "Perhaps your grandmother didn't do this."

"It was her." I walked past them, angling toward the far side of the breach where the only weed that grew still lay close to the ground without sign of flower or seed. At the back of my mind another of the Red Queen's blood-dreams replayed itself, not of Taproot in the palace forty years before I was born, but of Ameroth keep . . . another fortress that had exploded and where time had run in strange patterns.

Many people must have been killed but we saw no bodies as we crossed the courtyard, clambering over rubble. One could read that as good news—Grandmother having ordered their cremation, meaning that the Dead King would have no handy corpses to set chasing me for the key, or as very bad news, taking it to say that the Dead King had already gathered them into a single force, perhaps hidden amid the shattered walls of the stables, just waiting to pour forth . . .

"Jal!" Snorri's voice startled me from my imaginings. I jumped away, spinning, sword half-drawn.

"What?" Anger and fear mixed in my voice. Shadows filled the interior of the fort wall to wall. I could make out the northerners but the rest lay in a jumble of soft grey shapes.

"The beeping. It's slowing down. Was faster back there." He jabbed a blunt finger toward a group of outbuildings.

I nodded and started back. In truth I'd already tuned out the box's noise, too focused on my fears to hear it, only noticing it now that Snorri drew my attention to it. There are probably half a dozen lessons in that for a wise man.

As I approached the nearest of the outbuildings the box's beeps grew so rapid as to join together into a single tone which then, thankfully, ended. "Perhaps he died," I said. "We should go back to the horses now."

"We don't need a lantern, Jal."

I hadn't been planning to go back for a lantern—I wasn't planning on returning. But we did need light if we were intending to venture into the structure in front of us, and Snorri was right, we didn't need a lantern for that. "Fine." I pulled the orichalcum cone from my pocket and tipped it from its leather bag into Snorri's outstretched hand. The cold light that sprang forth as orichalcum touched skin revealed that the mist had caught us up again, faint tendrils of it curling about our ankles. What I'd taken for gravel underfoot turned out to be grain, the building before us a granary. Snorri stepped up to the shattered doorway and raised his hand. The light also showed a profusion of sacks, wreckage, and that whoever had gathered up the corpses—Grandmother's troops or the Dead King— hadn't been particularly thorough. The body of a stout, middle-aged woman lay trapped under one of the fallen roof beams. The sickly-sweet stink reaching out of the room suggested she had been lying there long enough to give birth to several generations of flies. I tried not to look too closely where her flesh lay exposed, not wanting to see it crawling.

"So, we're going in, then?" I asked as Snorri stepped through, Hennan and Kara crowding behind him.

"This floor is Builder stone." Kara knelt to set her hand to it, brushing away grain from split sacks.

"It will be below us," Snorri said. "The things that time wants to keep, it buries."

"Time might be playing different games around here," I said. The fireweed had shown a month's growth in less than two weeks, then become frozen in a single moment. Whatever had happened here broke something important and time itself that invisible fire in which we burn, had become fractured.

"I think there's a trapdoor over here." Kara called us from beside a pile of debris and fallen beams. "Bring the light."

"How on earth can you say there's a trapdoor?" I squinted through a gap in the crossed roof beams. Even with Snorri holding the light up I could see nothing but dust, wheat grain, and broken roof tiles. "I can barely even see the floor."

Kara looked around to meet my question, her eyes with that unfocused, "witchy" look to them.

"Oh," I said.

Hennan took hold of a beam and started to heave. An ant would have more luck trying to drag a tree. Snorri bent to help him.

"Is this a good idea?" By which I meant of course that it was a terrible idea. "Apart from whatever bad thing might be lurking down there, this place looks ready to finish falling down any moment." From what I could see several dozen sacks of grain formed the main structural support in lieu of the stone and timber now piled on the floor. Apparently Grandmother's men had agreed with me and decided to leave the sacks in place. "I said," I repeated myself more loudly. "The whole place could collapse any moment."

"All the more reason to work quickly and keep our voices down then." Snorri flashed me a look. He bent and, gritting his teeth, wrapped his enormous arms around a fallen roof beam, straining to move it. For a moment the thing held as Snorri passed from red through several shades of scarlet. Veins pulsed along the bulging muscles of his arms—I later described it to a young woman who seemed overly interested in the Northman as being like ugly worms mating—his legs trembled and straightened, and in a cloud of dust the beam gave up the fight.

I tried to retain a logistical role, explaining that such dangerous labour required coordination and oversight, but in the end the ignorant savages had me put my back into the effort. I set the ghost-box down in a corner and rolled up both sleeves. It took forever, possibly an hour, but eventually I stood sweaty, dirty, with my hands aching and torn, staring at six square yards of blank floor.

"There's no trapdoor." It had to be said. It's not my fault if I took a certain pleasure in saying it.

Kara knelt in the cleared space and started to tap the floor with a piece of broken tile. She moved methodically, checking the whole area, then returned to a patch to the left. "There, do you hear it?"

"I hear you making a racket," I said.

"It sounds hollow here."

"It sounds the same as the other two hundred places you whacked."

She shook her head. "It's here . . . but I can't see the trapdoor."

"There?" Snorri asked.

Kara nodded. The Viking handed her the orichalcum and stepped out over the splintered door into the night.

Hennan watched him go. "Where's he—"

Snorri came back almost immediately, a chunk of rock in his hands that clearly weighed considerably more than me. It looked as though it might have been blasted from the main walls. I recalled some debris up against the side of the granary.

Kara needed no warning to get out of the way. Snorri approached the spot, making the slow and deliberate steps of a man near the limits of his strength. With a grunt he hefted the rock up to nearly chest height, and dropped it. It hit the floor and kept on going. When the dust cleared I could see a dark and perfectly round hole where Kara had been knocking with her tile.

"I hope Dr. Taproot wasn't standing underneath that trapdoor waiting to be rescued . . ." I gestured for Kara to take a look.

"It goes down a long way." She knelt to take a closer look. "There are handholds built into the wall of the shaft." Without further discussion she swung her legs into the hole and started to climb down.

Snorri followed, then Hennan, shooting a glance back at me. He probably couldn't see much since our only light was vanishing down the shaft.

"Go on." I waved him forward. "I'll bring up the rear. Just don't want any of you lot falling on me."

I planned to find a comfortable grain sack and sit this one out. The thing about the stink of rotting corpse though is that you can never truly acclimatize to it. I'd blocked out the box's beeping almost immediately but drawing in a deep sigh of relief as Hennan vanished into the hole was all it took to remind me that I wasn't quite as alone as I might have hoped. The scuttling noise was almost certainly a rat: the place must be full of them. Corpse and grain—a rat feast! Even so, the possibility that it might be a dead hand suddenly twitching into action proved enough to make me a man of my word and six seconds later I was clambering down after the boy.

The descent put me in mind of our visit to Kelem in his mines, another ill-advised climb down into the dark unknown. The handholds in the poured-stone wall seemed to have been made when the shaft was lined, being moulded into the stone rather than hacked out, and proved considerably more trustworthy than Kelem's rickety ladders. And thankfully the bottom took less time to reach. I estimated we'd descended thirty yards, certainly not more than fifty.

I joined the others in a square chamber of poured stone. Dim red light pulsed fitfully from a circular plate in the ceiling, making our shadows grow and shrink. It put me in mind of Hell.

"Lovely." I drew my sword.

In the wall opposite a circular door of silver-steel a good six inches thick stood ajar on heavy, gleaming hinges. If ever a smith found a fire hot enough to melt the stuff there would be the wealth of a nation right there, just waiting to be forged into the best swords that money could just about afford to buy.

Corridors led off to the right and left, the left one blocked by an ancient collapse, the right by a more recent one, burn marks patterning the stone. I moved to peer past Snorri and over Hennan's head through the gap where the vault door opened. A single small room lay beyond it, also lit by a pulsing red light in the ceiling. It held four cubicles of glass, two against one wall, two others opposite. Four silver-steel domes were set in the ceiling, one above each cubicle. You could imagine each a great sphere of silver-steel, nine-tenths of which lay hidden in the rock above with just a fraction showing. The nearest cubicle on the right and the farthest on the left lay dark, the glass fractured in strange patterns. A dead man stood in the cubicle closest on the left, illuminated by some unseen light source, his flesh all the colours of rot, some peeling from his bones, some having dropped off and yet hanging unsupported partway to a floor spattered with decay. A kind of harness secured him to the wall. The last cubicle held Dr. Taproot, as motionless as the corpse, worry crowding the narrowness of his face, his hands locked together, long fingers entwined mid-wrestle. He looked much as he had when I last saw him in the flesh, dust marks on the blackness of his circus-master's coat, a white shirt across his thin chest, the buttons mother-of-pearl.

"What's wrong with him?" Snorri asked.

"He's stuck in time," I said. "Glued into one moment."

"And this one?" Hennan screwed up his face at the rotting body.

"I guess either he wasn't stuck so firmly and time is slipping by for him, just very slowly, or the machine was turned on and caught him like that."

"Machine?" Kara asked.

I nodded up at the silver domes. "Those, I guess."

Snorri walked over to Taproot's cubicle and opened the door, pausing to marvel at so large and flat and clear a piece of glass. He reached toward Taproot and I was glad to see some hesitancy in the move. I found it easier to like Snorri when he showed at least some sign of nerves. He frowned as his fingers met some resistance. He pushed and his hand seemed to slide around some second sheet of glass, this one curved and reflecting no light.

"I can't touch him."

"Can you break the glass?" I asked.

Snorri frowned. "I'm not sure there's any glass here . . . it doesn't feel like . . . anything. I just can't touch him."

Kara moved to stand with Snorri, looking tiny beside him—as most people do. "If he's locked in time, and where we are time is flow-ing . . . then there must be a divide between those two regions, a barrier through which nothing can pass because there is no time for it to do so. It would be pointless to try and break such a wall—there wouldn't be a meaning to the word 'break.'" She furrowed her brow, lips pressed into a thin line. "Even the light from him shouldn't reach us . . . perhaps the machine projects the last image of him for the benefit of those outside."

"Well, we're here to rescue him, aren't we? So we should get on and do it, or leave." I didn't much like the Builder hole with its pulsing red light, frozen corpse, and singular, easily blocked exit. In fact after my experiences in the Crptipa mines I was quite happy never to venture below ground again until my time came to be lowered in my coffin. "Hit it with your axe, Snorri. The way of the North!"

"There's got to be some way of releasing him . . ." Kara started to walk around the sides of the cubicle as if the glass would yield more information on closer inspection.

I left her to it and glanced over at the time-locked corpse to make sure it hadn't moved. I walked over to the doorway. If something the völva touched set the great metal disc swinging in on its hinges I would be the first to tumble out before the gap sealed. I stood beside the wall, had a yawn, scratched my nethers, and glanced at the corpse again. Still in the same position . . .

Kara had resorted to incantations, run out of those, and was swearing softly in Old Norse by the time I spotted the little silver buttons on the inner surface of the vault door, a grid of nine of them near the middle. I waited a while. She set her palms to the invisible surface that surrounded Taproot, closed her eyes, and began to concentrate, eyes screwed tight. After two minutes I could see the sweat on her forehead, like beads of blood in the pulsing red light. Another minute and she was trembling with the effort.

"*Hruga uskit'r!*" Kara threw up her hands. "Give me the damn axe." She reached for Hel, and Snorri moved it out of her reach.

"Or we could just push these buttons," I said. And reached to jab three at once.

"No!" Kara's shout to start with, Snorri's rising over her.

Too late to stop me, though. The lights went out, leaving us in total darkness. A moment later a noise that could only be the door swinging closed sounded just next to me, a dull and heavy clunk with as much finality as any judge's death sentence ever held.

"Ohgodwe'reallgoingtodiedownhere!" The words escaped me in a breath.

"Jal!" A sharp reprimand from Kara, protective of her young charge.

"You don't have the key?" Snorri asked in an even voice. "Without the key I'll agree, we might well all die down here."

"The key!" I reached for Loki's black little blessing, feeling over my chest for the lump of it beneath my jerkin. My moment of relief proved short-lived. Nothing! "It's somewhere. I put it somewhere!" Fear-blunted fingers began a wild search.

"Just wait!" Kara snapped. "I have the orichalcum. Let me get it out and we can see—"

"Got it!" I found the key. It had slid around on its thong and hung almost under my armpit. I pulled it out, lifted the thong over my head, and got a good grip on the key's glassy surface. As my hand tightened about it a distant laughter, perhaps imagined, seemed to mock me from the dark. "Hurry up with that light!" I held the key before me like a weapon, ready to ward off any unseen horrors, and stepped forward, swinging it. Somehow I'd managed to lose my bearings and the twenty-ton door was proving elusive.

Something ahead of me made a soft thump on the floor. I froze. Silence, save for Kara's muttered cursing in Old Norse again as she hunted her skirts for the orichalcum.

"What's that stink?" Snorri sniffed. "It smells like the hold of a long-ship in high summer."

I could smell it too. I had to pat myself to make sure it wasn't something those moments of blind terror had squeezed out of me—but this was something even less pleasant than sewage. It put me in mind of the rear dungeons at the debtor prison in Umbertide. The stink of death.

"Ah!" Light blossomed from Kara's hand, revealing the chamber once more.

The gleaming door stood behind me. Directly before me lay the remains of the rotting Builder corpse, now in a loose heap on the floor. I gagged and took a sharp step back.

"How did . . ."

"You unlocked him!" Hennan pointed at the key in my hand.

"Try it on Taproot." Snorri nodded toward the doctor still frozen in his own moment.

I glanced back at the door, wanting to secure our exit first, but Snorri waved me on. I shrugged and advanced on Taproot. Kara and Hennan stepped aside to give me access. "Do what you did over there," she said.

I jabbed the key at Taproot, expecting to hit something but feeling just empty air. "Well, it worked with the dead one . . ."

Kara frowned and reached out toward the motionless man in front of us. Her eyebrows lifted as her hand encountered no barrier. "I don't understand."

"He blinked!" A shout from Hennan at my side. "I saw him."

Kara stepped forward, extending her reach, and set her fingers to Taproot's arm.

"Dear lady!" Taproot pulled his arm back and swept into a bow that she narrowly avoided by means of a quick retreat. "Delighted to meet you. Prince Jalan Kendeth! Snorri ver Snagason! An unexpected pleasure. And who is this young man? A likely-looking fellow to be sure." He stepped smartly into the space vacated by Kara and out of the booth. "Now *that* is an interesting key, Prince Jalan!"

"What the hell are you doing down here, Taproot?" I waved my arm at our surroundings in case he might have missed them.

"Ah." He frowned and glanced across our number again. "Trapped by a witch. Minding my own business one moment and hexed the next. Happens to the best of us." Stepping past me with the fluid motion of an eel, Dr. Taproot angled for the door.

"We have a box with your image in it." Kara interposed herself. "That image directed us here—"

"That's right!" I raised my voice above hers, struggling to regain control of the conversation. "A little talking you. Younger, and speaking a lot of nonsense, but it said you were in danger and told us to come here."

"Really?" Taproot turned to peer at me as if I might be unwell. "A tiny me? Sounds like more witchcraft. I was trapped though, so you've been an enormous help. Now, if we could just get out of here—"

"You were in the Builder box, Taproot?" I made it a question.

"Yes, yes." Somehow he slipped between me and Kara and reached the door.

"You're a Builder," Hennan said. The words managed to stop Taproot where physical obstruction had failed. He froze, one hand halfway to the button pad at the centre of the door.

"Don't children have the strangest notions?" Taproot spun on a heel and faced us all, a wide smile on his narrow face.

"You were in Gholloth's court when my grandmother was younger than Hennan, and you're scarcely changed," I said.

"I have a common type of face. People are always mistaking me for . . ." Taproot slumped, his animation vanishing mid-sentence. "Well, you caught me. Knowledge is power. What do you plan to do with your power, Prince Jalan?"

I opened my mouth but no words came. I'd thought I was the one asking the difficult questions.

"You sleep years away here?" Kara pointed to the glass-walled cubicle Taproot had emerged from.

"Decades, madam. Once I spent a century in stasis. But I like to get out and about most generations, even if it's just for a week or two. In more interesting times I'll spend a few years topside, even take up a job maybe."

"To what end?" Snorri's first words since Taproot came back to life.

"Ah, Master Snagason, good question."

"And why," I interrupted, "don't you say 'watch me' any more?"

"A less good question, Prince Jalan, but still valid. Watch me!" A grin spasmed across his face. "An affectation. People remember such things long after they forget a face. It helps to adopt some quirk for each of my ventures into main time. If I stumble across some long-lived individual who has met me on a previous emergence they are more easily convinced that any resemblance is coincidental if the quirk has gone, replaced by something different." Again the grin. "I do worry that I overplay them sometimes. In your great-great-grandfather's employ I was an ear-puller. Watch me!" His hand came sharply to his ear and made a slow retreat, pulling the lobe between finger and thumb.

"To what end do you visit us?" Snorri repeated.

"Dogged! Dogged he is! Watch me!" Taproot spun to look up at the Northman. "I observe. I guide. I do what little I can to help. I wasn't chosen for this task—fate's fickle finger came to rest upon me on the Day of a Thousand Suns and I survived. I do what I can here and there . . ."

"And yet, when disaster threatens, here you are back in your hidey-hole," Kara said. "Did you think to sleep another hundred years and escape the second Ragnarok?"

Taproot's hands began his reply ahead of his mouth, signing their disagreement into the air between them. "Madam, there will be no hiding to be had if the Wheel turns past omega. Time itself will burn." He brushed at invisible nothings on the chest of his broad-collared shirt. "I came here to talk to the deepnet. Primitive, I know, but these days the mountain must go to Mohammed. When I tried to leave the upper door was jammed and the exterior sensors were dead. Satellite feed indicated an explosion of some sort. I hadn't brought any food down with me so I had little choice other than to put out a distress call then go into stasis and wait to see if help came." He spread his hands. "And here you are!"

"I understood about half of that," I lied. "But the main thing seems to be: you're a Builder and you're going to save the world so I don't have to go to Osheim. Right?"

"Would it were so, Prince Jalan." Taproot's eyes seemed drawn by the key in my hand. "My people didn't prove themselves particularly adept at saving the world though, did they? The IKOL Project was ill-conceived and its ramifications were not fully understood. The technology required to reach the control room safely is no longer available, and once there decommissioning the project is essentially an impossible task. Even at the time it would not have been just a matter of switching a dial to 'off.' With the transition so advanced it would require a whole new science to accomplish. The original staff might have succeeded given a decade of research. Maybe not even then. And they were the people who designed it, who understood the theory better than anyone on the planet." He looked wistful, as if overburdened by memory.

"This could do it?" I held up the key, reclaiming his attention. "A god made it."

Taproot cocked his head, staring at Loki's key. He frowned and reached into a pocket for a lens held in a silver hoop. Holding it to his eye, he leaned forward for a close inspection. "The one who made this gave me my first job." He straightened with a smile. "A remarkable piece of work." He looked around at us again. "It's clever. Very clever . . . It's possible. Not likely. But possible. How are you going to get it there?"

"We walk," Snorri said.

"Ride," I said. I'd done enough walking to last a lifetime.

Dr. Taproot's face fell. The change would have been comical if it didn't bode so poorly for me. "You've no help? No plan?"

"The plan appears to be walking to the Wheel and turning off the engines that drive it," I said, my voice sour. "Do you think it would be more of a one-man job, Taproot?"

"One, one thousand, it makes little difference." His hands returned to the wrestling they'd been caught in during his stasis. "Your dreams are what will tear you apart. Every man is the victim of his own imagination: we all carry the seeds of our own destruction." He tapped a long finger to his forehead. "It feeds on your fears."

"So we need another plan . . . We need to—"

"There is no other plan." Snorri cut me off. "Taproot has watched a thousand years go by. His people built Osheim, made this happen. The ancient machines speak their secrets to him. And he hasn't stopped the slow roll of this world into oblivion."

"It's true." Taproot hugged himself. "Go to Osheim. Perhaps the key . . ." A tremor ran through the chamber. "We should go."

I was already at the door, Loki's key pressed to the button pad. "Open!" The heavy valve slid back without a whisper.

"Well that's encouraging." Taproot at my side. "That is no simple lock."

We stepped aside to let Kara and Hennan through. I would claim chivalry but the truth is she held the light. I took a last glance at the room as shadows reclaimed it. The rotting horror of the dead Builder's head watched us go.

"I could have sworn . . ." That it had been looking the other way when it first fell. I followed hard on Snorri's heels, cursing him to hurry. Once through I held the key to the button pad on the outside and commanded the door to close.

Kara and Hennan were already climbing, an island of light above us. "Go on." I slapped Snorri's shoulder. "If the kid falls you can catch him."

I took the opportunity to plead my case alone with Taproot in the gloom at the bottom of the handholds. "Look, I can't go to Osheim. You said it feeds on fears. Christ, I'm all fear. Fear and bones. That's all I've got. I'm the worst person to send—the absolute worst. You should go with Snorri. Look, I'll just give you the key and—"

"I have other things to do. The data-echoes in the deepnet—"

"What?"

He drew in a sigh. "There are Builder ghosts in machines beneath the earth. They too will be destroyed if the Wheel turns too far. They can't stop the Wheel's engines safely but the engines only turn the Wheel because we use the power it gives us. They can't stop the engines but they can stop what's driving those engines on."

That sounded depressingly familiar. Grandmother had said something similar. "Us?"

"Yes. There is a faction—a faction growing in strength—that wants to use the remaining nuclear arsenal to wipe out humanity. Without people to exercise the . . . to use magic, the Wheel should stop turning."

"What can you do?" The Kendeth ghost that Garyus had summoned from the box had spoken of this. I had hoped he was lying.

"I can talk to them. Gather evidence. Politic. Delay. And that delay is only useful if someone else acts in it."

I reached up and found a handhold in the dark. "All I'm saying is that pretty much anyone would be a better choice for this than me." I started to climb.

"Fear is a necessary metric without which the modelling of risk and consequence would serve no purpose."

"What?" He'd gone back to talking nonsense.

"No man is without fears, Prince Jalan. The key is designed to unlock things. If it has gathered you four together then perhaps you're the best chance we have to unlock Osheim."

That made a kind of sense. I chewed on it as I climbed. By the top I'd lost the thread and was more concerned with the ache in my arms and the business of not falling.

TWENTY-FIVE

We stood with Dr. Taproot at the fort's shattered gates, an island amid a sea of mist, the skies above us bible black and strewn with diamonds.

"You have to come with us!" I said. "Who could be more help to us in stopping the Wheel than a real live honest-to-God Builder! Your people built the damn thing!"

"And I have spent a thousand years failing to turn off the machines that drive it," Taproot replied. "The key has assembled what it needs to do the job." He spread his arms toward the four of us. "If I were required for your success then the key wouldn't let me leave—it would find a way to keep me here. That's how the thing works. Loki's a tricky bastard. So stick with your plan. Go to Osheim and try the key."

"That's your best advice, Taproot? Try it?" Snorri seemed unimpressed.

"You must have more than that." I tried to keep the whine out of my voice. "Where's the wisdom of the ages? I ask you! I mean, you're older than my grandmother. Hell, you're older than Kara's." I waved toward the völva. Taproot made Skilfar's three hundred years seem youthful.

Taproot smiled apologetically and gestured up at the night sky. "The light of the sun is new-born, hot from the fires of heaven, and speaks cruel truths as the young are wont to—but starlight, starlight is ancient and reaches across an emptiness unimagined. We are all of us young beneath the stars."

"Very pretty," I said. "And not much help."

"My boss had it on a sampler behind his desk." Taproot shrugged.

"Loki?" Snorri rumbled, his face a mask. "You worked for Loki?"

"Trust me, it would do you no good to know." Taproot started to pick his way across the debris toward the rippled surface of the mist, lapping the slope just beneath us.

"Trust you?" I called after him. "Loki is the father of lies!" I thought of Aslaug. Even she had warned me against Loki.

"A lie may be built of many truths, and the truth fashioned from innumerable falsehoods stacked heaven-high." Taproot waved a long-fingered hand at us over his shoulder. "Good luck on your quest. I'll do what I can to buy you time. Don't waste it."

He stood knee-deep in the mist, the slow currents reaching up to wind the whiteness about him. Three more strides and he was gone.

I found his lens in my hip pocket late on the second day. Fingers hunting a coin discovered the cool smoothness of glass and I fished out the silver hoop. The old man must have slipped it in there—perhaps as we stood at the bottom of the shaft. I held it up to the sun, letting the light sparkle through it.

"What's that?" Hennan nudged his horse my way. He was a decent rider by now.

"Just some toy." *Watch me.* I held it to my eye and peered at the boy. He looked no different. With a shrug I let it slip back into my pocket.

Two more days took us through increasingly war-torn country. We reached the rearguard of the Red Queen's army and passed into the outskirts of Blujen. We camped in the rain, our tent pegs driven into mud made black by ashes. Fires burned in the woods, they burned on the ridges to the west, and in the ruins before the city walls and out beyond them. Flames guttered in the windows of empty stone shells that were once the homes of rich men.

We crowded four into a tent that would have been snug for just Snorri and me and, in orichalcum light, watched the rain dribble through the wax-cloth. Several companies of Milano skirmishers had their camps set around us. On the foremost tent pole we flew the crossed spears of Red March to dissuade patrols from skewering us through the cloth and asking questions afterwards. Come morning we would make the journey over the rubble of the city gates and into Blujen town to find the Red Queen. A trip better made in daylight if you hoped to survive it.

Occasionally a distant cry would break the night. Red March forces were still playing deadly games of hide and seek with the surviving Slov defenders amid the burning ruins. I hoped to be in and out with minimal delay, two Slov armies were rumoured to be only a day away, their out-riders already circling through the farmlands just a mile from Blujen's walls.

Sleep came quickly as it does at the end of most days on which you've covered thirty miles. I lay dreamless until Kara woke me, crawling over my blanket to the flaps, her hair brushing across my lips. She disappeared into the night and sleep went with her, leaving me stranded in the darkness, alone with my thoughts. Also a snoring Viking and a boy who kicked in his slumbers. Time passes slowly under such circumstances, but even taking that into consideration there comes a point when you realize that you're not getting back to sleep, the völva has been gone too long for just answering nature's call, and that no matter how you lie a rock will still be sticking into you.

I emerged to find that the rain had stopped and that Kara was sitting on a broken-down wall, watching the slow turn of the stars above the tattered clouds.

"Checking up on me?" she asked as I drew near, stumbling over the unfamiliar ground.

"I wish people would check on me more often," I said. "I could usually use the help."

"Your grandmother and her sister have the Blue Lady trapped in there." Kara nodded toward the glow above the roofs of Blujen.

"She deserves what's coming to her." I stood close to Kara now and leaned my hip against the wall she sat on. "She deserves all of it."

"Does she?" Kara pursed her lips and returned her attention to the stars.

I opened my mouth but it took a while for the words to come out. "Of course! She wants to burn the whole world, Kara! Not a barn or a village or . . ." I looked around. ". . . a city. The whole damn world. Just so she can be empress of the fire."

Kara sucked her lip. "The Wheel is turning. The wise say it can't be stopped. All the Lady Blue is doing is pushing it a bit harder. Choosing her own time for the end. A time when some few might survive. If the end's coming soon is it so terrible to make that end a little sooner?"

"Yes!" I spread my hands and gave her an incredulous look. "Hennan's going to die one day . . . so let's stab him now if there's some advantage in it? The Lady Blue deserves everything my grandmother is going to give her."

"I suppose she does, but that's not the same as being wrong. Have you thought about what we're doing, Jalan?"

"I haven't thought about much else. The last thing I wanted to do less than go to Osheim was walk into Hell."

She looked toward the tent at that. "Have you talked to him yet?"

"About Osheim?"

She narrowed her eyes at me. "About Hel. About what happened to him when you abandoned him."

"I didn't . . ." Her scowl made me give up my denial. "He says he's at peace. He doesn't want to talk."

"Men. Idiots all of you. Big or small. Young or old." She shook her head. "He needs to talk. It's not over until he tells his friends what happened. Any fool knows that. And you're all he's got left."

"Hmmm." I would place "having *that* conversation with Snorri" quite high on the list of things I didn't ever want to do. "What exactly did you mean before, about the Lady Blue not being wrong? The key can save us . . . right? This isn't entirely a fool's errand? I mean . . . I don't mind long odds . . ." Actually I did, I minded them very much. "But a suicide mission?"

"Skilfar says even if we manage to turn off the Builders' machine in Osheim it might only delay things. The machine is pushing us to destruction but when you stop pushing something it often rolls on a way by itself, and if it's reached a slope it can keep on going until it hits the bottom."

"Skilfar says? How would she know? And how would you know what she knows?"

Kara smiled, reminding me of how I had once doted on her. "Individuals like my grandmother can reach out to trained minds across any distance, and when she chooses to speak to me I can reply."

The warm feelings that had been stirring vanished in a moment as I imagined Skilfar watching me out of Kara's eyes. For a moment imagination painted wrinkles across Kara's face, tightened her skin there, loosened it here, pointed this, blunted that, and gave me the ice witch herself, weighing me with the coldest stare.

Kara ran a hand into her hair, as if looking for the runes she had once worn. It broke the spell.

"So we should just give up because it might not work?" I was less hostile to the idea than my question indicated.

"The key could be used to ease a passage from what comes before the conjunction to what comes after. Some might say it would be better to use the key to inherit the future rather than run such a risk to try to save the past."

"But when the Wheel turns too far everything is going to burn—that's what everyone keeps telling me!"

"The Blue Lady says there will be an afterwards. Unlike anything we've known. And those who pass through the conjunction will be gods in a new world. The Lady Blue isn't destroying this world, that's the Builders and their Wheel. She can't stop it. Your grandmother can't stop it. Skilfar can't stop it. We're all heading toward the falls and no matter how hard we paddle . . . we're all going over. All the Lady Blue is doing is paddling forward, building up speed to make the jump to something new. She doesn't care about the Dead King, she doesn't want what he wants. He's just the tool she's using to crack the world open sooner rather than later."

"You've been talking to her!" I knew it for truth as I spoke the words.

"I've seen her in my mirror." Kara shrugged. "She's not the devil, and I'm no sheep to be led by another's opinion. I listen. I consider. I make up my own mind."

"And?" I spread my hands.

"I'm undecided." She straightened and slid from the wall. Spots of rain began to fall around us.

"But she's evil! I saw her kill—"

"You say she's evil because one of the people her cause needed to die was your mother. But the Red Queen's cause has led to the deaths of thousands, plenty of them mothers. Look around you." She swung an arm at the ruins.

"I . . . I expect . . ." I tried to find the words to explain why she was wrong. "Most of them probably ran for it."

"Your people are the invaders. Snorri told me that he saw the one-armed man who tortured you—in a Red March tabard, here in Blujen, walking with soldiers."

"Cutter John?" I found I was hugging myself and the night seemed colder, more full of terrors. "I thought that bastard would be dead by now."

"Men who can get information from captives quickly are a valuable resource in war, Jal."

"It's a mistake. Red March doesn't have an inquisition. We're the good ones . . . I'll tell the queen. I'll—"

"Look behind the wall." Spoken softly to the night.

The rain fell harder now and I didn't want to look behind the wall.

"Make your own decision, Jalan. But do it with your eyes open." She brushed past me, bound for the tent.

The rain started to fall in earnest and clouds had stolen the light of moon and stars, but a tongue of flame still licked from a pile of blackened beams ten yards past the wall on which Kara had been sitting. With a curse I hunched my shoulders against the coldness of the raindrops and leaned over the wall where it stood at its lowest.

A girl's corpse lay curled at the foot of the wall. She lay there as she had lain for our whole conversation, as she had lain when we pitched the tent and while we slept, eyes to the sky filled with cold water. Half her face had been burned black, the skin peeling away in dark squares, but I could tell she had been young, pretty even, her hair long and dark like my mother's. I almost pulled away without realizing the bundle against her chest was a baby. I wish I had.

We came into Blujen on a grey morning beneath a cold rain. Tears for the dead.

A squad of ten Red March infantry escorted us along the town's high street. Fire had erased many of the signs of fighting but I didn't have to look hard to see them. In one place bodies lay in a heap, civilians uniformed in mud, a silent mound. The Dead King would have them hunting me if I stayed long enough for him to register the key. I saw soldiers bringing timbers ready to build a pyre, taking their leisure and complaining beneath their loads. If they had been at Vermillion's walls a week earlier they would be running to build it!

We spotted the tower before we saw any sign of the Red Queen or her forces. I say we saw the tower but in truth it was only the gleaming reflection of the sky, and as we drew closer, our own reflections warped, along with the surrounding ruins, across the surface of a mirror-wall. The men told me that the tower had been as any other, tall, rock-built, a ring of slit windows beneath a tiled conical roof. As the first soldiers had reached it the mirror-wall sprang up and had held ever since, immune to assault, reflecting back all violence.

The troops occupying the ruins, smeared with ash and mud, some bearing wounds, watched us with hard eyes. They must have known me as the marshal that let Vermillion burn. Some offered up a grim nod as we passed. Perhaps they knew how the Red Queen would deal with such failure and pitied me.

They took us to the royal pavilion, an edifice in scarlet dwarfing the campaign tents of the generals and the pavilions of her lords beyond them. Sir Robero, one of grandmother's seasoned campaigners from the Scorron conflicts, took the Norse into his custody while a pair of royal guards led me on. I surrendered my sword and dagger at the entrance.

Grandmother's pavilion had fared better than my tent: a silk outer skin, taut above a more durable waxed felt, seemed to have kept out the worst of the Slovian autumn, though I was gratified to see a collecting bowl to one side being fed by a steady drip-drip-drip from a seam high above.

Guards and officers drew back to clear a path to her wooden throne. The place smelled of wet bodies and old sweat. A dozen lanterns couldn't quite break the gloom and the rich rugs beneath my feet were thick with muddy tracks. Grandmother sat stiff-backed but older, as if ten years had passed since we last met, iron grey threading the dark red of her hair.

"Tell me of my city."

How much did she know already? I couldn't see the Silent Sister amongst the crowd. I straightened myself before the Red Queen, now hunched in her chair, and there in the half-light I told Vermillion's tale. And among all that talk of burning half the city to save what lay within the walls, of her son's treachery, and of my brothers' deaths . . . I quite forgot to lie.

"And now we're riding to Osheim with Loki's key on the steward's instructions." A silence followed my last words. I waited for judgment.

"It is what it is." Grandmother sounded tired. I'd never seen her tired before.

"I offer you the key, your highness." I went down on one knee and held the key up in both hands. The old desire to keep it had largely eroded since it became apparent that the key was my ticket to Osheim. "I'm sure it would unlock the Lady Blue's tower for you."

"When I most wanted this . . . you gave it elsewhere." She leaned forward, a gnarled hand reaching. "You seemed to have strong opinions regarding my brother's right to determine the fate of this key."

I kept my mouth shut, knowing it would only dig me a deeper hole. The key felt icy across my palms—as if it might slip away any moment.

The queen's fingers extended toward Loki's gift, lie-dark and gleaming. "No." The hand became a fist. "Garyus deserves our trust . . . my faith. You will take this to Osheim and undo the Builders' folly."

A sigh escaped me and looking up I closed a hand about the key. "Send someone more suited to the task?"

Grandmother favoured me with a rare smile, albeit a grim one. "It was you who reminded me of my brother's worth, Jalan. I wouldn't support his plan only to gainsay his choice of champion."

"Champion?" I widened my eyes at that, unable to entirely stamp out the burst of foolish pride rising through me.

"Besides," she said. "You have the Northman with you. He seems capable."

I begged for an escort north of course, but Grandmother insisted that Red March soldiers would draw more trouble than they averted while travelling through the fragments of empire. I countered that they could travel unmarked by uniform or device, but she repeated Garyus's non-sense about small groups passing unchallenged where larger ones would draw notice. The actual surprise came when she turned down my offer to unlock the Lady Blue's tower.

The Red Queen led me from her tent. "Mora Shival's wall will not withstand my sister for much longer."

It took me a moment to reconnect the Lady Blue with her name—I preferred to think of her as a title. A name made her too human. Once she was young, like me, like Kara. Thinking of her that way was uncomfortable. Time's river would carry us on, twisting with each eddy of the current . . . and what might we turn into?

"But . . . a twist of the key and . . ." I mimed the opening of gates.

We stood alone, a rain-laced wind tugging our cloaks, a score of guards ten yards back, and before us the mirrored finger of the Lady Blue's tower, aiming at heaven.

"They say no wrong-mage has ever left the Wheel." The Red Queen kept her eyes on the mirror-wall as if seeking some meaning in the distortion there. "They are incorrect. Two have. Mora Shival was one of the two who escaped. She has a gate within her tower. A marriage of her arts and the science of the Builders. A fractal glass. Most of her mirror-doors are broken now, and those that survive will break when this wall is broken. The fractal glass, though, that one will survive and it leads to—"

"Osheim."

Grandmother inclined her head.

"Wait. If she can run to Osheim why doesn't she go there now? You've said yourself armies are no use there. The Wheel is a better defence than this wall of hers."

"The heart of the Wheel is hard to endure, even for a wrong-mage. The lady has been weakened of late. She has lost too many reflections to wait in Osheim without great risk. She would only run there if no other alternative presented—or at the end of things when little time remains to the world.

"While we knock on her wall her attention is kept here, her strength employed to maintain her defences. You will have to find and destroy her exit in Osheim. That will be the time to fracture her barricades—when

THE WHEEL OF OSHEIM

she has nowhere to run. No bolthole. That is when we shall hold her to account." The Red Queen's jaw tightened as if she imagined that moment. "When you do it my sister will know, and we will act."

"You haven't seen Osheim—it's huge—how can I hope to find one mirror?" As if turning off the Wheel's engine wasn't impossible enough, now I had a needle to find in a haystack five miles wide.

"It will be at the heart of things. You'll find it."

Having failed to give Grandmother the key, failed to get her to send someone else, and failed to have her send an army to protect me I only had one place left to run. "What if she's right?" I summoned up Kara's arguments. "If we're all lost anyway, what does it matter if the world burns today or tomorrow? Why shouldn't the strongest, the cleverest, save themselves if they can save no one else? Have you considered joining her?" I let the "and saving me" go unsaid.

The slap didn't come as much of a surprise. Not even the force of it, which sent me to the ground clutching my face.

"We're Kendeths, Jalan!" She loomed over me. "We fight. We fight when hope is gone. We fight while there's blood left in us." She dragged me to my feet as if I were a child rather than a man topping six foot. "We fight." Her eyes fixed on mine, hard as flint. "That woman killed my grandfather. She spilled his lifeblood in my house. She tried to kill me and in defending me my brother and sister were changed . . . twisted into what they are now." She lowered her voice, the anger fading, her grip on me still iron. "That woman has lived too long and she'll sacrifice the tomorrows of a million to live herself lifetimes more. Yes, I want to save my city, my country, my people, and yes it's worth my life, and yours to give them another year, or month, or day. But truly? In my secret heart, Jalan? What drives me is that I will *not* let that bitch win. She has raised her hand against me and mine. She will die by my own hands. There's no life everlasting for that one. No new world. This is a war, boy. My war. I am the Red Queen—and I do *not* lose."

She let me go and I sagged back onto my heels. I'd known what she would say. I'd known she was right too. Or at least more right than the Lady Blue. Old habits die hard, though, and I had to at least try every escape route.

"If I see her in Osheim I'll kill her with the sword that killed my mother." I had my own revenge to take, my own fire, and my own measure of the Red Queen's blood.

"See that you do." A rare smile on Grandmother's lips.

I sighed and tightened my cloak about me. "Lucky I set off for Osheim with the key then. Or none of this would have worked."

Grandmother turned her head, looking past me. I turned too and followed her gaze. The Silent Sister had been standing at my back, uncomfortably close. She met my glance with her strange stare, one eye blind white and full of mysteries, the other dark as any hole. "Luck? We save luck for the endgame," the Red Queen said. "You're going to need every scrap of it for the Wheel. Nobody sees into that future, not a glimpse."

"I guess . . . I'll be going then." Bad as Osheim sounded I really didn't want to stand there between those two terrifying old women a moment longer. "And if . . . if it all works? What then?"

Grandmother made another of her rare smiles, as grim as the first. "The world will keep on turning. This ending will have been averted, or more likely delayed. The Gilden Guard will arrive within the month to take me to Congression and the Hundred will repeat the same arguments that have rumbled on since my grandfather's day. Perhaps this time we really will elect a new emperor and mend this broken empire of ours."

It took a moment to realize that the dry hissing beside me was the Silent Sister's laughter. I took it as my cue to leave.

Snorri and Kara were waiting for me with the horses by the largest of several supply dumps. The boy was nowhere to be seen. I envied his freedom to wander away.

"We're going?" Snorri raised his voice over the din all around us. Red March soldiers laboured in ant-like chains under the direction of roaring store-masters to break up and distribute the heaped stocks of food and equipment.

I nodded. "Meet me on the main road, up by the big church. I just need a moment."

"What?" Snorri cupped a hand to his ear but Kara was already pushing him away, her palm against his chest.

She looked back at me over her shoulder. "Don't run off now!"

I didn't reply but walked away wondering, and not for the first time, whether she could read my mind.

I wandered the ruins without direction, though remaining within the defensive perimeter. I'd no desire to explain myself to a vengeful Slovian mob. Grandmother had a strong position with a large number of seasoned troops but to hold this ground until I reached the Wheel of Osheim and sealed off the Lady Blue's last escape would require tactical genius, not to mention all kinds of luck. Her only real hope was that King Lujan would mistake her purpose and hold his strength up at Julana thinking her to be readying an assault against his capital.

I ducked into the roofless shell of a building to get out of the fine rain, blown on a cold autumn wind in such a way that it coats your face and fills your eyes. Standing beneath the arch of the entrance I pondered my options and discovered them to be limited. Somehow I'd found myself headed for the north once more, still bound to the Viking, and by chains I understood no better than the first time. I'd almost been dragged into Hell by the singular force of Snorri's good opinion of me, though it had taken the force of his arm to get me in there in the end. Now, somehow, the good opinions of many people—from the queen of Red March to that of a heathen child—were driving me into a hell on earth. Quite how so many people had sunk their hooks beneath my armour I wasn't sure. All I knew was that I didn't like it one bit. The Jalan who had jumped from Lisa DeVeer's balcony would have run and kept on running. Had a single year truly wrought that much change upon me?

Something drew my gaze into the sooty interior of the house. It had been a grand affair once. I started to identify objects among the clutter of black on black. The shattered bust of some family saint or elder, the jagged hulls of broken vases. I peered more closely—a sword broken into pieces as if it too had been ceramic. I moved the fragments with my boot, noting the bright edges. Stepping forward and leaning down for a better look, I saw that even the surviving pieces of wood, fallen roof timbers, flame-blackened and acrid in the rain, were jagged-edged as if they also had shattered, the breaks ignoring the grain. I stood up, making a slow rotation. Everything around me lay in sharp-edged pieces beneath its black coating, as if the whole room had splintered like glass beneath a single blow.

A framed picture leaned against the wall by the door arch through which I'd entered. The only whole thing in the place. I walked to it, reaching a finger to wipe a clean spot. The soot fell away the instant my fingertip made contact. Not just a patch beneath my touch, but every part of it, flowing down like a piece of black silk sliding from a polished table. And beneath it . . . a man's face, but not a portrait, my own, staring back at me in surprise from the smooth and unblemished surface of a large mirror.

"Hello, Jalan." I said it. I saw my lips move around the words. But it wasn't my voice.

"Get away from me!" Those were my words, and yet my reflection's mouth stayed closed. It watched me with eyes that were not my own. I tried to turn away but that stare held me.

"I'm not your enemy, Jalan. You want to escape. I want to help you escape. You're a piece on the Red Queen's board and she keeps pushing you into danger whatever you do. I can help you play your own game."

"You're my enemy," I said, though she was right about the escaping part. "Your hands are red with the blood of my family and my friends. Too much of it to be forgiven."

She smiled, her mouth more hers than mine now, curved as I remembered it from Grandmother's youth. "We show our weakness most when we look upon ourselves, Jalan. I've watched you watch yourself. I've heard the secrets spoken to your reflection—the doubts—the truths, each confession. We all knew you would be special. You or your sister. And we watched you, but while the Silent Sister studied the paths that might lead you through all your tomorrows, I made a study of the man, took his measure. A coward can forgive himself anything given the right excuse, Jalan. Believe me when I say that the sting of any treachery, whether to the living or to your dead, will last only a moment compared to the joys waiting for you. The freedom to do as you want, unconstrained by troublesome morality, unbound by that nagging voice of conscience which *others* have imposed upon you, infected you with."

"Lies," I said.

"The Wheel is turning, Jalan. It can't be stopped. The change can't be stopped. Everything we know will end. The decision is not how to fight it but how to survive it. I've watched you and you, Jalan Kendeth, are, above all else, a survivor."

"Lies," I repeated, but the worst of it was not that she was almost certainly right about the Wheel being unstoppable. The worst of it was that she was right about me. I could walk away. I could betray any trust to save my own skin. Oh it would hurt, and yes I would curse myself and mope . . . but after? I didn't think it would break me—not as it would break Snorri if he could ever do such a thing. I didn't run that deep. I wasn't made of the same stuff. Snorri was the truth. No give in him. Inflexible. Hold or break, nothing in between. And me? Prince Jalan was a lie I told myself, mutable, adaptable, lasting . . . a survivor. "How can anyone survive the end of everything?"

And there it was. As good as a betrayal. I'd asked the Lady Blue to plant a seed of hope in me. My reflection looked like both of us now—a mixture—her age on my bones, her words on my lips.

"There are ways known to those with power. True power that rests in the mind rather than in titles or lands or the command of great armies. I will bring those who serve me through the conjunction of the spheres and into a new world. But they have to be close at the last moment. Close enough to touch."

"All I have to do is come through your wall and join you in that tower, eh?" It had been a faint hope at best, but I hadn't expected it to sour so quickly.

"There is another way. For a man with Loki's key."

"I'm listening." My hand found the key.

"The heart of the Wheel is the centre of the storm. When the worlds shatter like mirrors and all the pieces come sliding down, anyone standing at the heart of the Wheel will pass through without harm." My reflection held little of me now, just my eyes staring from an old woman's face.

"I'm told it's not a place anyone would choose to wait."

"The engines of the Wheel continue to change the world. The Wheel continues to turn but that was never the Builders' intention. The engines were built to turn it so far and no more, to hold it in place, to give a little magic to each Builder and change their world from one set thing into another. The fact the Wheel kept turning, ever so slowly, was a mistake, an unforeseen event. It's us that turn the Wheel when we use the power it gives us, and the engines at Osheim help us to turn it considerably faster than we could on our own.

"Their war ended their interest in the matter, and a thousand years turned a little mistake that might have been corrected into a big one that cannot." The Lady Blue watched me from the mirror, no hint of my face there now. She looked old, though not as ancient as Grandmother and her sister. Her face however, held far less vitality—the skin stretched tight across her bones, paper thin, her eyes clouded. "Some think the key might be used to disable the Wheel's engines and that doing so might slow the inevitable conjunction. It's possible, though unlikely, and such a waste . . . the key destroyed to buy a handful of months, a few years at best. Better by far to turn it the other way—put those engines into overdrive, spin the Wheel as the Builders once did and bring about the end in moments. The man who did it would be assured a place in the new order of things and a clean, sharp transition would make it easier for those skilled among us to survive the change and bring through with them not just a few followers but dozens, scores, maybe hundreds."

"You sent Edris Dean to kill my mother." I held to the anger—at least that felt clean and uncomplicated.

"It wasn't an act of malice, Jalan. It was about survival. You know in your heart that when it comes down to burn or don't burn, you would choose to save yourself over others. That's honesty. That's the truth at the core of what we are. You need to—"

Something whizzed past my ear and the world exploded.

I opened my eyes an indeterminate amount of time later and discovered the world less exploded than I had imagined it would be, albeit decidedly odd-looking, as if the entire house had fallen on its side. It took a moment to work out that I was the one who had fallen over.

Some tugging and grunting indicated that someone was attempting to get me back into a sitting position, although they were doing a piss-poor job of it.

"I'm all right."

I sat up and drew a hand over my face, turning to find Hennan frowning at me. A glance down at my palm revealed it scarlet. "Shit! I'm not all right! I'm bleeding to death!" I staggered to my feet. Glittering shards of mirror lay all around, crunching under my boots.

"You've got a cut below your eye," Hennan said. "A piece of it must have caught you when I threw the rock."

"Threw?"

"The mirror was doing something to you. It was all blue—like the sky gone wrong. I threw a rock at it."

"Ah," I said. "Well." I glanced about. Just me and Hennan in the blackened shell of a merchant's house. "Good. Let's go."

TWENTY-SIX

I let Snorri and Kara navigate us out of Blujen's garden lands and on into northern Slov. Snorri's instinct for the outdoors seemed as keen among the woods and fields of the central kingdoms as it had amid the icy rocks of Norseheim. Kara also proved her worth, casting her runestones wherever the road offered us choices and selecting the path of least resistance.

Slov was of course in a state of high anxiety with rumours running rife through the countryside and any town with a wall, girding its loins for war. Suspicion ran deep that any stranger might be a Red March spy, but even the fevered imagination of the Slovs was hard-pressed to picture the Red Queen recruiting giant Vikings, blond völvas or red-haired northern lads as covert agents. I did my best to hide behind Snorri and say as little as possible during encounters. The approach worked well, becoming easier by the mile as we left the war zone behind us, and within a few days we had returned to the steady progress and comfortable tavern nights that we had enjoyed on the way.

Having consulted the maps at Grandmother's headquarters and discussed the matter with a dangerous-looking man of hers who described his employment only as "travelling widely on state business," we aimed to leave Slov along the Attar-Zagre border and pass swiftly into Charland, crossing the breadth of that ill-favoured nation before travelling the length of Osheim to the Wheel.

I'm not a man who likes travel. I do like to ride, it's true, but generally I'd prefer to end the day where I started, i.e. home in the palace of Vermillion. I don't approve of foreign places. Neighbouring countries are at best a necessary evil required to cut down on the amount of coastline, since the only thing worse than a long journey overland is a journey of any length over water. In short, even with the addition of decent roads, warm inns, and half-decent food, the business of getting from A to B is overrated.

I could regale you with a near-endless list of small towns passed through, lazy peasants encountered, provisions purchased, hooves shod, ale drunk, early morning frosts, the fiery colours of the fall, sunsets lingering in the west . . . but the truth is that by the time we met disaster nearly a hundred miles had passed beneath our hooves without a damn thing happening.

For a world reputedly on its last legs things seemed largely untroubled, at least to judge by what could be seen from the back of a horse in the middle of the Broken Empire. The sky remained variously blue or grey, showing no tendency to crack or burn. The land held the wet ochre hues of autumn with no sulphurous ravines opening up amid the stubbled fields, no tongues of fire licking from new-formed fissures. Even the hell that had been lapping at the walls of Vermillion seemed a distant dream now.

I tried on a couple of occasions to broach the subject of Snorri's journeying in Hel. I would have got to it in my own time without Kara making eyes at me. My own time, however, would have been when we were both old men. Fortunately he just shook his head and reached for his ale. "Done is done, Jal. Stories tell themselves when the time's right. And for some stories the time is never right."

For the first week of our journey each shadowed space hung thick with threat. I knew Edris Dean to be out there somewhere, having fled the siege when things turned sour. I knew that the Unborn Prince would be stalking the kingdoms, bound on the Dead King's business. And worse than Dean, worse even than the Unborn Prince, I knew my sister would be seeking me. Kelem had told me my sister required my death to seal her into this world. Marco had confirmed as much when we found him nailed to a tree in the drylands. My sister had escaped her long exile, breaking into our world through the wound left by the death of one brother. Unborn from hell and bound to a lichkin she would now be seeking the death of her last sibling to anchor her here. I needed something holier than my father's blessing on a cross to break my sister from the lichkin. I kept my eyes open as we travelled, but church relics are thin on the ground in most places, so mostly I kept my eyes open for skinless horrors trying to pounce on me from the hedgerows.

All that would be enough to keep any man a prisoner to his fears, viewing each night as a long horror when his foes might come upon him unannounced. But somehow, after so many days passing without incident, the normality of the road shrunk the fears that should have had me wide-eyed and shivering, to something almost abstract. Riding with Snorri on one side, Kara on the other, unexpected autumn sunshine on my back, the boy cantering ahead . . . it just didn't seem possible that the world could hold such nightmares.

"I think some Viking is rubbing off on me." I made a show of brushing at my sleeve as Snorri moved his horse slowly past Murder. The stallion had mellowed a touch on the journey and would allow the other nags to take a turn in the lead, presumably viewing them as heralds who go before a great king to announce his imminent arrival. "I'm not finding this trip north quite as dreadful as the last one."

"That's the magic of the fjords." Snorri grinned. "They call you back. None travel as far as the Vikings—but we go back—the North calls us home."

"Sentimental nonsense." Kara caught us up riding close on my left side. "There are more Vikings settled on the Drowned Isles and south of the Karlswater than live in all of Norseheim."

I could sense another of their interminable arguments coming on. The pair of them could debate the smallest issue for hours in that sing-song tit-for-tat way the Norse had. They would end up hair-splitting over some terminally dull point of Viking history. Suddenly the world would hinge on whether Olaaf Thorgulson, fourth son of Thorgul Olaafson, sailed from Haagenfast in the 28th year of the Iron Jarls or the 27th . . .

I glanced around hurriedly for something to distract them before they got started.

"Fuck me! It's the pope," I said, not really believing it, for meeting her holiness on a backroad along the Zagre-Attar border seemed no more real a possibility than an unborn lurching out from the hedgerows.

"That seems unlikely." Snorri stood in his stirrups for a better view. Ahead of us the road ran arrow straight, dividing the land, rising and falling with each undulation. Emerging from the hidden dip of the next valley a long caravan had begun to crest the next but one ridge. Even from a mile off I recognized the papal flag without difficulty, a purple cross fluttering horizontally on a white pennant. A dozen or more men carried a large sedan chair, its roof sporting a golden cross that screamed "steal me" across the intervening distance, and two squads of halberdiers, a score fore and aft, bracketed the affair, carrying enough pointy steel to make even the most hardened brigand turn a deaf ear.

"Well if it's not the pope it's someone damned important." Father never got such an escort despite being a cardinal.

"We should steer clear of them," Snorri said.

"Don't worry, the church gave up burning heathens years ago." I reached out to place a condescending pat on his shoulder. "You'll be fine. These days they only go after witches . . . oh." I glanced back at Kara. "Perhaps we should steer clear of them. A caravan that large is bound to have at least one inquisitor with it."

Of course when the people you want to avoid are ahead of you on the best road in an unfamiliar region, and going in the direction you want to go, only more slowly . . . that tends to mean reducing your own pace and following them.

We rode behind at walking speed, keeping a good half a mile between us. Every now and then the papal convoy would come back into view, cresting one of the folds in the rolling landscape. It started to rain.

"We could just ride past," Hennan said.

"The boy has a point," Snorri said. "At a canter we'd be ten seconds from rear to van."

"They're filling the road. They would need to stand aside for us," I said. "They might ask our business—and if there's an inquisitor with them then they would probably know it soon enough." My fingers found the lump Loki's key made under my jacket. Inquisitors had a nose for such things—though to accuse them of using enchantment would be little different from tying yourself to the stake and calling for a torch. Explaining the key to an agent of the Roma Inquisition was not something I wanted to have to do. Men had had their tongues torn out for even speaking the names of false gods.

The rain thickened as the light failed, and still the clerics and their guards showed no sign of turning from the road to seek shelter for the night.

"We'll be following them all the way to Osheim." I spat rainwater. The growing gloom felt oppressive, filled with all the threats that I'd become so adept at forgetting about of late. Unbidden, an image of Darin came to me, my brother lying dead by the Appan Gate . . . a moment later I saw my unborn sister's hand move beneath his skin, seeking a way out. I had given Darin peace with the sword at my hip, but my sister had found the gate she needed only hours later, carving her path into this world through Martus's still-warm corpse. Was she out there now? A creature of Hell, still raw from her false birth and hungry for my life?

"Jal?" A hand on my shoulder. Kara's hand.

I flinched and nearly lashed out. "What?" The word came out with a harsh edge.

"Someone's coming," she said.

The clatter of hooves drew closer as we pulled to the left side. A single horse, being ridden hard.

The man emerged from the murk and rain and was nearly lost from sight again before he pulled up, his mount rearing and whinnying a complaint.

"Has the cardinal's escort passed you by?" He threw his hood back. Black hair plastered his brow, the face beneath gaunt, teeth bared in exhaustion or threat.

"No," I said. "Which cardinal? What are they doing out here?"

The man ignored me, pulling his hood down and turning his horse back to the road. Perhaps the "out here" offended him. I keep forgetting people not from Red March tend to regard their own country as the centre of empire.

"Which cardinal?" I shouted.

"Hemmalung." A shout across his shoulder, almost lost amid the rain and hoof-beats.

"Why does it matter what his name is?" Hennan asked.

"Her name," I said. An idea had started to intrude, an idea so big that only a corner of it had managed to poke through my skull so far. "Hemmalung is Charland's second city." The truth was I couldn't name the first city, or any others, or any single fact about the kingdom—but I knew Hemmalung was a city because I knew the cardinal that kept her see there.

"And her name is?" Snorri leaned in to hear, drawing a hand down across the short black thicket of his beard as if to squeeze the rain out.

"Gertrude." I remembered her as a thickset woman in her late fifties, thin lipped, deep-sunken eyes, greying curls. She had visited Father at Roma Hall on more than one occasion. "I'm going to ride on ahead and reintroduce myself to the good cardinal."

"Why?" Kara looked as bedraggled as her horse, the rain dripping off the ends of both their noses. "We could find an inn. Take shelter for the night. Chances are they'll be out of our way come tomorrow."

"There's something she has that I need. Snorri can tell you what it is."

"I can't," he said.

"We were told about it in Hel . . ." I cocked my head expectantly, and finding Snorri still looking blank, and my ear filling with cold water, I cycled my hand. "By a dark soul deservingly nailed to a rather big tree . . ."

"Marco?" Snorri threw up his hands in exasperation. "You shouldn't believe anything he had to say!" He turned to Kara. "Jal thinks a cardinal's seal will split his sister from the lichkin that brought her out of Hel."

"It will!" I felt sure of it. "The dead can't lie." Then less sure. "Can they?"

"It's nonsense anyway." Snorri kicked his horse into motion. "If a cardinal's seal is so holy a thing then how do you expect to part Cardinal Gertrude from hers?"

"I'll steal it." I glanced toward Hennan. "I'm as god-fearing as the next prince, and scrupulously honest, but desperate times—"

"You stole Loki's key from Kara," the boy said.

"Ah, well . . . that was mine in the first place. Anyhow—stop confusing the issue. I'll take it."

"You'll 'take it'?" Snorri raised a brow. I've spent several hours trying to learn the knack of elevating a single eyebrow, but the talent eludes me. It's probably some inbred northern thing.

"How?" Kara asked. "You're not making sense."

"Post-coitally." Sitting there on a wet horse in the rain it didn't sound very appetizing. Remembering the last time didn't whet my appetite either.

"You slept with a cardinal?" Snorri leaned in, surprise and amusement warring for control of his features.

"Well, technically there was no sleeping involved." I aimed for the right tone of reserved nonchalance. I'm not sure I hit it. "But we knew each other in the biblical sense, yes."

"Aren't your cardinals . . . old people?" Hennan asked.

"How long ago was this?" Kara asked.

I nudged Murder to a faster pace, trying to shake off the curious Norse pressing me on all sides. "A long time ago."

"How long?" Snorri caught up. "Not long ago you were twelve. You weren't twelve were you?"

"Of course not. Much older than that."

"He's lying." Kara, back on my left.

"A little older." I could hear Snorri sniggering above the rain. "If you must know, Gertrude was my first. She was very gentle—"

Laughter from both sides cut me off.

"Damn you, heathens!" I spurred Murder into a canter. "I'll be back with the seal by morning. And if the guards catch you hanging around I'll recommend you're burned as witches."

I let Murder have his head. Rain and murk kept visibility to thirty yards or less but I've never known a road run so straight, and the locals kept it well surfaced, shingle in the main but in some stretches cobbles or even paved. There's something about galloping a horse that I'll never tire of. It's a sort of union that puts you in control of a power much greater than your own . . . control is too strong a word for it—if it were control much of the joy would go out of it—you're a guide, a conduit. I think it's as close to understanding sorcery as I've come.

Ten minutes later, soaked to the bone but flushed with the warmth of the ride, I knew I must be close to catching the cardinal. I slowed to a canter, not wishing to come on them by surprise and find myself accidentally impaled on a halberd before I could declare my intentions . . .

or rather declare my lies, since my actual intentions would very likely see me impaled on purpose.

I nearly missed the horse, standing as it was off in the margins of the road amid the pouring rain. A lone dark horse, head down, back against the fringes of a small wood not far from the roadside. I've always had an eye for horse-flesh and this piece seemed familiar. Looking around I saw one spot among the shingle that seemed darker than the rest . . . perhaps stained with blood. I rode closer to the horse. It cantered off, skittish, but I saw enough to feel more certain it was the beast the messenger who passed us had been riding.

"An assassin?" I spoke the words aloud though there was nobody to hear and the rain overwrote them.

I turned Murder back to the road and continued at a slower pace, perplexed.

It didn't take long to reach the column's rearguard, shadowy in the rain, their halberds across their shoulders, swaying to the rhythm of the march.

"Traveller, coming through!" I thought it best to keep my anonymity as long as possible. At first none of them gave any sign of hearing me. "Traveller, coming through!" I shouted again, and as one they all stopped. Without a head turning my way, the rearguard, some two dozen men in all, stepped to the roadside.

"Coming through . . ." I walked Murder past their ranks—eight lines of three, none of them glancing as I drew level, all with the blank-faces that soldiers on household duty often affect, affording the illusion of privacy to those they watch over.

The sedan chair was a large one, big enough to hold six people if they were squeezed side by side. Lanterns hung from each corner of the rectangular roof, but none were lit. Cardinal Gertrude would be travelling with a personal secretary, an aide, and a couple of priests at a minimum. Hopefully no space had been found for the inquisition.

"I'll pay my respect to the cardinal . . ." I spoke loud enough to be heard above the thunder of rain on the tarred black roof of the enclosed chair. Properly the captain of her guard should have presented himself by now and demanded my credentials. Instead the whole column just stood there, ignoring me. "Now, look here . . ." The bluster ran out of my voice as still not one face turned my way. Icy water ran down my back along with the surety that something was badly wrong here.

I turned Murder on the spot, a fancy move the stallion had been well trained in. With both legs clamped tight to his sides I could feel the nervous play of his muscles—the horse was scared, and given that he got his name from his normal response to threat . . . that made me scared too. I looked at the sedan's black and shiny door, the papal order blazoned there, beaded with water above the crown and scythe of Hemmalung. The bearers stood without motion, heads down, dripping, and suddenly no part of me wanted that door open.

As I watched, it seemed that the water pattering down beneath the door was darker than it should be, as if stained.

"I . . . uh . . . forgot something." I bumped my heels against Murder's ribs. "Sorry, my mistake."

The sedan's door began to open, slowly, as if the wind might have caught its edge and started to pull it wide. Some cold and ethereal hand sunk its fingers into my chest, lacing them between my rib bones and closing, tight.

A gust took hold and threw the door full open, slamming back against the sedan's wall. What light remained to the day proved insufficient challenge to the darkness within, revealing only one thing—a white enamel mask such as a rich man might wear to a masquerade. The eyes behind that slit remained invisible, but they cut like broken glass even so. The mask from the Vermillion Opera!

I slammed both heels into Murder's sides and he took off like a bolt loosed from a crossbow. The Unborn Prince left the cardinal's sedan with sufficient violence that splintered fragments of it winged past my ear as I bent to the gallop. He came after us with a rushing like a great wind tearing through a forest. A wet ripping sound chased us down the road. The halberdiers turned as we thundered by, trying to bring their weapons into play, but they proved slow and strangely uncoordinated, even for guardsmen of the more ceremonial variety. I had to duck low to avoid the blades of the last two halberds, and then we were free and clear, Murder and me against the darkness and the rain.

Glancing back is seldom advisable, especially when in full flight from danger. What are you going to do, run faster? It didn't work out well for Lot's wife and although I've learned few lessons from the bible, that one I should have hung on to. At least I hung on to my horse, though just barely. Perhaps the darkness saved me, concealing enough of the detail to preserve my sanity. As the Unborn Prince tore past the guardsmen, cardinal's robes flapping, each man ripped open in a red butchery of tattered flesh and white bones. The contents of their bodies vomited out toward the prince and where they struck they stuck, flowing, reorganizing, so that stride by stride he grew and changed.

"Dear God!" I kicked Murder to greater efforts but he was already giving all he had. He might be as vicious a stallion as ever ran the fields of empire, but in this instance the same mad terror made cowards of us both.

Whatever the Unborn Prince was becoming one thing was certain—it wasn't slow. The furious wet crunching thrash of the beast didn't seem to be fading away into the distance as Murder stretched his legs. In truth it was growing louder, closer, and more furious.

The thud of heavy feet began to drown out the thunder of Murder's hooves. Cold blood spattered across my back with each wordless roar of the monster. In moments a swing of its jaws would take me from the saddle. On the road ahead shapes loomed out of the murk, refusing detail to my rain-filled eyes.

"Save me!" A shout that emptied my lungs top to bottom.

With no alternatives left I veered right, hauling on Murder's reins and kicking him into a huge jump that carried us clear of both the ditch and the six-foot hedge standing behind it. At the height of the jump I glimpsed my pursuer, just starting to overhaul me, but still on the road, trying to follow, too heavy to match our turning circle. The thing that the unborn had built itself into looked for all the world like a dragon from myth. A huge, raw, skinless dragon whose wet and flapping mouth housed rib-bone teeth.

The last I saw of the unborn before the hedge took it from view was of bloody feet with thigh-bone claws scrabbling for purchase on the cobbled road as it sought to turn, starting to present a broadside to the three riders in its path, all of whom were now trying to throw themselves from their mounts to get clear of the collision.

We landed with a jolting impact and I narrowly avoided smashing my front teeth out on the back of Murder's head. Instinct told me to keep going, racing out in a straight line cross-country. Common sense could only muster a faint cry from the corner at the back of my mind where it had been relegated, but since that cry concerned the inevitability of laming Murder while crossing rough ground in the dark at speed, and being stranded alone, waiting for the corpse-dragon to find me . . . I listened. I tugged hard to the left and brought him toward a dip in the hedge.

The unborn monster must have lost its footing and smashed into the horses side on. Two lay on their backs on the verge, legs flailing. The Norse appeared to have got clear without being crushed. Snorri had hold of Hennan, dragging him out of range of the hooves as the nearest mare tried to right herself.

The third horse went down with the corpse-dragon and now lay entangled with it, dwarfed by the beast, screaming in a register that would have loosened my bladder if I hadn't passed that point several hundred yards back. As the unborn found its feet the horse, Hennan's chestnut mare, Squire, "peeled" and became part of the monster, its flesh and bones being drawn up and redistributed across the manufactured body. The lantern one of the riders had been carrying lay smashed in a pool of dancing flame, casting the unborn into hideous relief.

Snorri, pressing Hennan into Kara's care, returned on foot to the middle of the road.

"I have swum the River of Swords. I have whet my axe on jötnar bone in the cold places of the underworld. I am Snorri ver Snagason and I have slain your kind before." He lifted his axe and somehow the edge of it cut a glimmer from the night. "This night you return to Hel."

The corpse dragon shook itself, tattered flesh trailing beneath the muscular barrel of its body, supported on four thick legs. The head, its mouth wide enough to swallow a man, tilted first one way, then the other, bundled spines crackling deep within stolen flesh as it flexed. The porcelain mask now sat bedded in the beast's forehead, a single white scale amid all that rawness. Two eye-pits regarded the Viking. The eyes I had met long ago in Vermillion's opera house watched from their recesses—I couldn't see them but I felt their hate.

"You." At first it was the sound of blood gargling in a diseased throat, then somehow it was speech. "You dare to stand your ground against me?"

"Stand my ground?" Snorri looked very alone, there in the middle of the empty road, the rain dripping from every part of him. "Vikings don't stand their ground!" With axe raised above his shoulder the poor madman began to charge.

The unborn seemed as surprised as me and stood watching as Snorri covered the distance between them. The closer he got the more huge the unborn seemed, the more unequal the contest.

As Snorri raced across the last few yards, roaring his battle-cry, the unborn swiped at him, a bone-clawed foot of raw meat, half as wide across as Snorri was tall. The Northman threw himself under the swing, feet first, sliding across the wet stones and somehow rising to bring Hel down in a violent arc that terminated at the centre of the unborn's forehead, shattering the porcelain mask and burying the blade haft-deep.

The unborn, clothed in its body of many corpses, swung its dragon-like head, ripping Hel from Snorri's hands and catching him across the side from hip to armpit. The angle was wrong for biting but the force of the impact lifted the Northman from his feet, flinging him bodily through the air and hurling him on a trajectory that carried him off the road, through the top of the hedgerow, and into the field where he hit the mud about a yard in front of me with a dull thud.

In my limited experience, any blow that lifts a man off his feet tends to be the blow that kills him. One time I saw a stallion kick one of the stable-lads at the palace. His feet left the ground and he flew perhaps a fifth of the distance Snorri covered. I don't know if he was dead before he landed but if he wasn't it couldn't have been long after. They rolled him over and I saw the sharp fractures of his ribs all around where the hoof caught him. The rest of the bones had been driven into his lungs.

Compared to the unborn the hazards of galloping cross-country in the dark were nothing. I should have been out of both sight and earshot before Snorri hit the ground but instead I found myself kneeling in the mud, rolling him over. His whole left side was a mess of gore.

"C-could . . . have gone better." He croaked the words as air leaked back into his lungs.

"You're . . . hurt." I couldn't think of anything else to say. On the other side of the hedges the unborn roared and thrashed. It didn't seem to be getting any closer. Perhaps it was eating Kara. I'd imagined a lot of sorry ends for myself, but none had featured being slaughtered in the mud by a monster on a lonely stretch of road.

Snorri groaned and rolled onto his good side, grasping at his ribs. His hand came away messy and my stomach lurched.

"I'm in one piece." He managed a scarlet-toothed grin and I realized the gore had come from the unborn. "Odin's blood!" Snorri got into a sitting position, hunched like a man broken on the inside.

"How are you even alive?" I stood up, backing away a step. It seemed that the relatively slow velocity and large area of the impact had conspired to get Snorri airborne without turning his body to pulp.

I reached down to help him up but before he could gain his feet the hedgerow burst open, the unborn forcing a path.

"Shit!" I drew my sword: a toothpick would have been as much use. "What are you doing?" Snorri was still on the ground wrestling something glowing from the pack at his hip. "Put it away!" Light would just help it find us faster.

Too late, the huge nightmare head swung our way and the cold malice of those hidden eyes pierced me. I stood, paralysed, on the point of dropping my sword and running for it, abandoning all honour for the privilege of dying fifty yards further from the road. The thing lurched forward with a hideous gargle, but seemed unable to break free from the hedge. Black root-like loops had encircled its feet.

"Kara!" The völva must have been working on the entanglement spell that had had such marvellous effects against the Red Vikings near the Wheel of Osheim. The strength returned to my hand, fingers tightening on my sword hilt. I glanced down at Snorri. "What the hell?" He had the ghost-box, its glow making black silhouettes of his hands as he opened it, pointed toward his face.

"We need Baraqel!" He shouted it into the mouth of the box where a chaotic speckling of light and dark boiled.

At the hedge the unborn roared and threw itself forward, centuries-old roots groaned and creaked under the strain. Several burst apart with loud retorts. Elsewhere, dead flesh tore to let the bonds slip and reformed afterwards.

Snorri got to his knees. "The key, Jal, it's the way to let him out. He lives in here."

"It doesn't work like that, you stupid great . . . Viking." But even as I said it I pulled out Loki's key and pointed my trembling blade in the direction of the unborn, which was now uprooting the last hawthorn that had been anchoring it down.

"Yes it does!" Snorri stood, one arm clutching his side, the other holding the box out toward me. "Yes. It. Does." The look he gave me held such conviction I started to believe it too.

Bone claws dug into the mud and the unborn surged into motion. I dropped my sword.

"Baraqel!" I roared, taking the ghost-box and aiming its mouth toward the unborn. I thrust the key into the box's base and turned it.

The light that lanced out I had seen once before, though that time I had been inside a tent that had almost burst into flames. Now as then the Builders' Sun's light turned the darkness into the blind whiteness of dunes beneath the hottest sun. The unborn screamed, its flesh bubbling. In the next moment the impossible brightness of that unnatural illumination cut off and in its place Baraqel stood, as we had seen him once before at the wrong-mages' gate, a glowing angel with a sword cut from the sun, nine foot long and burning. In the instant he appeared I knew him. No one else quite managed that look of disapproval when their eyes found me.

A heartbeat later the unborn crashed into Baraqel, his sword descending upon it. Even a twelve-foot angel couldn't stop the creature dead. The dragon body it wore had been fashioned from the corpses of fifty men or more and Baraqel was thrown aside. But wings of bronze and gold spread to absorb the momentum and his furnace-bright sword struck the unborn's head from its shoulders in a single blow.

Dark crimson blood vomited from the unborn's neck in a lumpy torrent while the whole serpentine length of its body convulsed, whipping back and forth. A moment later it warped and tore like dough, corpse heads and disembodied eyes appearing along its back, new limbs forming, ending in rib-bone claws or half a dozen spinal columns thrashing like tentacles. Another convulsion and the mutated mass of it wrapped Baraqel in a coil, bearing him to the ground.

"Come!" Snorri snatched up my sword and, limping, ran into the fray.

"Come? You just took my bloody sword. What am I supposed to use? Bad language?"

I drew my dagger and stood watching. The fight confused my eye: rapid, furious coils of dead flesh black against the angel's brilliant limbs, bright wings fluttering, black claws tearing, and occasionally a glimpse of that burning sword sending shadows sprinting back across the field. I spotted Snorri here and there, like a mouse harrying an Indus python, Edris Dean's blade cutting through the necromancy that sustained the unborn, but surely with cuts too small to matter.

I looked at the four inches of iron in my fist, then looked back for Murder, only to find him gone, even his viciousness turned to terror at the sight and sounds of such a battle. The half-expected red tide of the berserker failed to rise in me, just a bitterness, an anger that this creature woven of the worst of men's hatreds that settle into the deepest rifts of Hell, had haunted me for so long. The unborn had been the start of my journey, breaking my life apart, and now it looked like being the end of it too. I held the dagger out before me. Die fighting alongside Snorri in the light—or alone a few minutes later in the dark? Sometimes the coward's choice aligns with that of the hero.

Kara told me I was screaming "Undoreth" when I charged. I don't have any memory of it, but I'm sure it would have been "Red March."

TWENTY-SEVEN

"Go away, damn you, and tell Ballessa I want kippers for breakfast." I screwed my eyes tight against the daylight. "And draw those damned curtains!"

"Time to get up, your majesty." The maid sounded sarcastic rather than respectful.

I tried to snuggle down into the bedclothes and found them wet and cold. "What the hell?" I opened my eyes, blinking against a bright light close to my face. All of me hurt. At least it had stopped raining.

"How are you feeling?" Kara, squatting at my side wet-haired and smeared with mud. She held the orichalcum up between us.

"I'm dying." With one hand I wobbled my jaw. "I think I broke my everything."

"He's fine," she called over her shoulder.

Snorri loomed out of the night and offered a hand to haul me to my feet. Hennan appeared from nowhere, more mud than boy, and got under my other arm to help me up as Snorri pulled.

I drew a deep breath and regretted it. "Smells like a funeral in a latrine."

"That's just you." Snorri clapped an arm around my shoulders and steered me toward the stinking ruins of the unborn. Long feathers littered the rutted ground, the light dying from them as I watched.

"Baraqel?" I asked.

Snorri shook his head. "They destroyed each other."

The box of ghosts lay bedded in the mud nearby, its glow drawing my eye. I gestured toward it. "Get that, Hennan." As he ran for it I added, "Don't let it touch your skin."

He returned, holding it gingerly, his sleeves over his hands. I shrugged

Snorri's arm off and stepped forward to take the box. Before it could summon some ancient relative I called into it, "Baraqel!"

At once that same fuzzy light lit in the box's depths and as I held it away from me a Builder ghost sprang into being above the opening. I could see something of Baraqel in the man before me, the same blade of a nose, the eyes somewhat hollow above prominent cheekbones, the broad expanse of forehead, but it was the way this ghost burned with many times the light of any seen before that convinced me this was Baraqel.

"Entanglement detected." The voice of the box. "Bareth Kell."

The ghost met my eyes and spoke with its own voice. "Call me Barry."

"I—" The things always unnerved me. "Are you dead?"

"I'm just a library entry, Jalan. Bareth Kell died many centuries ago in the third war."

"But I know you. You're Baraqel."

The ghost shone brighter still. I shielded my eyes. "When the world burned I was one of the few who could leave their flesh and pattern myself onto the energy flux. I became a wraith, a spirit if you like. The Barry who lived in the meat where my mind was born . . . he burned. It was a sad time."

"Baraqel? This is you, isn't it?" I tilted the box and the ghost tilted with it. There was more to this ghost than some "library entry"—he felt alive, charged with energy and personality. I saw it as he leaned with the box, a peevish frown, something judgmental in the way he pursed his lips. "It is you!"

Baraqel gave a nod and a grudging smile. "It's me. Or at least an echo of me resonating in this device. I won't last long. Where's the heathen? Bring him forward."

Snorri stepped into the light. "Baraqel. You fought well."

"You saved us." I frowned at the angel, now just the ghost of a man who died a millennium ago, a man in his fifties, slightly balding. You wouldn't remark him on the street—yet somehow he had through force of will set his stamp on the universe so deeply that it had carried his spirit all these years since his flesh had burned to cinders. "How . . . how did you get from this—" I tilted him back. Put a tunic on him and he could be a servant at the palace. "To *that*?" I nodded toward the unborn's remains and the great smoking wounds that Baraqel's sword had left in its flesh.

Baraqel grinned, waving a hand past his head in self-deprecation. "At the start it was as if we were gods, those of us who escaped into the . . . the elements you might call them . . . We ranged so far. This world is like one leaf and we had access to the tree. Years slipped by unnoticed. It was subtle at first. Men returned, just a few survivors emerging from bunkers after generations or spreading from the depths of places so remote they had suffered no direct damage. They drew us back. We thought it was our idea—that we'd come to watch humanity rise again, to guide it. But the truth was that their expectations reeled us in; and then their stories shaped us, degree by degree, so slowly we didn't notice it happening or understand the process, and we became the stories they told about us."

As Baraqel spoke the light from his data-ghost faded. "I've lived too long. So many years, so many regrets." He grew dim. "I used to love to watch the sunrise. Before the change. Before the world stopped being so simple. I used to wake up just to watch it rise over the Pyrenees." His voice grew soft, blurred around the words. "I didn't watch the sun rise that last day. I had wanted to . . . I regret that. Perhaps . . . more than the rest of it." He paused, more pale now than the ghosts the box normally produced. The box faded with him, its glow dying beneath my fingers. "I think sometimes that when the bomb vaporized me the real Barry Kell died that day, and all I am is an echo, a variation in the light." He looked up at me, wraith-like, faint lines suggesting the man. "And what . . . you see here is just an echo of that echo, rattling about in a box of tricks, old Baraqel . . . the angel superimposed on a simple AI to speak his last words."

"Thank you," Snorri said beside me. "It was an honour to fight beside you, Baraqel, an honour to hold back the night."

"I can see it." Words so faint now you might think them imagined.

"What can you see, Baraqel?" I'd mocked him, I'd thought him a pain in my royal arse when we were bound, but now my throat tightened around the words and I had to grit my teeth to speak them unbroken.

"The sunrise . . . can't . . . can't you . . . see it?"

"I can see it," Snorri said.

"It's . . . beautiful."

"Yes."

The box was dark in my hands. Silent.

◆   ◆   ◆

It's a strange thing to watch the death of a spirit that has shared your mind. Neither Snorri nor I spoke as we walked back to the road.

Stranger still to discover he was once a man with hopes and dreams like yours and all the foolishness that men carry around with them. I thought about what Baraqel had said in those final minutes—about how he had escaped the flesh and felt like a god, his potential without limit, only to find himself drawn into the stories people told about him, constrained by their expectations and finally fashioned by those tales, shaped into something new.

"I feel sorry for him," I said as I crossed the ditch and turned back to see the others kicking their way through the remnants of the hedge. "Never getting to be his own man . . . or spirit . . . or whatever."

Kara looked up at me as she passed, a faint smile on her lips. "You think you're so different, Prince Jalan?"

I frowned at that, about to contradict her, but the witch had the right of it. People's expectations drew me north, against every instinct I owned, a bond every bit as tight as the Sister's magic. The word "prince," the name "Kendeth," the story of the Aral Pass, all of them snares I'd been caught up in. Certainly I'd tried to use them, escape them, twist them . . . but as I twisted I'd turned into something new. Just like Baraqel. Just as unsuspecting.

The surviving horses proved easy to round up. Perhaps they were as scared of being alone out in the wilds as I was, but all three came nosing back onto the road not long after we assembled there. We rode on along the dark road, just to put distance between us and the unborn's remains. None of us liked the idea of sleeping with it lying out there, unseen but close.

"Come on." I hauled Hennan up behind me on Murder, noting quite how much heavier the lad had grown. I nudged the stallion into a walk, pulling him away from Kara's mount. "Easy. And no biting or I'm changing your name to Deserter."

A couple of minutes later we reached the ruin of the cardinal's procession. The road lay like the floor of a charnel house, spare pieces of men that the unborn hadn't the time to incorporate decorated a hundred yard stretch of the cobbles. Snorri closed his fist about the orichalcum and hid the worse of it from us.

"Wait." I drew up as we reached the shattered remains of Cardinal Gertrude's sedan. "I need a moment." I swung out of the saddle and remembered how all of me hurt. Careful placement of each foot brought me to the wreckage without stepping in anything that used to be a person. I turned over several of the larger pieces, picking up a number of splinters before finding what I was looking for. I wiped the corpse blood from my hands and hauled the cardinal's luggage over to the others.

"You're still hoping to find the seal?" Kara asked.

"It was the bait. The prince would have kept it to use again if this ruse failed. But he wouldn't have wanted it on him or any of his dead."

"He killed them all just to trap you?" Hennan asked, looking awkward perched on Murder's flanks.

"Probably enjoyed doing it. Good cover too for heading north, stand the dead men back up and walk the high road. Who's going to stop a cardinal? And the unborn know I need something like . . . this!" I pulled out the seal from a tight-bundled bag of purple vestments. "If I'm hoping to survive an encounter with my sister." I turned it over in my hand, a cubic inch of silver ornately wrought on four sides, formed into a ring on the fifth and carved into a seal on the sixth and opposite side. Stamped into a blob of cooling wax such a seal could authorize the burning of a heretic, found a monastery, or recommend a sinner for sainthood. I tried it on each finger, managing to work it past the knuckle of the ring finger on my left hand. Fortunately Cardinal Gertrude had been a woman of some girth and pudgy digits. "And of course the cherry on the top of this little plan was that the threat of a Papal Inquisitor, with their famously low view of heathens, was likely to mean I presented myself alone."

I stood, discarding the bag, having found no other symbols of the cardinal's office. I might have looted the golden crucifixes if I'd been alone, or perhaps even before an audience of non-believers, but heading toward Osheim didn't seem like a good time to rile the Almighty.

"This fine fellow saved me." I slapped Murder's neck. "Well, and you Snorri, and Baraqel."

Kara coughed into her hand.

"And Kara. Hennan too probably. And the other horses." I stared at her to see if she was satisfied. "Anyway. If Murder hadn't been quite so good at running away, the hero of the Aral Pass may have met a sticky end right here."

TWENTY-EIGHT

Charland reminded me of the Thurtans. Which is never a good thing. The peasants were muddier and rougher than one might encounter in more civilized southern climes but at least we weren't so far north that we'd slipped out of Christendom. By and large your Christian peasant knows his place better than the heathen, being more likely to tug the forelock and respect the God-given authority of a nobleman. In the north few jarls are more than two generations away from the bloody-handed reaver who carved out the miserable clutch of rocks they currently claim to rule.

Fortunately, apart from being dank and overburdened with streams, lakes, ponds, rivers, bogs, marshes, fens, and mires, Charland had been blessed with ten years of unbroken peace. This meant that with coin in one's pocket one could cross large distances in short order on well-maintained roads, and find half-decent accommodation each evening.

The closeness that had grown between Snorri and Kara, and between Snorri and the boy, on our journey south, started to grow again. There's a magnetism about the Viking that draws people in, and something in the man needed to be a father. Some women grow broody for a babe at breast; perhaps some men need a son to raise. At best I had served Hennan in the role of disreputable uncle, but Snorri took on a broader responsibility, teaching the boy without ever seeming to be a teacher, everything from tying knots to throwing knives, reading the lie of the land to reading the runes of the north scratched into the dirt.

Watching the three of them, I'll own to pangs of jealousy, but mixed with caution. In some ways it was like envying a man on a high cliff edge the view, whilst being thankful no such urge steered my own feet to any such precipice. Snorri loved too easily: that capacity for love, for unselfish giving of himself, drew people to him but at the same time opened him to the possibility of grave hurt. With axe in hand Snorri had proved himself nigh unstoppable, needing to fear nothing. And yet here he was handing the world a stick to beat him with. In Osheim a man has a hard enough time hanging on to his own skin. Taking a child in was bad. Taking a son in was like holding a knife to your throat and asking the world to cut you.

Only as the border with Osheim grew closer did the air of prosperity and good cheer start to wane. Villages grew fewer and farther between, fewer people kept to the roads, fields looked poorly tended and swathes of forest grew unchecked, their interiors dark and worrisome.

Hundreds of miles behind us, deep in hostile territory, my grandmother and the flower of Red March's army would be fighting a desperate battle to hold on to Blujen and maintain the siege of Lady Blue's tower. Little time could remain to them, and not much more remained to everyone else according to the oft-repeated prophecies of doom. And yet with each mile that passed beneath Murder's hooves I wanted to slow down, to drag the journey out, to do anything but step once more into Osheim and let the Wheel draw me down into the horrors at its midst.

"The world is changing." Kara rode alongside me as we forded a stream that cut across our trail through the ill-named Bright Forest. She had that tone she used when being profound—I think she copied it from Skilfar.

"It is?" I'd really rather it wasn't. Then we could go home.

"Can't you feel it?" She nodded up at the bright line where the trees failed to meet across our path. The sky had a brittleness to it. As if a sufficiently loud noise might shatter it and set the pieces tumbling down. "Everything is growing thin. Magic is spilling through the cracks."

"That spell of yours, trapping the unborn in the hedgerow, worked well."

"Better than it should. Better than I've seen outside the Wheel."

That night we camped in the woods, a cold, black night in which the whole forest seemed to move around outside the thin walls of the tent.

Somewhere on along the course of the next day, following old and overgrown lumber trails through a nameless expanse of woodland, we passed into the kingdom of Osheim close to the point where it meets with both Charland and Maladon. Already we were north of Os City where King Halaric cowered on the edge of his own domain as if scared to venture any farther into it.

After another day the trees also appeared to lose courage and their advance gave way to a miserable and blighted heathland where the only things to slow the wind were frequent heavy downpours, sometimes laced with wet snow.

In the distance a shadow loomed, a bruise on the sky, letting us know the Wheel waited, letting Hennan know he was coming home. That night I felt the pull of the Wheel for the first time in nearly a year, though it seemed then as if it had always been there, ever since it first sunk its hook as we fled the Red Vikings. I slept fitfully, a poor meal of dried meat and hardtack roiling around in my stomach, and in every moment I knew the Wheel sat out there in the distance, I knew exactly the direction, and I knew that my legs, restless with the need to take me there, would not let me spend long asleep.

The sunrise found us already up and about, readying ourselves for travel.

"It's stronger this time." Snorri crouched over a little fire, heating oats and water in a small, blackened cauldron.

In the east the sun hid behind a louring bank of cloud, sending rose-tinted rays fanning out across a pearl sky. To the north the Wheel waited, reeling us in.

"Much stronger," Kara said. "It's turning faster, approaching the break-ing point." She had an ethereal beauty in the dawn light, her eyes having that strange blurriness they take on when working witchcraft, stray hairs lifting up from her braids as if we stood in the midst of an electrical storm. The power of the Wheel echoed in her.

"How far now?" The land had run to the low hills and rolling valleys of Hennan's homeland, the sky above us bruised a yellow-purple, and swirled in some great spiral about a centre point directly ahead of us.

"About two miles less than when you last asked, Jal." Snorri led the way, swaying to the gait of his steed, offering me no view but broad shoulders beneath a leather cape, and thick black hair reaching down past his neck.

"Twenty miles, maybe." Kara took pity on me.

Hennan rode with me on Murder, perched on a collection of blankets secured to my saddle. His words had run out as we reached the margins of the Wheel-lands where his grandfather had once tended goats. Approaching from the south this time we saw no signs of life, either on four feet or on two, save once a pair of ravens flying west.

The countryside had not yet taken on the twisted and alien aspect encountered further in but everything about it felt wrong—the grass an unconvincing shade of green, the wind whisper-laden and beating strange patterns into the rushes that grew thick around the valley fens.

"Do you see them?" Snorri asked.

"No." I had been hoping they were figments of my imagination. "What are they?"

"Figments of your imagination," Kara said behind me, struggling to keep her nag from panic.

"Oh good." It had seemed that shadowy shapes had been pacing us on both sides, quite far off, and either vanishing when I looked directly at them, or refusing definition, remaining indistinct blurs in the middle distances, like a stain on the eye.

"It's bad. Very bad." Kara glanced around. "The Wheel is reaching out this far and starting to put flesh on our fears. I had expected something like this, but much closer in."

"Hell." Several weeks' worth of good intentions melted away like a snowball tossed into a furnace. "This is never going to work. We don't stand a chance." I'd spent my time worrying about what I might do if we really got to the heart of the Wheel, somehow allowing myself to gloss over the business of actually getting there. As I stared out at the indistinct shapes some of them started to look more solid, more sharply outlined. One in particular darkened and began to sprout long thin legs . . . "Shit! We need to run!" I hauled on Murder's reins. He'd galloped me to safety before, he could do it again.

"Jalan!" Kara's voice stabbed through me, taking the strength from my arms. "You need to calm down, empty your mind."

"Empty my mind? What the hell are you talking about?" My mind was a bubbling cauldron, I'd never been able to still its voices, even enjoying a goblet of wine out on a balcony after a tumble in the sheets my thoughts would be a seething mass of this and that and maybe and when. "I can't!"

"Then concentrate on something else, some good memory, something peaceful."

"I . . . I can't think of anything, damn it!" Every image that sprang to mind my imagination rapidly warped into some terrifying nightmare, and out across the grass yet another faint shadow grew darker and started to take on the shape of the horror in my head. I thought of Lisa DeVeer but no sooner had I pictured her, deliciously striped in light and shade, than my treacherous imagination started to speculate how the Wheel might hurt me with her—the flesh fell away around her mouth, revealing triangular teeth around a devouring hole. "I've got to go! I'll get us all killed."

I shook Murder's reins, but Snorri leaned across and took them in one hand.

"Jal!" He snapped his fingers beneath my nose. "You don't have to empty your mind, or fill it with something good, you just need to listen." Snorri steered Murder back toward the Wheel and walked his horse on, slowly. "A story will lead a man through dark places. Stories have direction. A good story commands a man's thoughts along a path, allowing no opportunity to stray, no space for anything but the tale as it unfolds before you."

"What story have you got, Snorri?" Hennan asked. "Is it the one about the jötun who stole Thor's hammer?"

"Christ don't tell one of your monster sagas!" I could see it now, frost giants shambling out of the mist just as Snorri described them.

"Oh, it's darker than that." Snorri turned in the saddle to look back at us. "But if I tell it true there will be no space in you for anything else. You won't think of Hel coming out of the Wheel for you, because I will have already laid it before you."

And like that, riding toward the Wheel of Osheim, Snorri ver Snagason spoke for the first time of his quest through Hel. Perhaps Snorri's story-telling had always been a kind of magic, and being so close to the Wheel had taken that gentle spellbinding and made something more powerful of it. All I know is that the words ran around me and like a bad dream I was back in Hell, seeing only what Snorri's tale laid before me.

Snorri turns from the many-pillared hall of the judges and looks out into the Hel-night, alive now with the rushing wind of her approach.

Jalan! The dry air shrieks it. *Jalan!*

There she stands before him, a child no older than his own sweet Ein-myria, ghost-pale but lit with some inner glow. Gone. Now the swirl of the wind reveals her on his right, a slim young woman, hollow-eyed, clothed only in the wisps of what rides her, her head cocked to one side, studying Snorri with alien curiosity. The wind speaks again in a voice that stings, grit-laden and cold. Now she's a baby, lying some yards to his right pale and silent, regarding him with eyes darker than Hel's night. Tendrils of the lichkin to whom she is bound rise about her like translucent serpents, their light devoid of warmth. The child who has never seen the world, and the lichkin to whom she was given, both woven together, waiting to be unborn into the living lands.

Jalan!

"I'm not him," Snorri says.

The unborn hisses, its shape twisting into some ugly thing without permanence or definition, the lichkin coming to the fore.

"You can smell it, can't you?" Snorri says. "The destruction of one of your kind? He came against me in Hel and now he's nothing." Snorri raises his axe. "Try me?"

The wind howls and the ghost-like unborn breaks apart, swirling away toward the judges' hall. Snorri shivers and lowers his axe, hoping he has bought Jal enough time to win clear.

In the distance, where the wind has dropped and the darkness fallen back to the ground from whence it was lifted, the dead-sky shows. It is the colour of sorrow and broken promises. Snorri starts to walk once more, the pain, thirst, and hunger of Hel woven into the meat of him so that each step is its own battle.

He hopes Jal will win through—the boy has grown in the time they have journeyed together. Less than a year, but the softness in him has been worn away to reveal some of the same steel so evident in the Red Queen, though perhaps Jal has yet to realize it. The afterlife feels too quiet without the prince's constant complaining. Snorri misses him already. A grin creases his face. Even in Hel Jal can make him smile.

Snorri walks on, out into the wilds where Hel's domain borders other places, the lands of ice and the lands of fire where the jötun dwell and build their strength for Ragnarok. Other places too, stranger places, all bound together by the roots of Yggdrasil. The land heaves and breaks as if frozen in its death agonies, mounded into compression ridges, scarred by deep rifts, stepping up toward daunting heights.

Few wander here, just the occasional soul bent around its purpose, and twice a troll-kin, hunched and moving swiftly through the scatter of rocks. In places monoliths stand, towers of black basalt, each carved with an eye as if to suggest the goddess watches even in the margins of her lands.

With Jal's departure the Hel that Snorri crosses has grown closer and closer to the tales the skáld would sing in the long night around the dying fire of the mead hall. Snorri knows that Hel herself sits enthroned at the heart of these lands, split like night and day, as if Baraqel and Aslaug had been sliced head to groin and half of each bound into one being. Snorri, despite the depth of his conviction, can't help but be glad his path has led him to the margins rather than to Hel's court. He means to break Hel's law, but he would rather not attempt it with her standing behind him.

In the distance hills rise from the blood-dust, dark with menace. The plain before them lies scattered with dead and twisted trees, ancient wind-stunted things, not one with a leaf on it, nor any hint of green across the whole swathe of the forest. Snorri sets off walking.

"Ccraaaawk!"

Snorri spins toward the sudden cry, axe ready. He sees nothing. Blood-dust rises around his feet, reaching his knees.

"Crawwk!" A raven, black and glossy, perched on a tree some yards back, long toes curled around a dry twig. "Here's an odd thing. A living man in Hel." The raven tilts its head first one way, then the other, sizing Snorri up.

"Odder than a raven that can speak?"

"Perhaps all ravens can, but most don't choose to."

"What do you want with me, spirit?"

"No spirit, just a raven, wanting what we all want: to watch, to learn, to fly back and whisper our secrets to the All-father. And perhaps a juicy worm."

"Truly?" Snorri lowers his axe, amazed. "You are Muninn? . . . or Huginn?" He recalls the names of Odin's two ravens from the priests' tales. Appropriately he recalled Muninn—memory—first, and Huginn— thought—took a little more thought.

The raven crawks, shakes its feathers, and settles. "Mother and father to us all. We all fly in their wake."

"Oh." Snorri's disappointment colours the word. "You don't speak to Odin then?"

"Everything that speaks speaks to Odin, Snorri son of Snaga, son of Olaaf." The bird wipes its beak on the branch beside it. "Why are you here? Why heading out into the wilds?"

Snorri knows his destination—he hasn't thought to question his path. "I'm here for my wife and children. It was wrong how they were taken from me."

"Wrong?"

"I failed them."

"We all fail, Snorri. In the end we all fail. Often sooner."

Snorri finds his hand pressed to his face, a weight of memory pushing him down, emotion choking him. "What was I supposed to do? Leave them? I could not let this stand. Win or lose, my fight is here. What else could I do?"

The raven shakes again, a stray feather floating down between dead branches. "Don't ask me for counsel. I'm just a bird. Just memory."

Snorri sniffs, ashamed of the tears he thought himself too dry for, feeling stupid and hurt. "I thought they would have gone before the goddess. I thought they would have gone before Hel and that she would have seen their goodness with her white eye and seen no evil with her black eye. They should be at Helgafell . . ." The holy mountain waited for the little ones and for those not slain in battle . . . though gods knew Freja must have fought to save her children. But Hel wouldn't separate her from Emy and Egil . . . surely that couldn't be the reward for her valour? Snorri's head spins and it seems that Hel rotates about him so that he and the raven become the centre of all things, all pivoting on this one question. "Why are they out here?"

Snorri wipes his forearm across his eyes and draws breath to repeat the question, but the tree is empty, the branch bare. For a long moment he wonders if the bird was ever there. Then he kneels and retrieves a lone feather from the rust-coloured dust. Standing, he slips the feather into his coin pouch, and continues through the dead forest toward the distant hills.

The sky seems closer here, and although it remains monotone some-how it bears the threat of a storm. The whole region does, as if it holds its breath, waiting. The Northman sets his gaze upon a high ridge and, with teeth gritted, he begins the long ascent.

Snorri climbs, scrambling up rough slopes, clambering over rocks that hurt for no reason other than that he touches them—as if they are made of pain itself. Visions of Eight Quays fill his mind as he reaches, grips, hauls himself up, and repeats the process. His village rising above the Uulisk, above the quays that give its name, the scatter of huts that he knows well enough to navigate around in the blind night, sometimes blind drunk. He sees his own home, Freja at the door, golden hair all around her shoulders, blue eyes smiling, small crinkles at the corners, one hand on Emy's shoulder, the other ruffling Egil's hair, red about her fingers. Coming up behind her, looming head and shoulders above his stepmother, Karl, white-blond like his true mother and promising to be as tall as his father. Even at fifteen he overtops most men.

How would Egil have grown from the scrawny energetic child, eager to investigate everything the world had to offer or to hide? Always into mischief of one sort or another. The boy had worshipped Snorri . . .

"I let him die." Another hold. A snarl of effort. Another few feet of elevation gained. "I let them all die."

Snorri looks up, blinking his vision clear. No pain he has suffered in Hel comes close to the ache that lodged in his chest the day he found Emy in the snow, mutilated by the ghouls that Sven Broke-Oar had brought to Eight Quays. That ache has grown around his heart—grown larger and tighter with each of their deaths, undiminished by passing time, an armour against what the world might offer, a prison too. *It will end though. Here in Hel, it will end.*

How long the climb takes him Snorri can't say. Without night or day, without food or water, with no living thing close enough that its distance might be measured in so slight a thing as miles, time runs its own strange paths. Snorri couldn't say how long the climb took but he feels, as he crests the ridge, that he has grown old somewhere along the way.

The ridge offers a view across a folded topography where a labyrinth of dry valleys, box canyons, and deep rifts stretches away toward a dark horizon. The sky lies tainted with shadow, as if faint streamers of cloud have been strewn across it, clinging to the underside of the world above Hel. Each line of shadow forms some part of a pattern, a great gyre, its rotation too slow for the eye and centred on some vertex miles out, above the labyrinth.

"I see it." Snorri sets his axe down for a moment, drawing a deep breath. "I'm coming for you, Freja." He wipes the blood from his hands. "I'm coming for all of you." He has a goal. Freja will be there with his children. All of Hel cannot stop him now.

Murder missed his footing on a loose rock and for a moment it jolted me from Snorri's story. We'd come deep into the Wheel-lands, perhaps almost as far as on our first incursion. Standing stones, each taller than a man, ran in five close and parallel lines, radiating like a spoke, passing close by us and rushing on ahead toward a convergence at infinity. Heather grew over-tall in sickly and twisted clumps. I heard my name called among the stones . . . a pale long-fingered hand reached around the side of one close by, ancient with lichen. I closed my eyes and the story caught around me once more, swirling me along a different path.

❖ ❖ ❖

A pale long-fingered hand creeps around the rock. The motion draws Snorri's eye, turning his gaze from the dusty floor of the gorge to the steep and craggy side. He's penetrated several miles into the labyrinth and overhead the shadow-stained gyre lies more pronounced than when he first saw it. And in all those dusty miles he hasn't seen so much as a stray soul.

"Best come out and show yourself," he calls, hefting his axe.

A narrow head peers over the edge of the jagged ledge, some thirty yards above the valley floor. At first Snorri takes it for a lichkin and his blood runs cold, but the thing is a sickly yellow rather than white, and its head is more like a bird's, an unhealthy fusion of beak and head, rather than the eyeless wedge of a lichkin. It hauls itself into view with a screech like nails on slate, revealing small triangular teeth in its fleshy beak, and a gangling skeletal body with a crest of barbs running along its spine.

"A demon." Snorri grins. "About time. Let's see what you've got." Behind the smile he knows this thing may make an end of him. The lichkin was overwhelming. He's fought trolls in the living world and barely survived—their strength many times that of a man and their speed startling. Even so, the red song of war rises in him and the pain flees his limbs as if in fear.

The thing raises its head and utters a cry that echoes down the gorge, the sound of a scream terminated by a cut throat. It clambers down the cliff-like wall, dropping a few yards here and there, catching on with claws as long as fingers and as white as malice, loose stones rattling down with it, striking the ground only moments before its two three-toed and broad-splayed feet.

As the demon closes on him, cautious, hopping from side to side like a bird of prey, Snorri hears its call returned in several voices, distant but not distant enough.

It rushes him and his axe takes it on an upswing, sinking home where neck meets head, carving through its windpipe and up into its brain. The demon falls, convulsing, and Snorri lets go his axe to keep clear of flailing limbs. Moments later he advances on the corpse through the cloud of dust raised in its death throes, takes hold of the axe haft, sets a foot over one side of the demon's face, and wrenches the blade free. Milky blood oozes from the wound with reluctance, stinking of corruption.

The first of the demons to answer their comrade's call come boiling around a sharp turn in the gorge several hundred yards away. The leaders, three of them, hold small similarities with the one that Snorri has slain, but no two are the same. Others can be seen dimly in the dust cloud raised behind the swiftest of them. Many others.

Lacking a bow, Snorri moves only to set his back to a boulder, then watches their approach, knowing their numbers will defeat him. The demons howl as they come, a motley bunch varying in hue from charcoal-grey to the white of curdled milk, some troll-tall and gangly, others squat and heavy, still others no larger than children and sporting vestigial wings.

Snorri rolls his shoulders and prepares to meet them all. It saddens him to die alone, at the hands of such ill-formed horrors, but he never expected to return from Hel, and an end in battle is perhaps the best he could have expected.

"Undoreth, we. Battle-born. Raise hammer, raise axe, at our war-shout let demons tremble."

In the last moments before the enemy closes Snorri knows a moment of peace. No parent should outlive their child. No hurt is greater than having sons and daughters die knowing that, at the last, you failed them. Snorri will die fighting to save them—this is as close as he can come to righting that wrong.

The first demon loses its raised forearm, and an instant later it loses its head to the same blow. The second demon, heavy-set and wolf-like, stops Hel's blade by bedding it in brain and skull. Snorri follows the swing down into a crouch and the third demon, leaping for him, sails over his head into the boulder behind. Then they are upon him, in their dozens and in their scores.

Snorri leaves the protection of the boulder almost immediately. With massed attackers it is important not to get pinned against anything. A whirling axe makes a good deterrent, but if it gets stuck in an opponent's body, even for a moment, then the wielder can go down under a wave of attackers. The Viking spins his way back across the uneven floor of the gorge, leaving severed demon limbs twitching in the dust. Their blood reeks of decay, making him retch as he retreats.

Snorri reaches the steep wall and fights close enough to it to keep his attackers to one side whilst still being able to swing, backing all the while. The dust cloud hides him from the bulk of his enemies, though they remain close, seeking him blindly, their hoots and howls filling the gorge.

Some huge creature with gangling arms, lumpen skin, and a boulder-like head strikes a blow that tears furrows down Snorri's chest, missing the veins and tendons in his neck by inches. Snorri catches it on a rising swing, slicing its chest in return and hewing away the lower portion of its jaw. He skips back, hammering the butt of his axe haft into the fang-filled face of another demon on his right. The larger one falls away, becoming a shadow lumbering through the dust cloud.

A clubbed hand punches toward Snorri's face, the owner black and well-muscled with hard shiny plates across its body and limbs. The Viking moves too slowly and a glancing blow sends him reeling toward the rock wall, vision doubled, blood running down his neck. More shapes crowd out of the dust, the noise and stink of them overwhelming.

A disembowelling swing opens two demons' bellies, a third, brown and scabrous leaps for him and fouls his axe as he tries to ward it off. A demon-child covered in thorns grapples his legs and Snorri falls back against the rocks, roaring defiance. He loses his footing, legs torn by the thorn-child and falls on his side in the loose stone. A dark shape looms above him, a creature of trollish proportions, flame guttering from its empty eye-sockets and spilling from its open mouth. This one hefts a dead-wood club studded with sharp pieces of flint. The scab-covered demon still wrestles with Snorri's axe and he hasn't the strength to tear the weapon free.

"Undoreth!" A last cry as the burning troll lifts its club to finish him.

A bright sword takes its head, the body starting to fall, flame gouting from the stump of its neck. A figure in shining armour moves by, sturdy boot stamping on the back of the thorn-demon's neck, sword reversing down in the scabbed demon's chest. A moment later the figure is gone, swallowed by the cloud, but from the changing tone of the demonic blares and barks Snorri knows that the newcomer is wreaking havoc out there.

Snorri tugs his axe free and kicks off the thorn-demon, just in time to meet a new foe blundering into view. For seconds, or hours, Snorri fights on. Faced by two opponents, the demons come at Snorri less frequently and in smaller groups. Even so, they almost take him down on several occasions. He continues to back away, hewing heads and limbs, whirling his axe before him in a figure of eight, swift and razor-edged. He is bleeding from half a dozen wounds now and his breath comes ragged, a weariness in his limbs, blood and sweat in his eyes.

Twice he almost falls, once tripped by a rock, the second time by a skull, black bone, fangs protruding. Within a few more yards bones are crunching under his feet every second or third step back.

The ground changes character slowly, step by step, becoming more stony, the dust cloud thinning. Snorri catches glimpses of the warrior who has joined him. A giant of a man, a Viking, long white hair streaming out beneath his helm. He looks to have stepped from the sagas, his armour finer than that of any jarl, scroll-worked, runed, the iron faceguard of his helm fearsome to behold, the many iron scales of his mailed shirt each chased with silver.

Snorri cuts down a pair of identical demons, both as gaunt as old trees, with gnarled hands and skin like bark. He spits blood and heaves in a breath. He can see the remaining demons now, a shadowy horde, perhaps a dozen in total.

"Come, Hel-spawn!" He meant to shout it but it escapes in a gasp. "Let's have you!" A glance at his shoulder reveals a ragged wound deep into the meat, pouring blood. He raises his father's axe, preparing to charge. "I said, let's—" But somehow his legs fail him and Snorri finds himself on his knees.

The demons send up a cacophony of roars, hoots, screams, and barks, surging forward for the kill. And the armoured Viking runs to intercept them. He spins into their midst, body-checking one, beheading the next, destroying a face with an armoured elbow, drawing the next into a devastating head-butt. Then somehow he is clear, in space, swinging his blade again. It takes a minute, and for that minute Snorri remains on his knees, slack-jawed, held by the sight. It's a dance, a violent, beautiful dance of steel, life taken at each beat, the warrior's victory as inevitable as it is perfect. Sixty killing seconds.

At the last the warrior stands, gore-splattered, stained with the blood of his enemies, their corpses strewn about him, his sword sheathed, and behind him the dust settles. It's like a fur drawn back from the bed, revealing three hundred yards, every step of the way littered with the dead, dozens, scores, many and more.

"What a tale we've woven here, brother." Snorri stands to meet the warrior as he returns. It takes all his strength but he's damned if he'll meet such a man on his knees. "Who are you? Did the gods send you?"

"The gods forbade me from coming." A deep voice, speaking Old Norse. Something in it familiar. Perhaps the accent or the tone.

Snorri looks down at his axe. His father's father's father had named it Hel. Perhaps some völva had seen its fate and suggested the title. Perhaps it was Skilfar, old even then. He looks up at the warrior, a man his own height, an inch taller, possibly. Snorri's father stood as tall, had the same hair. "You . . . can't be . . ." The hairs on the back of Snorri's arms stand up and a cold chill commands his spine, his mouth too dry to say the words. "Father?" Tears fill his eyes.

The man reaches up with both hands and removes his helmet, shaking the hair from his face. It is not his father, though he has the same look.

"They're waiting for you." The warrior nods back up the gorge. Demon bones litter the rocky ground as far as the eye can see, drifts of them in places, skulls rolled to the walls, shattered, broken. "I've been keeping them safe as best I can. I knew you would come."

Snorri blinks, seeing but not understanding. The warrior takes off his gauntlets and puts them in his belt. The hands beneath are scarred, the fingers crooked from old breaks. "They want the key," he says.

"What?" Snorri's face tingles, his mouth works but no words come.

"They want the key—the last words I spoke to you. I wanted to say more. To tell you I loved you. To thank you for finding me. To say goodbye."

"Karl!"

"Father."

The two men meet in a fierce hug.

Murder stumbled again and jolted once more from the story I glanced around—but I could see none of the Osheim's horrors: my eyes were too blurry.

"I could come with you, Father."

"No." Snorri sets a hand to his son's shoulder. "Your place is in Valhalla. They will understand . . . this." He lifts his axe toward the carnage stretching back along the gorge. "But more would be too much. We both know it."

Karl inclines his head.

"I'm proud of you, son." It doesn't seem real—to have Karl there before him and to be saying goodbye again. Snorri wants to take his boy home, but a man stands before him. A man with a seat waiting for him in Asgard, a seat at a table in Odin's own hall.

"We'll sit together one day, Father." Karl smiles, almost shy.

"That we will."

Snorri takes his boy in his arms one last time. A warriors' embrace. He lets him go. If he were to stay any longer he would be unable to leave. The child he raised has become a man. Even before he died. The Karl who had played on the shores of the Uulisk fjord, who had chased rabbits, tended goats, played with wooden swords, loved his father, laughed and danced, fought and raced . . . that boy had had his time and that time was good. Even before Sven Broke-Oar tore their world open, that boy was safe in memory and now a young man wears his clothes.

Snorri walks away, not trusting himself to speak further, not looking back, wounds forgotten, his arms remembering the feel of his son.

TWENTY-NINE

"Jal!" A tug at my arm. "Jal!"

"What?" I shook off the vision of Snorri and Karl. A desolate heath surrounded us, the horses plodding on, the wind blustery and promising rain. Just ahead of me Snorri rode with head lowered, wrapped in memory, still telling his story. I wanted to follow him back into it.

"Jal!" Hennan's voice at my ear.

Above us the sky had become a purple wound, a gyre that drew the eye. The dreary landscape about us hung thick with maybes, all of them bad. I turned in the saddle. Hennan, immediately behind me, pulled my sleeve again. "What?"

"We've passed over the Wheel!" He pointed back to a low ridge in the heath, like an ancient earthwork, stretching off in both directions in a straight line . . . though as I followed it with my eyes a slight curve revealed itself.

"You've been watching?" My gaze flitted to the monstrous shapes already starting to gather in the middle distance. They looked uncomfortably close to the demons Snorri had described. "How come you're not . . ."

"Dead?" Hennan shrugged. "This place doesn't trouble my family the way it does other people."

"Well it scares the shit out of me." I closed my eyes, trying to get back into Snorri's tale. "We're heading to the heart of the Wheel. Let me know when we get there."

"The centre of the Wheel is nothing but chaos." Urgency coloured Hennan's voice and that note of worry kept me with him despite the pull of Snorri's words. "The heart of the Wheel is in the ring, the place where the machine is controlled from."

I scowled. "How do you know all this?"

"Stories my grandfather told m—"

"Goat-herders' tales?" I spat, angry that the boy had risked my life for this. Already my imagination was conjuring fiends in the darkness behind my eyelids and very soon the Wheel would make them real.

"You never asked me who Lotar Vale was!" A shout now.

"Who?"

Hennan punched me in the kidney. Me! A prince of Red March, punched by some heathen peasant! "My grandfather's grandfather. Lotar Vale. He was the most famous wrong-mage of his time. He managed to return to the margins and raise a family there. He knew this place!"

"Shit! Snorri!" I turned Murder. "Snorri!"

Glancing back I saw Snorri lifting his head as if from a dream, Kara shaking herself free.

In the distance, about a quarter mile along the curve of the Wheel, a blocky shape broke the monotony of the landscape: a small building of some sort. "We need to get there!" I pointed. "Hold tight." I kicked Murder into a canter. Cold terror washed me, and rising with the fear came grey shapes, lifting from the heath like mist and congealing into more substantial forms as I looked. "Ride!"

Demonic shapes, dead men, clockwork devils with knives for fingers, witches, black and dripping tentacles reaching from tar pits, pine-men, vast devil-dogs, burning wolves, djinn . . . the products of my over-fertile imagination populated the heath so thickly there was scarcely room for them all.

"Jal!" Snorri from behind. "Jal! It's all you!"

He was right. There wasn't room enough in the Wheel for all my fears—no one else's nightmares stood a chance of gaining elbow room.

"Clear your mind!" Kara shouted. Advice as useless as any I'd heard. They should take away her cauldron.

The horrors converged on all sides, removing any clear path. I tried to ride down a half-formed Fenris wolf, but the thing, though misty, proved solid enough to shoulder Murder aside and we went down screaming.

Falling off a horse is a quick way to get yourself a broken neck. Having a horse fall under you will often add a broken thigh-bone to your

injuries. Fortunately I've had a fair bit of practice falling off horses and
the heather provided an almost soft and quite bouncy landing. I ended
up sprawled across a spiky green gorse bush, whimpering, more in fear
than pain.

"Jalan Kendeth." A cold and sibilant voice.

I looked up. Cutter John stood above me, pincers in hand, that same
skull's grin he wore when Maeres Allus told him to take my lips.

Something whirled above my head, its passage terminating in a meaty
thunk. Snorri's axe jutted at an angle from Cutter John's chest, one of
the twin blades buried up to the haft.

Cutter John took three quick steps back, then stopped. He looked
down at the axe, curious, then bringing up the ugly elbow stump of the
arm Snorri severed so long ago, he knocked the axe free. "No interrup-
tions this time, Jalan." Cutter John returned his pale, overlarge eyes to
me, the wound in his chest bloodless.

On all sides the monsters from the dark corners of my mind stood
waiting, bleeding mist, one into the next. They walled away Snorri and
Kara. I couldn't see Hennan among the press of them. I couldn't even
see Murder, though I heard his panic. Of all of them only Cutter John
seemed truly solid, as real as the ground he stood upon.

I hadn't the strength to get up. I'd come halfway across the world to
be gruesomely murdered by my own worst fears. Everything I'd predicted
had come true. The Wheel had given me the rope and here I was, hanging myself.

". . . yourself . . ." Kara's voice, growing further away, almost drowned
out by Murder's whinnying, half-fear, half-anger.

Cutter John raised the pincers in his hand again and stepped aside
to reveal the stained wooden table to which I had once been tied in
Maeres Allus's poppy-filled warehouse.

". . . defend . . ." Kara, strident and penetrating despite the distance.

Defend? I staggered to my feet, drunk with terror, and drew my
sword. Cutter John knocked it to the ground with a backhand blow. I'd
need an army to stop him! For some reason an image of Skilfar's army of
plasteek guardians flashed into my mind. "Christ! Help me!" A despair-
ing wail, and one that expected no answer. But all of a sudden there she

stood, a plasteek mannequin, nude, pink, stiff-armed, between me and
Cutter John.

"Pathetic." A swipe of his arm and she was flying away, her torso
separating from her legs.

I backed away, arms raised to shield my head. I needed more. And
in an instant there were half a dozen more mannequins between us,
arrayed in a variety of nonchalant poses. "More!" I moved away at speed,
concentrating on creating more of them, remembering how it had been
in the train den where all the tunnels met.

In an instant all the half-formed horrors were gone and I stood at the
centre of Hemrod's plasteek army, hundreds of them radiating out from
where I stood; the only disturbances in the pattern being Snorri and Kara
on their horses fifty yards back, looking amazed, Murder, who had already
knocked over a dozen of the statues in temper, and Cutter John striding
toward me, knocking my useless guardians aside.

"Defend me!" I dug deep for whatever it was that made the Wheel
answer my call.

As one the plasteek army turned their heads toward Cutter John, and
wordlessly those closest to the torturer threw themselves upon him, grap-
pling his arm and legs, clawing at his eyes with hard plasteek fingers. He
went down beneath them with an animal scream, more and more of my
naked defenders throwing themselves upon the mound of bodies, burying him completely.

As the bulk of the army streamed toward the growing mound, the
heath cleared sufficiently for me to see Hennan standing close by and
gazing at my faithful warriors striding past him. Snorri and Kara rode
up, following the mannequins.

"Only you, Jal." Snorri shook his head, trying to hide a grin.

"What?"

"The power of the Wheel at your beck and call . . . and you make
five hundred nude women?"

"You could have made a dragon," Kara said. "Anything you can think
of is possible."

"Why didn't *you*?" I may have sounded a little cross. "Here, boy!" I
went across to Murder, making the tutting noise that calms him.

Kara nudged her mare along behind me. "It's much easier for you to fight your own creations. It's very dangerous for two people to set their imaginations loose against each other. That's how most wrong-mages die."

I looked around, feeling inordinately pleased with myself. "I imagine I could do with a drink."

The closest of the mannequins still guarding me turned to face us, holding out a golden goblet brimming with dark wine.

A faint grinding sound escaped the mound of warriors heaped upon Cutter John. I imagined they were reducing his bones to powder.

"This doesn't feel right." Snorri dismounted beside me, staring at the confusion of bodies where Cutter John went under.

"I think I need to sit down." I turned around to discover a richly upholstered reclining couch, rather like one I used not to be allowed to sit on as a child in Roma Hall. I fell into it, sinking in thick red velvet.

"Ha! We're like gods here!" I could have anything. The mannequin approached with my wine. She grew more like Lisa moment by moment. She had long black hair now, falling around her shoulders, and her flesh looked softer, less like plasteek. I took the goblet. "Come here, Hennan! I've got cake." And I did, a towering edifice on five silver tiers, decorated with sugar paste and white almonds. I grabbed a handful and crammed it into my mouth.

Hennan joined me, returning my sword.

"We should go." Snorri reached to pull me up.

I slid aside. "Calm down. You've got this place wrong." I raised my palms, both cake-smeared. "I'll admit I was a little worried back there too. But look." I paused to swallow sugary goodness, and nodded to the mannequin approaching with his axe. I'd modelled her on one of the dancers we met at Taproot's circus.

One of the mannequins from the pile shot back, turning over twice in the air before it landed.

"Get on your damned horse, Jal. We need to go." Kara gestured irritably toward Murder.

I sipped my wine and watched her. They'd made such a song and dance about the Wheel bringing your fears to life that I'd quite forgotten the good side of the equation. If this was any kind of taster for what things would be like after the Wheel had turned past the breaking point, then I was all for it.

The grinding noise from the pile had grown louder so I had to raise my voice over it. "Come on down, Kara. Let's enjoy ourselves. It's not often the world does what you want for once."

Two more of the mannequins were blasted away from the mound, both snapped into several pieces. A torso landed close by, thumping down amid the heather. I patted the couch and the Lisa-quin sat beside me. She was perhaps more generously proportioned than the original but one can't control one's imagination.

Kara moved her big, smelly horse right up to us. "We have to go now! People die here because however wonderful the things they can imagine, the bad things are always worse. The self-destruction in us always wins out."

A roar interrupted her and the heaped mass of my mannequin soldiers heaved and began shedding plasteek bodies. A moment later Cutter John emerged from it, half a dozen perfectly-formed plasteek women still clinging to him.

"Shit!" I pictured a dragon, all gleaming scales and gouting flame, swooping down on my enemy. A moment later a column of orange-white fire hammered down on the spot where Cutter John stood. The heat of it washed over us. The horses bolted, whinnying in panic, I dropped my wine into my lap, and the couch went over backwards.

I crawled back to the couch, knees squishing on the damp ground, and peered over it. Cutter John stood scorched and blackened, rivulets of molten plasteek running down him, the coils of my huge dragon hemming him in. It opened jaws wide enough to encompass a shire horse, and scooped him up. Teeth like short swords, bright as silver-steel, crunched down. In moments the bastard was gone, swallowed away into the gullet of a vast serpent scaled in fire-bronze and gold.

I should have felt safe—but I saw how those oh so fine and shiny teeth failed to shear Cutter John into pieces, and just before he slid away down that throat, he met my gaze, his pale eyes unafraid and full of awful promise.

Looking around, I saw Snorri and Kara had regained control of their steeds and were veering toward the building I'd seen. Hennan was running for the same place and had covered about a third of the distance. I pursed my lips, thinking that he might have shown a little more faith in the Marshal of Vermillion. I did oversee a successful defence of an entire city against an army of the dead . . . Behind me my dragon collapsed, falling onto its side and scraping at the shiny scales over its stomach as if it had eaten something that disagreed with it. Actually I suspect dragons tend to eat everyone that disagrees with them . . . but by the time that thought popped into my head I was already running.

I got to the blockhouse moments after Hennan, my stomach churning with a mixture of cake and raw fear. Kara had caught Murder's reins on her way to the building and led him along with her. Snorri had dismounted and set his strength against a large slab of Builder stone that looked as if it might be covering a doorway. If it wasn't then the place had no entrances—for all we knew it might just be a solid block of poured stone put there to waste people's time while their own imaginations plotted to kill them.

I glanced back. A familiar and unwelcome figure was running toward us. Behind him the heath still burning fitfully where my dragon had scorched it. The beast itself lay on its side, an ugly hole torn in its stomach.

"What are you doing?" I shouted at Snorri.

He looked around, red-faced with effort, his expression dangerous.

"Get out of the way," I said, and, without waiting for him to do so, waved my hand, willing the slab to slide. "Damn Wheel's trying to kill us—may as well make it work for us too." Nothing happened. With gritted teeth I tried harder, staring at the door, feeling the blood pound in my head and prickle in my eyes.

"Not working very well, is it?" Snorri growled.

"If it wasn't shielded from the wrong-mages it wouldn't have lasted long, would it?" Kara said. "Why don't both of you try?"

Normally I try to leave physical labour to the peasant classes, but with Cutter John bearing down on me I didn't need a second invitation. Hennan and I joined Snorri, throwing our weight against the slab. I strained hard enough to rearrange several internal organs. Panic lends a

man strength though and something gave with an unpleasant combination
of snap and squelch. For a moment I was sure it was part of me that had
broken, but it turned out to be the slab moving. Once started it moved
more smoothly and moments later the slab stood a yard to the left in the
muddy furrow it had cut through the sod. Revealed behind it was a dark
rectangular opening.

Kara jumped down, orichalcum in hand, and entered the building.
I spared a glance back at Cutter John. He ran with a degree of awkwardness due to his shortened arm, steady rather than sprinting, as if wanting
to milk as much terror from me as possible.

"We're going to have to leave the horses." I hated to say it, and not
just because Murder was so good at running away.

"I know." Snorri ducked through the doorway, Hennan behind him.

I raised my hands, turning my palms up in a mixture of outrage and
astonishment, but nobody was left to see it. Just me, and Cutter John, a
hundred yards off now. "They're not just fucking cows that you ride, you
know!" I shouted at the Norses' backs. No response. "Ah, shit on it!" I
waved one hand at the horses, blinking my eyes to focus. A screeching
eagle dived out of nowhere, sending all three bolting. I had the bird swoop
again and turn them so they ran away from the Wheel. The other hand
I held toward Cutter John and opened my fingers. A huge pit yawned
underneath him and he vanished into it. I closed the hand again and the
pit walls slammed together. It wouldn't delay him long. With a last look
at the fleeing horses I turned and followed on into the blockhouse.

"It's a hole." I meant it on several levels. The blockhouse was a bare box,
its corners dark with wind-blown detritus, bits of twig, grey rags, small
bones. A stink of old urine hung about the place. Directly before us a
ragged hole had been hacked through a yard of steel-reinforced Builder
stone, and through it I could just make out the top of a circular shaft
leading down.

"Wrong-mages must use this place for something, otherwise the years
would have covered it over long ago." Kara stepped to the edge of the
shaft and peered down, holding the orichalcum out. "There are rungs."

Kara went down first and I was happy to let her. Snorri followed, then Hennan.

"Why am I last?"

"It's your imagination that's trying to kill us," Snorri called back from the shaft.

Kara's illumination reached past the other two, casting a confusion of light and shadow on the ceiling above the hole. I shuffled my feet and waited for the boy to get out of the way so I could join them in the shaft. "Why is that?" I called after them. "Why me?"

I couldn't make out the reply but I knew the answer already. My imagination had been attacking me my whole life—only here it had the weapons it needed. A vast underground machine, the crowning glory of the Builders, and all those engines deep below us now waking from their slumbers and devoting their energies to allowing my fears to make war on my hopes.

A quick look through the doorway showed the ground starting to heave in the spot where I buried Cutter John. Moments later I was on that ladder down into the unknown, with Hennan complaining I was stepping on his fingers.

"Are we safe here?" I peered around the tunnel, suspicious of every shadow.

We stood a little over a hundred yards beneath Osheim's surface in a pipe-like tunnel perhaps six yards in diameter. Running along the centre, above our heads, a black pipe just a yard wide stretched away into the darkness. I could see no means of support for it. Bands of silver-steel ringed the tunnel every few paces, each six inches across, like some kind of re-inforcement. A hum, at first barely audible, filled the whole place, though after a short while, even though it grew no louder, you could feel it in your bones.

I coughed to check that everyone hadn't gone deaf. The sound echoed away into the darkness. "I said—"

A sound from above cut me off. Someone missing a foothold.

"No," Kara answered.

"How's he even climbing? He's only got one fucking arm!" It wasn't fair. I'd escaped Cutter John twice, against all odds, only to deliver myself to him on the third occasion. Not even to him—to my own worst fears concerning him, wrapped up and made flesh by the power our idiot ancestors had left us.

"I left Karl and walked up the valley where he had stood guard," Snorri said, moving away into the shadows. "In places the bones were heaped chest-high."

Kara and Hennan followed. I stood for a moment, ears straining for Cutter John's descent but heard only Snorri's voice and that old magic of his folded about me, drawing me on. I walked after them, my feet pursuing the ancient passage the Builders had left us, while my mind followed the Norseman back into Hel, too busy with his tale for the moment to bother plotting its own destruction.

THIRTY

Snorri moves up the gorge, past the remains of the demons his first-born son has slain in defence of his step-family.

Above him the gyre in the sky tightens and narrows. Soon, Snorri knows, he will stand beneath its centre, at the eye of an invisible storm.

The gorge widens into a valley, angling down now, out of the highlands. Snorri hobbles on, his wounds stiffening, the injury to his shoulder still pumping blood, the pain all through him like white wire.

Ahead the valley reaches a neck after which it falls away too swiftly to be seen again, and beyond this narrow point a view opens up such as Snorri never imagined to see in Hel. He stands, his eyes filled with the Uulisk Fjord, soft with mist, its slopes spring-green, black woolly goats dotting the Niffr slopes high on the far side where the sun touches the land with gold. There should be a village here, houses scattered all the way down to the water's edge—but all Snorri can see are the eight quays stretching out their slim fingers across the fjord, and a hundred yards back up the slope, a single house. Familiar even at this distance. His house.

Ice fills his veins. The gyre in the sky centres above that lone house. The great turning in the heavens, the labyrinth of stone beneath it, all have led him here, to his past, his present, a place with no future. Snorri sets his jaw, holds his axe close against his chest, and walks on, so full of broken emotions that he seems a man on fire, and yet the hand around his heart clutches colder than ever.

As he walks Snorri sees that slaughter has been done here too, the carnage strewn about. An arm here in the shadow of the rocks, a head there, offal strewn across a broad swathe of stone. Not misshapen demons but men, or beings like them, and not just men, but women too, shieldmaids armoured in the fashion of the north and bearing axes, spears, hammers. Each of them though, whether tall or short, broad or narrow, shares one trait that speaks of their origins. Every person there lies white-fleshed on the right, black on the left, the same with their armour, each axe or sword cast in a metal white as milk, their shields so black they might be holes cut into the day.

"Servants of the goddess." Snorri kneels, wincing, to inspect a shield-maid. An axe blow has sheared through the side of her helm. Hel must have sent her and the others to retrieve Freja's soul and those of the children. Whoever killed them has not been gentle, but this was not the work of Karl's sword. Snorri studies the woman's white eye, reflecting the gyre above his shoulder, and her dark one, like a polished black stone. Her lips are drawn back in the snarl she wore when struck, the teeth behind serrated like a sawblade. Not human, then.

Though Hel has no sun there is a sun here in this memory of the Uuliskind, and it is setting. Ahead of him in the neck of the valley, black against the sunset, a lone warrior, wide, armoured in ill-matched pieces, arms spread, a buckler held in one hand, an axe in the other, its blade a wedge for piercing mail.

"Sven Broke-Oar?" For a moment Snorri knows fear. The giant is the only man to have bested him: his strength is not human. Weak from loss of blood and crippled by his injuries, he knows this fight to be beyond him. Still on his knees the Northman whispers a prayer, the first to pass his lips in an age. "All-father, I have done my best. Watch me now. I ask only that you give me the strength that has left me." The prayer of a man who has met his challenges with an axe and a brave heart. The prayer of a man who knows this will not suffice. The prayer of a man who will not live to speak another.

Snorri rises with a snarl, careless of his wounds, knowing that the gods are watching him. He stands, clothed in the ichor of demons and the scarlet of his own blood, hardly distinguishable from the beasts he has slain in such numbers.

"I am ready." If Hel has set Sven Broke-Oar between him and his family then Sven Broke-Oar will die the second death. "Undoreth!" he roars, and as if his shout is a spear launched at the heavens themselves the sky turns red as blood behind him. And then he charges.

The warrior holds his ground as Snorri races toward him. He wears an outsized shoulder guard of spiked black iron, a pot helm, visored to offer only a slit for his eyes and perforations at the mouth. Black bands of iron around his chest and middle girdle a thick shirt of leather and layered padding. Iron plates sewn to leather trews defend both legs. Every part of his armour bears the signs of battle, bright cuts, dull crimson splashes, dented metal, torn leather.

Twenty yards remain between them. The warrior raises his axe above him. Ten. The warrior tilts his head. "Snorri?" Five. And lets the axe fall.

Snorri, filled with battle-rage, swings his own axe in a decapitating arc, razored steel driven with the force of both arms. At the last moment mind over-rides muscle, and screaming with effort he pulls the blow, able to rob it of most of its power. Hel's blade strikes the warrior's gorget, coaxing a bright sound from the metal collar before falling away.

"Snorri?" Gauntleted hands fumble with the helm's hinged faceplate.

Snorri lowers his axe and uses it to support himself, heaving in laboured breaths.

The faceplate comes free.

"Tutt?"

"I knew you'd come." Tuttugu smiles. He lacks his beard, his chins raw where it was ripped away. The red slice Edris Dean's knife made still marks Tuttugu's throat, his face pale. His eyes though, they shine with joy. "I knew you'd make it."

"What in Hel's name? What . . . Tuttugu . . . how?"

"Ssshhh!" Tuttugu raises a hand. "Don't speak her name—not here. She'll send more of her guards, and they're hard to beat."

Snorri looks back at the body-strewn valley. "You did all this?"

Tuttugu grins. "They didn't all come at once."

"But still . . ."

"I couldn't let Freja and the children be taken, Snorri."

"But Karl . . ."

"Karl could fight the demons, they're just beasts following their instincts to hunt down stray souls. But to go up against Hel's servants as they carry out their orders? That could get him thrown out of Valhalla. We couldn't have that."

"But you . . ."

"I haven't taken up my place yet, so they can't throw me out. When you're bound for the halls you keep your body in Hel . . . or a copy of it I guess . . . Anyway, I went looking for Freja instead of going where I was supposed to."

Snorri reaches out and sets his hand on Tuttugu's shoulder. "Tutt." He realizes that he hasn't any words.

"It's all right. You'd do the same for me, brother." Tuttugu clasps Snorri's wrist then moves on to lead the way.

Snorri looks once more, out across the gorge that Tuttugu has held against all comers, then follows his friend down the slope toward the still waters below.

A rowing boat lies close to shore, tied to a boulder in the shallows. Just beyond the rock the fjord's bed shelves sharply down, becoming lost in clear dark water. Snorri wades out and takes the rope. The awful thirst in him cries out to drink, but he hasn't come for water.

Snorri climbs in, takes the oars. Tuttugu scrambles over the side to sit in the stern, and Snorri rows them out across the lake. There are no signs of pursuit back where the valley joins the fjord. The sky is the sky of the living world, dark with cloud, swirled as if by a god's finger into a great spiral right above them. Thor's work perhaps. Will the thunder speak before this journey ends?

An evening mist clings to the waters. The freshness of the air speaks of early autumn, carrying hints of wood smoke, fish, and the distant sea. Each dip of the oars draws him closer. In the valley fear had seized him—fear that his strength would not be enough to win through, and that at the last the way of the warrior would not bring him to his heart's desire. Now a new fear grows in him, its voice louder with each pull of the oars. What will he find? What will he say? What future is there for them? Snorri came to save his children, and instead feels more a child himself with each passing moment—scared to face the family he has failed—scared that he will be unequal to whatever task might be required of him now.

Instinct slows his oars. He raises them, dripping, and the boat bumps gently against the Long Quay. Snorri loops the rope over an ancient post and clambers onto the walkway, his injuries making an old man of him.

The slopes before him are those he was born upon, where he was raised from cot to manhood, where he raised children of his own. Tuttugu and Snorri fished from the quays as boys, ran riot among the huts when the longboats sailed in spring, chased girls. One in particular. What had her name been? A grin twists Snorri's mouth. Hedwig, Tuttugu's sweetheart when they had been nine. She'd chosen Tutt over him, perhaps his only victory in all those years, and Snorri had taken it with poor grace.

Tuttugu stands with Snorri at the foot of the climb, waiting. Snorri catches himself delaying. Only his house lies on the slopes. His path is clear. And yet he stands here, not moving. The breeze tugs at him. Grass bends to its tune. High above on the ridges, goats move along their slow paths. Out over the fjord a gull slides down the wind. But none of them make a sound, not one single sound. And the house stands, waiting.

"I'll watch the lake," Tuttugu says.

Courage comes in many forms. Some strains come harder to one man than the next. Snorri digs deep for the courage he needs to do this thing that has held him for so long, drawn him so far and by such strange paths. He puts one foot in front of the next, does it again, and walks the beaten path that he has walked so many times before.

At the door to his house Snorri has to dig again. Images of the night Sven Broke-Oar brought the dead to Eight Quays fill his vision. The sounds of their screaming deafens him, their screams as he lay helpless beside the hut, buried by the snowfall from the roof.

Blind he puts his hand to the door, fumbles the latch, pushes through.

The hearth lies cold, the bed beneath furs and the furs beneath shadows, the kitchen corner tidy, the ladder to the attic in is proper place. They stand, all three, with their backs toward him, Freja between her children, a hand on Egil's shoulder, the other on Emy's head. All three silent, unmoving, heads bowed.

Snorri tries to speak but emotion grips his throat too tightly and he can form no words. The air comes from him in sharp panting breaths—the kind a man might make when a spear runs him through and he seeks to master the pain. He feels his face twist into a grimace, cheeks rising as if they might somehow hold back the tears. In the doorway of his house Snorri ver Snagason falls to his knees, pressed there by a weight greater than the snow that held him down, his strength stolen more effectively than by any venomed dart. Wracked by sobs, he tries to speak their names and still no sound will break from his lips.

Freja stands, golden hair coiling down her back, the woman who saved him, who was his life. Egil, fire-haired terror, cheeky, mischievous, a boy who loved his father and believed Snorri would wrestle trolls to keep him safe. And sweet Einmyria, dark as her father, beautiful as her mother, sharp, and clever, trusting and honest, too wise for her years, too short a time spent playing by the Uulisk.

"Only their sorrows are here." Tuttugu steps in beside his friend, reaching down to put a hand upon his shoulder. "They didn't need them any more. They won't turn—their sorrow can't see you, because you're no part of it. When you leave this place they'll be gone. But while you are here Freja and the children can hear you. What you speak here will reach them."

Snorri wipes his face. "Where are they?"

Tuttugu sighs. "A völva told me this. One you've met before. Ekatri. She came here."

"She's dead?"

"I don't know. Yes. Maybe. That doesn't matter. What she told me is the important thing, and it's complicated so don't interrupt me or I'll forget parts and get it wrong.

"The magic that we see in the world—the necromancers, mages like Kelem, all that . . . it comes from the Wheel. It's what the Builders did to us, to themselves. It made each of us capable of magic through nothing more than focusing our will. The Wheel allows wants to become real. Some of us are better at it than others, and without training none of us seem to be very good at it.

"The thing is—that even though most of us aren't good at wielding the magic the Wheel gave us . . . together we can move mountains. When someone tells a story and that story spreads and grows and people believe it and want it . . . the Wheel turns and makes it so.

"All this." Tuttugu flaps an arm at the fjord. "It's here because we were told it was here, we wanted it to be here. I'm not just talking about this place. I mean all of Hel. I mean the souls, the rivers, every rock and stone, each demon, Hel herself, all of it. It's not real—it's what the Wheel has given us because the stories we tell ourselves have bound about us so tight, we believe them, we want them, and now we have them."

Snorri heaves in a deep breath, his mind turning in great circles, as slow as the gyre above the house. "Where are my family, Tutt?"

Tuttugu grips his shoulder. "Before the Wheel there was an older magic, far deeper, less showy, more impressive. There still is. Nobody understands it. But we feel it's there. Everyone has their own ideas about it, their own story to tell about it. Our ancestors told a story about Asgard and the gods. Perhaps it's true. But this." He waves again. "Is not it. This is the dream of men. Made for us."

"Freja and the children are waiting by a gate that won't open until the Wheel of Osheim is broken. Beyond it is whatever has always waited for us when we die. The true end of the voyage.

"You've seen this place. Didn't it strike you as wrong? Is this really what we have waiting for us for all eternity?" The fat Viking slumps. "I'm no sage, Snorri. I can hardly pronounce 'philosophy,' let alone make sense of it. But is this place where you want your children until the end of time? Even if Hel sends them to the holy mountain . . . Helgafell's a place you can visit just like this one. Don't you want something for them that is beyond our imagination, not a copy of it? That's what Freja wants . . ."

"Who . . ." Snorri clears his throat, his words hoarse. "Who brought them to this gate?"

Tuttugu sighs again. "Ekatri. She said she knew you would come here, and that if you found Freja and brought her out, along with the children, it would be an awful thing for all of you, worse than death, not at first, but slowly, by degrees, you would start to hate each other, and in the end that hate would consume you all, utterly.

"Also you might break the world doing it."

Snorri hangs his head. A hollow pain fills him, and next to it the complaints of cut and torn flesh are nothing.

"Speak to them, Snorri. They know you're here. They've waited for you, and they will hear you. Go on," Tuttugu says, his voice gentle. "They stayed because they knew you would come. Not because they needed you to come." He turns to go, axe in hand.

Snorri glances through the doorway, down the slope to the lake. Three tall warriors are climbing from a scaled boat, each of them black on their left side, white on the right.

"Stay, speak," Tuttugu urges. "I'll deal with them."

Snorri moves to stand by Tuttugu's side, reaching for his own axe.

Tuttugu shakes his head, closing his faceplate. "You didn't come here for this." He turns away. "Neither of us can count the number of battles you saved me in. Now it's my turn. Go."

Snorri looks once more at his friend and nods.

"We'll meet again in Valhalla." Tuttugu grins. "I'm not facing Ragnarok without you beside me."

"Thank you." Snorri inclines his head, eyes full once more.

Tuttugu squeezes Snorri's shoulder a last time and leaves the house.

As the long silence wore on I began to glimpse the tunnel, Kara's orichalcum light throwing our shadows across the curve of the wall, no sound, our footsteps deadened by the dust of a thousand years.

"Did you speak to them?" My voice came rough and echoed ahead, following the arc of the Wheel, vanishing into the darkness.

"I did," Snorri said. "And it gave me peace." The Viking paced a hundred yards before he spoke again, and while he held quiet I started to hear distant hints of pursuit from behind us.

Snorri cleared his throat. "When I came out of the house Tuttugu was waiting for me. He said he would guard them as long as he could. I told him I would stop the Wheel's engines and free Freja and my children from Hel. Or die trying."

"Where will they go?" I hadn't quite followed that part, or thought Tuttugu capable of delivering such a speech. But then, I'd underestimated the man time and again.

"To whatever has always waited for us beyond life," Snorri said. "They will be free of the Wheel. Released from man's dreams and stories and lies. You've seen it yourself, Jal. Is that where you want those you love to spend eternity?"

My mother was assuredly in Heaven, but on the other hand my father, cardinal or not, was definitely in Hell if the rules he occasionally preached held any truth. Most importantly though, it was not where *I* wished to spend forever.

"What's this?" Hennan pointed to a sign fixed to the wall, so covered in grime that we had nearly passed it by.

"We don't have time!" I stared back into the darkness, ears straining for those sounds again. At any moment Cutter John could race into view.

"International . . ." Kara was already rubbing dirt away from the sign with her sleeve. "Kollaboration . . ."

"It looks like gibberish to me, come on!" The lettering was alien, though faintly familiar.

"It's an old version of Empire tongue, very corrupted." She rubbed away more of the dirt. The sign seemed to be enamelled metal and in many places corrosion had broken up the surface beneath the grime. "I can't read the rest. The first letters are bigger though. I.K.O.L. That last word might be 'Laboratory.'"

"What's a laboratory?" Hennan asked, looking up at me for some reason.

"It's something that wastes your time while monsters creep out of the dark to kill you," I said.

"There's a picture here too." Kara wiped at it with her filthy sleeve. "It can't be . . ."

Despite my fears I moved to join her. Beneath the large title running several feet across the top of the sign were three pictures, side by side, head-and-shoulders portraits, painted with exquisite detail. A balding grey-haired man with glass lenses over his eyes; a middle-aged man, black-haired and serious, his face divided by a beak of a nose; and a young man with a wild shock of brown hair, his features narrow, eyes large and dark.

"Professor Lawrence O'Kee," I read, puzzling through the twisted lettering. "Dr. Dex—no, Fexler Brews, and Dr. Elias Taproot!"

"Taproot was in charge of the Wheel?" Snorri asked, looming over us as Hennan wriggled between Kara and me for a closer view.

"Important enough to be on this sign," Kara said. "I'm guessing this one is in charge, though." She set her finger to the oldest of the three, the professor.

The sound of running brought an end to the questions, feet pounding the dusty tunnel, coming up fast behind us. I started off without the others, sprinting into the darkness and got about twenty paces before hitting something very solid. I saw a dim outline with just enough time to get my arms up—even so, the next thing I knew I was being helped up off the floor by Snorri.

"Where is he?" I threw my head left and right, hunting the gloom for Cutter John.

"The footsteps vanished when you hit the bars." Kara stood behind me with the light.

"Bars?" I saw them now, gleaming pillars of silver-steel, each as thick as my arm.

The sound of charging feet started up again behind us, maybe fifty yards back. I pushed Snorri away and fumbled for the key. It slipped from my fingers, treacherous as ice, but the thong held it and I caught it again. "Open!" I tapped it against the closest bar and all of them slid back into their recesses, the top half into the ceiling, the bottom into the floor.

I stepped over before they sunk from sight and turned, sharpish, the others following. The shadows spat Cutter John out at a dead sprint. "Close!" I slapped the key against the gleaming circle of a bar, now flush with the floor. I stood, frozen by the sight of that goggle-eyed monster racing toward me. Snorri jerked me back, but not before I saw Cutter John leap for the narrowing gap . . . and miss. He hit with awful force and I swear those bars rang with it.

"Come on." Snorri dragged me forward.

"The bars will hold him," I said. I almost believed it.

Fifty yards on the tunnel entered a chamber as big as the new cathedral at Remes. The black tube that had run along the tunnel core continued through the centre of the open space and vanished into a tunnel mouth on the opposite side. Its path took it into the jaws of a vast machine that sat upon the chamber floor fifty feet below us and extended another fifty feet above the point where the black tube passed through it.

Lights set into the ceiling, too bright to look at, lit the chamber from top to bottom as if it were a summer's day. The air smelled of lightning, and throbbed with the heartbeat of huge engines.

We stood at the edge where the tunnel gave out onto a sheer fall to the floor far below. If there had ever been any supporting rail or stairs they hadn't been made of such durable material as the bars back along our path or the titanic machine before us, and perhaps now accounted for the brownish stains down the walls and across the floor.

"There's someone down there." Hennan pointed.

At the base of the towering block of metal an alcove had been set into the bulk of the machine, an alcove lined with plates of glass all aglow with symbols and squiggles. In the middle of it, from our angle only visible from the shoulders down, stood a man in a white robe or coat of some kind, his back to us.

"He's not moving," Kara said.

We watched for a whole minute, or at least they did: I kept looking back in case Cutter John caught us up and pushed us over the edge.

"A statue?" Hennan guessed, stepping to the edge of the drop.

"Or frozen in time, like Taproot in that Builder vault." Snorri pulled Hennan back.

Far behind us a dull clanging started to sound. "We should get down there and find out," I said.

"How?" Kara approached the edge less boldly than Hennan, on hands and knees.

"Fly?" I flapped my arms. "We're wrong-mages now after all!" I willed myself off the ground, lifting my shoulders, standing on tiptoes. Nothing happened save that I was forced to take a stumbling step forward to keep from falling, and was very glad I hadn't tried closer to the drop. "Why won't it work?"

"The Builders' machines must place counter-spells to protect them-selves. How else would they still be working after so many years?" Kara leaned head and chest out over the edge. Snorri beat me to the job of holding her legs. "There are rungs set into the stone of the wall, just like in the shaft we came down."

She inched back, shook her legs free, then spun around to back over the edge, feet questing for the holds. With the strong suspicion that the clanging noise was the bars back along the tunnel surrendering to Cutter John, I slipped over the edge directly behind her.

A minute or so later all four of us stood on the chamber floor, feeling like ants, both in scale and significance. Snorri led the way to the alcove in the base of the machine. The towering silver-steel engine, through which the black core of the Wheel passed, occupied most of the chamber but a good twenty yards stood between the wall of the chamber and the outer skin of the machinery. The thing looked like no engine I'd ever seen. There were no wheels or cogs, no moving parts, but the structure seemed to be built of many sections and various pipes snaked across its surface, meeting and separating in complex patterns. The whole edifice hummed with power—not a comforting hum but an ungentle sound that carried within it unsettling atonal harmonies that could not have come from any human mind.

"It's that man from the sign." Hennan walked at Snorri's side, a large knife that the Viking must have given him ready in his hand.

"Professor O'Kee," Kara said.

He stood, frozen as Taproot had been, studying one of the glass panels and the pattern of lights glowing from it. Also in the alcove, somewhat surprisingly, was a messy pile of dirty bedding, a scattering of books, half-eaten food on a plate, and a stained armchair. Just before him, perhaps knocked by the hand resting on the semi-circular desk that ran along the length of the alcove, a small object, a slim cylinder, narrower and slightly longer than my finger, had been captured just after falling from the flat surface. It hung in mid-tumble about three feet off the ground.

I drew my sword and moved forward to prod it in the old man's direction. I ran into the invisible wall well before I'd expected it, almost smashing my face into it as I'd only just begun to raise my blade.

"It's big!" I said, to cover my embarrassment.

"Taproot called it stasis," Kara said. "A stasis field."

Snorri set his hand to the smoothness of the boundary between time and no time. "Use the key."

"He's not frozen," Hennan said.

"Yes he is." I patted myself for the ever-elusive key.

"That . . . thing . . . falling from the table is lower down now."

I looked. The stylus did look a little closer to the ground, but it could easily be a trick of the eye. "Nonsense."

"He's right."

It took me a moment to realize that I didn't recognize the voice backing Hennan's opinion. I turned to find that Snorri already had his axe uncomfortably close to the newcomer's neck. "Who are you?" A Viking growl.

"You don't recognize me?" The man wore the same long and close-fitting white coat as O'Kee, with black trousers and shiny black shoes beneath. He was in his twenties, perhaps a few years older than me, dark hair in disarray, standing up in tufts as if he was in the habit of tugging on it, and thinning at the crown. His wide eyes sparkled with amusement, certainly more than I would show with a barbarian's axe just inches from my face. Something about him did seem familiar.

"No," Snorri answered. "Why should I recognize you?"

Kara stared at the man, brow furrowed. "You're a Builder magician."

"Oh come on! I'm staring you in the face." He waggled his fingers under his chin and gestured with the other hand toward the alcove. "See?"

O'Kee had his back to us so it was far from obvious, but that was where the familiarity came from. He looked a bit like the older man, or at least how I remembered him from the picture. "You're his son? Brother?"

"Son. In a manner of speaking." A broad smile. "Call me Larry. In any case, your lad is right. Look, the pen has reached the floor."

We all turned, except for Snorri, too much the warrior to fall for simple misdirection. The cylinder had indeed hit the floor and was perhaps in the process of bouncing.

"It's slo-time," Larry said. "A year spent in there sees a century pass
out here."

"We need to speak to the professor," I said.

"You could ask me?" He smiled.

"It's a pretty big question," I said. "We really need to talk to the man
in charge. We're going to turn it off."

"What are you going to turn off?" Larry asked.

"This." I waved my hand at the machine, which was nearly as big as
a castle keep. "All of it." I gestured toward the tunnel mouths at either
side of the chamber. "The Wheel."

"The professor can do it for us." Snorri's voice left no room for choice.
"It's his creation."

Larry shrugged. "It's the creation of hundreds, if not thousands, of
the brightest minds of his age, but yes, he oversaw the project. He's been
working at turning it all off for the past thousand years—ten years in his
time—but without success. There are a great many processes that must
be exquisitely balanced for a successful termination of the operation. The
smallest mistake in calculations could see the effect accelerate . . . or
worse."

"Even so, we will talk to him." Snorri set a palm to the surface where
the professor's time met ours.

"Be my guest." Larry opened his hands toward the professor. "But
you'll need the key. And if you don't have that I'm afraid I'll have to see
you out."

I glanced at Snorri, his face set in a grim frown, then back at Larry.
Most people find an enormous Viking intimidating. Larry somehow conveyed the impression that he considered us all to be naughty schoolchildren.

"I have the key." I pulled it out and was rewarded with the smallest
hesitation from Larry before his grin broadened.

"Marvellous! Really marvellous. You've no idea how long I've been
waiting to see that again."

"Again?" I shook my head at his nonsense and turned to the professor.
"Open!" I jabbed the key at the barrier . . . and found no resistance.

The "pen" bounced once more and rolled under the armchair.

Professor O'Kee tutted. He tapped the glass plate he had been look-ing at—across which lights and lines and numbers were moving in bright and colourful confusion—and turned, bending to retrieve the fallen pen, only to be arrested halfway through the action by the sight of three hea-thens from the savage north and a prince of Red March.

"Oh thank God!" he said. "Larry, put the kettle on."

"We're here to turn the Wheel off," Snorri said. "Will the kettle help with that?"

"Of course you are." The professor offered us a genial smile and nodded toward my still-outstretched hand. "You've brought back my key."

"Your key? This is Loki's key. It was made in Asgard." Snorri bristled.

"I'm sure it was." The professor nodded and hobbled to his armchair. He didn't look well. "I'd offer you all a seat, but I've only the one I'm afraid. Age before beauty and all that."

Larry, who had been standing at the desk back in the alcove, now returned with a cup of steaming brown liquid. He offered it to the pro-fessor who took it in a hand that quaked with old-man's palsy, threaten-ing to slop the contents over first one side, then the other. He got it to his lips without incident and took a noisy slurp.

"That's tea!" I said. The others looked at me.

"Well done, lad." The professor took another slurp and made a satis-fied "ah."

I nodded my head curtly, accepting the praise. My mother brought the leaves of the tea plant with her from the Indus, dried and pressed, and used to drink an infusion of them in hot water.

The old man looked up at Snorri. "There's no kettle, just a hot water dispenser and very old teabags. It's an expression—language clings onto things long after we've forgotten what they were."

"You say it's your key," Kara challenged.

"In a manner of speaking. In several manners of speaking in fact."

"You're Loki?" I asked, allowing just a hint of mockery into the question.

The professor shot me a look that had some steel in it, and, blowing on his tea, drank deeply. "I guess we should get to it. I can't spend too long outside slo-time or the rats will get me."

"Rats?" I glanced around.

"Yes. Can't stand the things." He put down his cup. "It's what the part of my mind that wants to kill me summons up to do the job."

"But we're shielded down here? We can't work magic like we could on the surface . . ." I looked back up at the tunnel mouth high in the wall, expecting to see Cutter John standing there with his pincers at the ready.

"There's a dampening field, yes, but the, ah, the unfortunate side-effects of the experiment can still manifest, they just take a little longer. Inside the slo-time bubble I'm completely safe, but too long out in the chamber and the rats start creeping in."

"Larry was out here," I pointed out.

"Yes." The professor looked at Larry. The family resemblance was quite remarkable now the young man stood beside the professor's chair. "Well, Larry . . . Larry is—"

"A marvellous mechanical man," Larry said, and executed a sharp bow.

The professor shrugged. "I built Larry to carry my data-echo—he is, as he says, an automaton, housing . . . well, me, or at least the copy of me that the machines hold. We have our little joke: I'm the father—"

"I'm the son," said Larry.

"And Loki is the Holy Ghost," the professor finished.

"I don't understand," Kara said. None of us did of course, but the völva valued knowledge above pride.

"You've met Aslaug of course?" The professor struggled out of his chair, falling back once and waving off Larry's help on his second attempt. The automaton—some sort of clockwork soldier, I assumed—gave us an embarrassed look. "A number of my contemporaries escaped their bodies when the nuclear strikes went in, both starting and ending the war over the course of a few hours. They were able, with the help of the changes that our work here had wrought on the fabric of things, to project their intellects into various different forms. Aslaug was Asha Lauglin, a brilliant physicist. She projected onto negative energy states in the dark-matter field. The projections all think they survived. They didn't of course, Asha Lauglin was carbonized in a nuclear explosion. She died eleven hundred years ago. Aslaug is a copy, just like Larry here, only one that became corrupted over the years, caught up in the folklore of the people who repopulated. Reshaped by their beliefs and the joint will of the believers—"

"And Loki?" Kara interrupted. I was pleased of it. I thought that the professor must be a teacher in addition to his other duties—few other people are so in love with the sound of their own voices.

"Loki is the copy of me that I projected. Only I didn't die. That's not a necessary part of the equation—although the effort involved, and the pain of it, are such that without the threat of imminent death to spur you few people are ever likely to undergo the process."

"Loki is you?" I asked unnecessarily—my lips just wanted something to say.

"Not me, a copy of me. I don't control him and we have . . . grown apart. But we share the same core and many of the same goals. His power to influence events is both enhanced and constrained by the trap into which he has fallen though."

"Trap?" Becoming a god was a trap I would happily step into.

"The myth of Loki. It pre-dates me by a very long way, however old I may appear to you, young man. I fear my . . . let's call it my 'spirit-echo' may have fallen into that particular trap owing to something as puerile as word-play."

"I don't follow."

"My contemporaries at school used to call me Loki. I suppose I might have been somewhat of a joker back in those days, but really it was just how my name appeared on the register. Lawrence O'Kee. You see? L. O'kee. Simple as that."

"So your spirit copy thinks he's Loki . . ." Kara said.

"Yes."

"And he isn't."

"No. But because he's trapped in stories that a great many people believe, he has access to the power of their belief, which in turn is backed by what you call the Wheel. The changes our machines here have made to reality allow the belief of all those people to give Loki real power. Just as immediately above us those changes allow each of you to summon fire or fly or accomplish whatever it is you wish to accomplish. Before your imagination creates monsters to kill you of course."

"What about the key?" I asked, holding it up.

The professor tapped it with a finger. For an instant it became a small silvery key of peculiar design and no more than an inch long. I nearly dropped it. By the time I stopped fumbling it the key was back to its usual black glassy appearance, reaching from the base of my palm to the tip of my index finger.

"It's the authorization key for the manual control panel on the central processor complex. I gave it to my projection—to Loki—as a kind of back-up plan if my efforts to terminate the IKOL project didn't succeed in the time available. To be honest it started off as more of a joke than a serious attempt to solve the problem. At that point I thought it might take me six months to close down the accelerator ring. I hadn't imagined that I would spend the next ten years of my life working at it . . . and run out of time before the damn thing went critical." The old man ran a hand through his thinning white hair. Exhaustion lurked in the wrinkles at the corners of his eyes. "Now the key looks as if it's our only hope. I sent the key out with Loki to gather belief. The idea was to weave it into stories, to make it part of mythology. The more deeply it became embedded in the consciousness of the people the more strength it could draw from their collective will, from their sleeping imaginations. So, you see, the key has become a symbol that indirectly draws on the Wheel's own power. If it works, the Wheel will effectively turn itself off."

"Give him the key, Jal." Snorri stepped up close, looking down on both of us. "The professor will know what to do with it to turn the machine off."

My hand closed of its own accord, fingers clenched about the coldness of the key. Giving up the key at this point felt like having my options taken from me. Turning the Wheel's engines off now would supposedly give Snorri's family a chance to slip into the unknown that awaited dead people in Builder times. Snorri wanted that . . . but an afterlife on this Holy Mountain didn't sound so bad. And turning off the engine wouldn't stop the Wheel turning, only slow it. Without the engines at Osheim the only thing to turn the Wheel and keep changing the way reality works would be us—every time a mage used magic it tore at the fabric of the world. The cracks would spread, the Wheel would turn, more slowly than before, but turn none the less, carrying us all toward the end. The world would still shatter—just in a few years' time rather than a few weeks. Turn the key the other way and those last few weeks would compress into a last few seconds and, according to the Lady Blue, I'd face the end of the all things standing in the single most secure place, guaranteed safe passage into a new world, poised to rule not as a king or emperor but as a new god. The Blue Lady might have lied: I didn't trust the bitch further than I could spit her, but she had made this her last hidey-hole for a reason.

"Jal?" Snorri smacked my shoulder.

"Sorry—drifted off there." I uncurled my fingers, eyes on the key. "Well—"

"Access to the central processor complex is rather awkward." The professor pressed both palms against his chest as if to preclude the possibility of anyone placing the key in his hand. Perhaps when he poked it the thing bit him back. "The real work was always done remotely in the control room." He nodded toward somewhere high above us. "But for the super-fine control we need it's best to be right there where the main processors are."

I nodded as if any of that made sense.

"To reach the right chamber requires climbing seven or eight ladders and several tight squeezes. If I were a younger man . . . Besides, I'm not sure I could last long enough out of my slo-time to reach it." His gaze fixed on a point over my shoulder. "I'm rather afraid it's already started."

I turned, following the professor's stare, and found myself looking at a large black rat which was perched on a ledge on the side of the engine, a few yards above us. It watched us, unmoving, its eyes gleaming.

A loud thud behind me drew my attention from the rat.

"Shit."

Cutter John uncurled from the hunched ball into which he'd been compacted by the fifty foot drop from the tunnel edge. I backed into the alcove, hauling Hennan with me by the shoulder. The professor moved to join me. Larry took a few paces forward and stood guard before the alcove. Kara drew her knife, sliding to one side as Snorri stepped forward to intercept. Cutter John ran straight for me at a flat sprint.

The Viking waited, perfectly still, until in the last split second he spun aside, bringing Hel round in a rising arc to take the monster beneath the chin.

The shout of triumph died in my throat as instead of hitting the floor in two pieces Cutter John was simply lifted by the force of the blow, the axe blade failing to bite into him. He landed heavily, but rose even as Snorri brought Hel overhead for a second chop.

"Larry is very reliable, but I would feel safer if . . ." The professor reached over to a nearby panel and tapped a glowing square. "There."

I didn't have time to say, "There what?" Immediately the scene outside accelerated to a pace that would have seemed comical if the contents weren't so disturbing. With blinding speed Cutter John fended off a flurry of blows and struck one of his own that sent Snorri sprawling boneless across the floor. Somewhere in all that Kara must have come in from behind to have her own stab at Cutter John. I spotted her lying in his wake as he blurred toward us. The fight with Larry lasted a while longer, fists flying, neither man giving an inch. For a second, that must have been a minute or more outside, the two were locked together in a test of strength. Suddenly, in a blaze of sparks, Larry's arm flew across the chamber. Cutter John backhanded him into the metal wall of the engine, and there he was, the torturer, his face pressed against the wall of our slo-time bubble.

I had been holding Hennan back. Now I didn't have to. Cutter John's face held an ugliness in it that would unman anyone.

"Oh this is bad," the professor said. "Very bad."

"Can't you do anything?" Hennan yelled. "We need to help them!"

I echoed the sentiment—though it was mainly me I was thinking of when it came to help. I couldn't speak, though. Fear had stolen my voice. And I couldn't look away.

"Well," the professor said behind me. "There's always this . . ."

"A stick?" Hennan said. "How will—"

Something cracked around the back of my head. I saw two pieces of splintered walking stick fly by, one to either side of my face. After that it was all falling.

THIRTY-ONE

"Ouch!" Something hit me in the face. And again. "God damn it!" I lifted my head and another metal rung passed within a finger of my nose. "Where the hell . . ." I appeared to have been slung over someone's back. "Put me down!"

"If you want." Snorri's voice, very close to my ear. "But it's probably better if I wait until we're at the top. It's a long drop from here and you might damage something important."

I looked around, immediately regretting moving my head. When the white flashes of pain faded I could see we were in a vertical metal pipe, dimly lit by a glowing strip running its length. Below me Kara and Hennan were climbing, and below them the shaft ran perhaps another ten yards. I tightened my arms around Snorri's neck, despite the fact that my wrists already appeared to be tied together.

"That old bastard hit me!"

"He said it was the only way to get rid of the one-armed man you keep conjuring up. Well, he said killing you would work too."

"You don't even recognize him, do you?"

"Who?"

"The one-armed man!"

"Should I?"

"Well, you're the reason he's one-armed!"

With a grunt Snorri heaved himself over the top of the ladder and shrugged me off onto the floor of a small chamber. I lay groaning as Kara and Hennan joined us. Screens and access panels dotted the walls, the remaining space being thick with pipework. Three narrow tunnels ran off, one vertically.

"Where are we?" What I really meant was where was Cutter John?

"Inside the machine," Kara said. "The professor gave me a map to the place where we can use the key." She peered down the shaft we'd just come up. "He said that the shielding is stronger in here, so your friend might take a bit longer to find us."

"Except where it's not," Hennan added.

"Sorry?" I had a quick glance over the edge myself. Nothing.

"The shielding is stronger in most places. But there are unshielded areas too," Kara said. "They're marked with yellow warning signs."

I clambered to my feet, using the wall for support, and pulled my hands free of their bindings. "Let's get on with it then." I gestured for Kara to lead on. She consulted the paper in her hand and led off down the passage to the left.

I walked at the rear, rubbing the back of my head. If having a walking stick broken over my skull hadn't given me a headache then the pulsing of the dim lighting and the pervasive throb of the hidden machinery would have. The cramped conditions were claustrophobic on their own but it managed to be much worse than that. The still air held a sickly-sweet stink and the walls pressed close, as if at any moment the Builders' engine might flex its muscles, snapping shut the already-tight voids within it.

Up ahead the passage opened into a chamber just big enough for the four of us to stand together, then led on. As I squeezed in Kara had just set her fingers to an irregular-shaped mirror panel set into the wall. The reflection it offered seemed fuzzy at the edges and several smaller reflections of Kara jumped into being where her fingers made contact. Without warning her face vanished from the mirror to be replaced by the professor's.

"Ah, I see young Jalan has recovered! Let him be the one to use the key. An imagination as overactive as his has . . . drawbacks . . . as we've seen, but it should allow a strong bond with the key and enhance the effects of—"

"What is this thing?" I interrupted.

"What thing?"

"This!" I leaned past Kara and jabbed at the professor's image. "It was a mirror."

"Well." The professor puffed himself up like a tutor about to dispense wisdom. "It would take a very long time to list all its functions, but it serves a variety of important uses in the main analysis suite, perhaps communication being the most minor. You'll see numerous such panels as you follow the route to the central processor, but they're all actually the same object. It's very difficult to explain . . . we call it a fractal mirror—"

"Break it, Snorri! Quick!"

Convinced by my tone, for once Snorri did as he was told, and with a violent thrust drove the horns of his axe into the professor's face.

"You can't break it!" The professor favoured us with an indulgent smile as the axe slid over his image, leaving no mark. "Why would you even want to?"

"The Lady Blue is going to use the mirror to come here . . . if she's not here already. She can watch through mirrors and if she sees us, well, we're in trouble: she doesn't want the Wheel stopped."

"If you break the mirror the magnetic confinement will become unstable. All manner of processes may drift beyond their designated bounds . . ."

"We're here to turn the engine off. It doesn't matter if we damage it a bit beforehand." The Lady Blue could glance our way at any moment. The mirror was her last escape route from her tower in Blujen: she would hardly ignore it. The panic that had been bubbling away in me, up to about chest height, ever since I regained my senses now started to rise toward my eyes.

"Well . . ." Professor O'Kee pursed his lips. "You would have to go down to the original mirror in Hall E. It's marked on the map. But if you break the prime image you might only have minutes left."

"Before?"

The professor knotted his fingers into a single tight fist. "I would hurry."

"Kara?" I turned to the völva, cold in my sweat.

She looked up from the map. "Follow me."

I kept close to her heels, urgency nipping at my own. Three tight corridors, one left turn, two right, a ladder up, a ladder down. We passed facets of the mirror at three points, each time with the professor's nervous face watching us pass. Each time my heart beat out the rhythm of my panic against my chest. Each facet was a window through which any number of horrors could be watching.

"We're close," Kara said, crouching to edge beneath another of the mirror facets.

"I need to see," I said.

"What?" Kara's mouth was a tight line.

To be observed and not know whether you are being studied or not is to be prey. The predator stalks from cover. "I need to see," I repeated, taking the key. I moved to the mirror. For a moment it showed scattered images of Prince Jalan shimmering about the main reflection, each as pale with fear as the next, vanishing down the scale into insignificance. The professor's face reappeared, frowning. Before he could speak, I set the key to the mirror. "Show me."

The scene changed, from the alcove at the base of the engine and the bare stone floor beyond, to a luxurious room deep with woven carpets, lined by elegant sideboards, an inlaid box on one vomiting strings of pearls and golden chains across the polished top. And on every wall, mirrors, dozens of them, all sizes, all shapes, framed in silver, in wrought iron, elaborately carved timber gilded and gleaming, in bleached pine, splintered with misuse . . . nearly all of them shattered, their shards hanging like broken teeth, littering the floor.

"That's her tower. Now we can see her too, if she comes in to spy on us." I felt a little better. Not much.

Kara grabbed my arm and jerked me past the mirror. "Come on."

Another corridor and a short descent brought us to a locked silver-steel door. I tapped it with the key. Nothing happened.

"What's wrong?" Snorri stepped off the last rung, cramming himself in behind us.

"I don't know." I looked for a keyhole. Normally the key made its own.

"Try again." Hennan hissing from behind me.

"Really?"

"Yes." Sarcasm is wasted on children.

I pressed the key against the door, flat between my palm and the steel. "Open!"

The portal shuddered and a noise like a giant grinding his teeth started up beneath us, vibrating through the soles of my boots. "Open, damn you! In the name of Loki!"

I felt a sharp pain deep between my eyes and somewhere in the thickness of the wall an unbreakable something broke. The door grated back into a recess in the wall.

"Builder locks were made to hold," Kara said and pushed me forward.

The room beyond lit as I stepped over the threshold. A great mirror dominated the far wall. I say it was a mirror, though it showed only the Lady Blue's sanctum, and nothing in that room moved, so one might think it a painting. It stood maybe nine feet tall and as wide across as my spread arms. The edges fractured in strange patterns, breaking into tendrils of mirror and finally into a peculiar sparkling dust or smoke.

I took one more step before stopping, arms pinwheeling as I tried not to take another—not easy with the others crowding behind me. "Stop!"

"Why?" Kara at my shoulder.

I swept my arm around in answer, index fingers extended to point at the bright yellow crosshatching painted in a band across the floor, following up each wall and across the ceiling. "It's not shielded."

"How bad can that be?" Snorri grabbed my shoulder and thrust me forward.

In a heartbeat I found myself face to face with Cutter John, his face broken by his skull-grin that was far more terrifying than rage. Iron-hard fingers closed on my upper arm and collarbone. Snorri jerked me back and I came free with a scream, flesh torn and bruised where Cutter John's grip had almost got a proper hold.

Snorri and I both fell back, the Viking stumbling into the wall while managing to slow my descent to the floor. Cutter John threw himself forward . . . and flattened against the invisible shields, spreading and dissipating like a liquid against glass.

"He's gone," Snorri said, heaving me up.

"What the hell were you doing?" I screamed.

"Testing."

"Well test with your own damn self next time!" I straightened my shirt, then rubbed tentatively at the scrapes Cutter John's fingers had left on me. They hurt. Wincing, I looked up to see Snorri taking my advice, stepping forward, axe-haft held across his chest like a bar to ward off attack.

The figure rose almost immediately, the ground opening, swallowing itself to reveal a fissure like that at the back of Eridruin's Cave on the Harrowfjord, the one that had swallowed Kelem's shade back into Hell.

Out scrambled Einmyria, muddy and howling, an awful noise that made me want to drive a knife into each ear to kill my hearing. As Snorri's child raised her skinless face to us flies rose all about her, vomited from the pit in tens of thousands. I saw her hands, the end of each finger darkening into a cruel black claw. And then I saw nothing but buzzing flies until Snorri hurtled back across the yellow crosshatching and the whole nightmare broke into fading wisps like smoke rising into still air.

Snorri, back against the wall once more, stood doubled over, his face hidden behind the dark fall of his hair. For a long minute no one spoke. I watched the mirror, the false calm of Mora Shival's inner sanctum, praying that the Lady Blue would not return from whatever business kept her elsewhere in her tower and see us as we saw her.

"I'm sorry." Snorri spoke at last. "It was wrong of me to push you forward. It can be hard to understand the depth of another person's fear."

"We could throw something to break the mirror . . ." Hennan suggested.

"I'm all out of rocks," I said. "And I'd rather not lose my sword. Plus, there's no guarantee the mirror will break . . ." I shot Snorri a sideways glance. "An axe is a good throwing weapon . . ."

Snorri scowled and, stepping away from the wall, plucked the dagger from its scabbard on my hip then flung it at the mirror. It hit dead centre with enough force to bury it hilt-deep in a man . . . and bounced off to come skittering back over the painted boundary.

Kara moved between us as I picked up my dagger.

"If I set this to the mirror," Kara opened her palm to reveal an iron rune tablet no larger than my thumbnail, "and say *brjóta*—which means 'break' in the old tongue, it will break."

I gestured toward the mirror. "Be my guest."

Kara narrowed her eyes at me, then advanced toward the boundary, arm extended, one finger reaching out to touch. She moved so slowly that sometimes I thought her motionless. Even so, the effect proved sudden. Darkness blossomed where her fingertip brushed the shield's limits, spreading like drops of ink in water. Within moments night had swallowed the space beyond and a pervasive silence wrapped us.

No sound. I held my breath. And then the faintest creak. Perhaps a floorboard beneath a foot.

Kara pulled her hand back as if bitten. "I can't go in there," she whispered. I shivered at the thought of a darkness that could scare a dark-sworn mage. The fear made her look older, as if something precious had been sucked from her. She drew a deep breath as the darkness evaporated.

"I'll go."

I whipped around.

"I'll do it." A small voice, but firm. Hennan held out his hand to Kara. "Give me the rune."

"You can't." Snorri shook his head. "You saw what it's like in there. And it's not what you saw that you should be worried about, it's whatever is in you that's going to come out. The effect is so much stronger down here than it was on the surface . . ."

Hennan ignored Snorri, holding Kara's gaze. "You told them I should come. You said, 'what could be more valuable than someone whose family has resisted the pull of the Wheel for generations?'"

"Yes but . . ." Kara faltered. "This is something different. You saw—"

"Anyone who comes close to the Wheel can call themselves a wrong-mage." Hennan spoke over her. "Jal made the ground open up and swallow someone." He mimed it with his hands. "But most of them aren't wrong-mages for very long. The Wheel kills them."

"Too right!" I said. "And it's not a good death either. You're mad if you want to go in there." I found I didn't want to watch the boy die.

"My grandfather's grandfather was Lotar Vale. He worked his magics closer to the Wheel than almost any before or since, and he did it for ten years—then found the strength to leave! That's why my family don't feel the pull. Lotar's blood runs in our veins. The horrors don't come for us." It would take a practised liar to spot the hesitation, but I could tell he was just guessing.

"You don't know what you're saying," Kara said.

"Let him try," Snorri rumbled.

"What?" Kara took the boy's arm, as if he might throw himself across the boundary at any moment.

"He's old enough to know his own mind. In two years he'll be a man. Unless we fail here in which case nobody will be anything in two years' time." Snorri waved at the mirror. "If we don't break it and the Blue Lady sees us, you think she's going to take him on as her little helper? Or kill him with the rest of us?"

Kara said nothing but held out her hand, the iron tablet dark against the whiteness of her palm. Hennan took it, brushed a hand up through the red shock of his hair, glanced nervously back at Snorri and me, then put a foot over the boundary. Took another step. Wholly inside the unshielded area now, he looked back, lips twitching toward a smile.

"Hurry!" Kara waved him on.

The air began to seethe around Hennan as he turned back toward the mirror, with quick steps, hands out in front of him as if he were breaking through cobwebs. Half-seen shapes moved around him like figures made of glass, seen only as a confusion of surfaces catching and distorting the light.

As he neared the mirror one of the shapes darkened, taking on colour. Something snake-like wrapped his wrist as he reached out with the tablet.

"No!" Hennan sounded angry rather than scared. The snake, or tentacle, or tendril became glassy as he stared at it, turning insubstantial again, and Hennan pressed the tablet against the mirror's surface.

"*Brjóta.*" For a moment the word hung in the air, trembling through the half-glimpsed horrors as the Wheel tried to give them form. In the next moment the mirror cracked with a splintering bang that left my ears ringing. A spiderweb of fractures ran across it, top to bottom. Immediately a klaxon rang out, strident, the light turning from a constant white to a pulsation of reds in shades from hot coals through to scarlet.

Hennan spun away, shaking off translucent hands, brushing past or through figures that loomed on all sides. He ran for us, each step slower than the next as if he were wading through a swamp. The air grew misty around him, but red as blood with the light's warning.

"Don't stop!" I roared.

A yard to go now. A thin crimson line opened along his cheekbone as a glassy claw sliced him. The mist took on a deeper stain.

All three of us stood at the boundary, screaming for him to push on.

He made it another foot, moving with agonizing slowness, before another cut opened up, this one deeper, running across his forehead, leaking blood.

We reached for him, though thankfully I had the sense to do it a split second later than the other two. Kara was quickest, lunging shoulder deep into the profound darkness that bloomed the moment her fingers crossed the boundary. Dark or not, she caught the boy and dragged him to us. I caught her in turn as she fell back. Her arm seemed unmarked but she lay in my lap, trembling as though dipped in the Norseheim sea, unable to catch her breath, eyes wide and staring.

"You're all right." Snorri lifted her from me.

I got up, pulling Hennan to his feet. With a rag from my pocket I wiped the blood from his eyes. We stood for a minute, all of us waiting for our hearts to stop trying to batter their way out of our chests. Kara shook herself free from Snorri and started to treat Hennan's wounds with some paste from a leather pouch, the frightened girl banished once more to whatever part of her mind Kara kept her in, the völva back with us again, all business.

"We need to move." I started back out through the door. Grandmother said the Silent Sister would know when the mirror broke. They would be beginning their final assault on the tower now and I wasn't keen to find out if the Lady Blue had any more tricks up her sleeve.

Hennan brought up the rear and, glancing back, I saw the air around his shoulders mist briefly then fade, as if the shields that had once held to the painted boundary might now be failing, fractured as profoundly as the mirror.

Once I had them moving I let Kara lead the way with her map, and slipped into the middle of our little group just behind Hennan. "Good work there, lad." I punched his shoulder in the way I'd seen Snorri dish out approval. "If I'm still marshal when I get back to Vermillion I'll recommend you for a medal." I rolled the word "when" silently in my mouth.

I still didn't know for sure what I would do once the key was in that final lock. I might have cut the Lady Blue off from coming to visit through the fractal mirror, but her words could still reach me. I could be a god in the new world—or burn with the peasants in the old . . .

"Look!" We reached one of the facets of the fractal mirror, finding it covered by a radial web of cracks, but Kara was pointing to the room beyond rather than the damage.

"I don't see—" Then I did. The whole room gave the faintest of shudders and fine white clouds of plaster dust began to sift down over the polished furniture. "Come on!" Everyone's time had been running out faster and faster. Now the Lady Blue's time had run out, and somehow I didn't think she would go gentle into her last goodnight.

THIRTY-TWO

Kara led us through the bulk of the sleeping leviathan, the engine that had broken free the Wheel that once steered the ship of the universe on its straight path through the unending night. The engine that even now nudged the Wheel further and further from true, threatening at any moment to steer us over some precipice into a fall that could shatter worlds.

The pulsing light throbbed throughout the structure, the siren penetrating all corners, making speech almost impossible.

"We have to hurry!" I shouted the words at Kara's back in order to be heard. "We don't have much time." Since we broke the mirror I had been hearing various parts of the great engines come to life, or rather feeling it through the soles of my boots. Beneath the siren the labouring mechanisms groaned and whined, an unhealthy edge to the sound.

Kara turned away from the door in front of her and narrowed her eyes at me over Hennan's head. "Perhaps the person with the key that opens everything should go first?"

I could hand the key over, but that would feel like handing over my choices. Instead I squeezed past and held key to door until the hidden locks surrendered and the metal slab slid out of my way.

We passed half a dozen facets of the mirror, positioned as if they might be windows into the interior of the Builders' creations, but each showing the Lady Blue's sanctum. Twice more I saw the room shudder and on the second time larger pieces fell from the ceiling, along with several mirror frames, and innumerable glittering shards as the broken mirrors had their teeth shaken from them.

"Up?" I looked up the narrow shaft, pulsing red.

"Up." Kara nodded.

"Will Snorri make it? He's quite fat."

Snorri growled, the light gleaming on muscles slick with sweat as the temperature rose around us.

I drew a deep breath, and regretted it. "Smells like the rest of the Builders came in here to die."

The tight confines of the shaft muted the siren, but as I clambered into the small chamber at the top it returned with full force. I stumbled to the mirror facet set into the wall and slapped the key onto one of the dead screens below it. "Make it stop!"

That last "stop" burst out into a silent room. Kara looked up at me as she climbed out of the hole.

"Well done." Rubbing her ears, she stepped back to let Hennan out.

"Thank the gods for that." Snorri squeezed out of the shaft, flexing his shoulders.

"We're close now. The central chamber is next but one. Through there." Kara pointed to a peculiar opening, tall, narrow, leading into what looked to be a small cupboard.

The sound of a door crashing open spun us all around. The Blue Lady stood in the doorway of the room beyond the mirror, arms spread as if about to cast some terrifying spell, grey hair in disarray, a cloak of midnight blue swirling around her. Her age shocked me. I knew her to have more than a hundred summers under her belt, but I'd not seen her like this, like something that might be piled in the corpse cart at the back of a debtors' prison: bones wearing old skin that wrinkled up around each joint. Worse than her age was the way she moved, possessed of unnatural vitality, avid, eyes full of fever. She sprang at the surface between us, covering the distance in a moment. Her face filled the mirror, shrieking curses at us in a language I was glad I didn't understand.

I took a step back as two gnarled hands covered the mirror facet and the whole thing grew dark. "What's she doing?" Mora Shival might look a shadow of herself—not a shadow, more as if she had been scraped too thinly across the day—but she still scared the hell out of me. "What's she doing?"

"I don't know," Kara said. "We should keep going though."

"Where?" I asked.

Kara pointed to the slot she had indicated before.

"But it's just a cupboard or something . . ."

"The map says it's through there." She glanced down at the paper in her hand, frowning.

"Fine." I pushed past Snorri and stuck my head through the slot. "There's room for one person to stand in here, and no other way out."

"Maybe it goes up," Snorri said.

I didn't like the sound of that.

"Get in there and try it." At least he refrained from pushing me in this time.

"That should do it." An unfamiliar voice behind me.

Turning, I saw the hands draw back from the mirror facet, revealing the Lady Blue's haggard face and bright eyes once again. "That should do it," she repeated, her voice like a rasp, no trace of the culture and humour I remembered from the Red Queen's memories.

"Do what?" I wanted to ask but my tongue stuck as my mouth went dry. I could see some of the thinnest hairline fractures closing up.

"The mirror's healing itself." Kara stepped back. "Go! Hurry!"

Keen to be away now, I slid into the space past the slot, folding my arms across my chest. I stood in a vertical tube a little taller than myself. A silver panel with no markings was set into the curving wall before me. Lacking any other ideas, I pressed the key to it. "Open." The structure shuddered. "Open!" The panel turned black. "Open, damn you!" Something began to move with the sound of tortured steel, an awful scraping noise that put my teeth on edge.

"Jal!"

I turned my head just in time to see Snorri vanish as the inner cylinder rotated, with me inside, sealing away the opening slot. I kept the key pressed to the panel and prayed hard to any god that would have me. The light stuttered and died. I've known weeks pass more quickly than the thirty seconds that followed. Eventually a bright vertical line appeared, broadening with agonizing sloth into a gap wide enough for me to press myself through as the slot in the inner cylinder rotated into alignment with the slot affording access into the next room.

"Decontamination cycle complete." A lifeless voice spoke in the cylinder as I stepped out.

The first thing to hit me was the stink, as if something had crawled in here to die. Fortunately that was also the only thing to hit me. The chamber was larger than I had expected, with irregular walls giving on to narrow convoluted passages trailing off beyond the reach of the pulsing red light. A time-star floated at head-height in the centre of the chamber, burning blue above a black disc set in the silver-steel floor. I kept myself from looking at it, sensing the thing could hook a person, leaving them to spend the rest of their life staring at it.

A facet of the fractal mirror had been set in one of the few flat sections of wall. The spiderweb of fractures continued its slow healing process and for a moment the Lady Blue turned her attentions to her sanctuary's door. On the walls around her a dozen or more unbroken mirrors now hung in spots where the original occupant of the space had been shaken down. All of them the same: a plain mirror in a cheap pine frame . . . The same mirror I had seen hanging in a score of places in Tuttugu's cell as he lay dead.

In the section of wall directly opposite me was a valve like the one I had just come through, next to a large black rectangular panel. I pressed the key to the outer casing of the valve that had admitted me. "Keep turning." The thing ground on with agonizing slowness, fighting every inch of the way.

In the mirror the Lady Blue's door shuddered beneath a great blow. Then another. On the third hit it shattered as if it had been made of glass, wickedly sharp chunks flying in all directions. The Silent Sister stood revealed in the doorway, stooped in her greying rags as always, the hint of that enigmatic smile gilding the thinness of her lips, one eye dark and penetrating, the blind eye glowing as if her head were full of light. Behind her, taller, broader, armoured in crimson half-plate, the Red Queen, smoke rising from the mantle about her shoulders as if she might at any moment burst into flames.

"Alica." The Lady Blue tilted her head to acknowledge her visitors. "And your sister. I never did quite catch her name."

Behind me Kara slipped out of the valve which kept on turning, rotating its opening back toward Snorri and Hennan. "Don't look at the star," I hissed, pushing her face away from it with one hand.

"Perhaps you'll introduce us?" the Lady Blue said.

My grandmother made no reply. The Silent Sister stepped into the room, and as she did so, reflections of the Lady Blue leapt from the new mirrors on the walls, each racing toward the original, running into her, somehow becoming one with her. Each joining painted Mora Shival more firmly into the world, adding definition to her, making the blue of her robe deeper, more intense, more vibrant, making her flesh more solid over her bones.

"No." The Silent Sister spoke only that word and every mirror exploded into fragments, glittering clouds blooming before each frame. Even the cracks across the fractal mirror spread for a moment rather than healing. I couldn't tell you what she sounded like—I only know that the word was spoken.

"That was foolish." The Lady Blue wiped her mouth where a flying shard had cut her. "To spend your power so."

"You're not running away this time." My grandmother stepped around her sister. She held a long, thin sword with runes along its length.

"You can't stop this, Alica." The Lady Blue stepped back toward the fractal mirror. "This world is broken. Death is broken, along with the darkness and the light. There's a better life waiting for those of us with the strength of mind to take it. The herd is lost either way, but the shepherds can survive." She faced the old women before her but I knew her words were for me.

"The people can be saved." Grandmother raised her blade, the tip pointed at her enemy's heart. "And I will fight to save them, however slight the hope of success."

Mora Shival shook her head. "You speak about the people, girl, but it's always been about keeping power in your own two hands. It's fear that keeps you fighting. Fear of what you might be without history, without throne and crown to fill your peasants' throats with cheers. You were born to power. You stepped up to it over the broken bodies and broken minds of your siblings. Somewhere behind those fierce eyes the dream of being Red Empress still burns, doesn't it, Alica? You've been planning a route to the all-throne for so many years you can't let it go even when you try. You broke Czar Keljon's power in the east, neutralized Scorron, put the fear of

God into the Port Kingdoms at your back . . . and here you are, advancing
through Slov on a pretext, bound for Vyene. You're piling corpses up faster
than the Dead King—so don't talk to me of 'the people.'"

Snorri joined Hennan behind me and gestured voicelessly to the valve
opposite us.

"The last chamber," Kara hissed. "You can end all this."

I hurried, hunched and fearful, across the chamber, skirting the blue
star burning at its heart. The valve proved identical to the first. I pressed
the key to it, causing the same trembling as whatever held it in place
struggled to deny me, then came the same slow and grinding revolution
of the inner cylinder. Over the grating I heard a last snatch of the con-
frontation back in Mora Shival's tower in Blujen.

"How is that dear boy you broke getting rid of me back in Vermillion?
Shouldn't he be the third Gholloth? If anyone has a right to be emperor
it's him. The last emperor, twisted and drooling in the all-throne as he
watches the world die around him."

I wanted to shout that Garyus would make a good emperor—better
than any of them—but the entrance narrowed to an inch and then vanished, sealing off sound and plunging me once more into darkness.

The whole structure shuddered, a deep-voiced groan resonating
through the metal superstructure. Throughout the vast machine, in
engines that the best minds among the Builders had conceived and
wrought, one element battled the next, running wild now that the mirror
which was both one and many lay cracked through.

I turned with the cylinder and eventually the slot reappeared in front
of me, first a dark-grey sliver, then a finger-width only a shade lighter than
the midnight all around me, a hand-width, wider . . . I stepped through.

A single light panel in the ceiling struggled into life, replacing the
near-impenetrable gloom with a flickering red half-light, chasing the
shadows toward the corners only to fall back and let them regroup. Four
thick, square pillars occupied the middle of the room, each face covered
with screens, all dark.

I saw immediately that the small amount of light I had first seen in
the room came through the window beside the valve. I'd thought it a
black panel but it was really a thick glass window that had been giving

me a view of a dark room, and now showed Snorri and the others waiting at the far side of the valve.

To my left a dirty grey cloth hung over something on the wall. I twitched the thing off and found I held a cloak, tattered and stained by hard use. It had been covering the room's mirror facet. The Lady Blue stood close to the mirror now, her back toward it, both hands raised. The lamps in her sanctum threw her shadow across me, the rest of their light spilling into the chamber. Grandmother and her sister stood before the Lady, their faces tight with concentration. I had seen that expression before, back in Grandmother's memories when they both struggled against their reflections as children. Silver, glimpsed between the Lady Blue's fingers, confirmed that in each hand she held a small looking-glass, angled toward her enemies.

The strain upon their faces held me. It kept the breath locked in my chest. It kept me silent. That's when I heard the footstep behind me.

"Oh God. It's Cutter John." Fear's cold hand knotted its fingers in my innards.

"Whoever that bogey-man is, he's your creation. He can only hurt you in ways you can imagine. I, on the other hand, am going to hurt you in worse ways. Ways you can't imagine."

I turned on legs almost too weak to hold me up. Edris Dean stood there, devilish in the pulsing red glow, the dark crest of his hair night-black between widows' peaks. The pale scar, horizontal below his right eye, seemed to underscore his words. A darker scar, thick and ridged, ran along the side of his neck where Kara had nearly taken his head from his shoulders.

Motion at the corner of my eye drew my gaze to the window for a moment. Dead men were emerging from the twisting corridors that ran into the depths of the machine in the chamber behind me. I could see Snorri's mouth open in a roar, Kara shouting, or screaming, but no hint of the sound reached me.

"The Blue Lady sent me through the mirror ahead of her . . . with some friends . . . to secure the Wheel and make sure nobody tried any-thing foolish, like turning it off." Edris smiled. He held a curved sword of black iron, its point resting lazily on the floor between us. It reminded me of the blades the Ha'tari carried in the depths of the Sahar.

I glanced at the window once more. There were a lot of dead men. All in leather armour trimmed with blue. They moved with worrying quickness, faces full of fury and dark with old blood. Snorri's axe carved a path through two of them, splattering the window.

"They're the Lady Blue's men," I said. "You killed them."

Edris inclined his head. "Dead men are better at obeying orders."

In the mirror the Lady Blue thrust her hands toward the Silent Sister and the Red Queen. "You were foolish to bleed your army here for so many weeks, Alica." She hissed the words as if forcing them past gritted teeth. Grandmother fell to her knees with a cry, hands before her, wrestling with the invisible. The Sister went to her knees slowly, by degrees, first to one, then to both, as if a great weight were upon her, increasing from one moment to the next. "You spent so many lives and so much of your strength . . . and for what? To die at my feet." The Lady Blue shook her head. "You were not the only one the years made stronger."

"You should have defended the mirror," I told Edris, and set my hand to the hilt of my sword—the blade I'd taken from Edris back in Frauds' Tower in Umbertide. "Now your mistress is locked away."

"I thought you might make it here," he said. "You and the Northman." He nodded to the blood-spattered window. Not much could be seen through it save the outlines of men, all in violent motion. "And the bitch." He rubbed absently at his neck and the black scar above the collarbone. "Thought you might break it for me, so I did. You see, I never did much care for the Lady, and she never did quite trust me, what with my refusal to show in any future the wise can read. I'm for her plan, and all. It's just I'd rather see myself at the head of the table when the new gods meet in the world that comes after this one. Edris, Lord of Creation. It has a nice ring to it, so it does." He raised his wicked sword, its point a hand-span from my belly. "If you could pass over that key now, and I'll do the honours." He nodded beyond the pillars. The light from the mirror revealed the back wall, projecting its own cracks across the many screens set there, cracks that were still healing, perhaps halfway now to a full repair. In the middle of the back wall was the silver plate the professor described, the legend "Manual Over-ride" above it. A dark line in the middle that must be the key slot.

I looked down at the sharp point level with my navel then glanced back at Grandmother and the Silent Sister, on their knees, straining to stand but being pressed inexorably down, blood starting to leak from the corners of their eyes. I thought of Hennan in Frauds' Tower with Edris Dean's blade against his neck. I'd given the boy Loki's key to give to the necromancer and he'd thrown it back at me. Refusing to let me purchase his freedom. My eyes returned to the sword point before me. At the last it always comes down to the sharp end. Edris had threatened me with horrors I couldn't imagine. I couldn't properly imagine seeing that black iron slide into my gut.

A sharp cry of agony rang out behind me. An old woman's hurt. Something dark and bloody hit the window beside me, sliding away without a sound. It had been a slight figure . . . perhaps Hennan . . .

I threw the key and, the Lord have mercy on my impious soul, I prayed to Loki, even though I knew him to be nothing more than an imprint of an old professor, stamped onto the stuff of the world and shaped by legend. I prayed and followed the key's rotation through the air with a single word, "Off!," chosen for no better reason than that I wanted the opposite of whatever Edris Dean wanted. We would all still be bound for Hell in a handcart if the engine shut down: the Wheel would continue to roll, albeit more slowly, driven by man's inability not to use power for personal gain. But more than anything I wanted Edris Dean to go to Hell first.

You can't of course throw a key at a small keyhole ten yards away and expect it to hit, let alone stick in and turn. But Loki is the god of tricks.

There's one benefit of doing very stupid things. They surprise people. Throwing the key across the room surprised Edris Dean just enough for me to clear my steel and sweep his belated thrust away from my belly whilst leaping backwards. A hot wet feeling across my hip let me know I hadn't escaped unscathed, but at least Edris's sword wasn't sticking through me.

Edris thrust again and I turned his blade. Behind him all the panels in the far wall lit, torrents of numbers rolling down across them as if a river of digits were pouring over a cliff. The key, now bedded in the lock, started to smoke gently, as if the obsidian was giving off darkness as a vapour. All the previous grindings, groanings, and shuddering seemed as nothing compared to the tortured sounds now reaching through the metal floor. Somewhere, deep in the heart of the Builders' engines of calculation a cryptological war of codes and cyphers was being fought, as the key sought both to over-master the security that guarded the Wheel's prime function, and to solve the problems that had defeated Professor O'Kee for so many years, allowing the engines to wind down in such a way that they didn't pitch us over the fall we were seeking to avoid.

Edris swung at my head. I parried, the clash of steel almost lost in the cacophony around us. At the end of things, with so many ways to die surrounding me, I found fear to be less important to me than the fact that the man who butchered my mother stood before me. I parried again and lunged, cutting through his tunic and leaving a bright scratch across the mail underneath.

"If you kill me you won't have time to force the key the other way!" I shouted. "And if you try to do it before you kill me I'll cut your head off."

Edris made a wild swing and leapt back. He wiped his mouth, bloody from a bitten tongue, and regarded me, breathing heavily.

Through the mirror facet on the wall between us I glimpsed Grandmother and the Silent Sister, both on all fours, their arms buckling under invisible weight, the Lady Blue stepping toward them in triumph.

"You came to save the world, Alica," she hissed. "But you neglected to bring anyone to save you."

The Sister managed to raise her head, her dark eye a hole into midnight, her blind eye a hole onto the noon-day sun. Snorri's goddess, Hel, had such eyes. The old woman managed to raise a hand, fingers clawed, and for a moment the Lady's advance halted, but only for a moment. The Sister's head dropped once more, face lost behind grey straggles.

Edris watched, as fascinated as me by the spectacle. The hands that had played us across their board our whole lives now met for a final reckoning.

"They didn't bring me. I came." A figure at the Lady Blue's doorway, covered in masonry dust, ghost-grey. At first it didn't look human: too bulky, too many limbs at odd angles.

A step forward and the new figure collapsed, now making a kind of sense. One man carrying another. The man on his knees, short, stocky, dark beneath the dust, the face of a clerk rather than a hero, despite his uniform and the sword at his hip. Captain Renprow, adjutant to the marshal in Vermillion, my right hand in organizing the defence.

"No!" If the mirror had truly been a window I might have thrown myself through it. The smaller figure, sent sprawling, rolling among the mirror shards, was twisted as cruelly as any victim upon Cutter John's table. An old man, deformed, barely able to turn himself, and yet, in that moment as he raised his misshapen head, more noble than any man I've seen upon a throne.

"Madam." Garyus's voice came rough from his throat. The journey from Red March could not have been easy on him—the journey from the base of the tower still less so. "You underestimate how much a son of Kendeth is prepared to sacrifice for his sister."

One twisted hand reached out and old fingers with over-large knuckles wrapped around the Silent Sister's ankle. I saw the pain of even that small action in his face—the cold had always troubled Garyus's joints, and in Slov the winter has teeth.

The Silent Sister flexed her shoulders then straightened her arms, head still lowered. The sound of shattering filled the air. She got to her knees, drawing in a rattling breath.

"Down!" The Lady Blue brought both hands together as if crushing something between them.

The Silent Sister stood, a slow, deliberate motion, accompanied at each stage by the sound of glass breaking until there was nothing left to break. In the Lady Blue's hands the last two looking-glasses shattered. The Lady spread her fingers with a gasp and shards of mirror tinkled down amid dripping blood, her palms sliced by the fragments.

Alica Kendeth, the Red Queen, surged to her feet with a roar of fury, sword swinging.

With a cry the Lady Blue broke away from the contest, turning on a heel, somehow fast enough that the point of Grandmother's sword only ploughed a furrow through her shoulder, and threw herself toward her last mirror. toward Osheim, and me. For a split second her image filled the facet. She hit the remaining fractures and they cut her like wires through cheese. And she was gone—nothing remaining on the mirror save a crimson wash, the room beyond seen dimly through it. Blood trickled down across the image of the Red Queen, her sword extended, the point against the mirror that her enemy had leapt through. I had little doubt that a visit to the fractal mirror far below us would reveal a wet heap of cleanly sliced body parts—the last remains of a woman who would have sacrificed one world to be a god in another.

Edris's blade flickered my way. I almost didn't turn it from my chest. My inattention earned me a shallow cut across my upper arm. The panels on the far wall burned red now and I thought I saw a figure moving beyond them, as if each were a window through the wall to some space beyond. The sound had died somewhat, reduced to deep metallic groans and the slow noise of a ratchet as one tooth after the next is drawn through it.

Edris feinted at me, our blades scraping edges. "I don't have time to kill you," he said. "Fortunately I brought someone with me who does." He backed away and the unborn unfolded itself spider-like from the darkened ceiling where it had hidden in the shadows behind the pillars. It descended into the space Edris opened between us, a horror built from fresh meat rearranged about the bones of the men the Lady Blue had sent with Edris. A torso on thick legs, lowered by five raw and skinny limbs emerging from its open chest, each reaching two yards or longer, jointed in a dozen places, and ending in a sharp bone spike.

Edris turned his back and walked to the far wall and the key. "With that sword you stole from me maybe you'll even send her back to Hell. But she'll still be bound to the lichkin. Either way, it will buy me the time I need and I'll deal with you myself afterwards if I have to." He set his hand to the key and gasped as its lies wrapped him. "Though there isn't going to be an after." His wrist turned, forcing the key the other way, and the great engines howled a new note. "This is the way the world ends. No bangs, no whimpers, just the turning of a wheel."

In the end there are few things more likely to squeeze stupidity and courage from a man in equal measures—if indeed they are not both the same thing. Family will do it, and so will the sight of someone you hate with a passion about to seize their moment of triumph.

"Never underestimate what a son of Kendeth will sacrifice for his sister." The words came from my lips without any hint of fear.

It wasn't a berserk that took me. I think the rage that enveloped me the day I cut Maeres Allus's throat had never truly let go, never bundled itself back into the tiny and forgotten space where I had once kept it, but mixed with my blood as with any other man, sometimes quiet, sometimes loud. The anger that raised my hand was all mine, owned and paid for. I threw Edris's sword hilt over tip, turning through the air just as the key had. And just as Loki's key struck home, Edris's unholy blade did so too, taking him between the shoulder-blades.

The unborn reared between us, its arms closing around me like the fingers of a hand. Somehow Snorri had seen the essence of his son within the unborn that attacked us inside the Black Fort's vault. I hadn't understood it then—how he saw his own inside that corrupt travesty of corpse flesh and wept to end it. I couldn't see it now, but I knew my mother would have seen her daughter, and that was enough. It wasn't my knife I plunged into the open heart of the unborn but the cardinal's seal from that road far away, running along the Attar-Zagre border. And it wasn't my faith that tore them apart, the child that never saw the world from the monster that was forged in Hell. It was the faith of the million and more, huddled in their churches, hiding from uneasy dreams in their beds, cowed by signs and portents, clinging to their god as the end of days drew near. That faith, that will, that belief, given power by the Wheel itself, split child from horror, and left the dead flesh shredded on the ground.

I hadn't felt the spikes pierce me. I didn't feel the pain until I rolled and, finding myself on the floor, tried to rise. The blood flooded from puncture wounds in my shoulders and side, running hot down my back. I slumped to one side and lay there, watching. Edris faced me now, his face contorted with fury, the point of his own sword emerging from just beneath his ribs.

I didn't care about Edris any more. I looked around and saw them both, the lichkin and my nameless sister. She stood, a pale spirit, grown into the woman I had glimpsed when I cut her from the Hel-tree. She held both Mother and the Red Queen in her, beautiful, strong, undaunted. The lichkin, nerve-white and naked, hiding in the blind spot of my eyes, reached to clothe itself in my sister's ghost. She took its finger in hers and wound its whole body swiftly into a ball, larger than a head, then compressed the ball until it grew smaller, smaller, the size of a fist, an eyeball, a pea . . . gone.

Her image rippled like a reflection on water, changing, fading, shrinking, a younger woman, a child . . .

"Don't go." I tried to raise a hand to her.

Edris loomed behind her, blood drenching the grey shirt across his abdomen. "Don't go," he echoed me. "I'm sure I can find you another master." His fingers worked to spell runes into the air, weaving a new web of necromancy to snare her once again.

My sister, a little child now, offered her tormentor a scowl I knew from the Red Queen's face on the walls of Ameroth. She stamped her foot, punching down with both fists, and in an instant Edris was flung down, groaning alongside me in the fetid mess of the unborn remains. The groan became a snarl and he got to his knees, facing the faint traces that were all that was left of my sister, blocking them from my view. My sword still jutted from between his shoulders, the hilt offered to me, swaying just out of reach.

I didn't have the strength to move. But I had the desire, and I moved anyway. With one last burst of energy, I yanked the sword free and took his head with a wild swing, more by luck than judgment.

Edris knelt for a moment longer, blood spraying, then keeled over.

Of my sister, there was no sign.

It took me an age to reach the rear wall, crawling, inching through the filth whilst all around me the engines of the Builders screamed for the end of the world. Somehow my hand closed around the end of the key and I turned it to the middle, neutral, position.

And there, at the end of all things, I hesitated. Let Loki's key finish its work and I would be guaranteed safe passage into the new world that the Lady Blue had so desired. A god. The status I had always sought, all that and far more, delivered into my lap. No longer the superfluous princeling eking out a life at the margins of my grandmother's court. Turn the key back to the left, and the great engines would shut down, the magic would leave this place, and with nothing to drive it forward, the Wheel that the Builders set turning, changing the balance between desire and the solid stuff of the world, would slow and eventually stop. Perhaps it might even turn back and return us to the lives men had known all those long years since some fool scattered us across the face of the Earth.

Listen to the wise, though, and you would know they saw a doom postponed, not ended. The Silent Sister saw that same Wheel turn under the pressure of man's greed for power and crack everything apart, pitching us minor mortals into fire and destruction. I could save myself now and end countless nations . . . or consign myself and all those people to the fire in a few short years. Beneath my hand the key smoked and all around me the engine whined and roared. The key still battled the lock, fighting for control, and the engine, without the fractal mirror to moderate its energies, ran wild.

The many screens to either side of me continued to show their portions of a larger scene, as if they perforated the wall, revealing what was happening in the mind of the machine beyond.

"I need—"

"Men don't know what they need." A figure turned, cutting across the first and unseen speaker. "They barely know what they want." He looked like a short man, though there was nothing to measure him against and the screens showed him larger than life. Neither young nor old, his dark hair standing as if in shock. He wore a coat of many colours. But as he turned it became a golden jacket sewn all over with innumerable pockets. In the next moment, the blacks of a Florentine modern, replete with three-tiered hat. Whatever he wore, he looked familiar. "Me? I'm just a jester in the hall where the world was made. I caper, I joke, I cut a jig. I'm of little importance."

"Professor . . ." I saw the old man's face there, traces of him behind Loki's confidence and cunning.

The god continued to address his unseen target. "Imagine though . . . if it were *me* that pulled the strings and made the gods dance. What if at the core, if you dug deep enough, uncovered every truth . . . what if at the heart of it all . . . there was a lie, like a worm at the centre of the apple, coiled like Oroborus, just as the secret of men hides coiled at the centre of each piece of you, no matter how fine you slice?"

I clutched the key tight and the black ice of it slid beneath my grasp. The screens went dark.

"Wouldn't that be a fine joke now?" Loki stood beside me.

"W-what do you want?" I tried to move away without releasing the key.

"Me?" Loki shrugged. "I'm finished when you break my key, and it will break when its job is done. Turn it left, turn it right. Make up your mind, Jalan."

"I . . . I don't know." Sweat ran down me, my hand pale from loss of blood, trembling. "Was the Lady Blue telling the truth when she—"

"Truth?" Loki threw up his hands, fingers fluttering. "Lies are our foundation—we each start with a lie and build a life upon it. Lies are more durable than the truth, more mutable, able to change to meet requirements."

"I *need* the truth. You set me on this path with the truth when you showed me my mother die. The key didn't drop me in the desert at random . . . it was all part of a plan. Meeting Jorg Ancrath, finding the steel to kill Maeres Allus. You were building me for this task, just as you built the key and sent it out in the world to gather strength."

"Perhaps." Loki shrugged. "The facts are a liar's best friends. So many truths are uncovered in the search for a plausible lie. Why not work with them?" He turned to gesture at the chamber, a hall of wonders, strewn with death. "*What a tangled web we weave when first we practise to deceive.* The Great Scott wrote that, back when the moon wore a younger face." A sigh. As the darkness smoked about the key in my grasp Loki seemed to diminish, growing older, the light within him fading. "This was my first work and it is, I will admit, tangled. *Where's the coward that would not dare to fight for such a land?* Another of the Great Scott's lines—and here you are, my coward. Do you dare?"

"But should I—"

"I don't care!" Loki boomed across me, haggard now, and ill. "Only know that you don't need the truth. The truth didn't set you free. It was a lie. You didn't see your mother die. You weren't in the room. You weren't even in Roma Hall that day."

"What?"

"I lied to you."

"What . . ."

"Hate, courage, fear . . . all lies. Don't look for reasons. Do what you feel. Not what you feel to be right—just what you feel."

"I have the scar . . ." My free hand moved toward my chest where Edris's sword had caught me that day.

"You did that climbing a fence."

"You lying bast—"

"Yes, I know. Now hurry up could you? I'm falling apart here."

I looked back past the false god, a thing made real by the dreams of men, and saw, standing at the blood-smeared window to the other room, the hulking figure of my friend, only his eyes clearly visible where a hand had wiped the glass clean.

I turned the key.

THIRTY-THREE

Garyus was buried as a king in the cathedral of Our Lady in Vermillion. The funeral procession wound from Victory Plaza in the palace out across the city, along the Corelli Line overlooking the river and down toward the Appan Gate. We had snow, the first snow to fall in Vermillion in eight years, as if the city had dressed for the occasion, covered up its scars and stains and dirt for just one day to see the old man laid to rest.

I carried the coffin with my cousins, and Captain Renprow filled in the sixth space. The Red Queen appointed him to the honour for carrying Garyus up into the Blue Lady's tower through magics no other soldier had survived, and for the heroics he displayed in getting my great-uncle to Blujen in the first place a week earlier, against Renprow's own strong advice, it must be said.

"For this, Marshal Renprow, we thank you. We thank you for carrying our brother."

"He carried me, your majesty." Renprow bowed. "And it was my honour."

"He carried us all." The Red Queen nodded and bowed her face. "For many years."

We set his coffin in a sepulchre of white marble within the cathedral, bound by magics that would secure him from any necromancy. I said the words over him in his resting place. I think I spoke them clearly and with meaning.

"Be at peace, my brother." Grandmother laid her hand upon the cold stone, and beside her, seen by no one else but me, the Silent Sister put her own pale hand where her twin's name was graven, and from her dark eye a single tear fell, sparkling.

I came to see Snorri leave from the river docks. I had bought him a boat. A good one, I hoped. I called it *The Martus*. Darin left a child to carry his line and a wife who loved him. Martus needed something, and a boat to carry his name into the world was the best I could offer.

Snorri stood at the wall beside the stone steps we had once run down, escaping Maeres Allus's thugs. The wound on his face was healing, and his broken arm was hidden beneath a thick bearskin cloak fastened with a heavy golden clasp—a gift from the queen.

"We have snow here! Why are you leaving?" I spread my arms to encompass the unreal whiteness of Vermillion. Dockhands shivered around us in their too-thin coats as they loaded the last of his stores.

"The North calls me, my friend. And this isn't snow—this is a frosting. In the North we—"

"Dance naked on such days. I know! I've seen it." I clapped a hand to his good arm. "I'll allow it . . . but come back, you hear? As soon as you've had your fill of frostbite and bad food, come back and warm up again."

"I will." A grin, white teeth in the bristling blackness of his short beard.

"Seriously. I mean it. Life will be too dull without all your nonsense." I had more to say but it left me, along with the air from my lungs, as Hennan shot up the steps and bundled into me. "Ouch! Careful! Wounded hero here!" I put an arm round him and ruffled his red hair in the way that used to annoy me so much when my father did it to me. "Kara! Rescue me!"

The völva came up from the boat at a more leisurely pace, casting an amused eye over the three of us. "The boat's ready. The river too," she said.

"Look after these idiots for me," I said. "The only thing Snorri knows in Trond are the docks and the Three Axes. And Hennan has never had the chance to appreciate the true horror of a Norseheim town."

"I'll see they get there safe enough," she said. "After that I have things to do."

I shrugged and smiled. I didn't know much about boats, but what I did know was that very often the people who stepped off them at the end of a long voyage were not the same people who had boarded them.

And that was that. Snorri crushed the breath out of me with a one-armed hug, and the Seleen took them away, running west toward the sea.

The weeks that followed saw the continuing rebuilding of the outer city, a labour that would keep the people of Red March busy for years to come. If we have years to come. But who knows how long they have? We stopped the engines driving us to destruction. All that turns the Wheel now is us. More slowly, yes, but the destination is the same. We purchased time and time is a wonderful thing. Me, I intend to waste it hand over fist until it's time to panic again. And even then it will be someone else's task to fix the problem. My adventuring days are over—a neat parcel of memories sealed with a bow and shoved into some dark corner of a cupboard to gather dust and never see the light of day again.

Weeks later when the maid arrived at my rooms to stow away my laundered clothing, she came with Dr. Taproot's lens laid neatly on the top in its silver hoop.

"It's lucky they found that, your highness," she said, beaming beneath her curls. "A delicate thing like that could easily come to harm."

I was tempted to grind it to dust beneath my heel there and then. Loose ends warrant stamping on if they're the kind that connect with people like Dr. Taproot. In the end though I feared summoning trouble and settled for wrapping it up and finding a literal rather than metaphorical seldom-used cupboard with dark enough corners to hide the thing away. Then went off to the kitchens to demand a huge lunch with plenty of wine.

Grandmother shook up the palace. Hertet, who miraculously survived the night of horror at Milano House, she sent into exile as permanent ambassador to the eastern czardoms. To quell any future manoeuvring over succession she officially named an heir. She even summoned me to a private session of court to discuss the matter. I backed her selection.

Cousin Serah had showed in the siege that Grandmother's blood ran deep in her. When at last the Red Queen met her end our people would shout "The Red Queen is dead! Long live the Red Queen!"

Which just leaves me, here in the guest wing of the Inner Palace, watching from a high window as Barras Jon limps off to one or other of his duties. They found him alive on the morning when the Dead King broke his siege. He lay trapped amid a heap of broken corpses at the base of the city wall where we had fought together. His leg proved to be too badly shattered for a full recovery, but with the aid of a cane he gets about, overseeing his father's affairs in Vermillion. Indeed, these days his business interests see him called hither and thither across the length and breadth of Red March. He says I saved him that day, and if I ever want anything from him I just have to ask. So really, my only crime is having forgotten to ask . . .

"Get into bed, Jal. I told you he wasn't coming up."

I turn back to my companion. She's sitting up, wearing nothing but satin sheets and a smile. I echo the smile and unclasp my velvet robe. It drops into a purple heap behind me. I reach toward my head . . .

"Leave the hat on," she says. "I like it . . . Cardinal Jalan."

"Oh my child," I say, pulling off my left boot. "You're such a sinner." I kick off the other boot and start unbuttoning. "Time for some genuflexion. Let's get ecumenical." I slide into bed beside her. I've been picking up the clerical language as the bishops desperately try to train me. I pull Lisa DeVeer to me. "Or even ecclesiastical." Neither of us know the definition of the word—but we both know what it means.

And in the end neither the lies nor the truth matter.

Just what we feel.

I'm a liar and a cheat and a coward, but I will never, ever, rarely let a friend down.